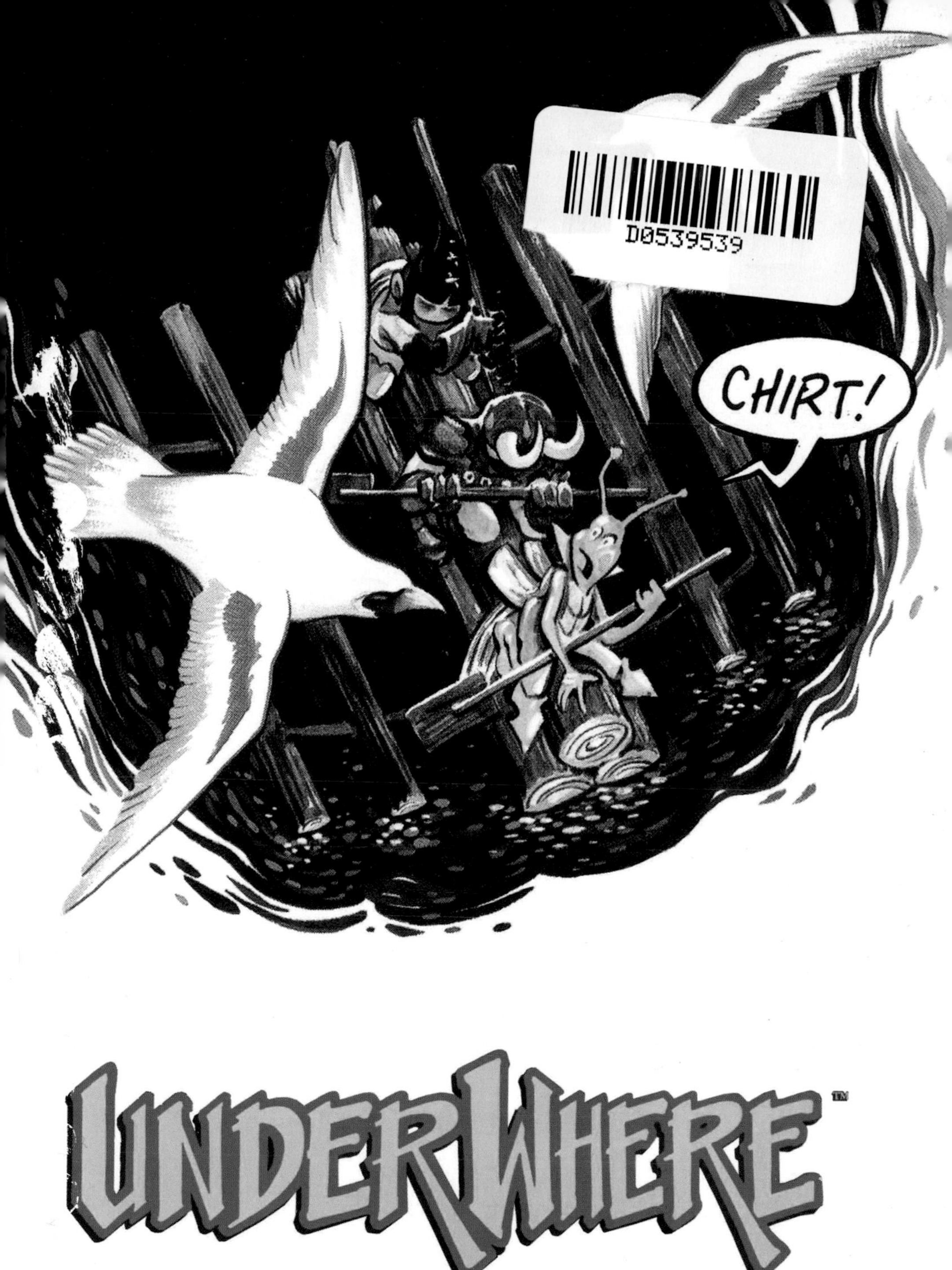
CHIRT!

UNDERWHERE™

4 4 0017983 7

Become our fan on Facebook **facebook.com/idwpublishing**
Follow us on Twitter **@idwpublishing**
Subscribe to us on YouTube **youtube.com/idwpublishing**
See what's new on Tumblr **tumblr.idwpublishing.com**
Check us out on Instagram **instagram.com/idwpublishing**

COVER ART BY
KEVIN EASTMAN

COLLECTION EDITS BY
JUSTIN EISINGER
AND ALONZO SIMON

PRODUCTION ASSISTANCE BY
SHAWN LEE

PUBLISHER
GREG GOLDSTEIN

ISBN: 978-1-68405-204-2   21 20 19 18   1 2 3 4

Greg Goldstein, President & Publisher
Robbie Robbins, EVP & Sr. Art Director
Chris Ryall, Chief Creative Officer & Editor-in-Chief
Matthew Ruzicka, CPA, Chief Financial Officer
David Hedgecock, Associate Publisher
Laurie Windrow, Senior Vice President of Sales & Marketing
Lorelei Bunjes, VP of Digital Services
Eric Moss, Sr. Director, Licensing & Business Development

Ted Adams, Founder & CEO of IDW Media Holdings

For international rights, please contact
licensing@idwpublishing.com

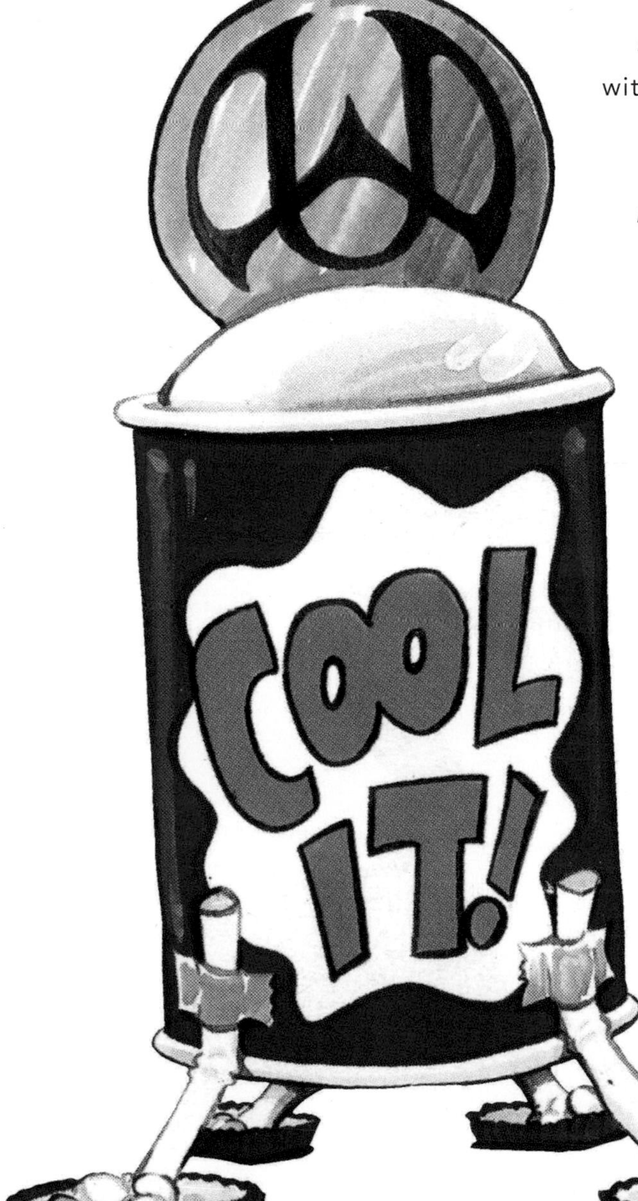
COOL IT!

Created by
KEVIN EASTMAN

Written by
KEVIN EASTMAN
with **PAUL JENKINS**

Storyboards by
KEVIN EASTMAN

Painted by
MARK MARTIN

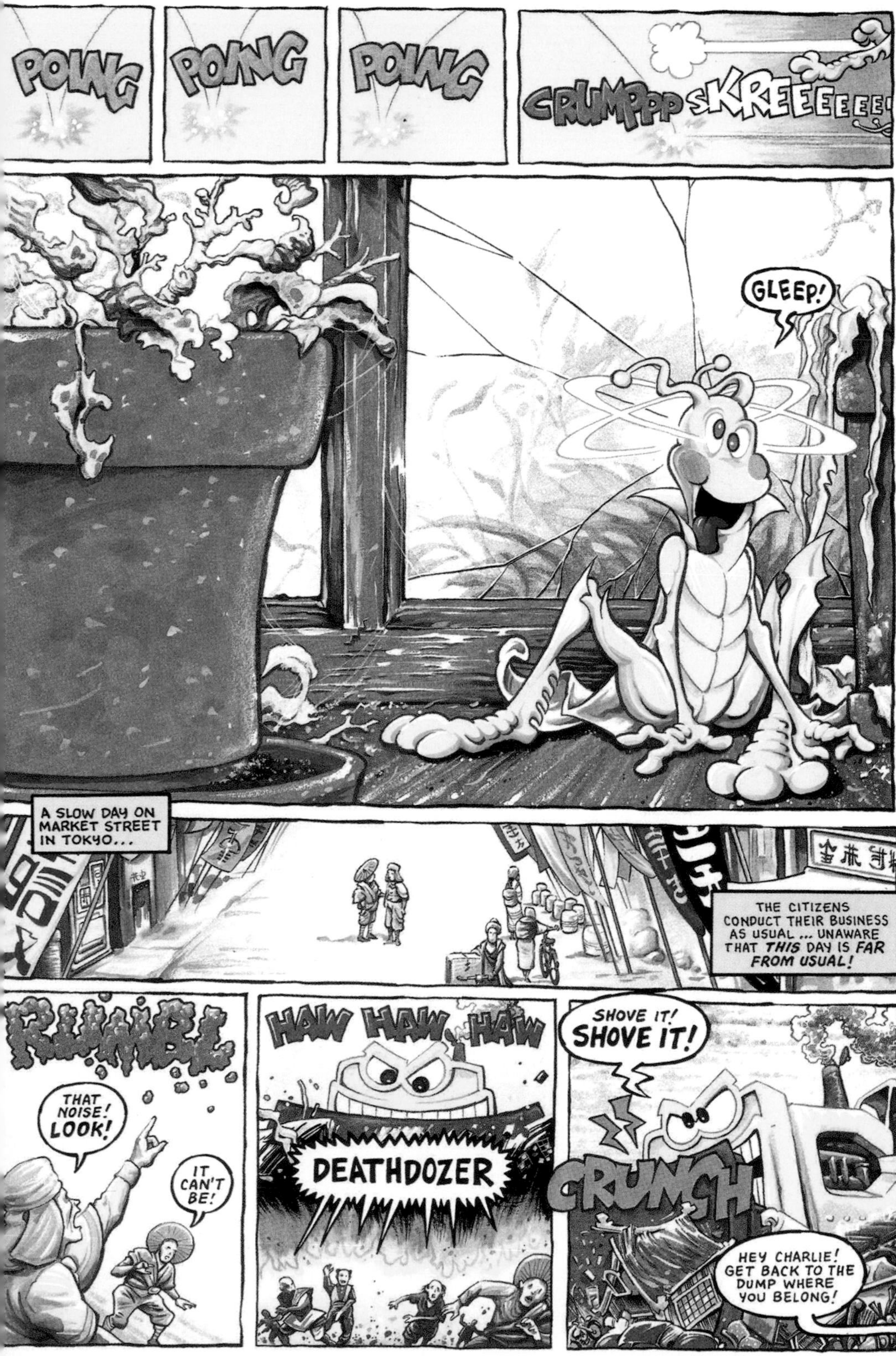

POING
POING
POING
CRUMPPP SKREEEEEEE
GLEEP!
A SLOW DAY ON MARKET STREET IN TOKYO...
THE CITIZENS CONDUCT THEIR BUSINESS AS USUAL ... UNAWARE THAT *THIS* DAY IS *FAR FROM USUAL!*
RUMBL
THAT NOISE! LOOK!
IT CAN'T BE!
HAW HAW HAW
DEATHDOZER
SHOVE IT! SHOVE IT!
CRUNCH
HEY CHARLIE! GET BACK TO THE DUMP WHERE YOU BELONG!

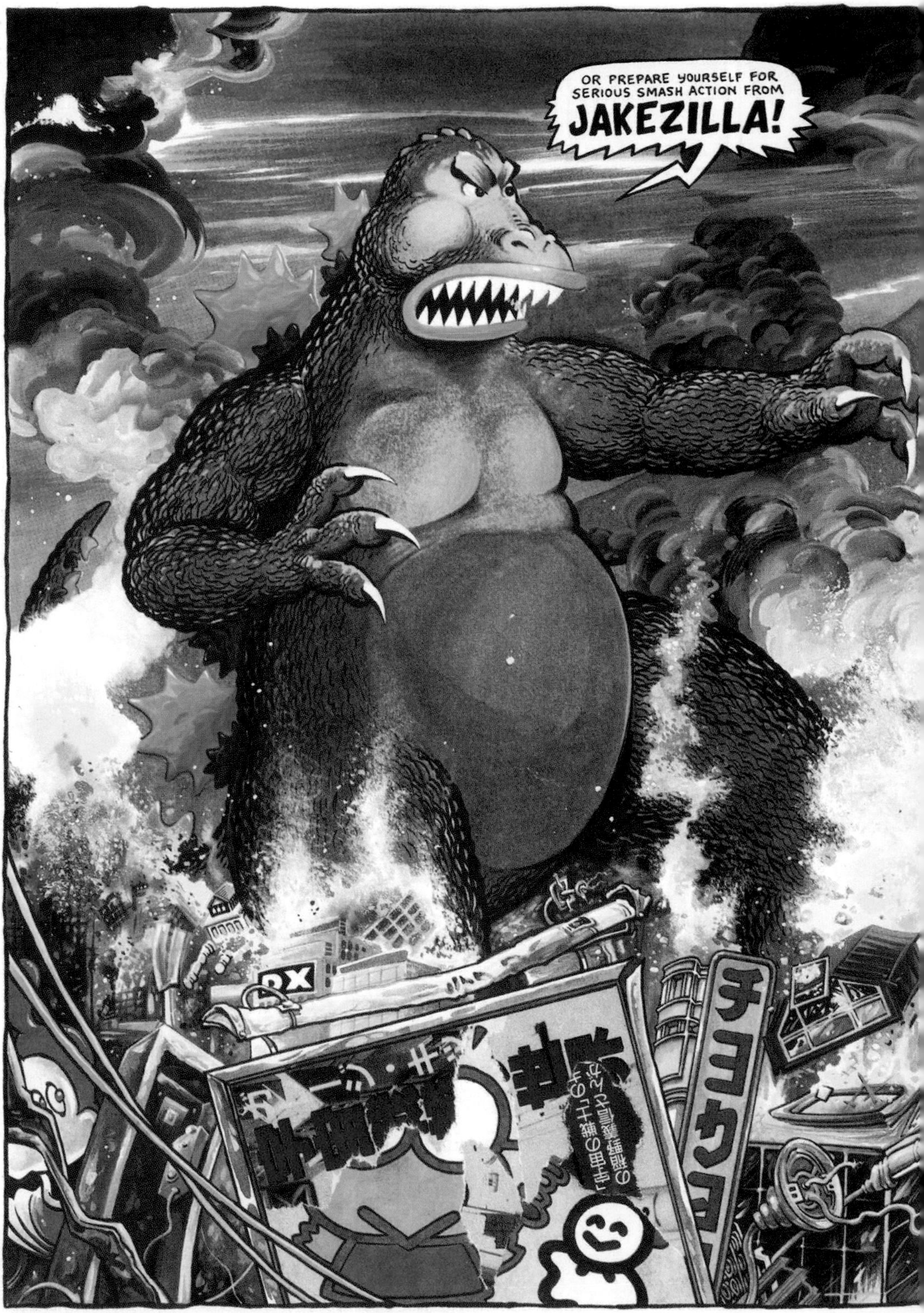
OR PREPARE YOURSELF FOR SERIOUS SMASH ACTION FROM JAKEZILLA!
DX

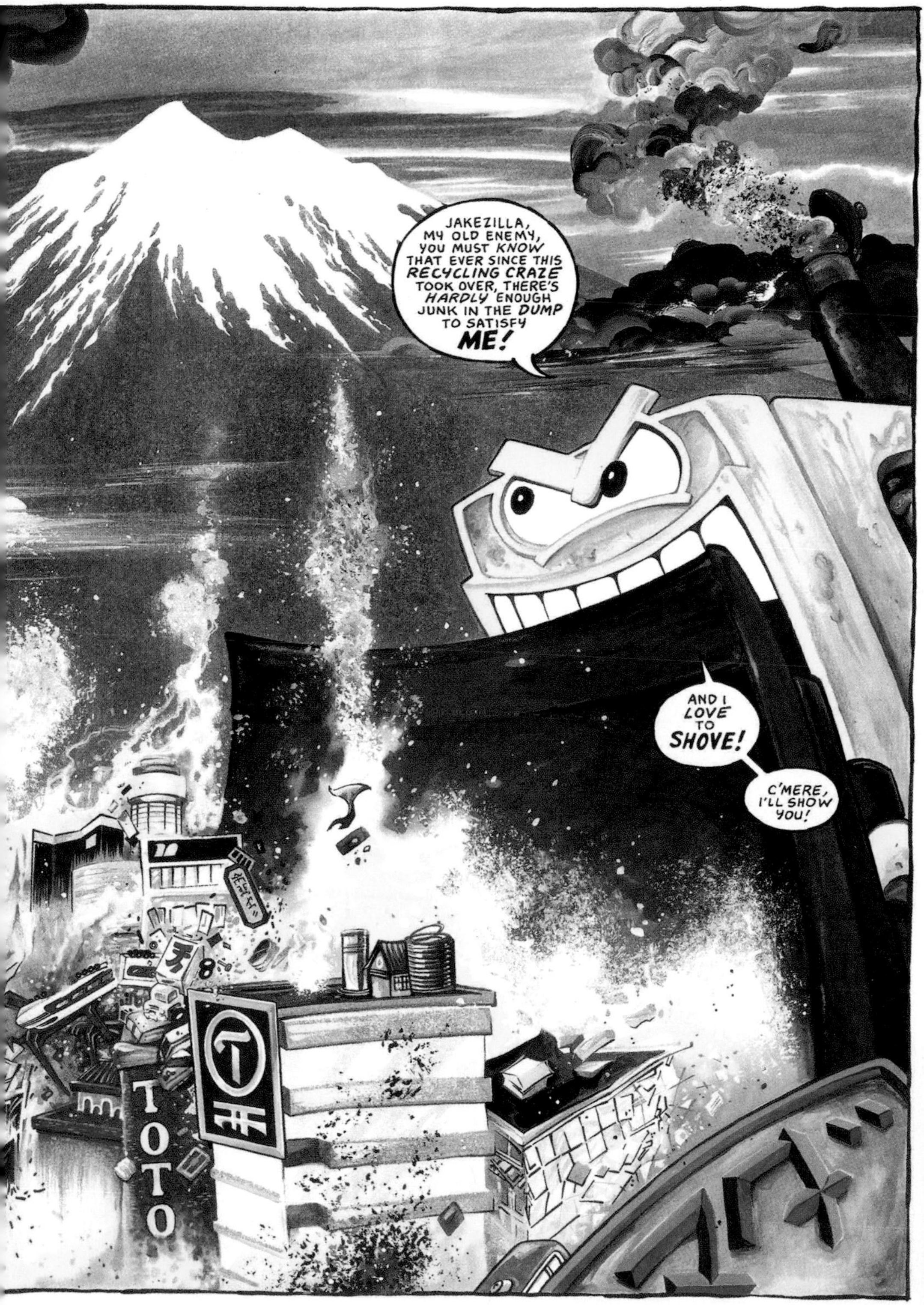
JAKEZILLA, MY OLD ENEMY, YOU MUST KNOW THAT EVER SINCE THIS RECYCLING CRAZE TOOK OVER, THERE'S HARDLY ENOUGH JUNK IN THE DUMP TO SATISFY ME!
AND I LOVE TO SHOVE!
C'MERE, I'LL SHOW YOU!
TOTO

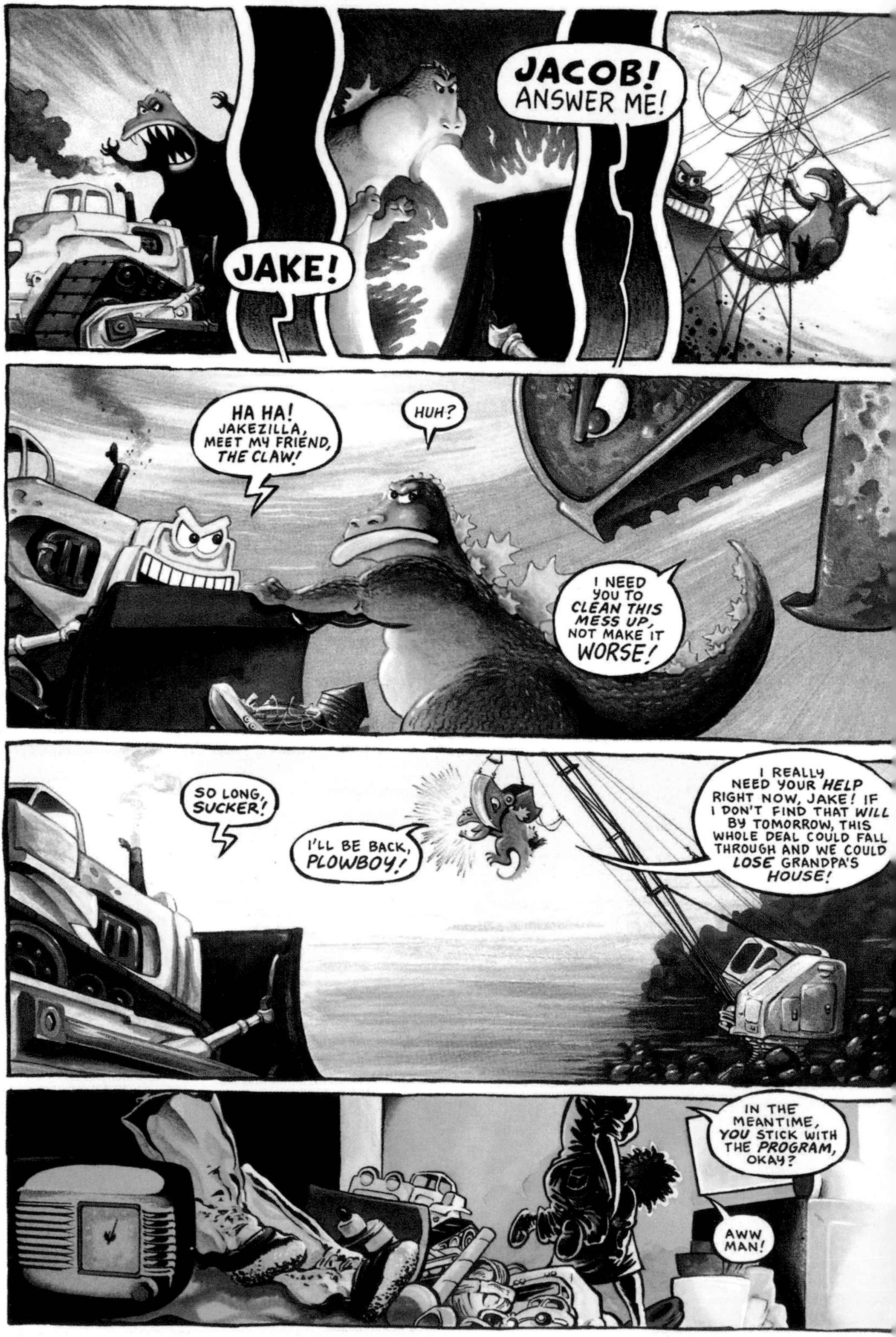
JAKE!
JACOB! ANSWER ME!
HA HA! JAKEZILLA, MEET MY FRIEND, THE CLAW!
HUH?
I NEED YOU TO CLEAN THIS MESS UP, NOT MAKE IT WORSE!
SO LONG, SUCKER!
I'LL BE BACK, PLOWBOY!
I REALLY NEED YOUR HELP RIGHT NOW, JAKE! IF I DON'T FIND THAT WILL BY TOMORROW, THIS WHOLE DEAL COULD FALL THROUGH AND WE COULD LOSE GRANDPA'S HOUSE!
IN THE MEANTIME, YOU STICK WITH THE PROGRAM, OKAY?
AWW MAN!

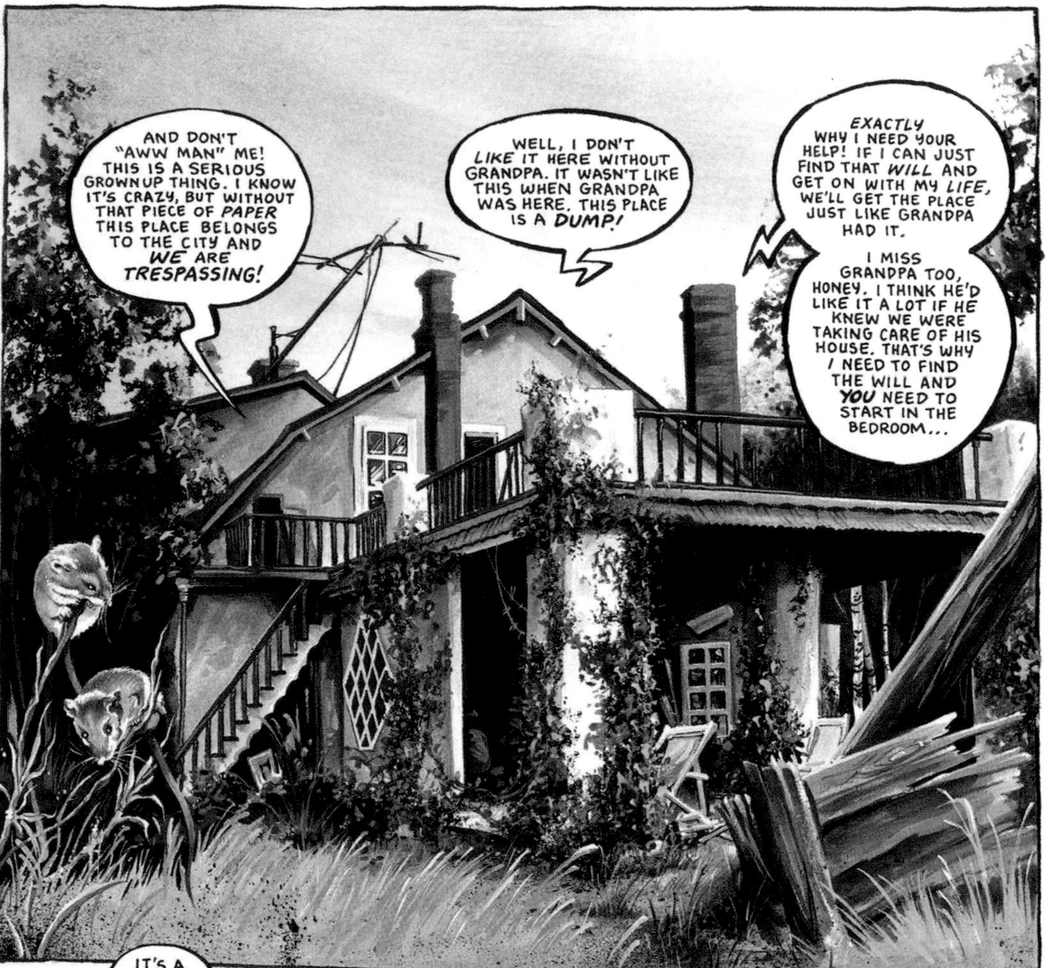
AND DON'T "AWW MAN" ME! THIS IS A SERIOUS GROWNUP THING. I KNOW IT'S CRAZY, BUT WITHOUT THAT PIECE OF *PAPER* THIS PLACE BELONGS TO THE CITY AND *WE* ARE *TRESPASSING!*
WELL, I DON'T *LIKE* IT HERE WITHOUT GRANDPA. IT WASN'T LIKE THIS WHEN GRANDPA WAS HERE. THIS PLACE IS A *DUMP!*
EXACTLY WHY I NEED YOUR HELP! IF I CAN JUST FIND THAT *WILL* AND GET ON WITH MY *LIFE,* WE'LL GET THE PLACE JUST LIKE GRANDPA HAD IT.
I MISS GRANDPA TOO, HONEY. I THINK HE'D LIKE IT A LOT IF HE KNEW WE WERE TAKING CARE OF HIS HOUSE. THAT'S WHY *I* NEED TO FIND THE WILL AND *YOU* NEED TO START IN THE BEDROOM...

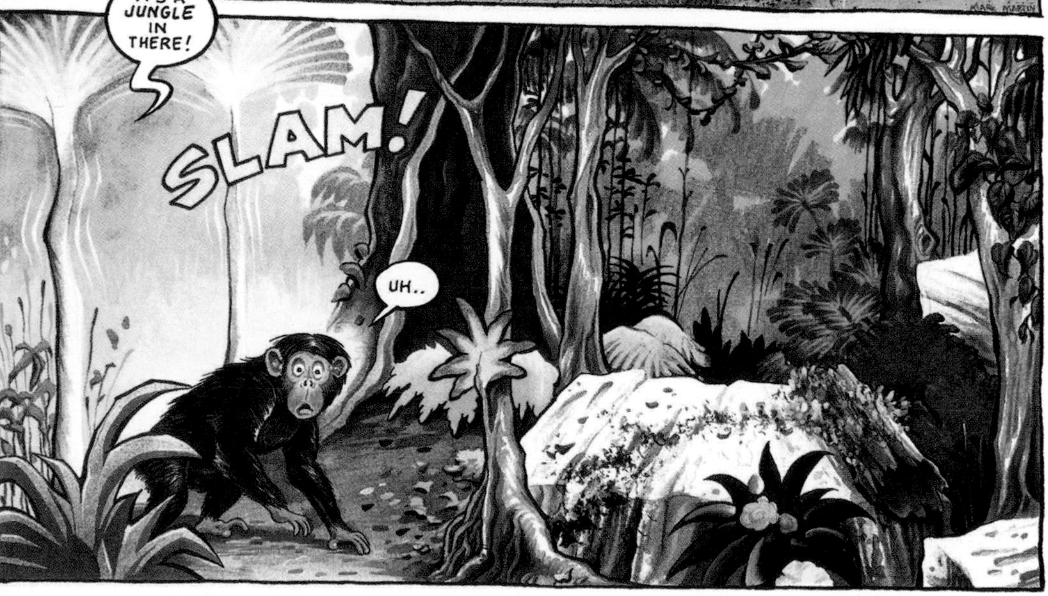
IT'S A JUNGLE IN THERE!
SLAM!
UH..

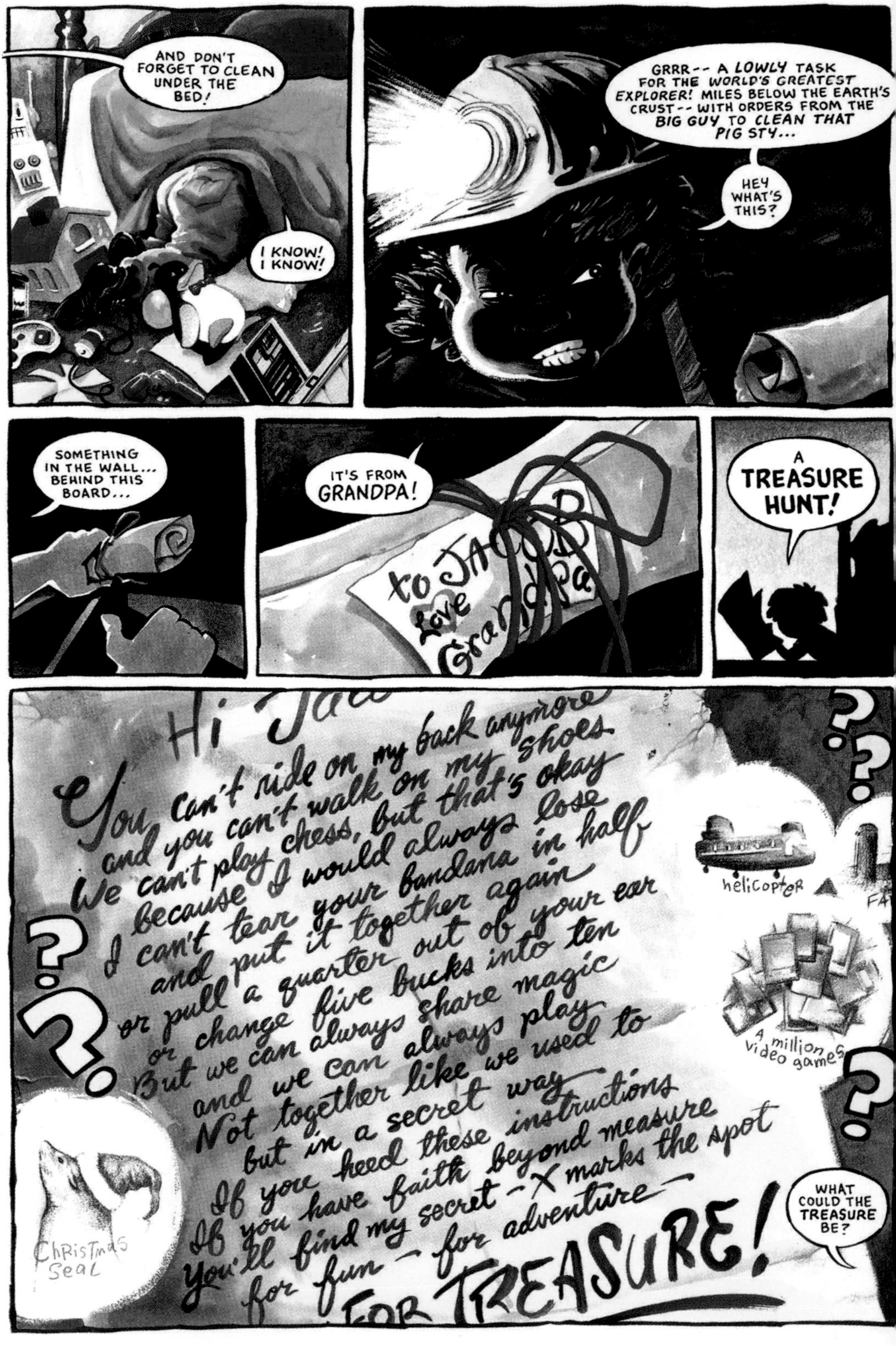
AND DON'T FORGET TO CLEAN UNDER THE BED!
I KNOW! I KNOW!
GRRR-- A LOWLY TASK FOR THE WORLD'S GREATEST EXPLORER! MILES BELOW THE EARTH'S CRUST-- WITH ORDERS FROM THE BIG GUY TO CLEAN THAT PIG STY...
HEY WHAT'S THIS?
SOMETHING IN THE WALL... BEHIND THIS BOARD...
IT'S FROM GRANDPA!
to JACOB Love Grandpa
A TREASURE HUNT!
Hi Jac
You can't ride on my back anymore
and you can't walk on my shoes
We can't play chess, but that's okay
because I would always lose
I can't tear your bandana in half
and put it together again
or pull a quarter out of your ear
or change five bucks into ten
But we can always share magic
and we can always play
Not together like we used to
but in a secret way
If you heed these instructions
If you have faith beyond measure
you'll find my secret - X marks the spot
for fun - for adventure -
FOR TREASURE!
helicopter
A million video games
Christmas Seal
WHAT COULD THE TREASURE BE?

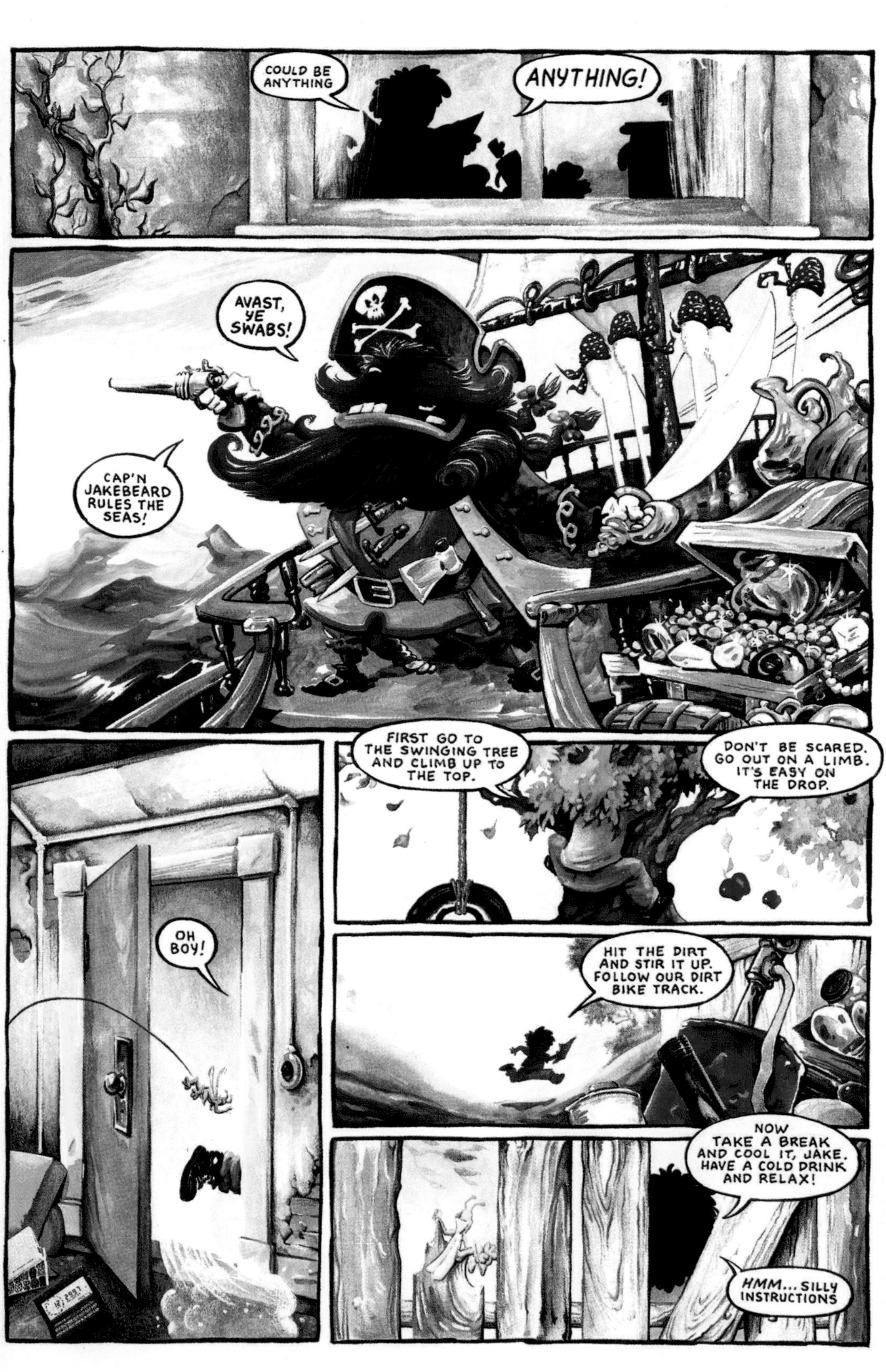
COULD BE ANYTHING
ANYTHING!
AVAST, YE SWABS!
CAP'N JAKEBEARD RULES THE SEAS!
OH BOY!
FIRST GO TO THE SWINGING TREE AND CLIMB UP TO THE TOP.
DON'T BE SCARED. GO OUT ON A LIMB. IT'S EASY ON THE DROP.
HIT THE DIRT AND STIR IT UP. FOLLOW OUR DIRT BIKE TRACK.
NOW TAKE A BREAK AND COOL IT, JAKE. HAVE A COLD DRINK AND RELAX!
HMM... SILLY INSTRUCTIONS

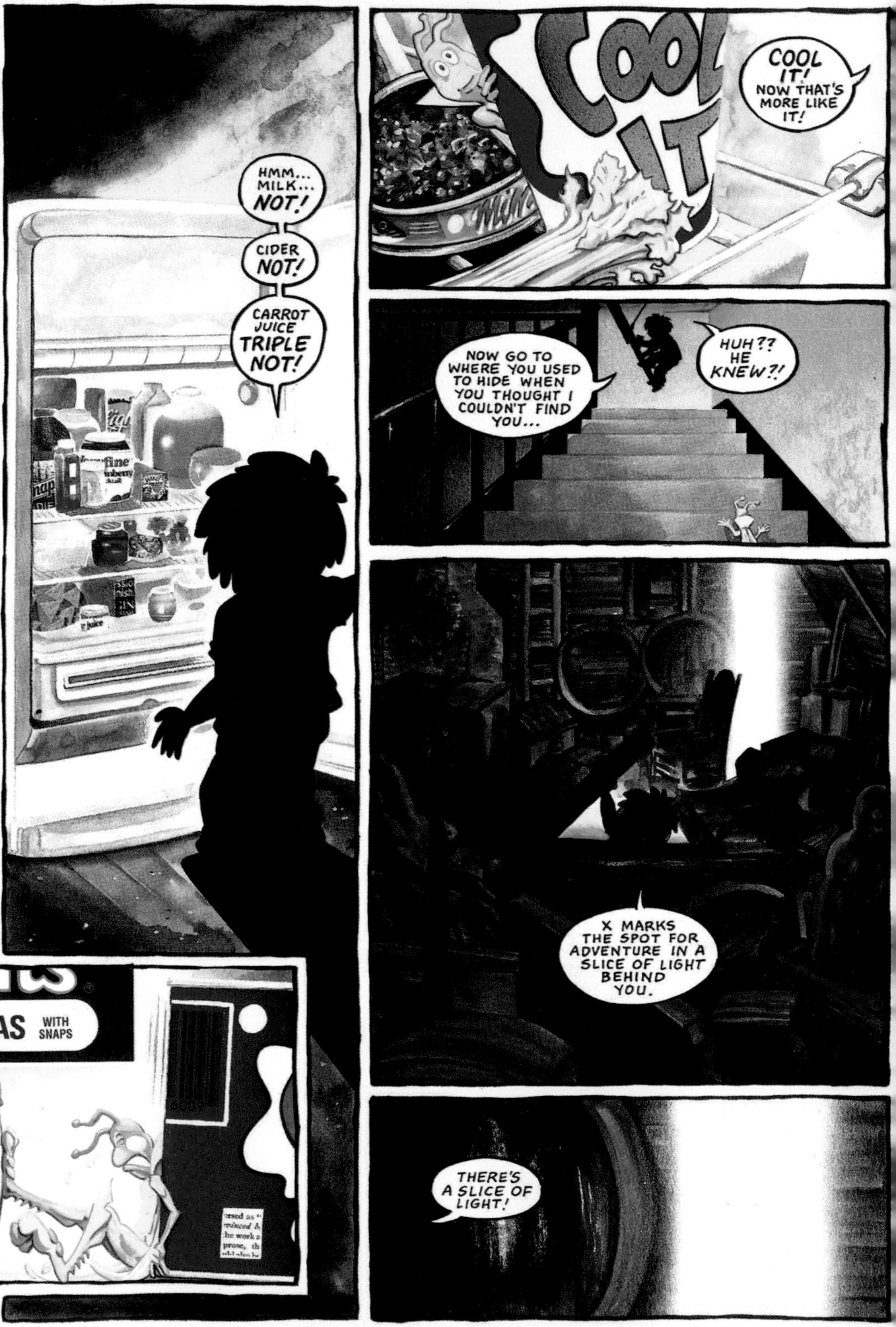
HMM... MILK... NOT!
CIDER NOT!
CARROT JUICE TRIPLE NOT!
COOL IT! NOW THAT'S MORE LIKE IT!
NOW GO TO WHERE YOU USED TO HIDE WHEN YOU THOUGHT I COULDN'T FIND YOU...
HUH?? HE KNEW?!
X MARKS THE SPOT FOR ADVENTURE IN A SLICE OF LIGHT BEHIND YOU.
WITH SNAPS
THERE'S A SLICE OF LIGHT!

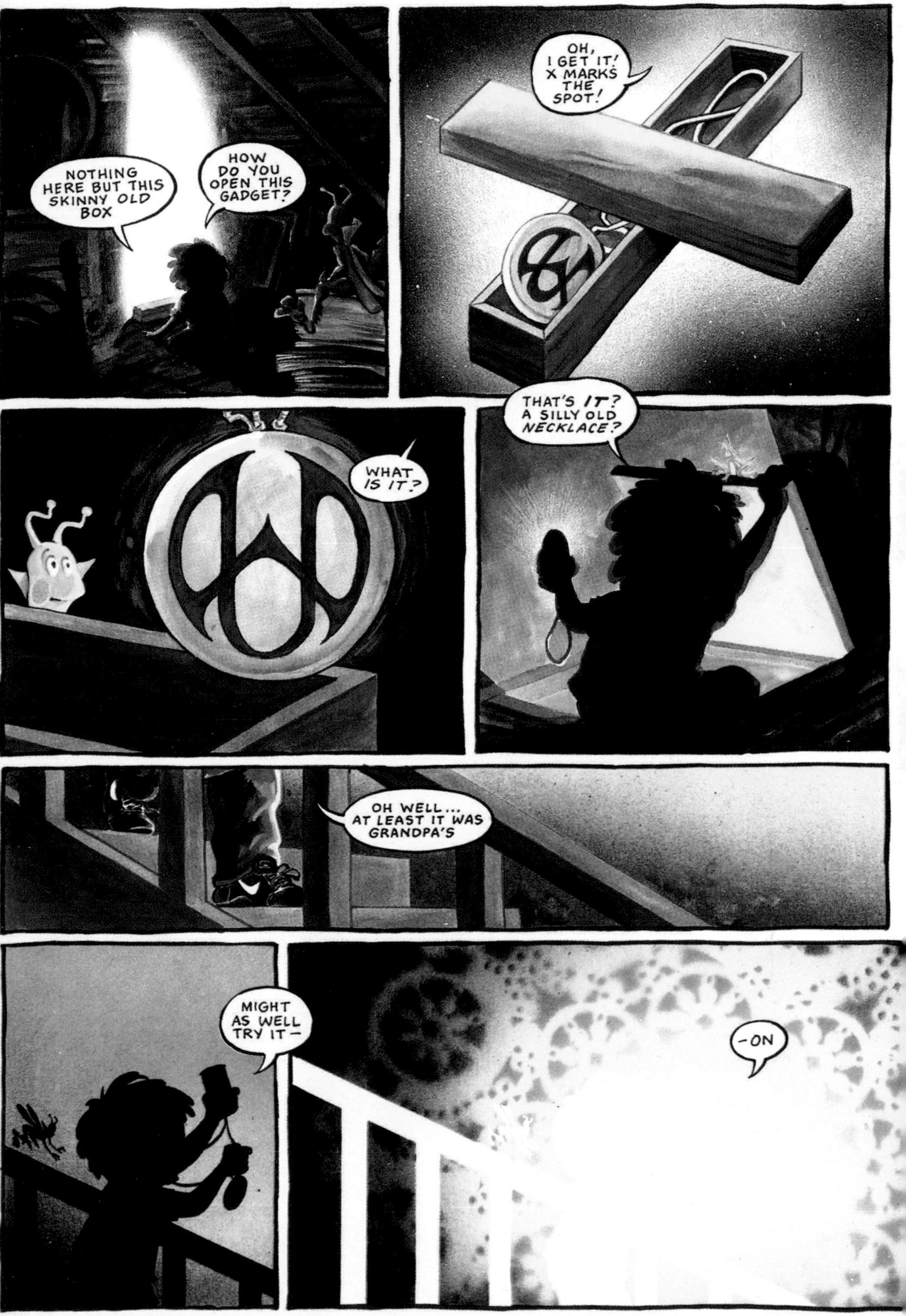
NOTHING HERE BUT THIS SKINNY OLD BOX
HOW DO YOU OPEN THIS GADGET?
OH, I GET IT! X MARKS THE SPOT!
WHAT IS IT?
THAT'S IT? A SILLY OLD NECKLACE?
OH WELL... AT LEAST IT WAS GRANDPA'S
MIGHT AS WELL TRY IT—
-ON

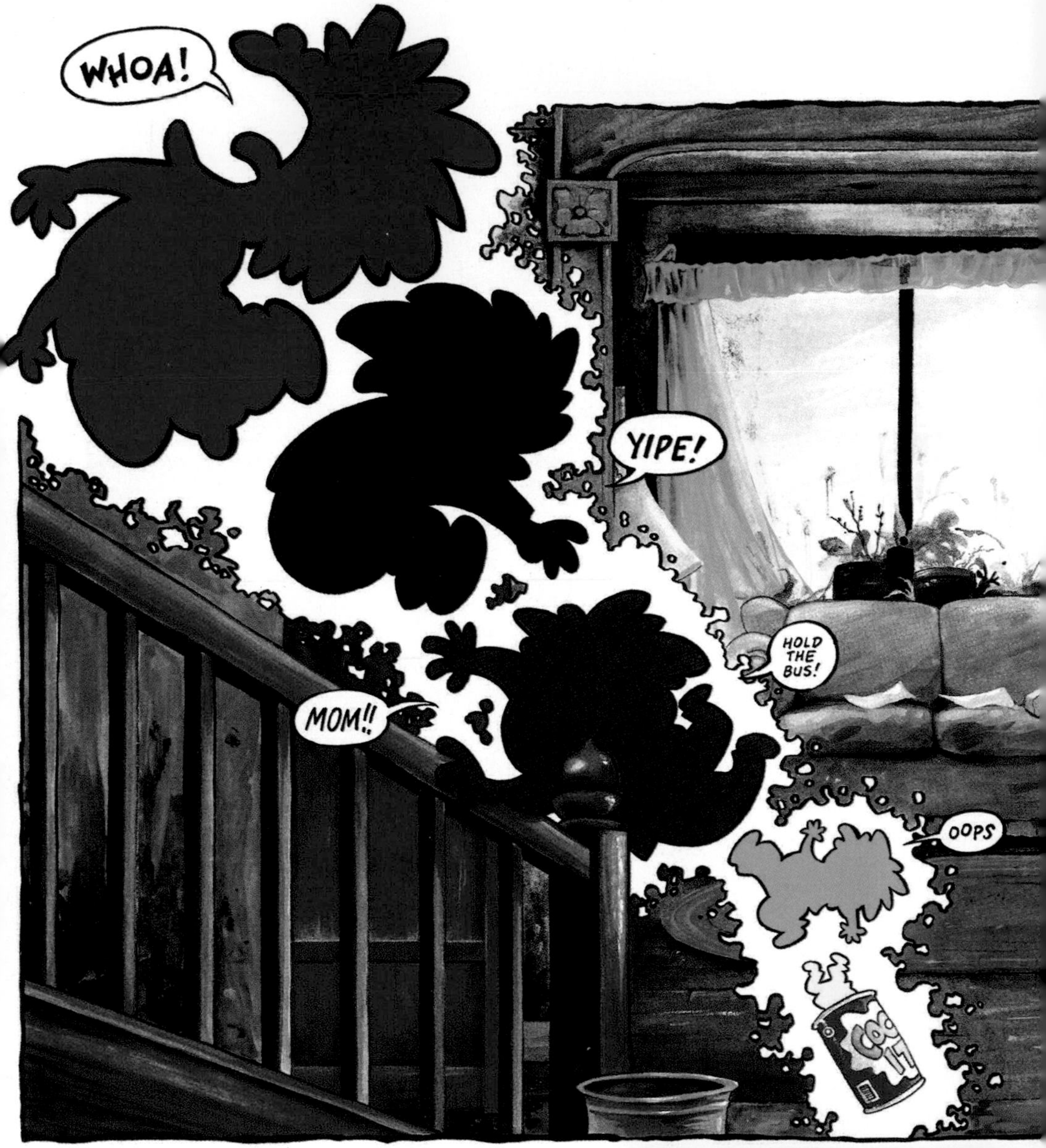
WHOA!
YIPE!
MOM!!
HOLD THE BUS!
OOPS

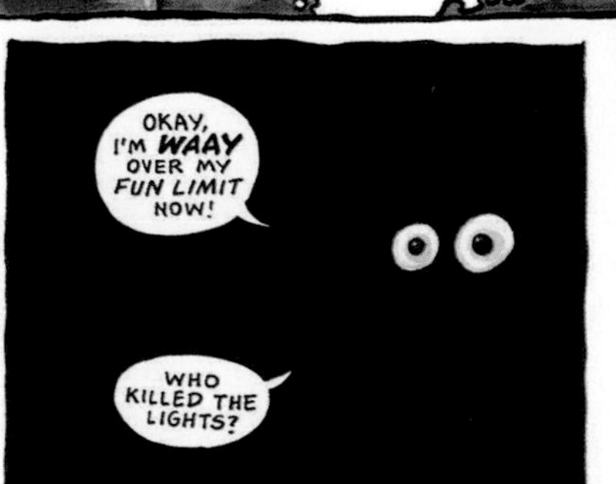
OKAY, I'M WAAY OVER MY FUN LIMIT NOW!
WHO KILLED THE LIGHTS?

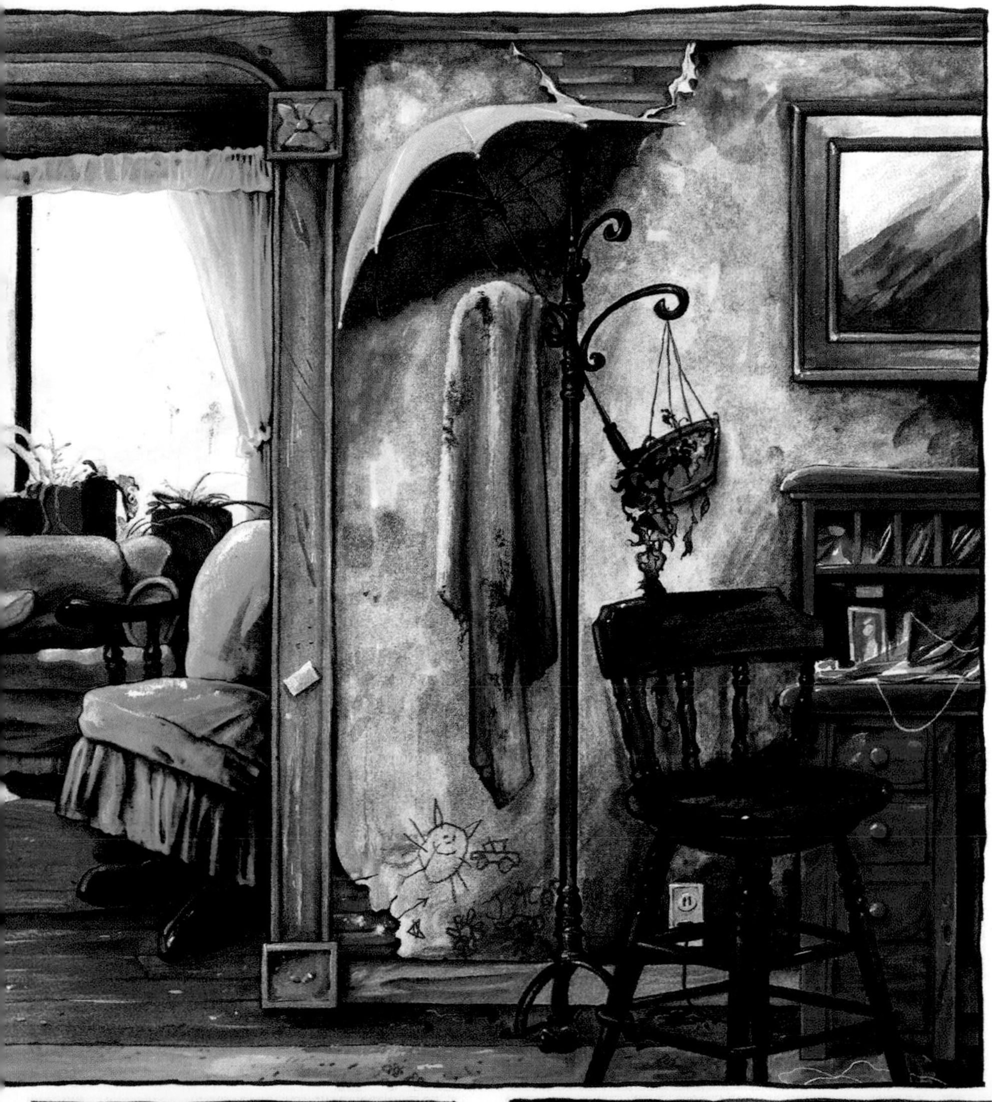

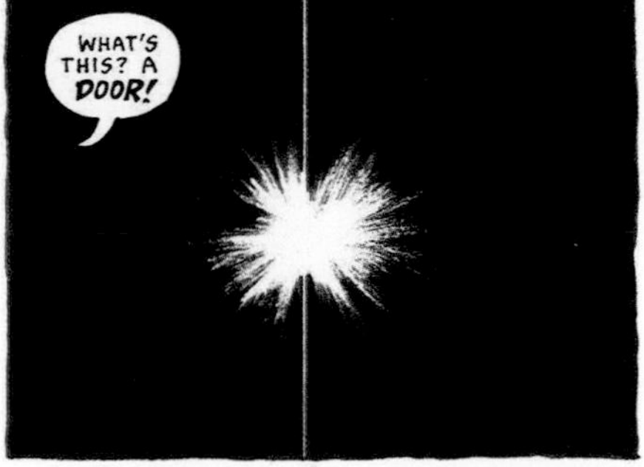
WHAT'S THIS? A DOOR!

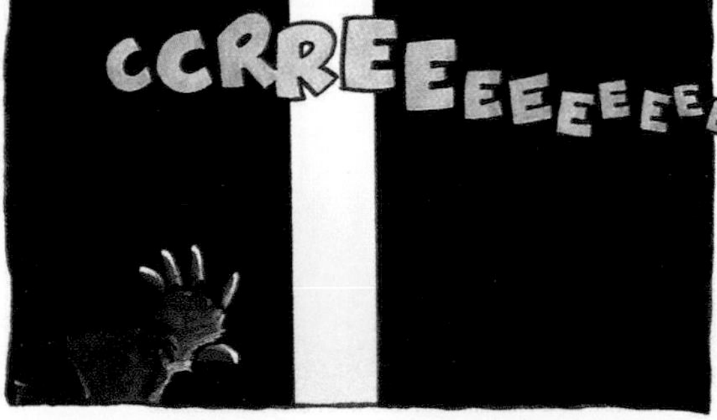
CCRREEEEEEEEE

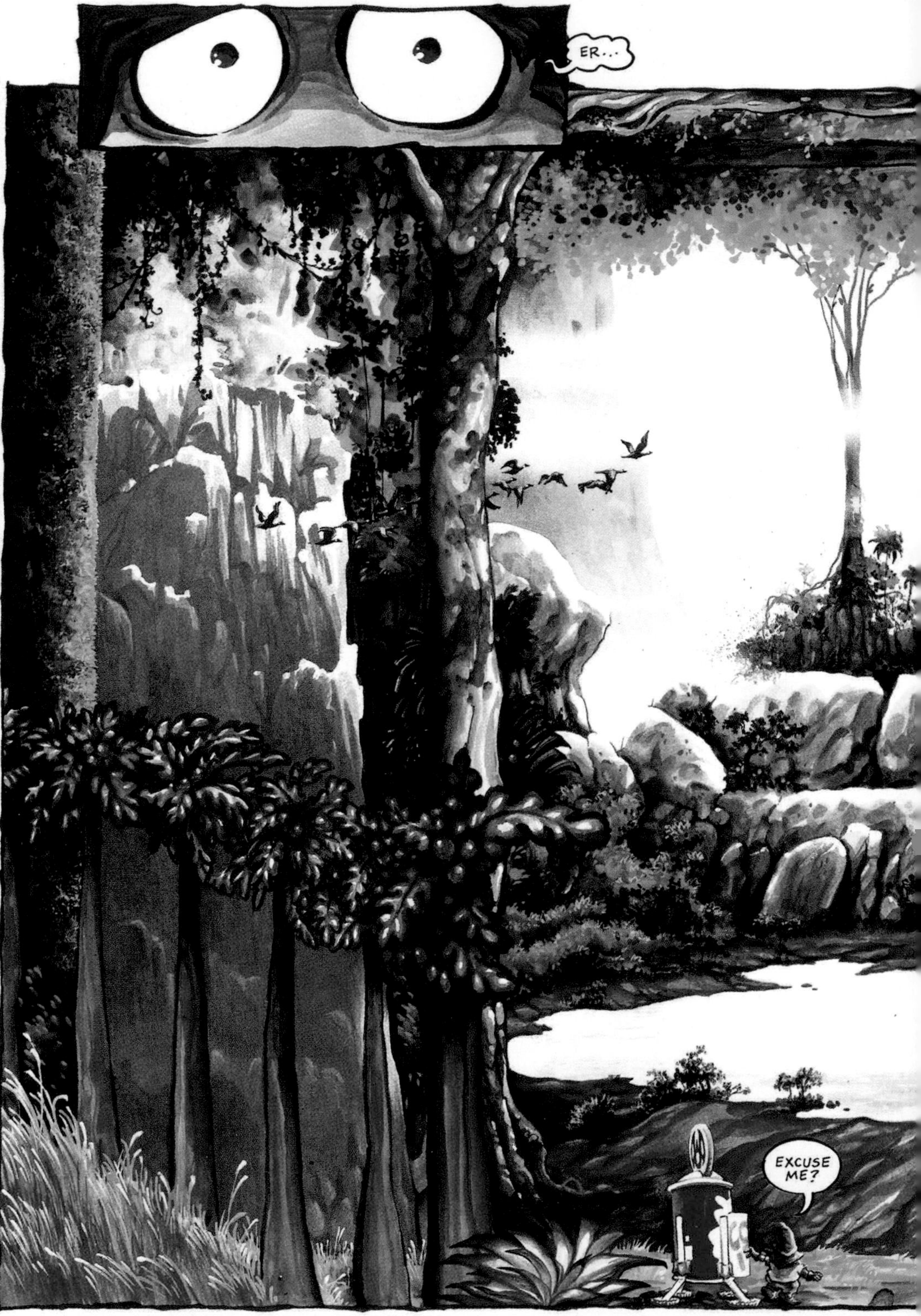
ER...
EXCUSE ME?

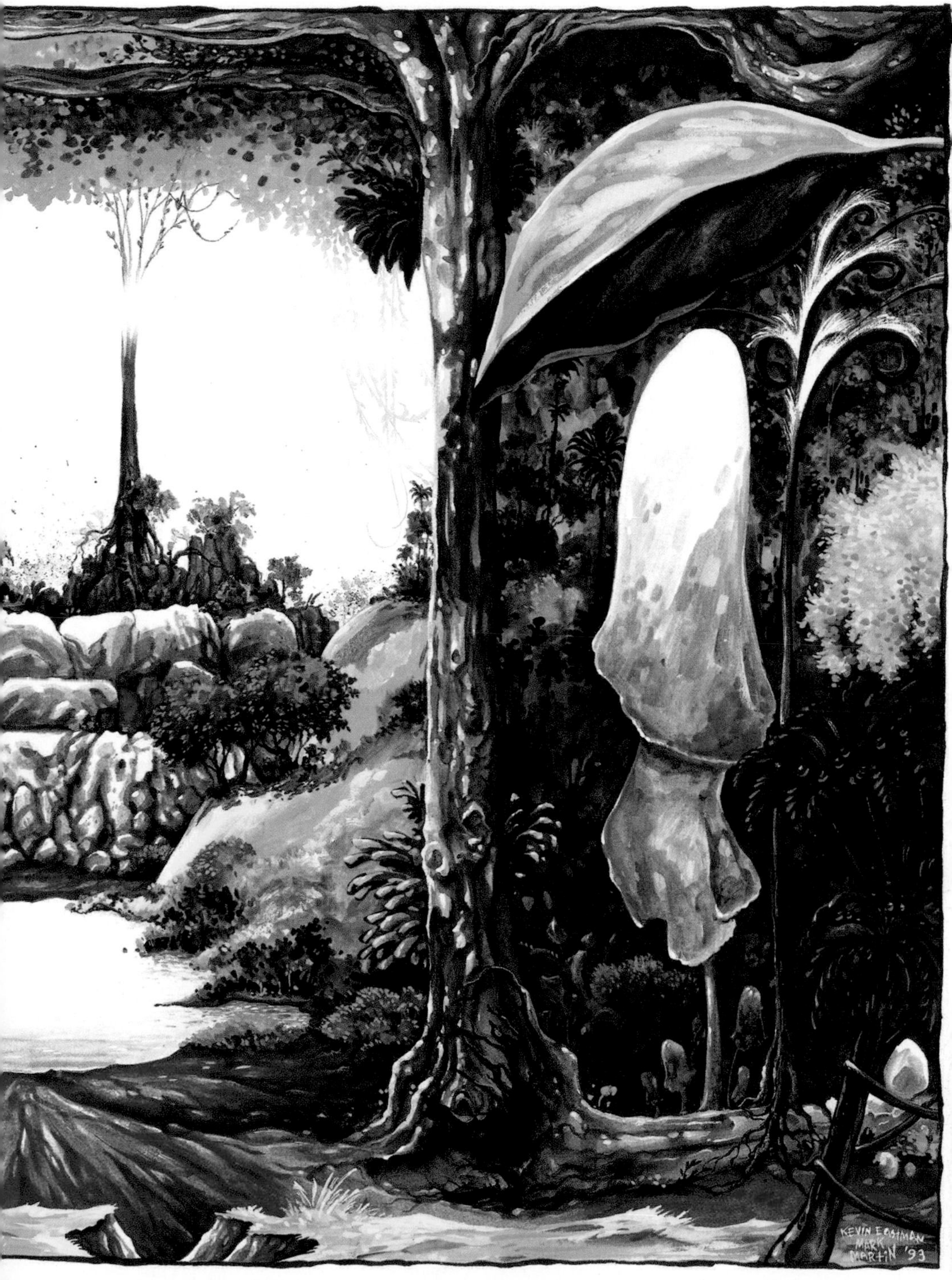
KEVIN EASTMAN
MARK MARTIN '93

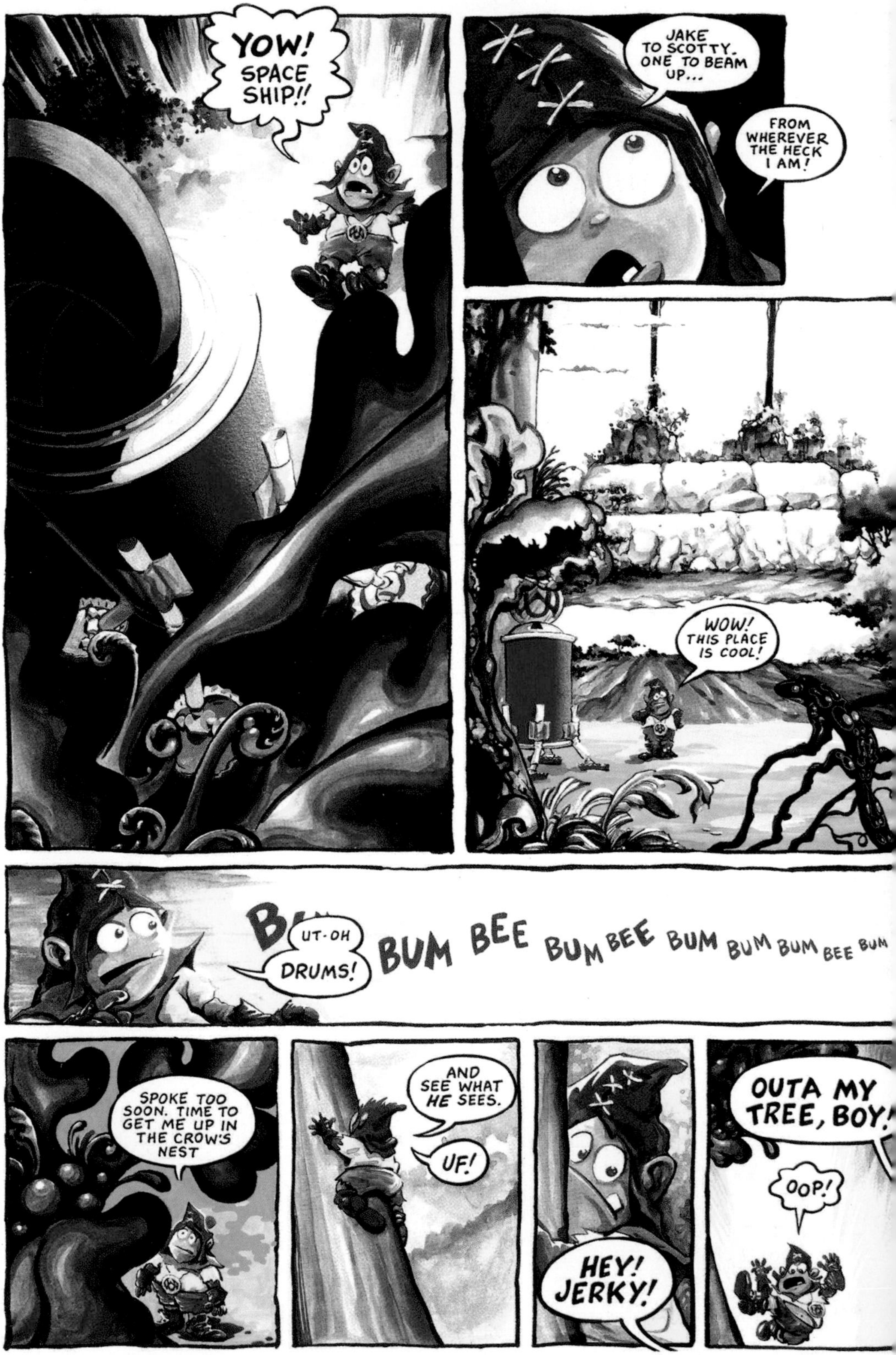
YOW! SPACE SHIP!!
JAKE TO SCOTTY. ONE TO BEAM UP...
FROM WHEREVER THE HECK I AM!
WOW! THIS PLACE IS COOL!
UT-OH DRUMS!
BUM BEE BUM BEE BUM BUM BUM BEE BUM
SPOKE TOO SOON. TIME TO GET ME UP IN THE CROW'S NEST
AND SEE WHAT HE SEES.
UF!
HEY! JERKY!
OUTA MY TREE, BOY!
OOP!

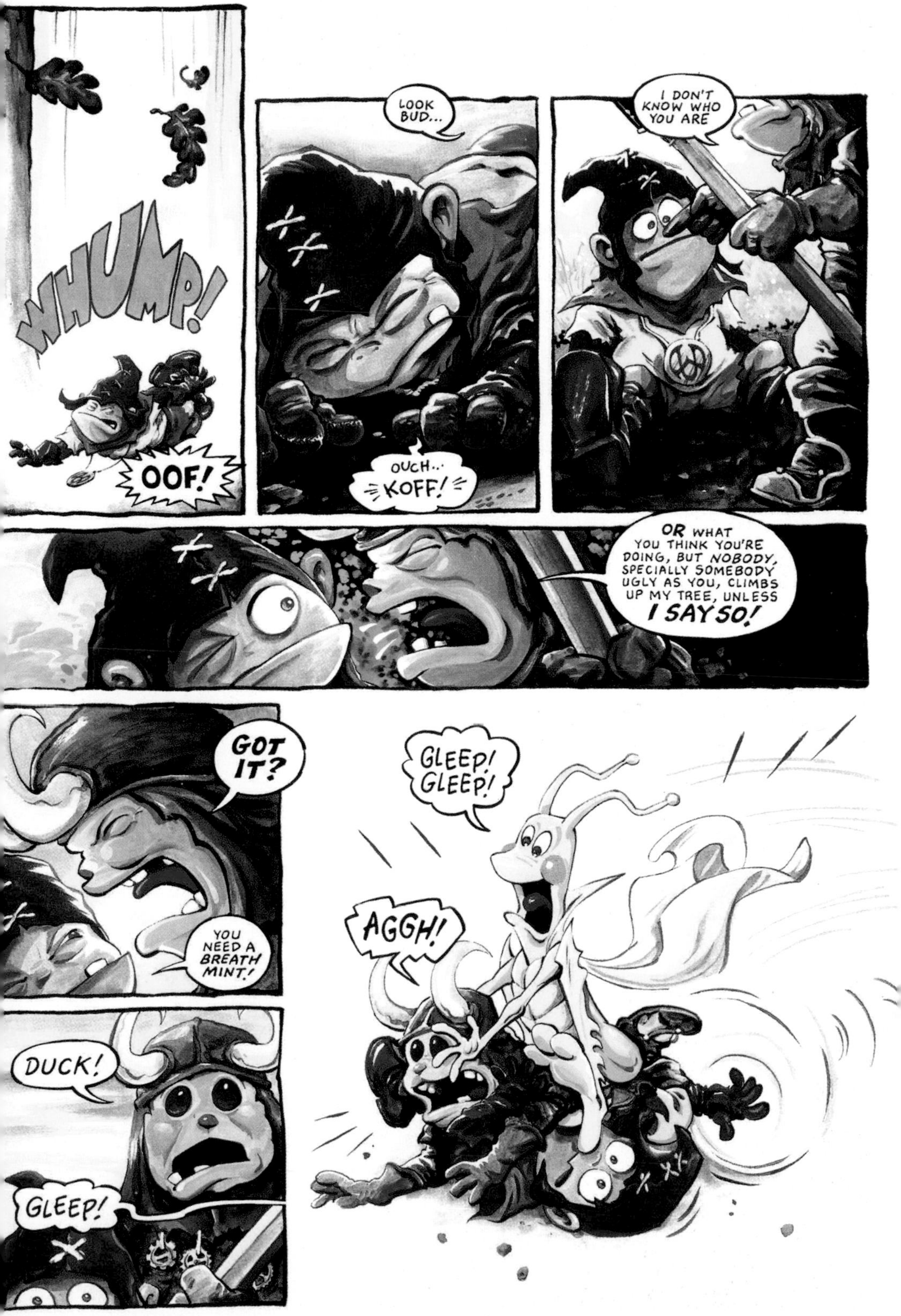
WHUMP!
OOF!
LOOK BUD...
OUCH... KOFF!
I DON'T KNOW WHO YOU ARE
OR WHAT YOU THINK YOU'RE DOING, BUT NOBODY, SPECIALLY SOMEBODY UGLY AS YOU, CLIMBS UP MY TREE, UNLESS I SAY SO!
GOT IT?
YOU NEED A BREATH MINT!
DUCK!
GLEEP!
GLEEP! GLEEP!
AGGH!

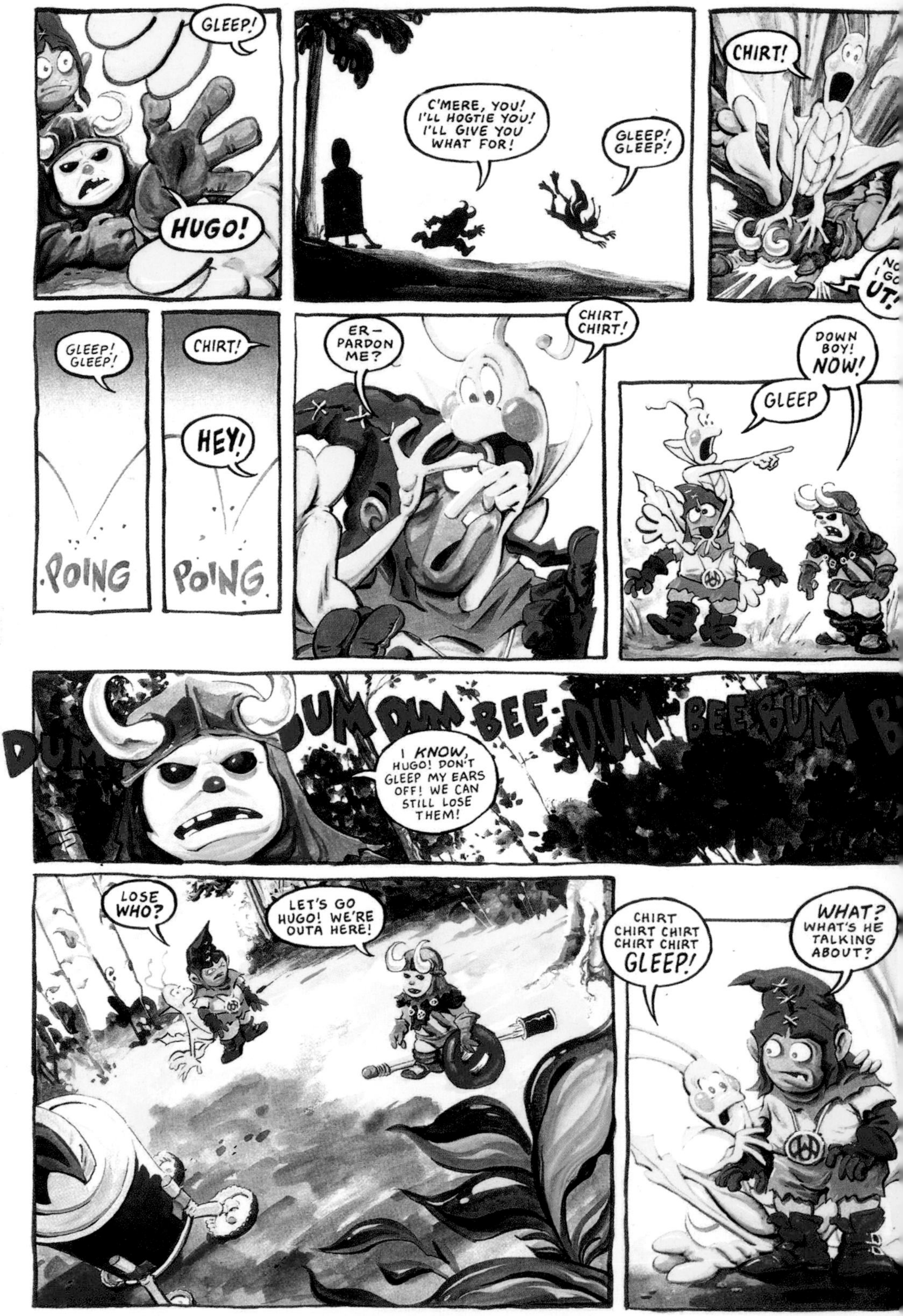
GLEEP!
HUGO!
C'MERE, YOU! I'LL HOGTIE YOU! I'LL GIVE YOU WHAT FOR!
GLEEP! GLEEP!
CHIRT!
GLEEP! GLEEP!
POING
CHIRT!
HEY!
POING
ER—PARDON ME?
CHIRT CHIRT!
DOWN BOY! NOW!
GLEEP
DUM DUM DUM BEE-DUM BEE BUM
I KNOW, HUGO! DON'T GLEEP MY EARS OFF! WE CAN STILL LOSE THEM!
LOSE WHO?
LET'S GO HUGO! WE'RE OUTA HERE!
CHIRT CHIRT CHIRT CHIRT CHIRT GLEEP!
WHAT? WHAT'S HE TALKING ABOUT?

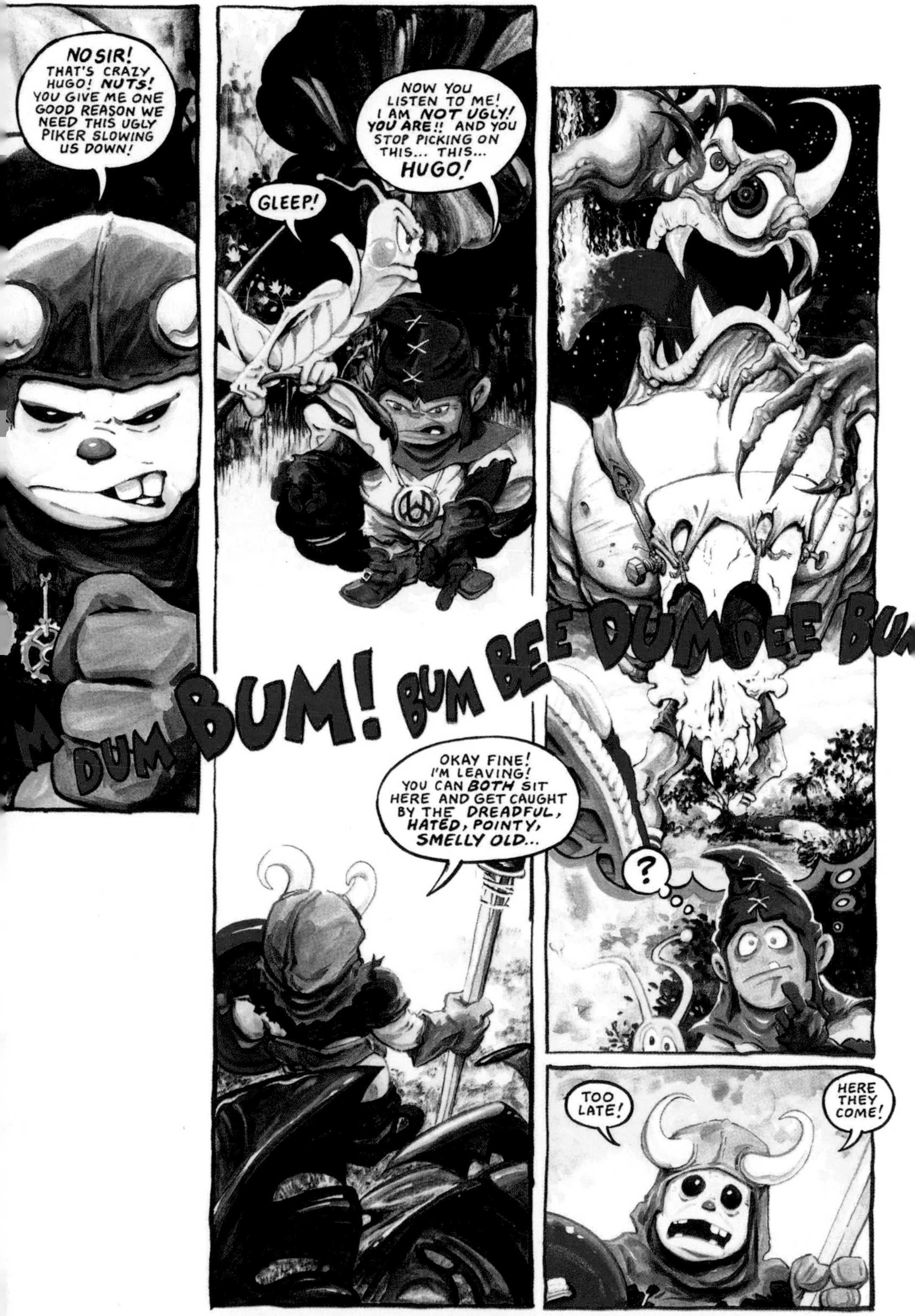
NO SIR! THAT'S CRAZY HUGO! NUTS! YOU GIVE ME ONE GOOD REASON WE NEED THIS UGLY PIKER SLOWING US DOWN!
NOW YOU LISTEN TO ME! I AM NOT UGLY! YOU ARE!! AND YOU STOP PICKING ON THIS... THIS... HUGO!
GLEEP!
DUM BUM! BUM BEE DUMDEE BU
OKAY FINE! I'M LEAVING! YOU CAN BOTH SIT HERE AND GET CAUGHT BY THE DREADFUL, HATED, POINTY, SMELLY OLD...
?
TOO LATE!
HERE THEY COME!

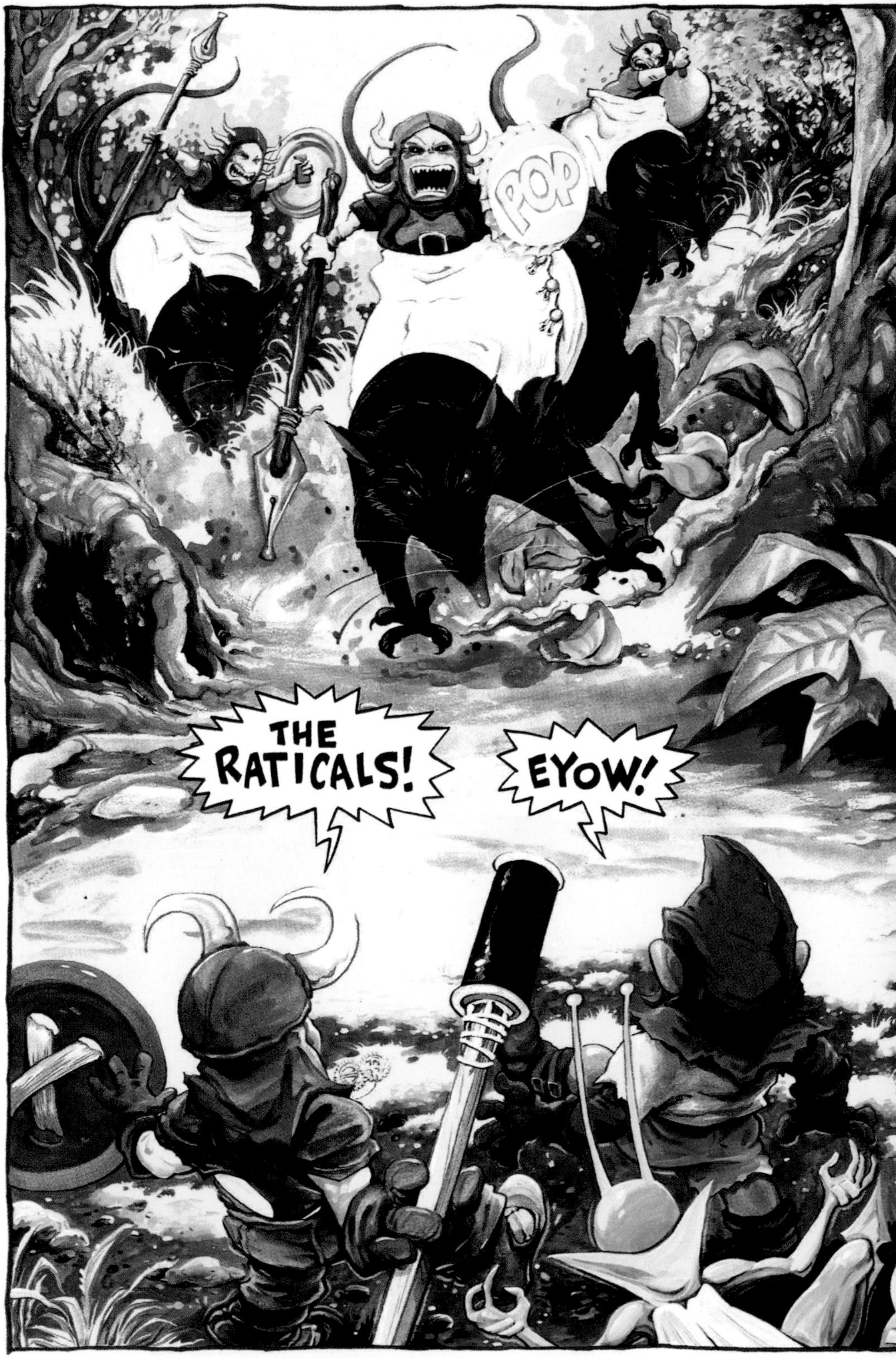
POP
THE RATICALS!
EYOW!

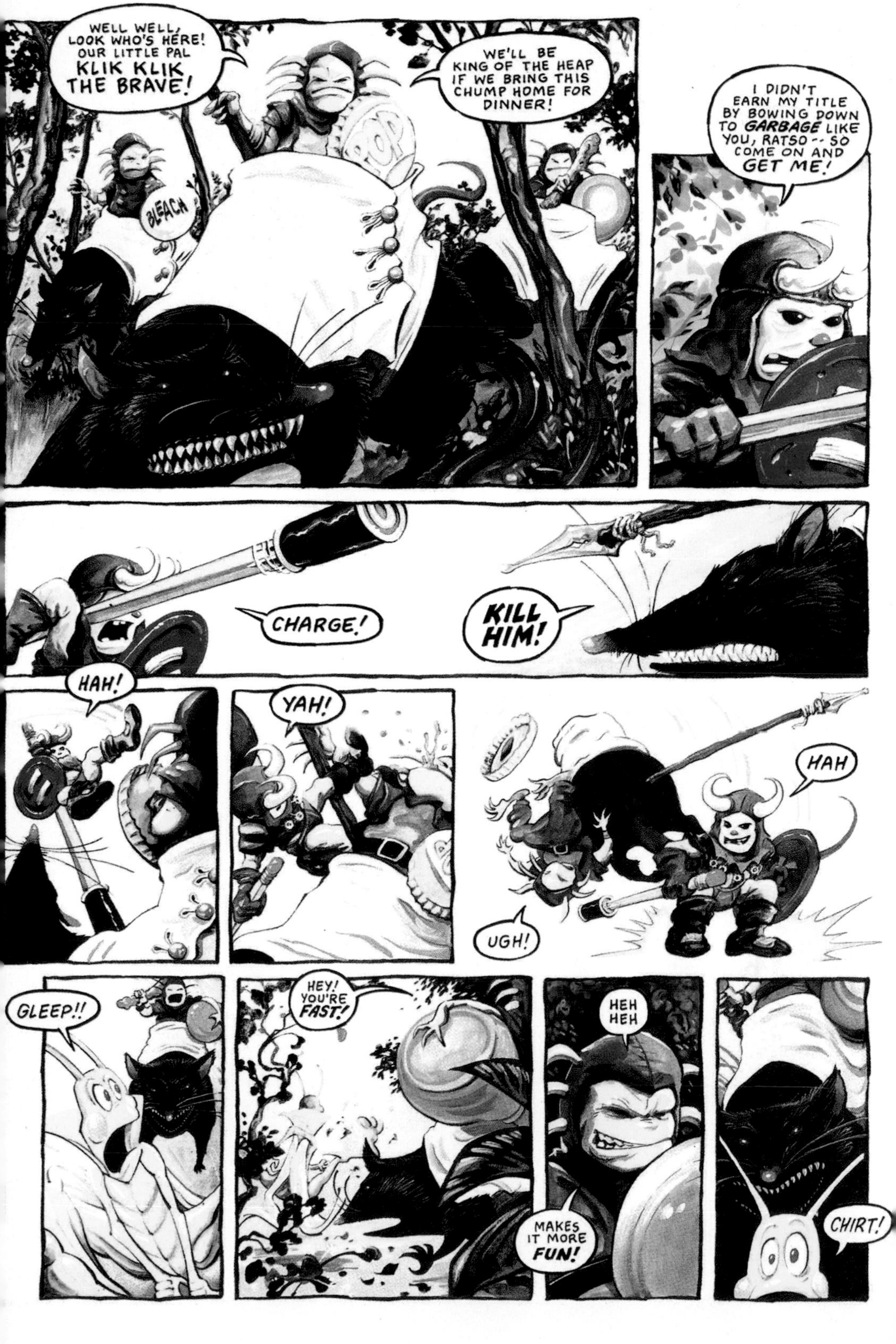
WELL WELL, LOOK WHO'S HERE! OUR LITTLE PAL KLIK KLIK THE BRAVE!
BLEACH
POP
WE'LL BE KING OF THE HEAP IF WE BRING THIS CHUMP HOME FOR DINNER!
I DIDN'T EARN MY TITLE BY BOWING DOWN TO GARBAGE LIKE YOU, RATSO -- SO COME ON AND GET ME!
CHARGE!
KILL HIM!
HAH!
YAH!
HAH
UGH!
GLEEP!!
HEY! YOU'RE FAST!
HEH HEH
MAKES IT MORE FUN!
CHIRT!

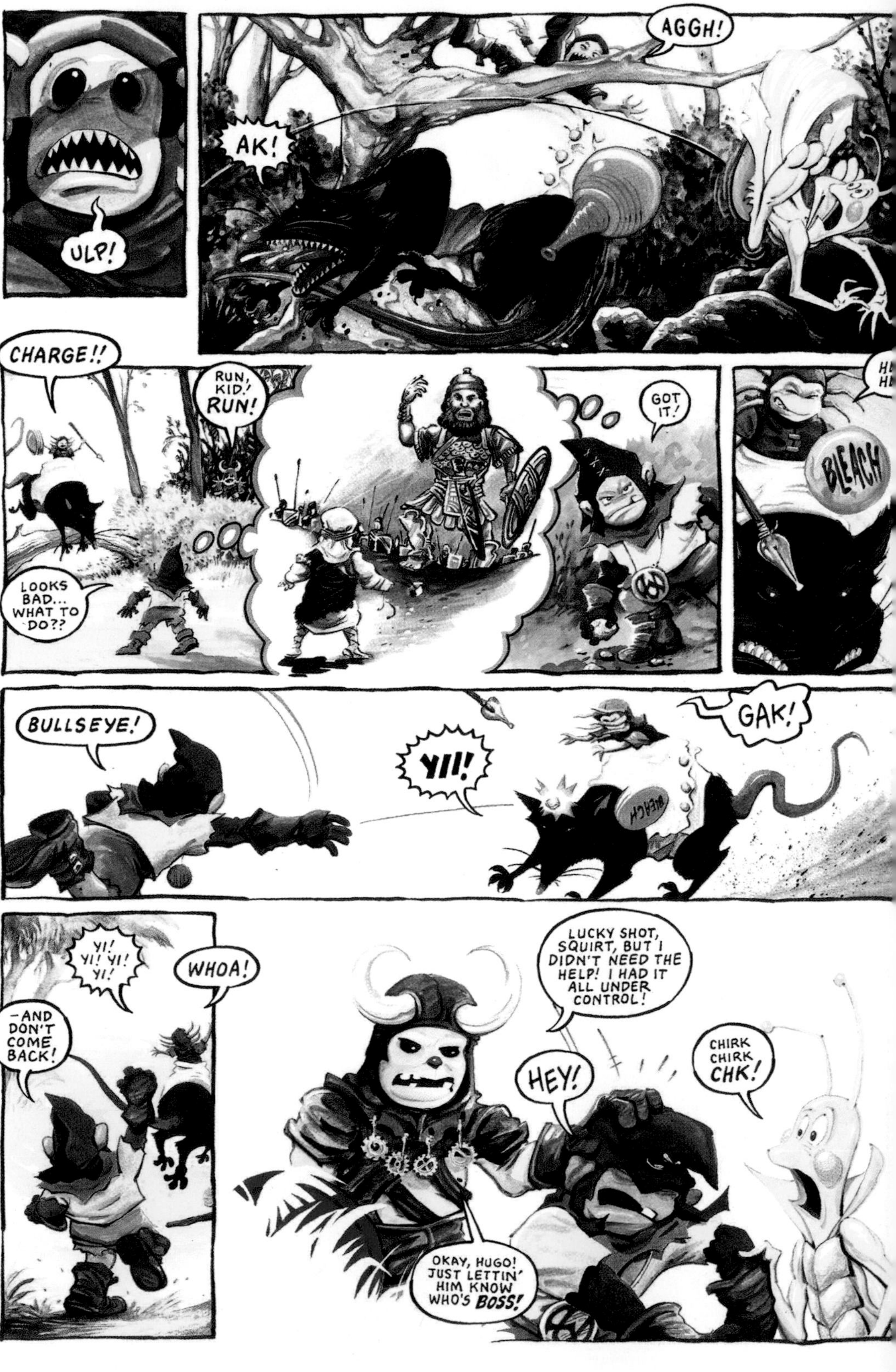
ULP!
AGGH!
AK!
CHARGE!!
RUN, KID! RUN!
LOOKS BAD... WHAT TO DO??
GOT IT!
BLEACH
BULLSEYE!
YII!
GAK!
BLEACH
YI! YI! YI! YI!
WHOA!
-AND DON'T COME BACK!
LUCKY SHOT, SQUIRT, BUT I DIDN'T NEED THE HELP! I HAD IT ALL UNDER CONTROL!
HEY!
CHIRK CHIRK CHK!
OKAY, HUGO! JUST LETTIN' HIM KNOW WHO'S BOSS!

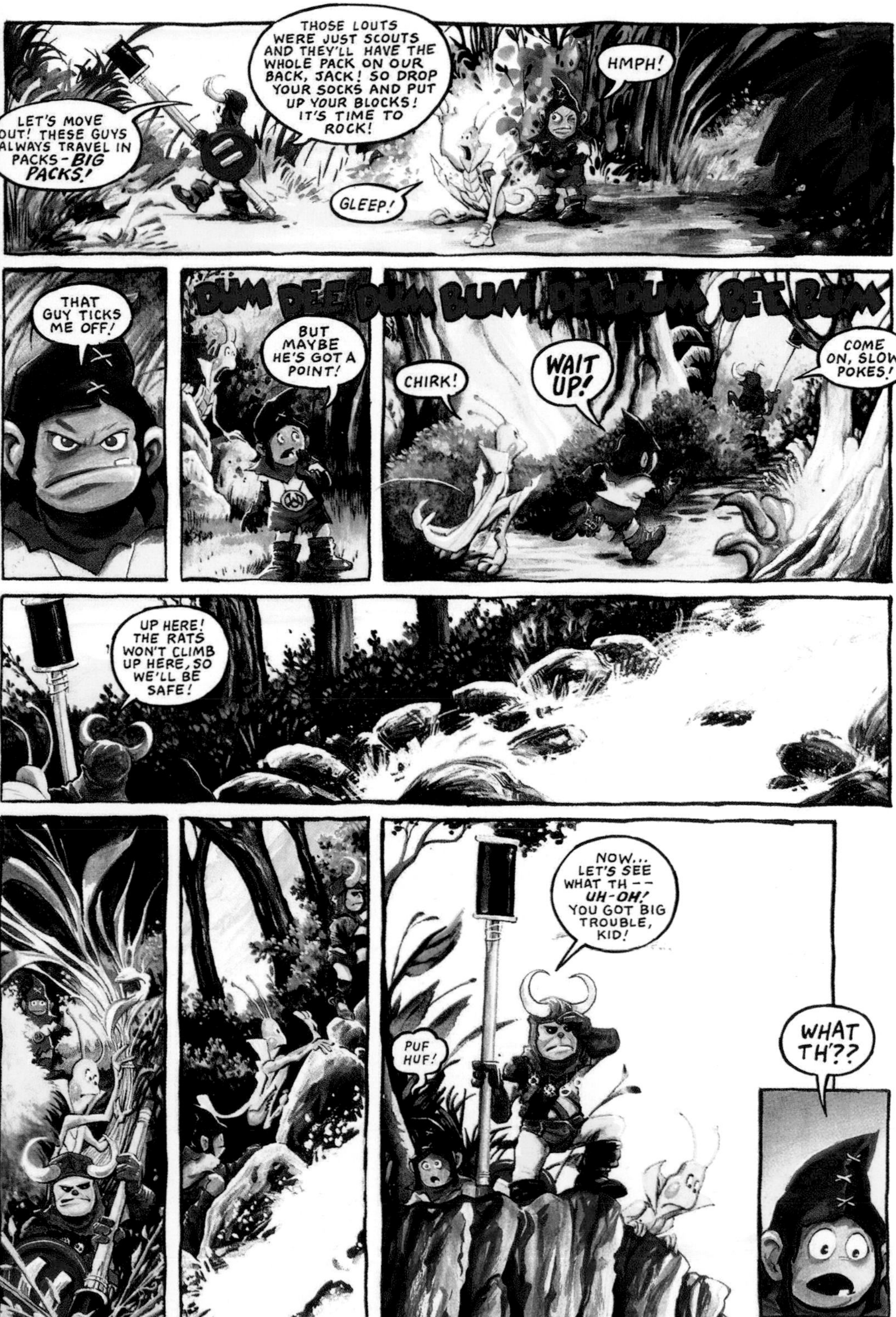
LET'S MOVE OUT! THESE GUYS ALWAYS TRAVEL IN PACKS-BIG PACKS!
THOSE LOUTS WERE JUST SCOUTS AND THEY'LL HAVE THE WHOLE PACK ON OUR BACK, JACK! SO DROP YOUR SOCKS AND PUT UP YOUR BLOCKS! IT'S TIME TO ROCK!
GLEEP!
HMPH!
THAT GUY TICKS ME OFF!
BUT MAYBE HE'S GOT A POINT!
DUM DEE DUM BUM DEEDUM BEE BUM
CHIRK!
WAIT UP!
COME ON, SLOW POKES!
UP HERE! THE RATS WON'T CLIMB UP HERE, SO WE'LL BE SAFE!
NOW... LET'S SEE WHAT TH -- UH-OH! YOU GOT BIG TROUBLE, KID!
PUF HUF!
WHAT TH'??

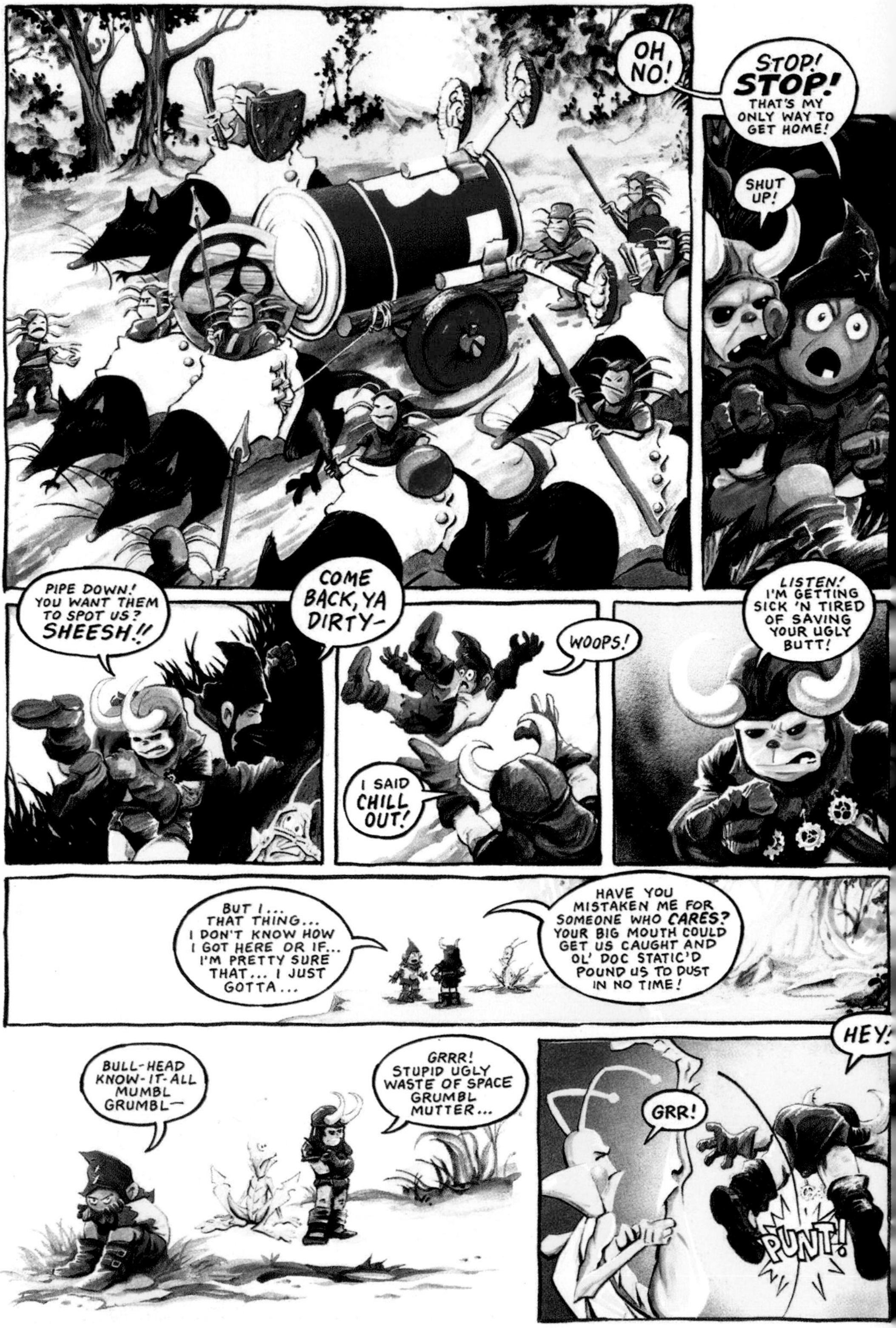
OH NO!
STOP! STOP! THAT'S MY ONLY WAY TO GET HOME!
SHUT UP!
PIPE DOWN! YOU WANT THEM TO SPOT US? SHEESH!!
COME BACK, YA DIRTY-
WOOPS!
I SAID CHILL OUT!
LISTEN! I'M GETTING SICK 'N TIRED OF SAVING YOUR UGLY BUTT!
BUT I... THAT THING... I DON'T KNOW HOW I GOT HERE OR IF... I'M PRETTY SURE THAT... I JUST GOTTA...
HAVE YOU MISTAKEN ME FOR SOMEONE WHO CARES? YOUR BIG MOUTH COULD GET US CAUGHT AND OL' DOC STATIC'D POUND US TO DUST IN NO TIME!
BULL-HEAD KNOW-IT-ALL MUMBL GRUMBL—
GRRR! STUPID UGLY WASTE OF SPACE GRUMBL MUTTER...
HEY!
GRR!
PUNT!

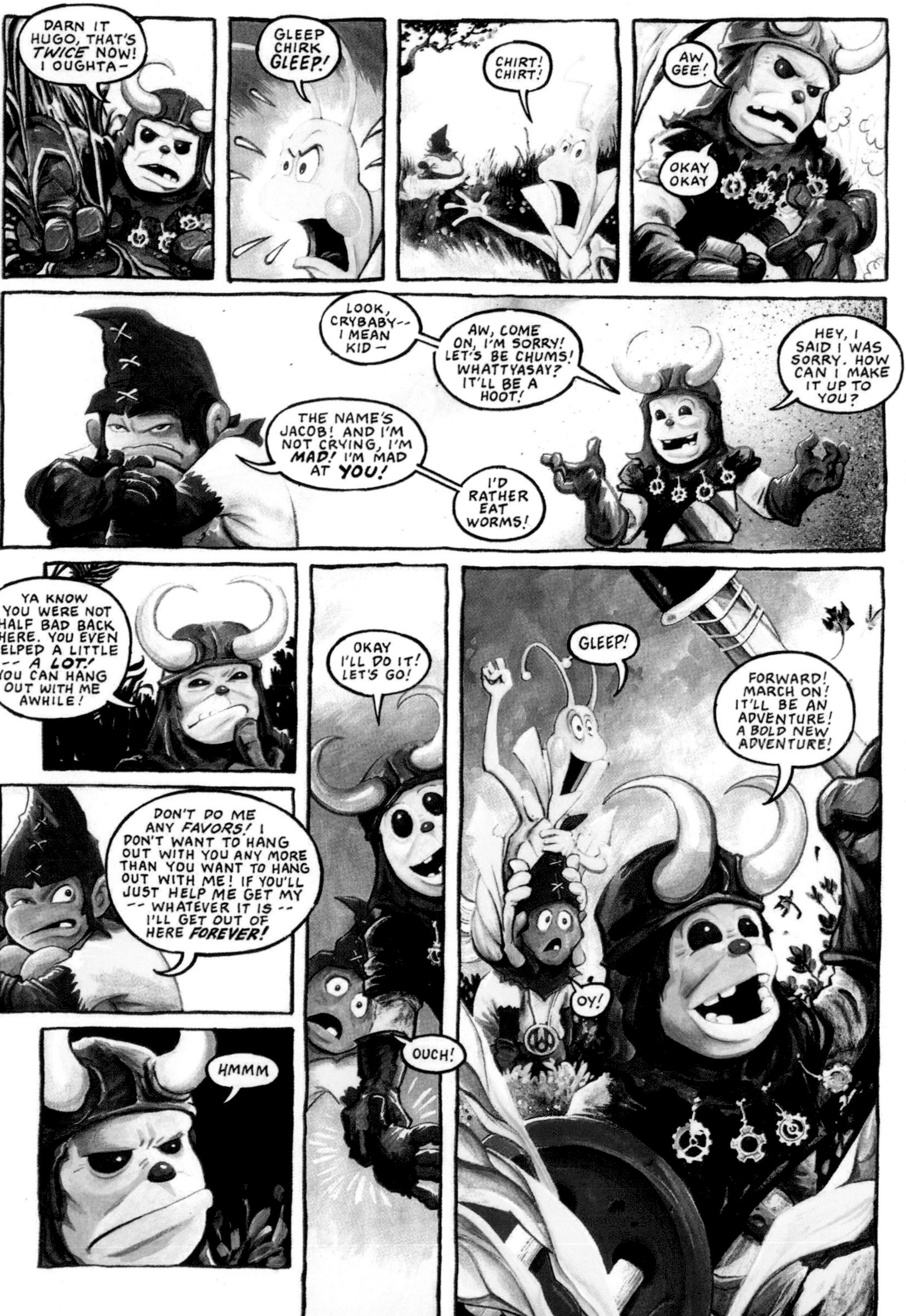
DARN IT HUGO, THAT'S TWICE NOW! I OUGHTA-
GLEEP CHIRK GLEEP!
CHIRT! CHIRT!
AW GEE!
OKAY OKAY
LOOK, CRYBABY-- I MEAN KID-
AW, COME ON, I'M SORRY! LET'S BE CHUMS! WHATTYASAY? IT'LL BE A HOOT!
THE NAME'S JACOB! AND I'M NOT CRYING, I'M MAD! I'M MAD AT YOU!
HEY, I SAID I WAS SORRY. HOW CAN I MAKE IT UP TO YOU?
I'D RATHER EAT WORMS!
YA KNOW YOU WERE NOT HALF BAD BACK THERE. YOU EVEN HELPED A LITTLE -- A LOT! YOU CAN HANG OUT WITH ME AWHILE!
DON'T DO ME ANY FAVORS! I DON'T WANT TO HANG OUT WITH YOU ANY MORE THAN YOU WANT TO HANG OUT WITH ME! IF YOU'LL JUST HELP ME GET MY -- WHATEVER IT IS -- I'LL GET OUT OF HERE FOREVER!
HMMM
OKAY I'LL DO IT! LET'S GO!
OUCH!
GLEEP!
FORWARD! MARCH ON! IT'LL BE AN ADVENTURE! A BOLD NEW ADVENTURE!
OY!

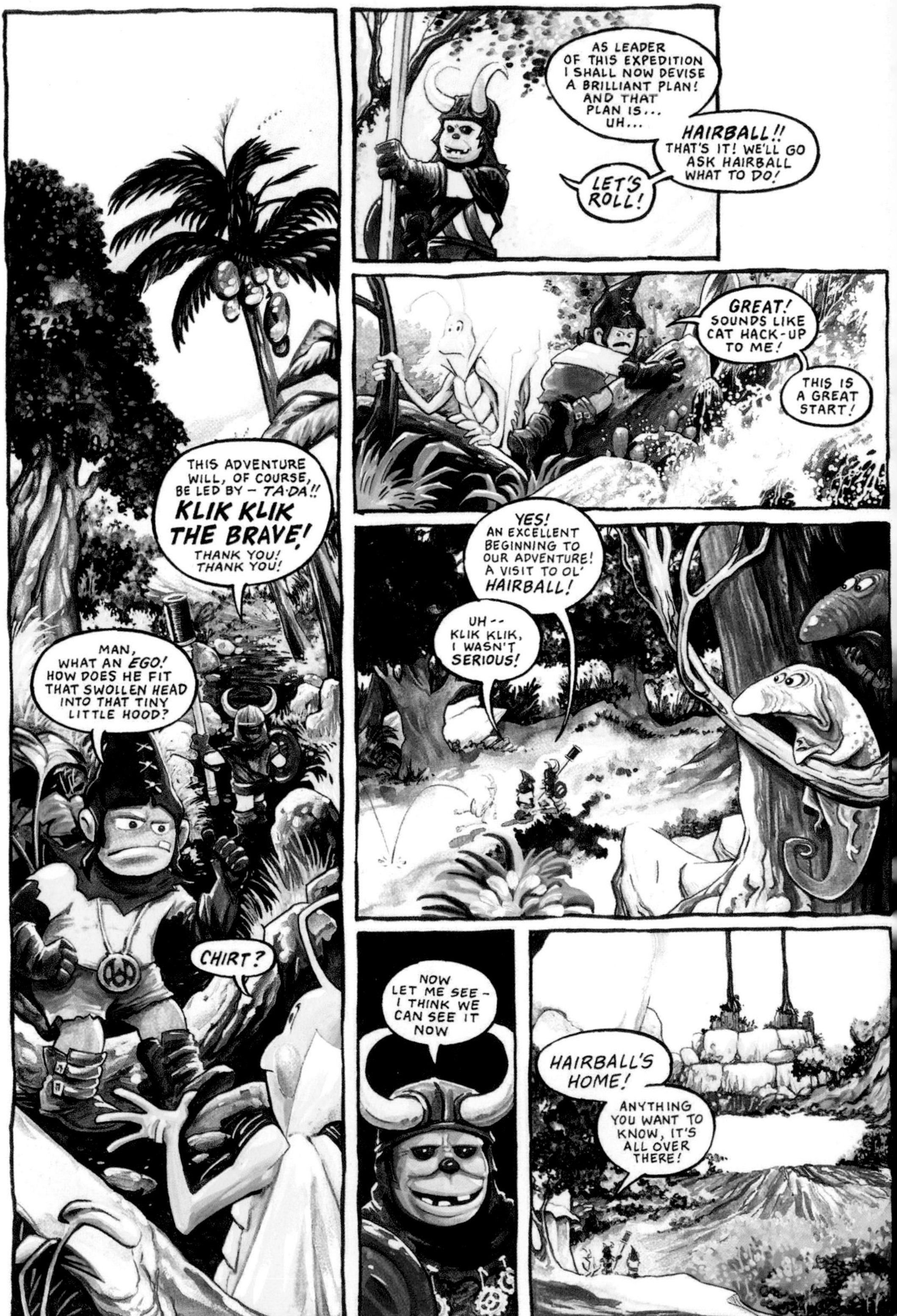
THIS ADVENTURE WILL, OF COURSE, BE LED BY – TA-DA!! KLIK KLIK THE BRAVE! THANK YOU! THANK YOU!
MAN, WHAT AN EGO! HOW DOES HE FIT THAT SWOLLEN HEAD INTO THAT TINY LITTLE HOOD?
CHIRT?
AS LEADER OF THIS EXPEDITION I SHALL NOW DEVISE A BRILLIANT PLAN! AND THAT PLAN IS... UH...
HAIRBALL!! THAT'S IT! WE'LL GO ASK HAIRBALL WHAT TO DO!
LET'S ROLL!
GREAT! SOUNDS LIKE CAT HACK-UP TO ME!
THIS IS A GREAT START!
YES! AN EXCELLENT BEGINNING TO OUR ADVENTURE! A VISIT TO OL' HAIRBALL!
UH -- KLIK KLIK, I WASN'T SERIOUS!
NOW LET ME SEE - I THINK WE CAN SEE IT NOW
HAIRBALL'S HOME!
ANYTHING YOU WANT TO KNOW, IT'S ALL OVER THERE!

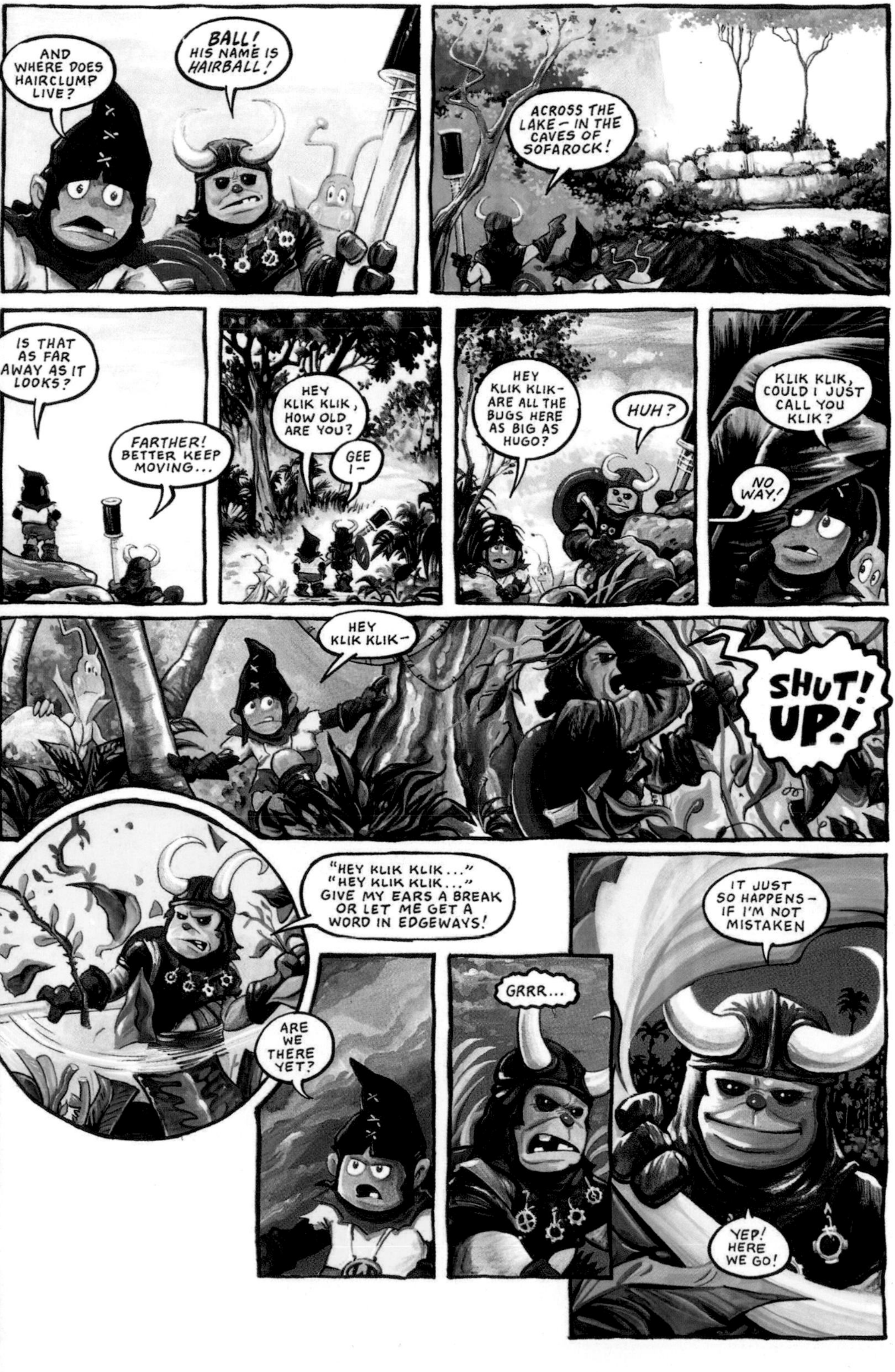
AND WHERE DOES HAIRCLUMP LIVE?
BALL! HIS NAME IS HAIRBALL!
ACROSS THE LAKE—IN THE CAVES OF SOFAROCK!
IS THAT AS FAR AWAY AS IT LOOKS?
FARTHER! BETTER KEEP MOVING...
HEY KLIK KLIK, HOW OLD ARE YOU?
GEE I—
HEY KLIK KLIK—ARE ALL THE BUGS HERE AS BIG AS HUGO?
HUH?
KLIK KLIK, COULD I JUST CALL YOU KLIK?
NO WAY!
HEY KLIK KLIK—
SHUT! UP!
"HEY KLIK KLIK..." "HEY KLIK KLIK..." GIVE MY EARS A BREAK OR LET ME GET A WORD IN EDGEWAYS!
ARE WE THERE YET?
GRRR...
IT JUST SO HAPPENS—IF I'M NOT MISTAKEN
YEP! HERE WE GO!

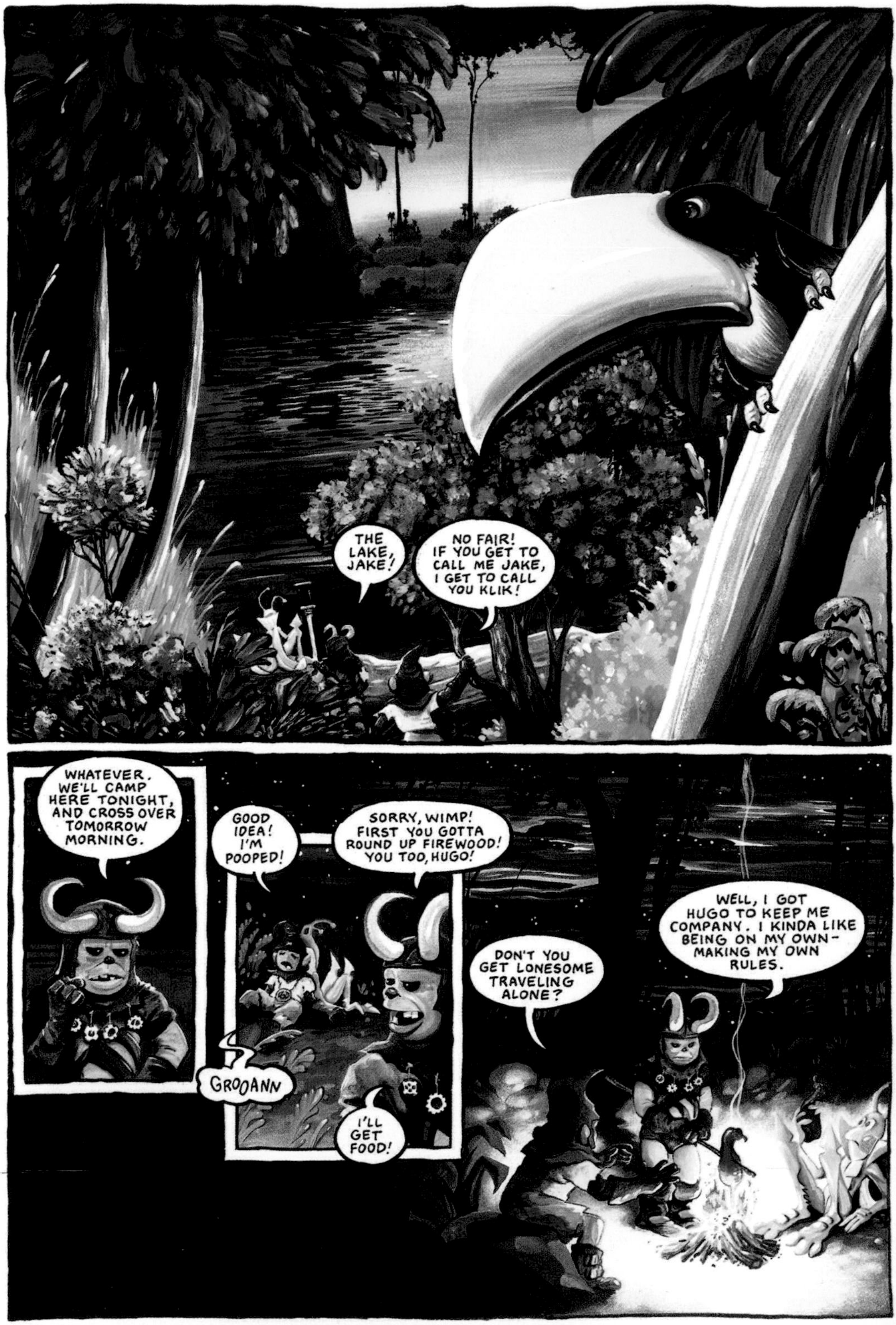
THE LAKE, JAKE!
NO FAIR! IF YOU GET TO CALL ME JAKE, I GET TO CALL YOU KLIK!
WHATEVER. WE'LL CAMP HERE TONIGHT, AND CROSS OVER TOMORROW MORNING.
GOOD IDEA! I'M POOPED!
SORRY, WIMP! FIRST YOU GOTTA ROUND UP FIREWOOD! YOU TOO, HUGO!
GROOANN
I'LL GET FOOD!
DON'T YOU GET LONESOME TRAVELING ALONE?
WELL, I GOT HUGO TO KEEP ME COMPANY. I KINDA LIKE BEING ON MY OWN- MAKING MY OWN RULES.

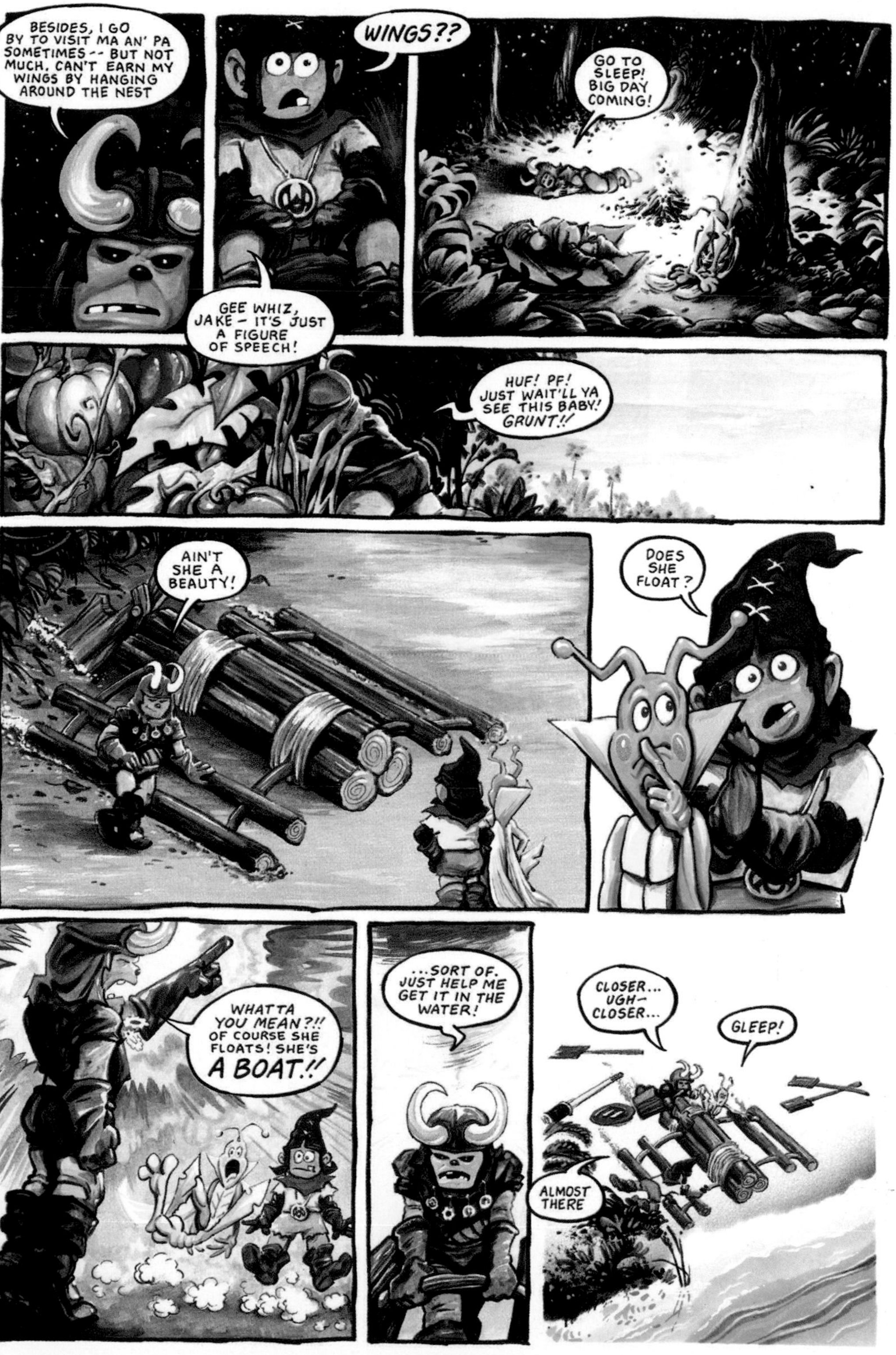
BESIDES, I GO BY TO VISIT MA AN' PA SOMETIMES-- BUT NOT MUCH. CAN'T EARN MY WINGS BY HANGING AROUND THE NEST
WINGS??
GEE WHIZ, JAKE - IT'S JUST A FIGURE OF SPEECH!
GO TO SLEEP! BIG DAY COMING!
HUF! PF! JUST WAIT'LL YA SEE THIS BABY! GRUNT!!
AIN'T SHE A BEAUTY!
DOES SHE FLOAT?
WHATTA YOU MEAN?!! OF COURSE SHE FLOATS! SHE'S A BOAT!!
...SORT OF. JUST HELP ME GET IT IN THE WATER!
CLOSER... UGH- CLOSER...
GLEEP!
ALMOST THERE

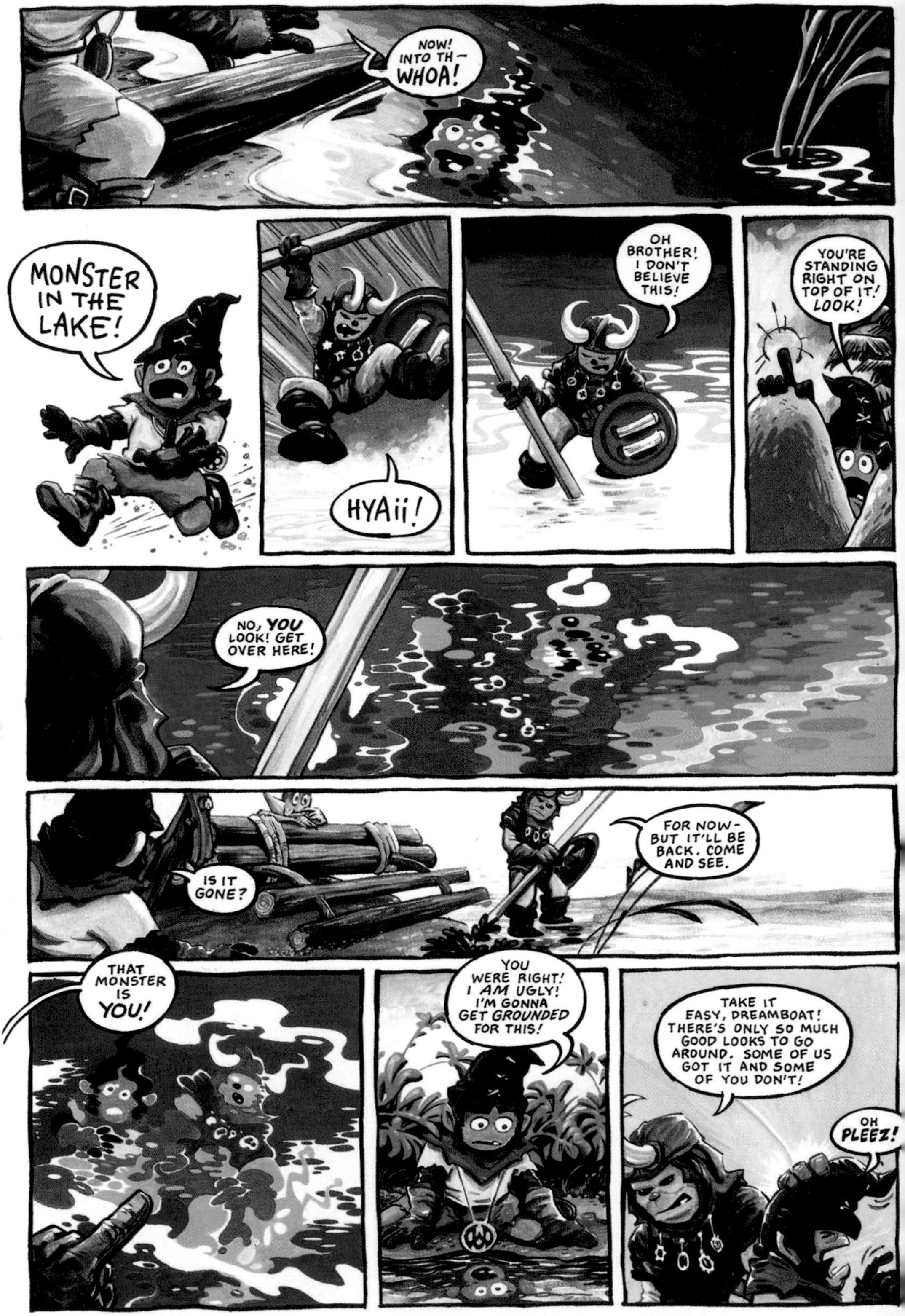
NOW! INTO TH— WHOA!
MONSTER IN THE LAKE!
HYAii!
OH BROTHER! I DON'T BELIEVE THIS!
YOU'RE STANDING RIGHT ON TOP OF IT! LOOK!
NO, YOU LOOK! GET OVER HERE!
IS IT GONE?
FOR NOW- BUT IT'LL BE BACK. COME AND SEE.
THAT MONSTER IS YOU!
YOU WERE RIGHT! I AM UGLY! I'M GONNA GET GROUNDED FOR THIS!
TAKE IT EASY, DREAMBOAT! THERE'S ONLY SO MUCH GOOD LOOKS TO GO AROUND. SOME OF US GOT IT AND SOME OF YOU DON'T!
OH PLEEZ!

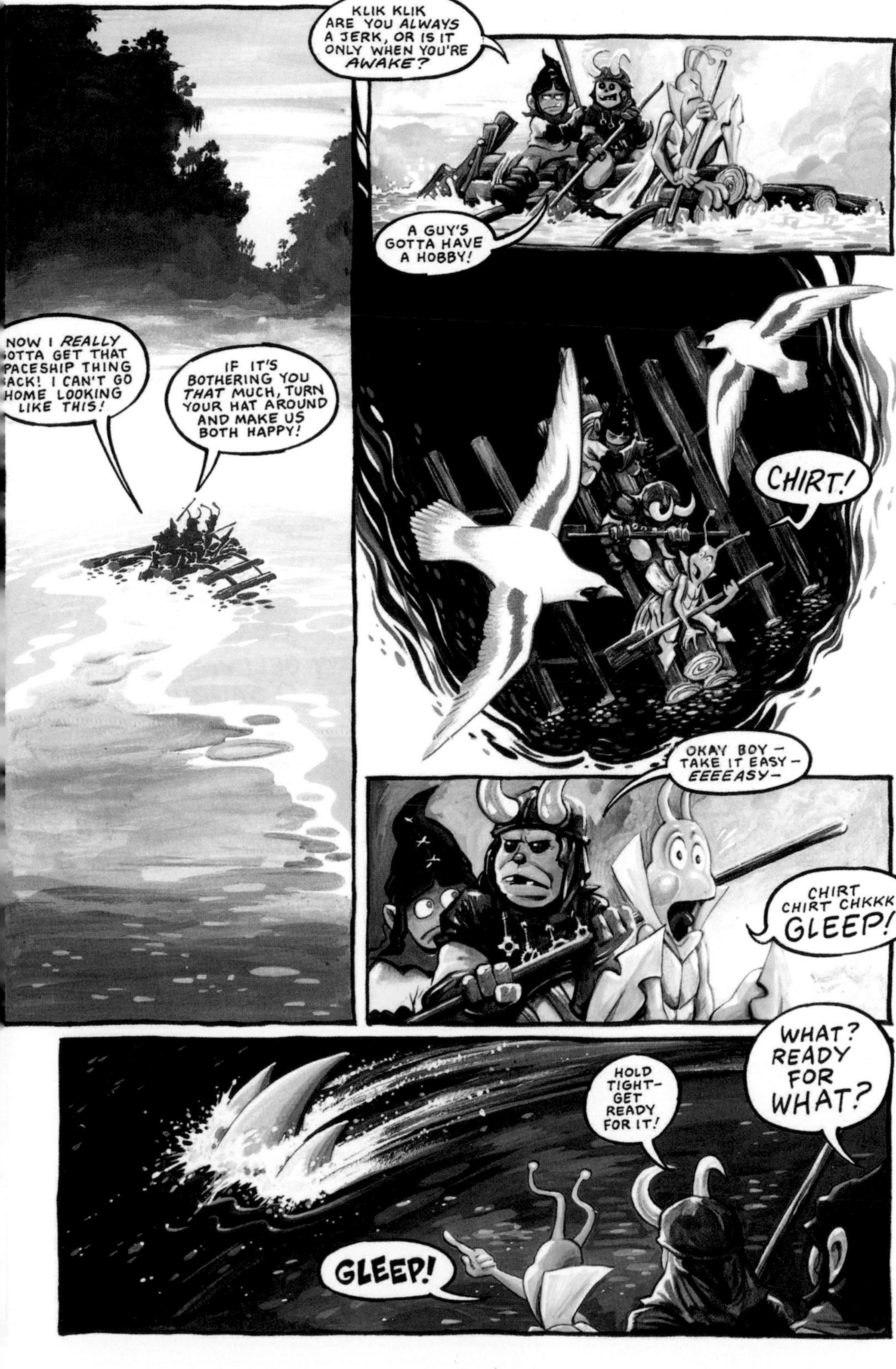
KLIK KLIK ARE YOU ALWAYS A JERK, OR IS IT ONLY WHEN YOU'RE AWAKE?
A GUY'S GOTTA HAVE A HOBBY!
NOW I REALLY GOTTA GET THAT SPACESHIP THING BACK! I CAN'T GO HOME LOOKING LIKE THIS!
IF IT'S BOTHERING YOU THAT MUCH, TURN YOUR HAT AROUND AND MAKE US BOTH HAPPY!
CHIRT!
OKAY BOY— TAKE IT EASY— EEEEASY—
CHIRT CHIRT CHKKK! GLEEP!
HOLD TIGHT- GET READY FOR IT!
WHAT? READY FOR WHAT?
GLEEP!

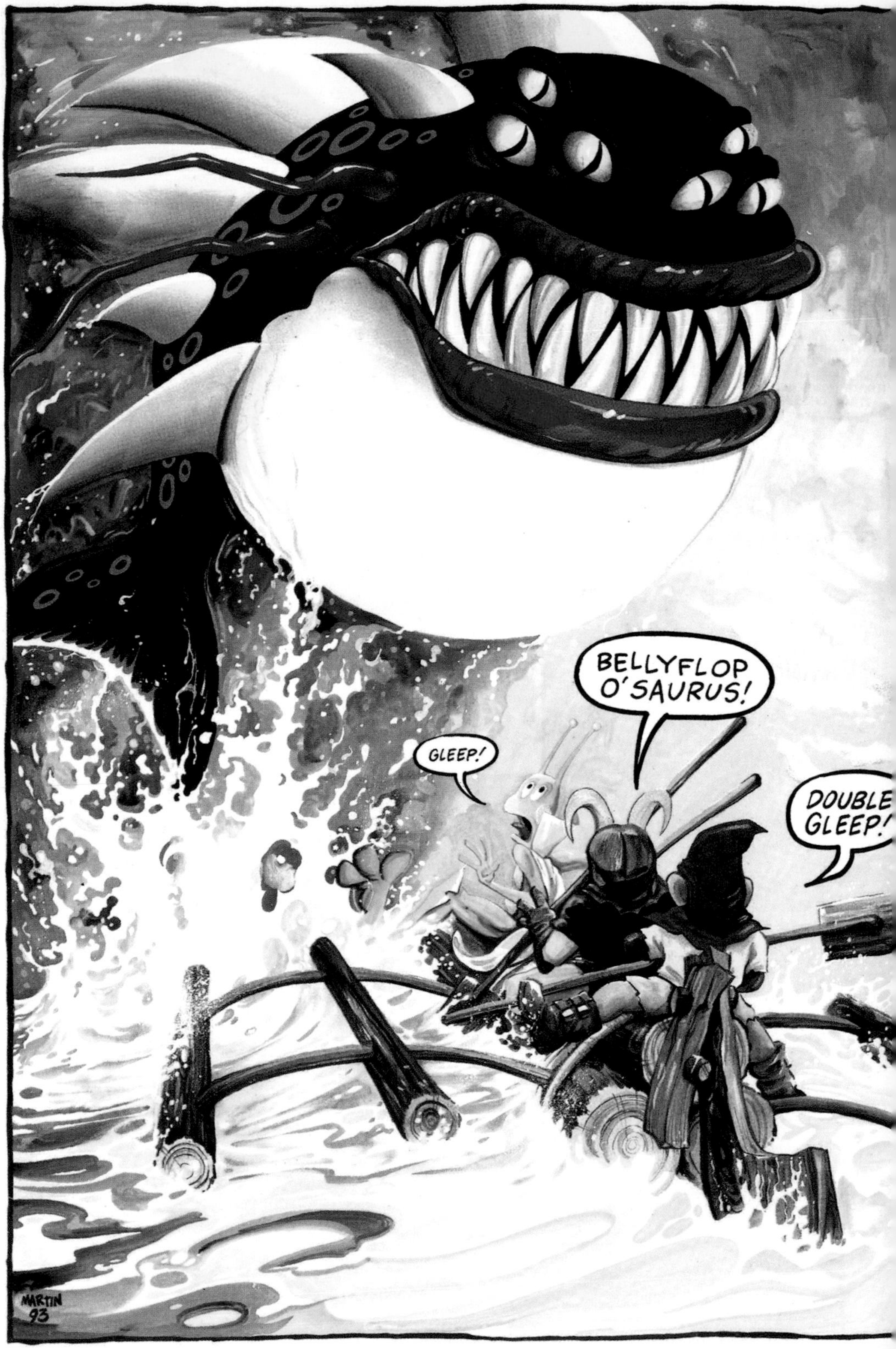
BELLYFLOP O'SAURUS!
GLEEP!
DOUBLE GLEEP!
MARTIN 93

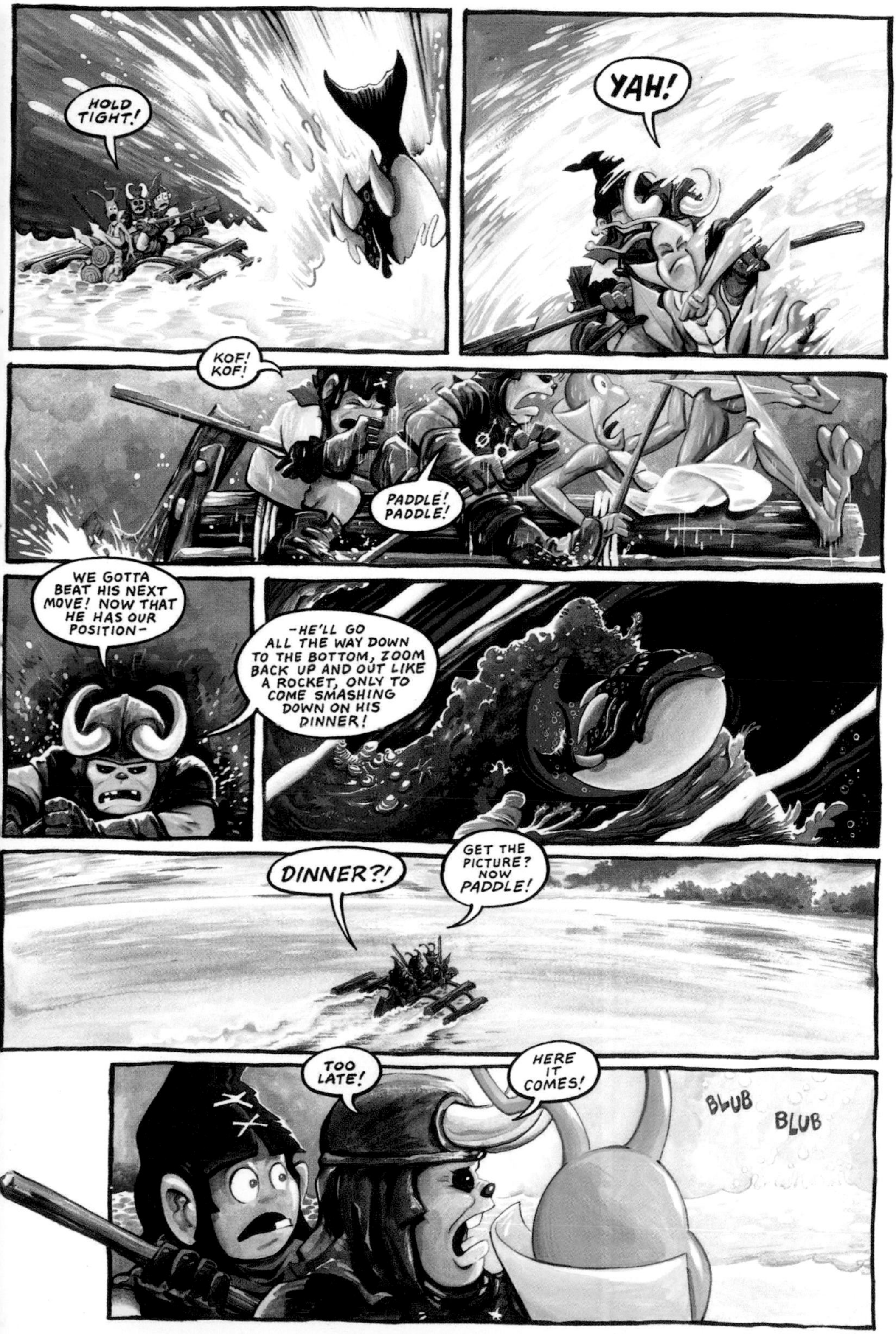
HOLD TIGHT!
YAH!
KOF! KOF!
PADDLE! PADDLE!
WE GOTTA BEAT HIS NEXT MOVE! NOW THAT HE HAS OUR POSITION–
–HE'LL GO ALL THE WAY DOWN TO THE BOTTOM, ZOOM BACK UP AND OUT LIKE A ROCKET, ONLY TO COME SMASHING DOWN ON HIS DINNER!
DINNER?!
GET THE PICTURE? NOW PADDLE!
TOO LATE!
HERE IT COMES!
BLUB
BLUB

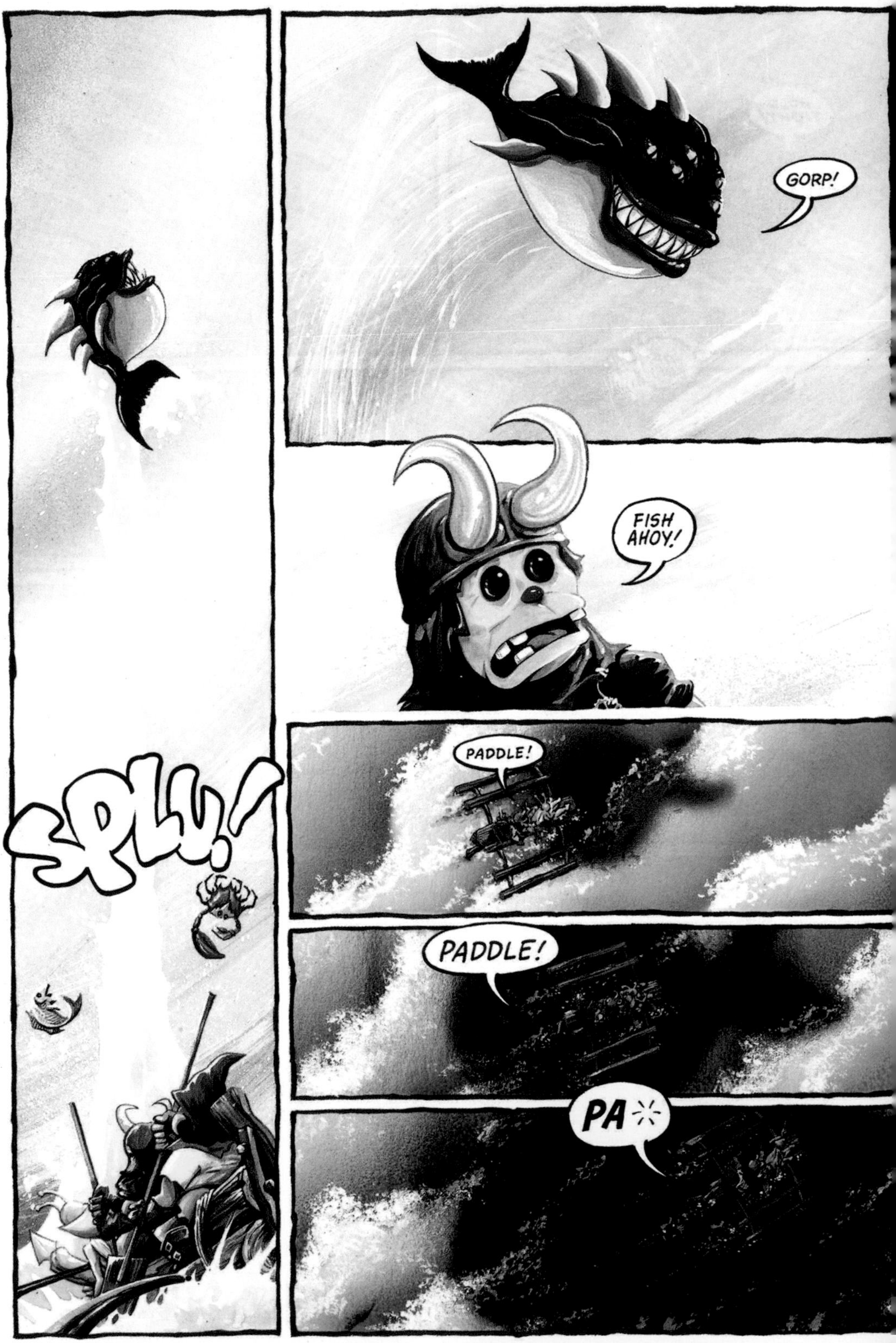
GORP!
FISH AHOY!
SPLU!
PADDLE!
PADDLE!
PA

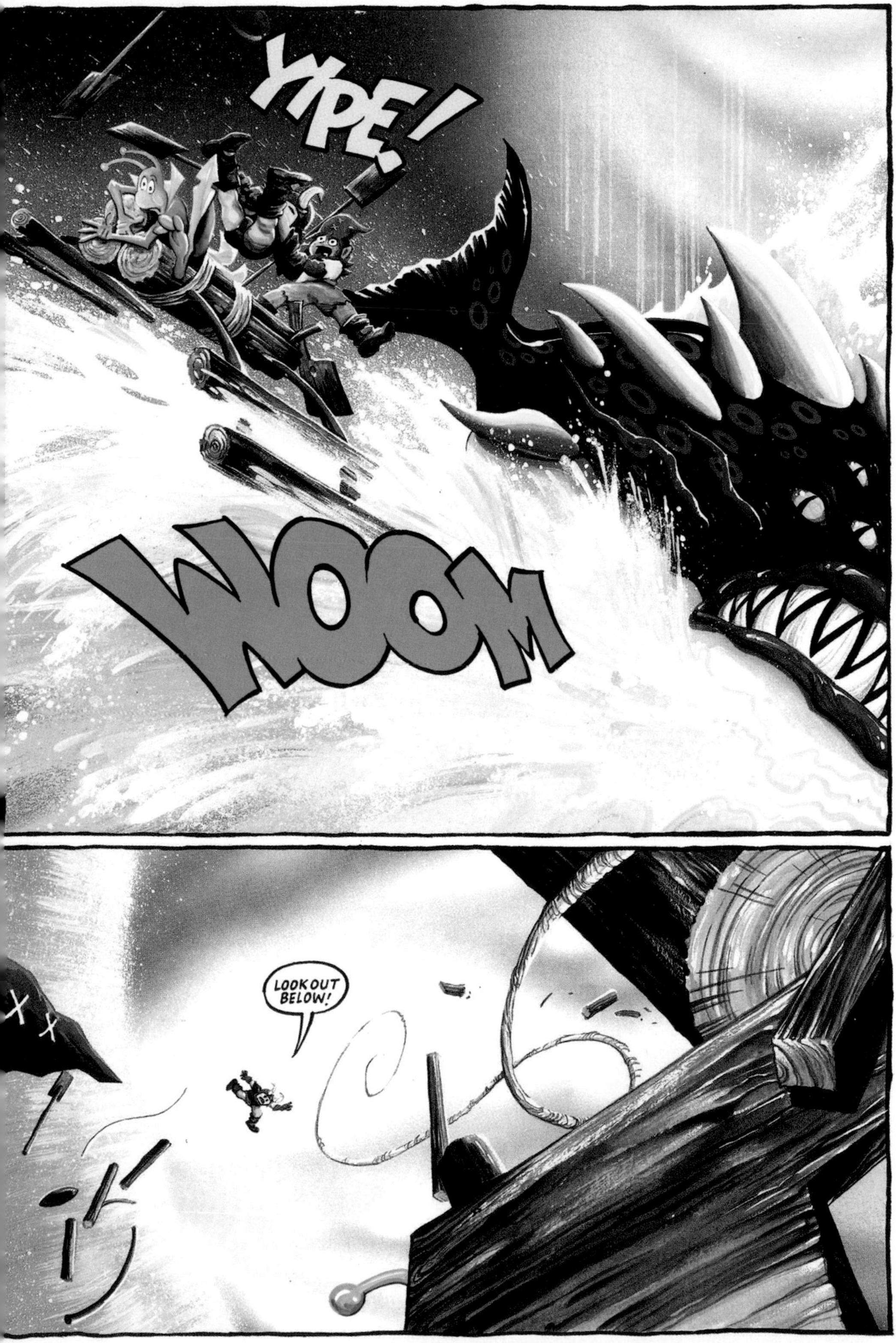
YIPE!
WOOM
LOOK OUT BELOW!

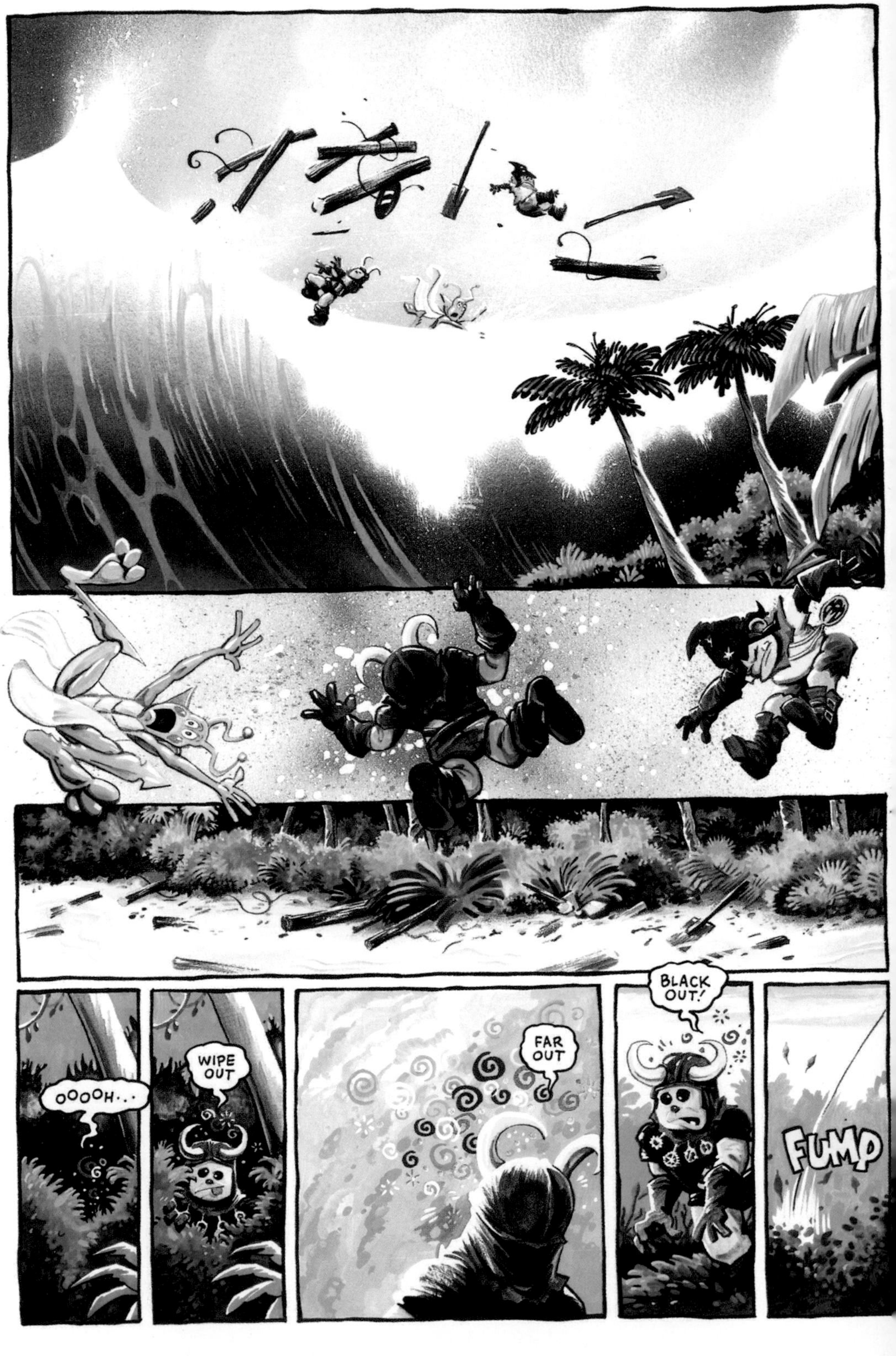
OOOOH...
WIPE OUT
FAR OUT
BLACK OUT!
FUMP

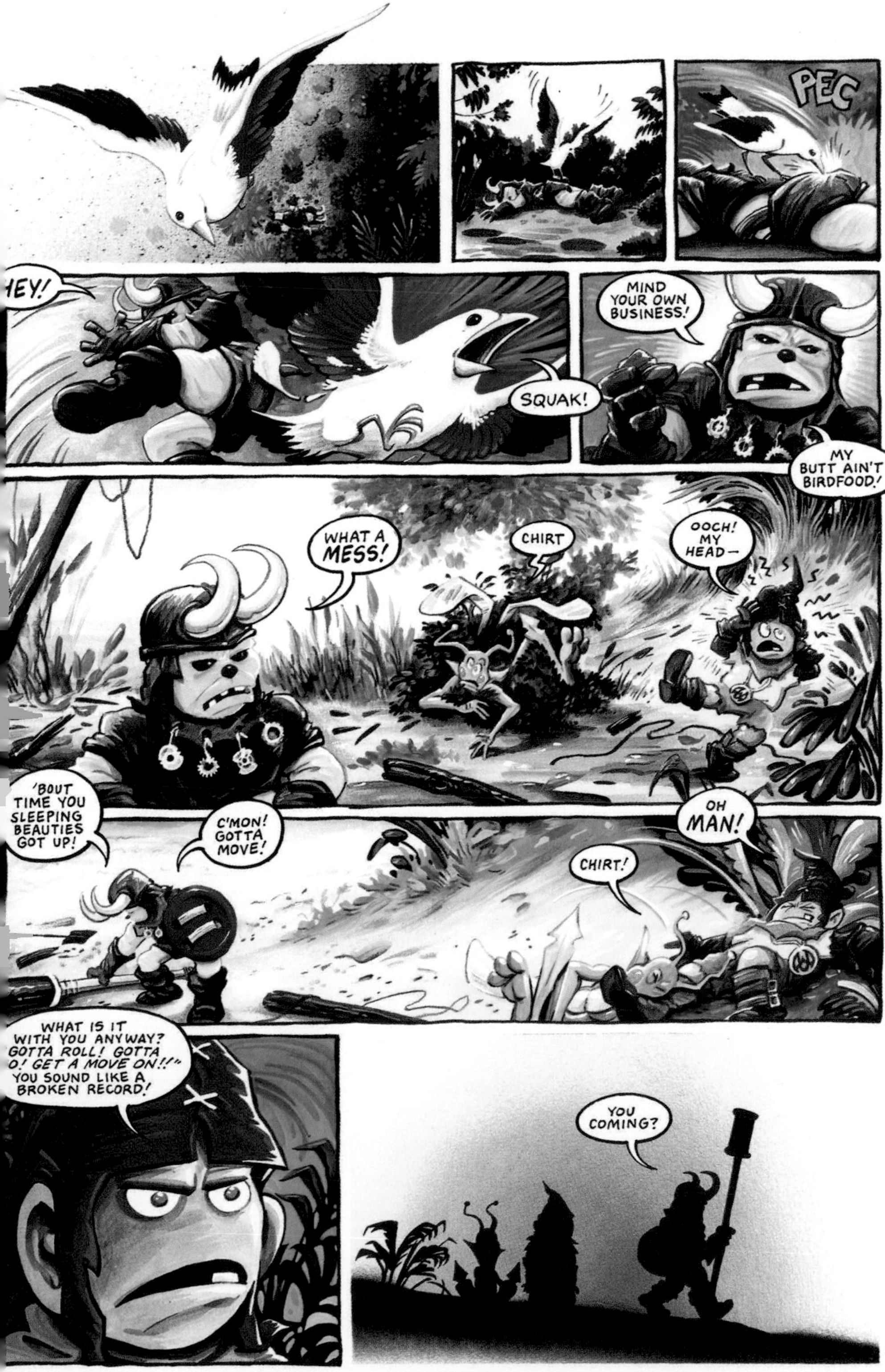
PEC
HEY!
SQUAK!
MIND YOUR OWN BUSINESS!
MY BUTT AIN'T BIRDFOOD!
WHAT A MESS!
CHIRT
OOCH! MY HEAD—
'BOUT TIME YOU SLEEPING BEAUTIES GOT UP!
C'MON! GOTTA MOVE!
CHIRT!
OH MAN!
WHAT IS IT WITH YOU ANYWAY? GOTTA ROLL! GOTTA O! GET A MOVE ON!!" YOU SOUND LIKE A BROKEN RECORD!
YOU COMING?

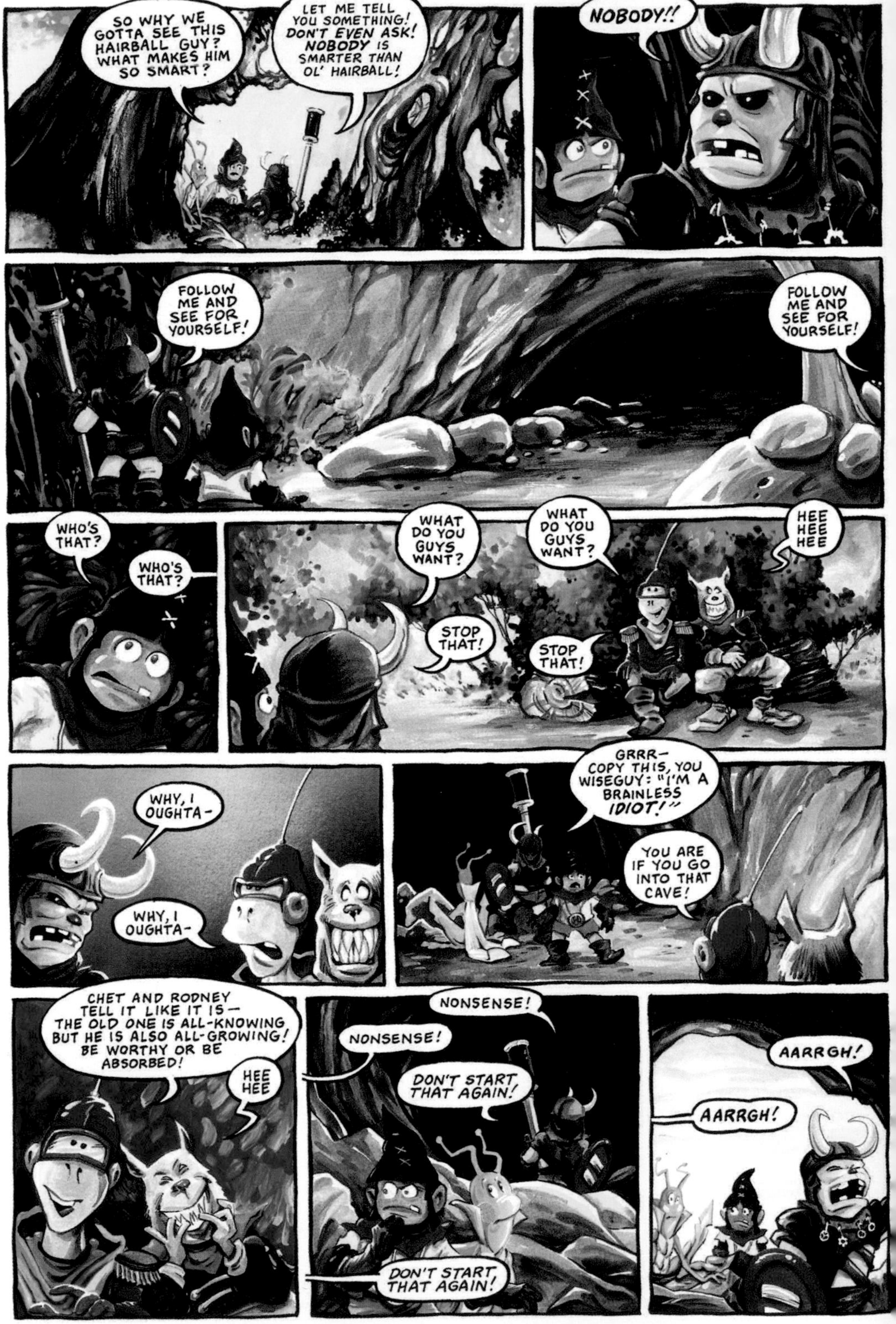
SO WHY WE GOTTA SEE THIS HAIRBALL GUY? WHAT MAKES HIM SO SMART?
LET ME TELL YOU SOMETHING! DON'T EVEN ASK! NOBODY IS SMARTER THAN OL' HAIRBALL!
NOBODY!!
FOLLOW ME AND SEE FOR YOURSELF!
FOLLOW ME AND SEE FOR YOURSELF!
WHO'S THAT?
WHO'S THAT?
WHAT DO YOU GUYS WANT?
WHAT DO YOU GUYS WANT?
HEE HEE HEE
STOP THAT!
STOP THAT!
WHY, I OUGHTA-
WHY, I OUGHTA-
GRRR– COPY THIS, YOU WISEGUY: "I'M A BRAINLESS IDIOT!"
YOU ARE IF YOU GO INTO THAT CAVE!
CHET AND RODNEY TELL IT LIKE IT IS— THE OLD ONE IS ALL-KNOWING BUT HE IS ALSO ALL-GROWING! BE WORTHY OR BE ABSORBED!
HEE HEE
NONSENSE!
NONSENSE!
DON'T START THAT AGAIN!
DON'T START THAT AGAIN!
AARRGH!
AARRGH!

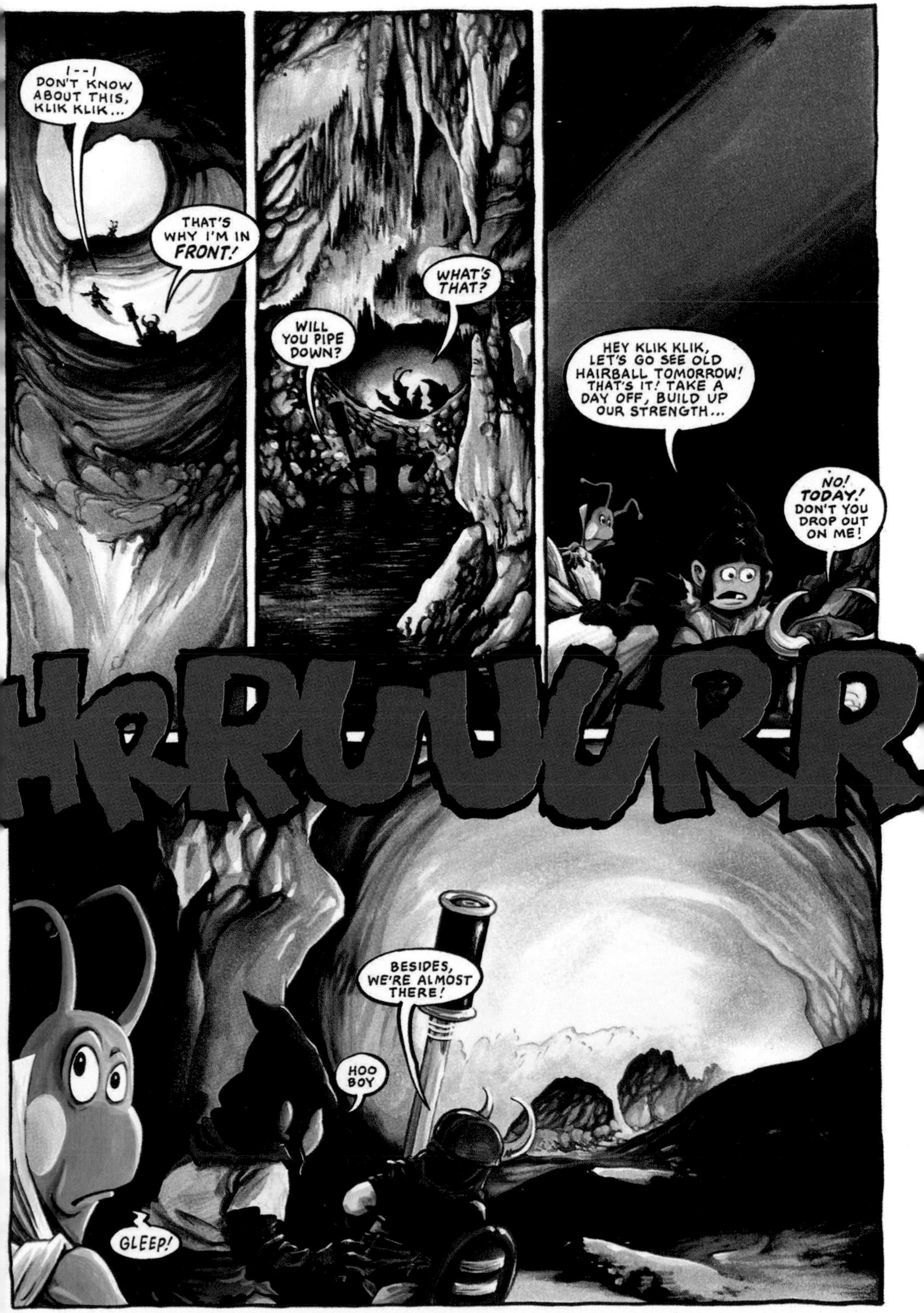

I--I DON'T KNOW ABOUT THIS, KLIK KLIK...
THAT'S WHY I'M IN FRONT!
WHAT'S THAT?
WILL YOU PIPE DOWN?
HEY KLIK KLIK, LET'S GO SEE OLD HAIRBALL TOMORROW! THAT'S IT! TAKE A DAY OFF, BUILD UP OUR STRENGTH...
NO! TODAY! DON'T YOU DROP OUT ON ME!
HRRUUGRR
BESIDES, WE'RE ALMOST THERE!
HOO BOY
GLEEP!

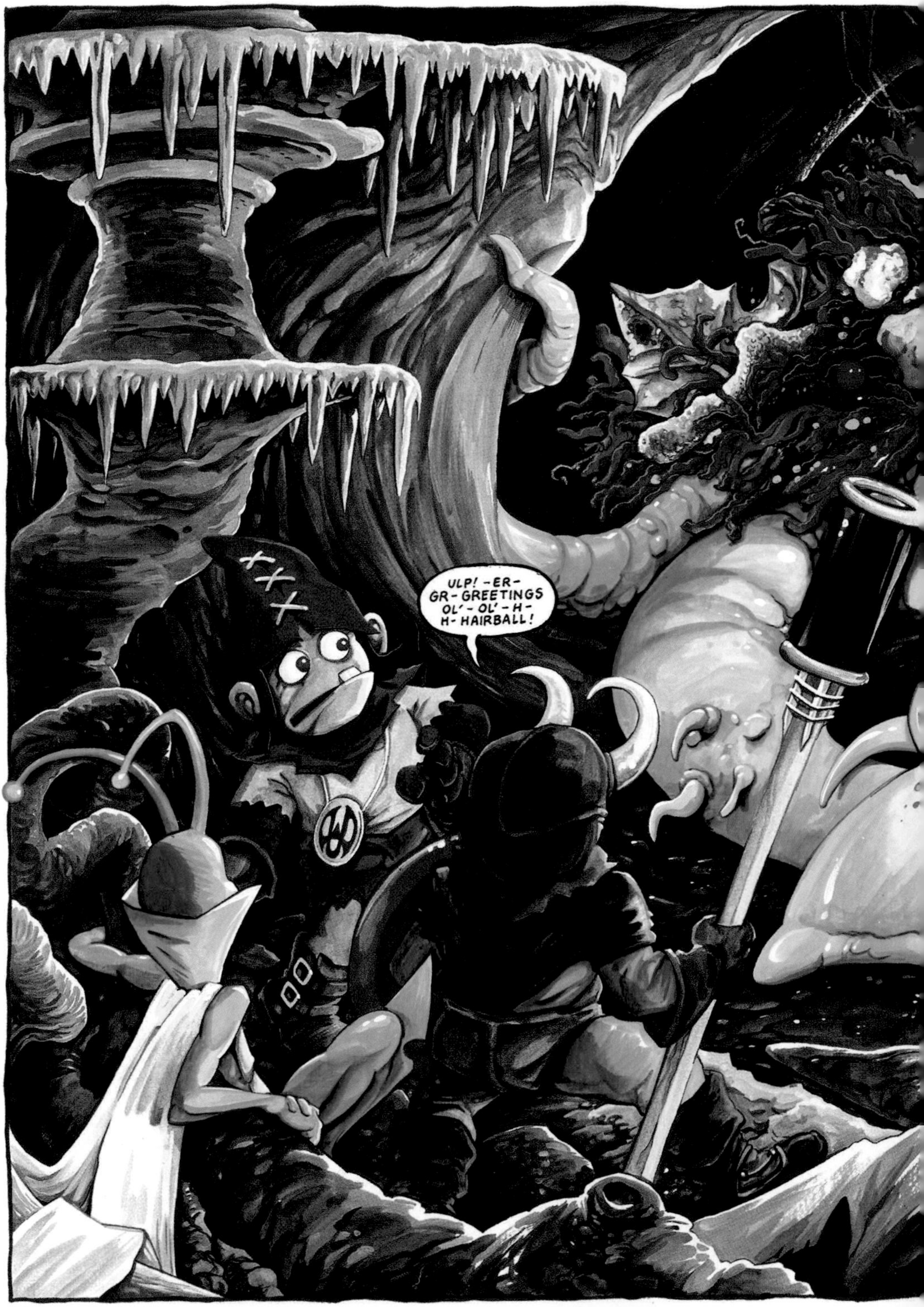
ULP! -ER- GR-GREETINGS OL'-OL'-H- H-HAIRBALL!

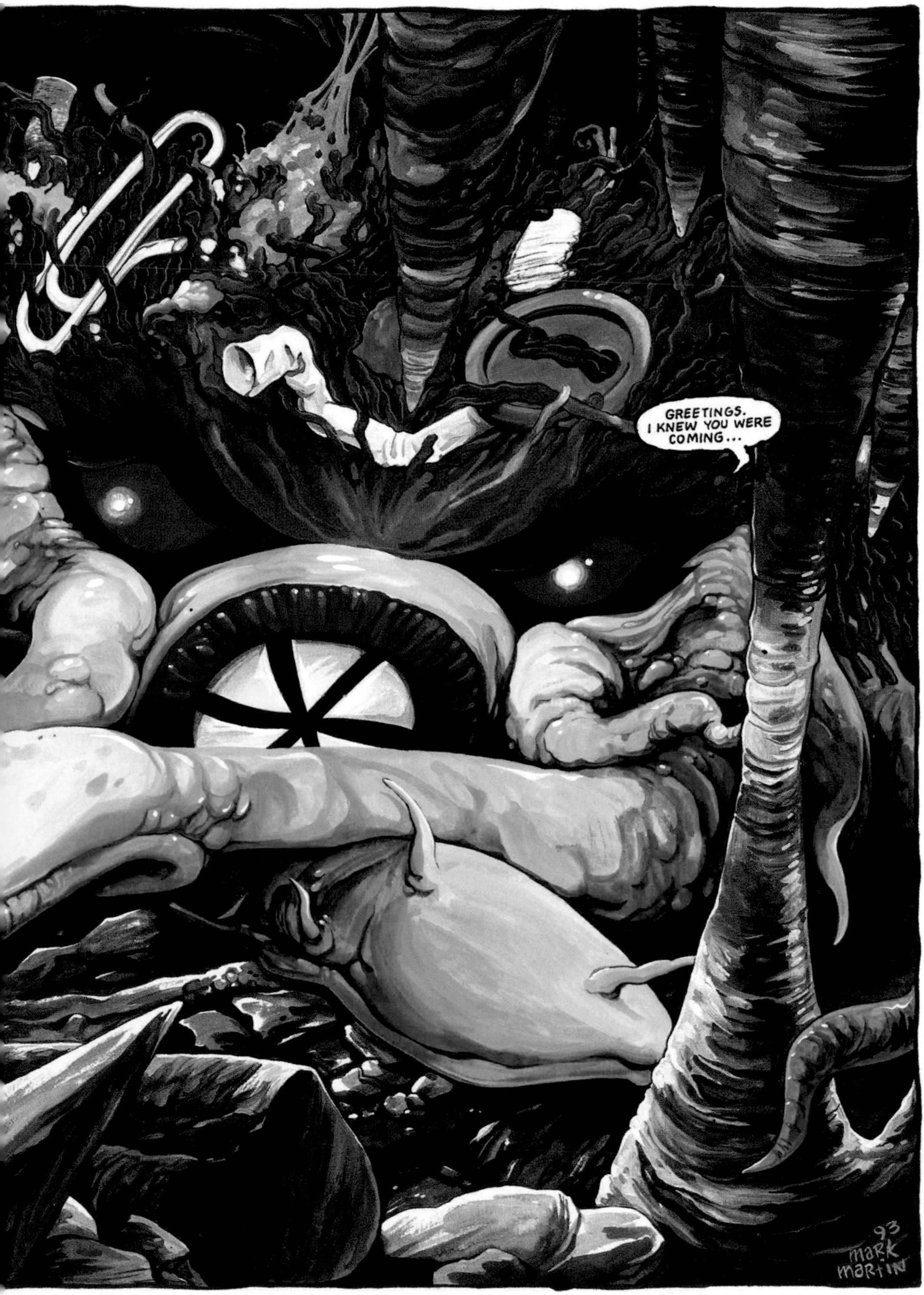
GREETINGS. I KNEW YOU WERE COMING...
93 mark martin

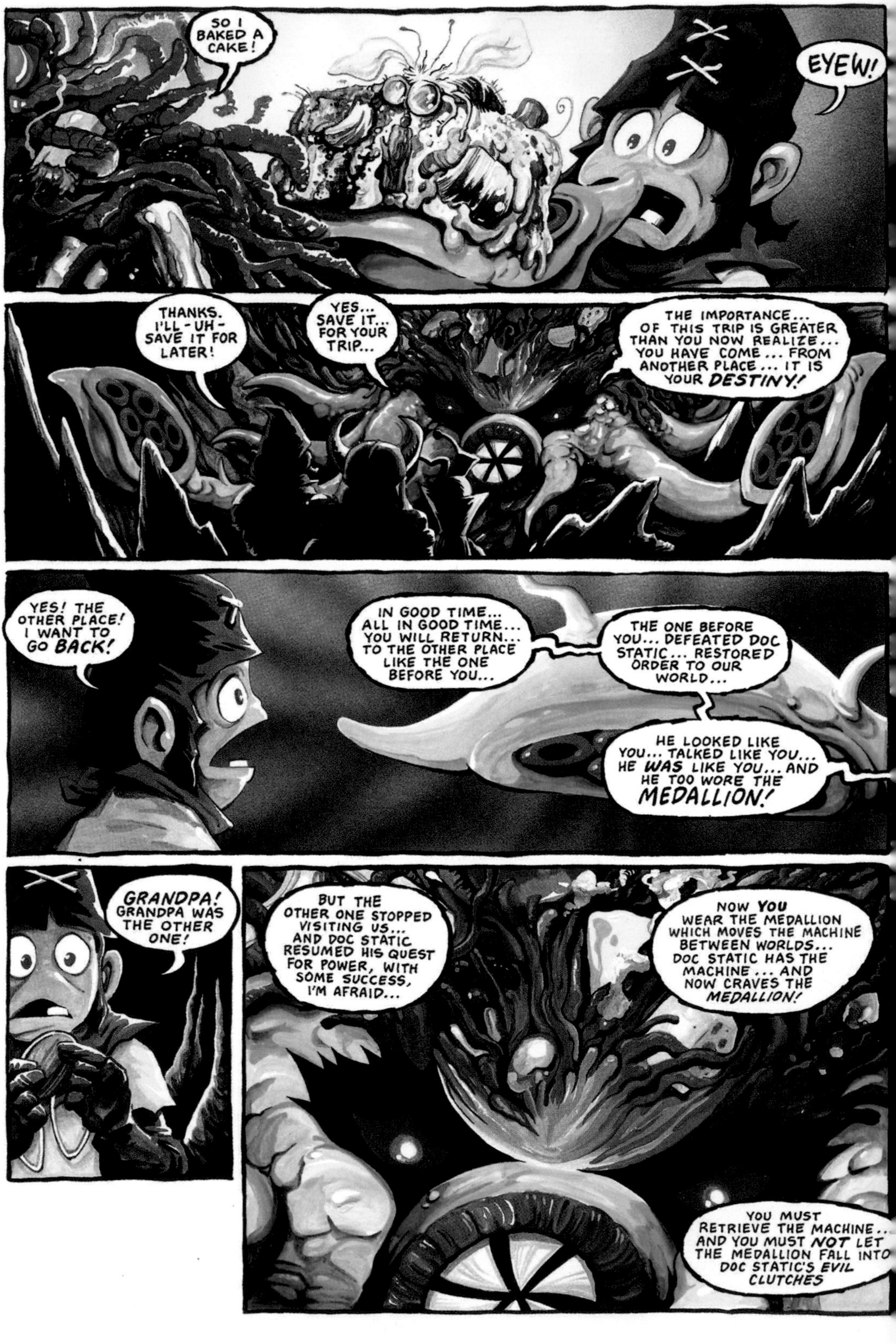
SO I BAKED A CAKE!
EYEW!
THANKS. I'LL - UH - SAVE IT FOR LATER!
YES... SAVE IT... FOR YOUR TRIP...
THE IMPORTANCE... OF THIS TRIP IS GREATER THAN YOU NOW REALIZE... YOU HAVE COME... FROM ANOTHER PLACE... IT IS YOUR DESTINY!
YES! THE OTHER PLACE! I WANT TO GO BACK!
IN GOOD TIME... ALL IN GOOD TIME... YOU WILL RETURN... TO THE OTHER PLACE LIKE THE ONE BEFORE YOU...
THE ONE BEFORE YOU... DEFEATED DOC STATIC... RESTORED ORDER TO OUR WORLD...
HE LOOKED LIKE YOU... TALKED LIKE YOU... HE WAS LIKE YOU... AND HE TOO WORE THE MEDALLION!
GRANDPA! GRANDPA WAS THE OTHER ONE!
BUT THE OTHER ONE STOPPED VISITING US... AND DOC STATIC RESUMED HIS QUEST FOR POWER, WITH SOME SUCCESS, I'M AFRAID...
NOW YOU WEAR THE MEDALLION WHICH MOVES THE MACHINE BETWEEN WORLDS... DOC STATIC HAS THE MACHINE... AND NOW CRAVES THE MEDALLION!
YOU MUST RETRIEVE THE MACHINE... AND YOU MUST NOT LET THE MEDALLION FALL INTO DOC STATIC'S EVIL CLUTCHES

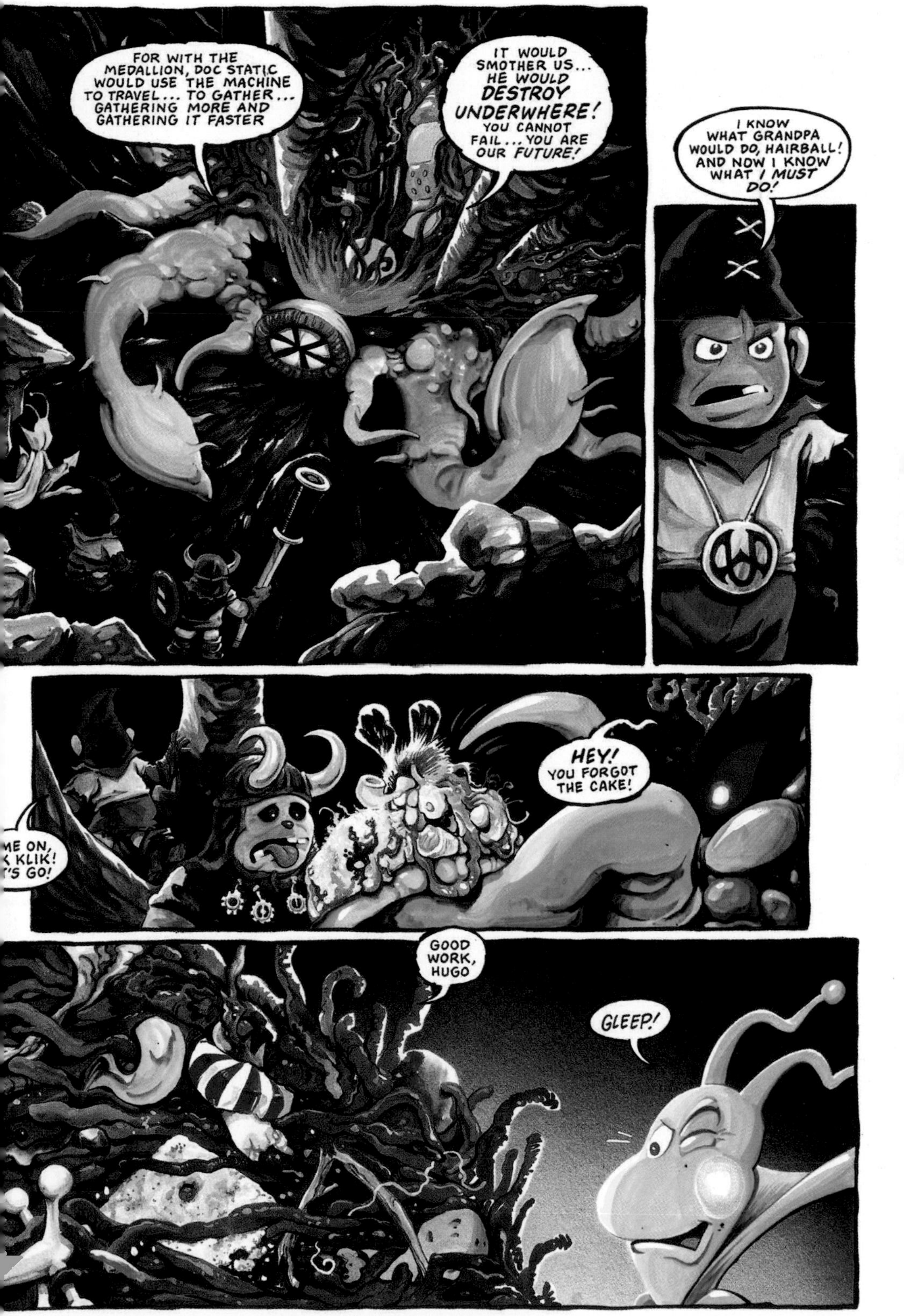
FOR WITH THE MEDALLION, DOC STATIC WOULD USE THE MACHINE TO TRAVEL... TO GATHER... GATHERING MORE AND GATHERING IT FASTER
IT WOULD SMOTHER US... HE WOULD DESTROY UNDERWHERE! YOU CANNOT FAIL... YOU ARE OUR FUTURE!
I KNOW WHAT GRANDPA WOULD DO, HAIRBALL! AND NOW I KNOW WHAT I MUST DO!
ME ON, K KLIK! T'S GO!
HEY! YOU FORGOT THE CAKE!
GOOD WORK, HUGO
GLEEP!

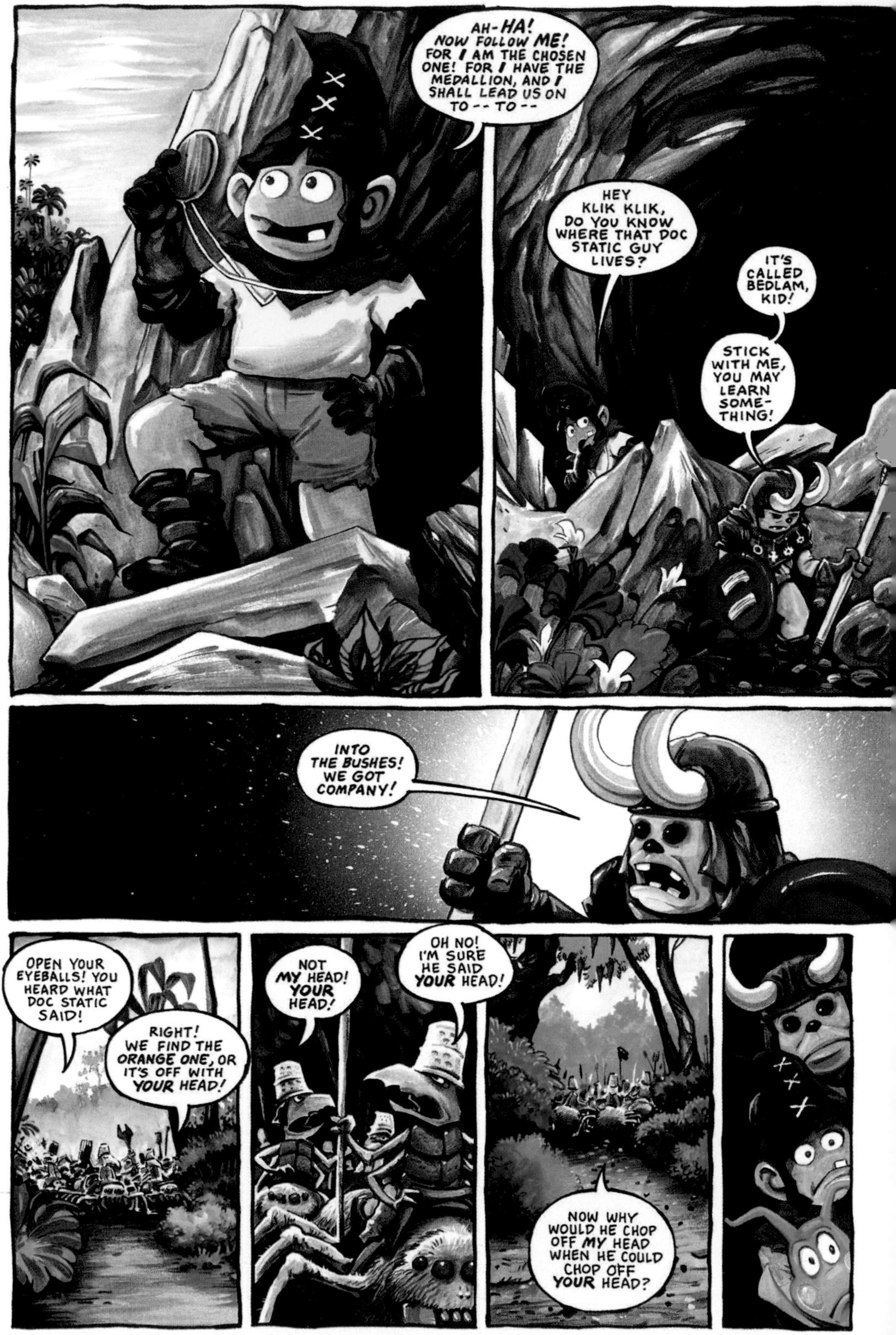

AH-HA! NOW FOLLOW ME! FOR I AM THE CHOSEN ONE! FOR I HAVE THE MEDALLION, AND I SHALL LEAD US ON TO -- TO --
HEY KLIK KLIK, DO YOU KNOW WHERE THAT DOC STATIC GUY LIVES?
IT'S CALLED BEDLAM, KID!
STICK WITH ME, YOU MAY LEARN SOME-THING!
INTO THE BUSHES! WE GOT COMPANY!
OPEN YOUR EYEBALLS! YOU HEARD WHAT DOC STATIC SAID!
RIGHT! WE FIND THE ORANGE ONE, OR IT'S OFF WITH YOUR HEAD!
NOT MY HEAD! YOUR HEAD!
OH NO! I'M SURE HE SAID YOUR HEAD!
NOW WHY WOULD HE CHOP OFF MY HEAD WHEN HE COULD CHOP OFF YOUR HEAD?

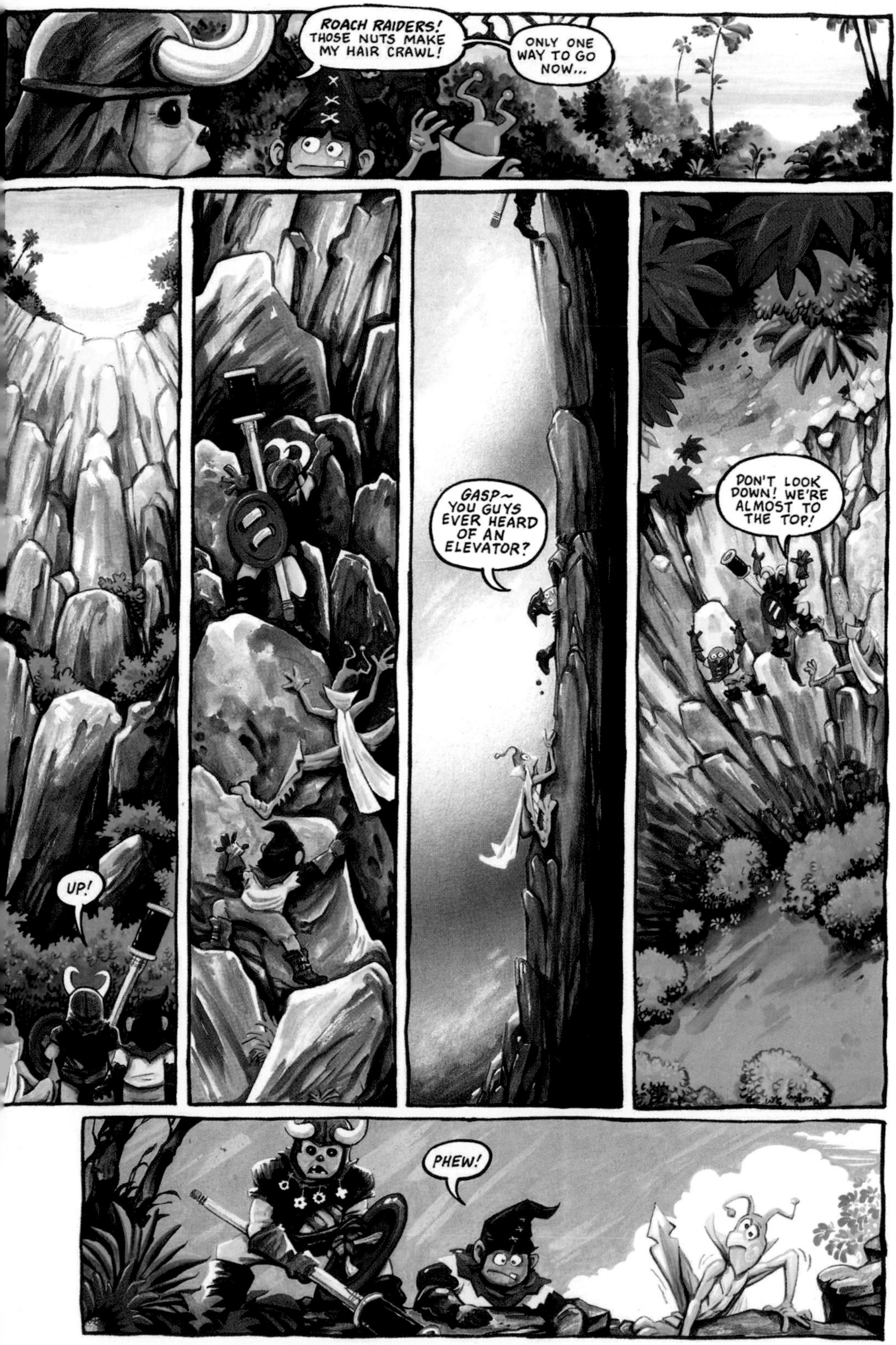
ROACH RAIDERS! THOSE NUTS MAKE MY HAIR CRAWL!
ONLY ONE WAY TO GO NOW...
UP!
GASP~ YOU GUYS EVER HEARD OF AN ELEVATOR?
DON'T LOOK DOWN! WE'RE ALMOST TO THE TOP!
PHEW!

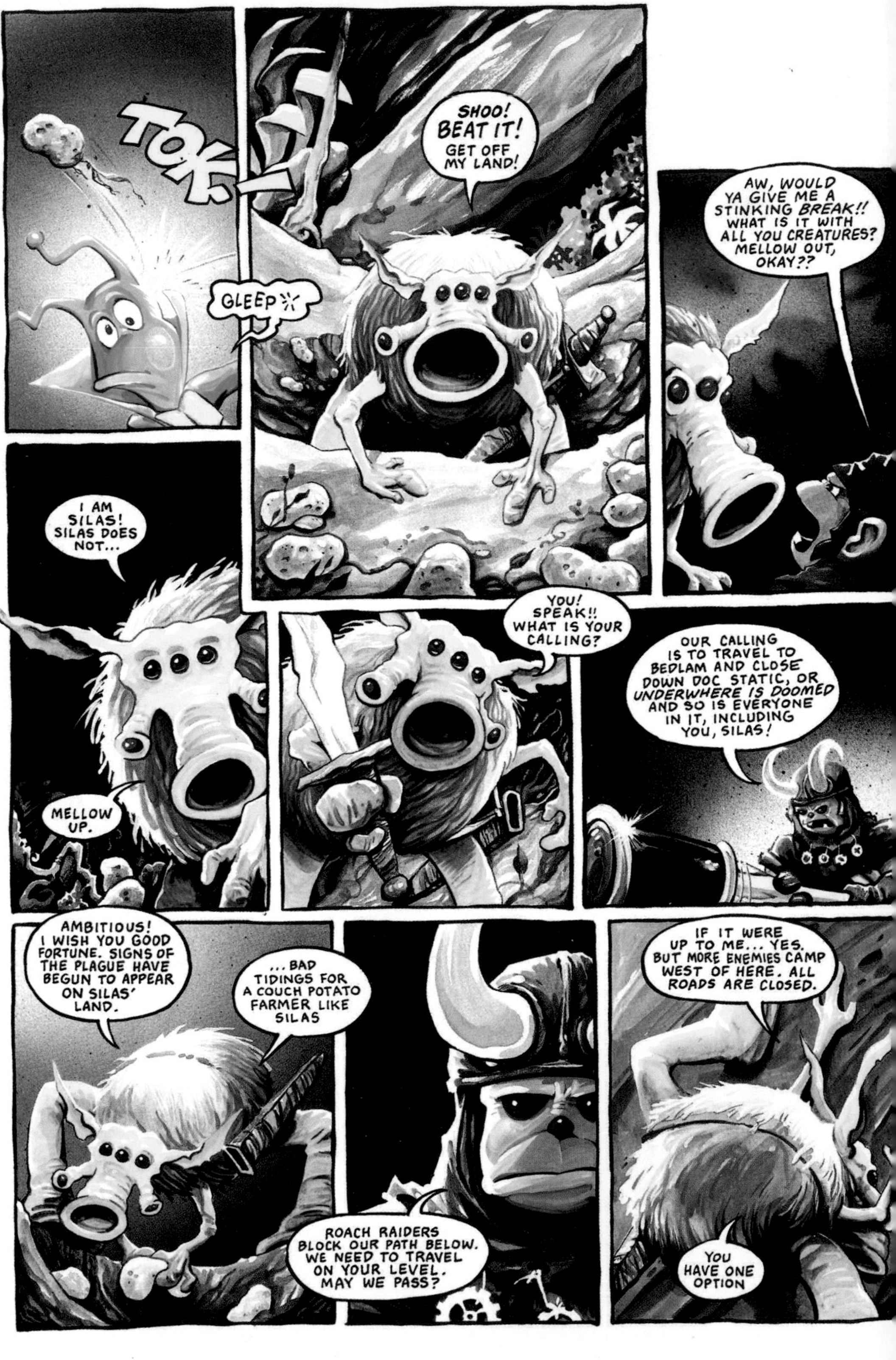
TOK!
GLEEP
SHOO! BEAT IT! GET OFF MY LAND!
AW, WOULD YA GIVE ME A STINKING BREAK!! WHAT IS IT WITH ALL YOU CREATURES? MELLOW OUT, OKAY??
I AM SILAS! SILAS DOES NOT...
MELLOW UP.
YOU! SPEAK!! WHAT IS YOUR CALLING?
OUR CALLING IS TO TRAVEL TO BEDLAM AND CLOSE DOWN DOC STATIC, OR UNDERWHERE IS DOOMED AND SO IS EVERYONE IN IT, INCLUDING YOU, SILAS!
AMBITIOUS! I WISH YOU GOOD FORTUNE. SIGNS OF THE PLAGUE HAVE BEGUN TO APPEAR ON SILAS' LAND.
...BAD TIDINGS FOR A COUCH POTATO FARMER LIKE SILAS
ROACH RAIDERS BLOCK OUR PATH BELOW. WE NEED TO TRAVEL ON YOUR LEVEL. MAY WE PASS?
IF IT WERE UP TO ME... YES. BUT MORE ENEMIES CAMP WEST OF HERE. ALL ROADS ARE CLOSED.
YOU HAVE ONE OPTION

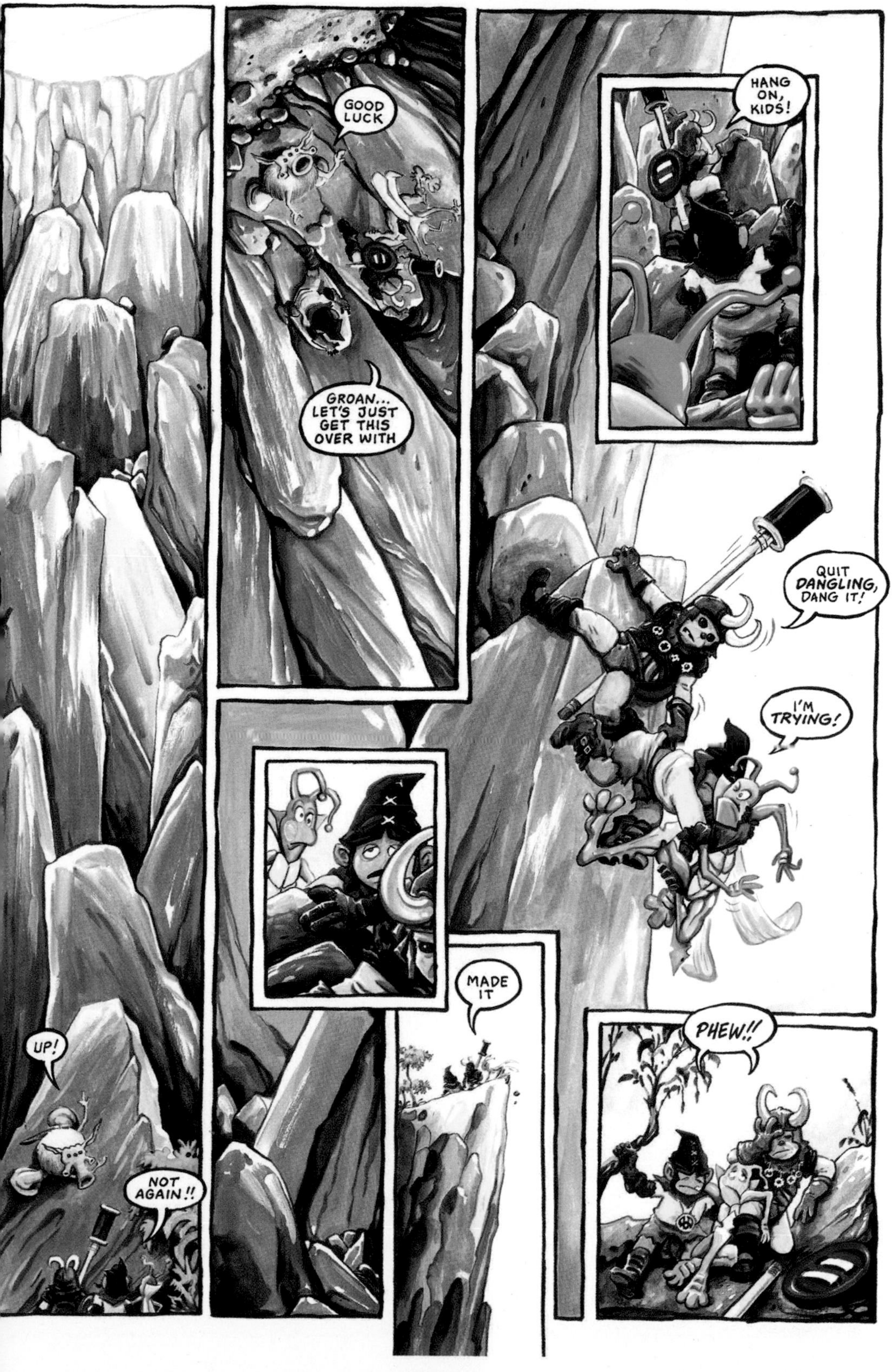
UP!
NOT AGAIN!!
GOOD LUCK
GROAN... LET'S JUST GET THIS OVER WITH
MADE IT
HANG ON, KIDS!
QUIT DANGLING, DANG IT!
I'M TRYING!
PHEW!!

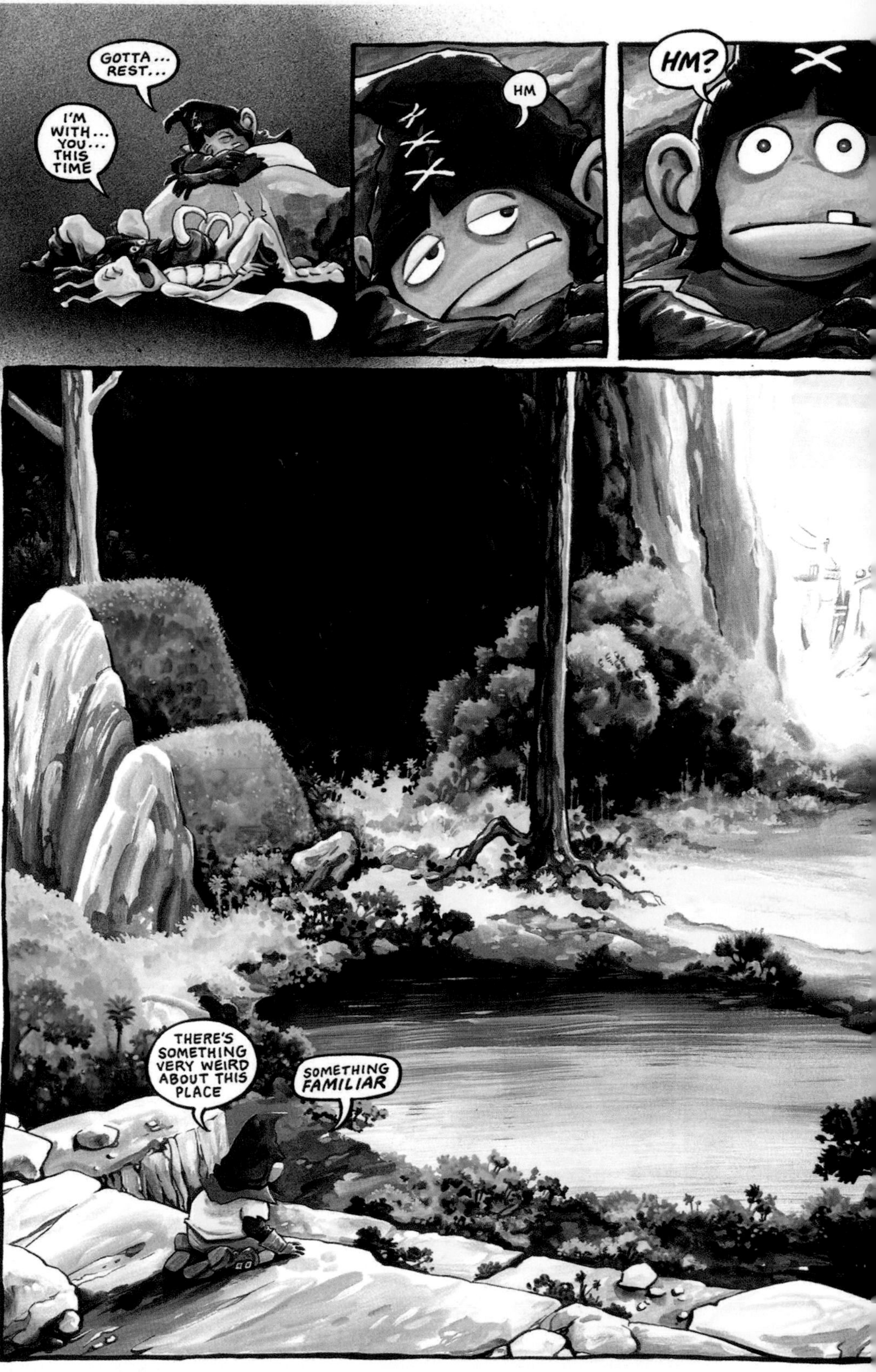
GOTTA... REST...
I'M WITH... YOU... THIS TIME
HM
HM?
THERE'S SOMETHING VERY WEIRD ABOUT THIS PLACE
SOMETHING FAMILIAR

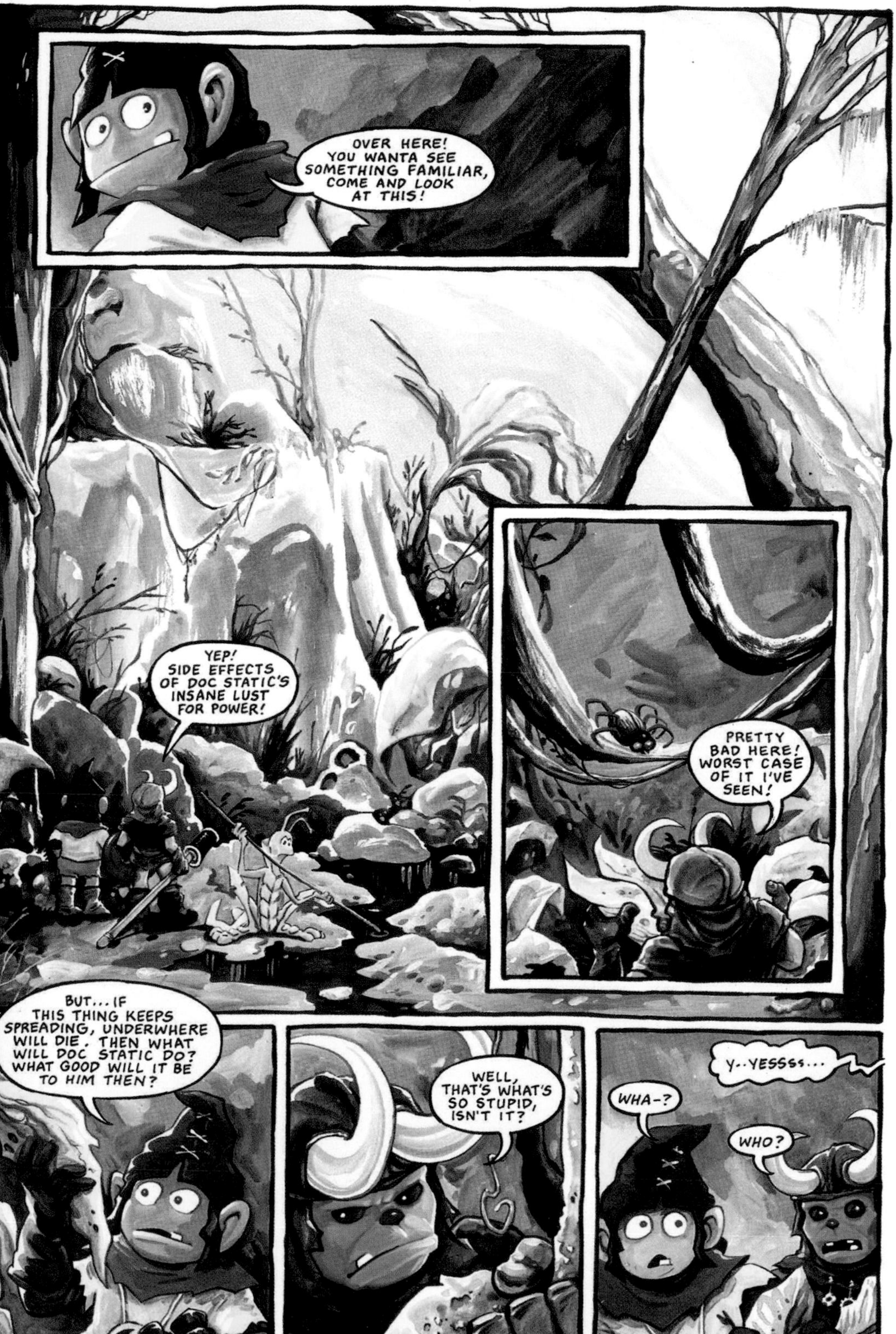
OVER HERE! YOU WANTA SEE SOMETHING FAMILIAR, COME AND LOOK AT THIS!
YEP! SIDE EFFECTS OF DOC STATIC'S INSANE LUST FOR POWER!
PRETTY BAD HERE! WORST CASE OF IT I'VE SEEN!
BUT... IF THIS THING KEEPS SPREADING, UNDERWHERE WILL DIE. THEN WHAT WILL DOC STATIC DO? WHAT GOOD WILL IT BE TO HIM THEN?
WELL, THAT'S WHAT'S SO STUPID, ISN'T IT?
Y-YESSSS...
WHA-?
WHO?

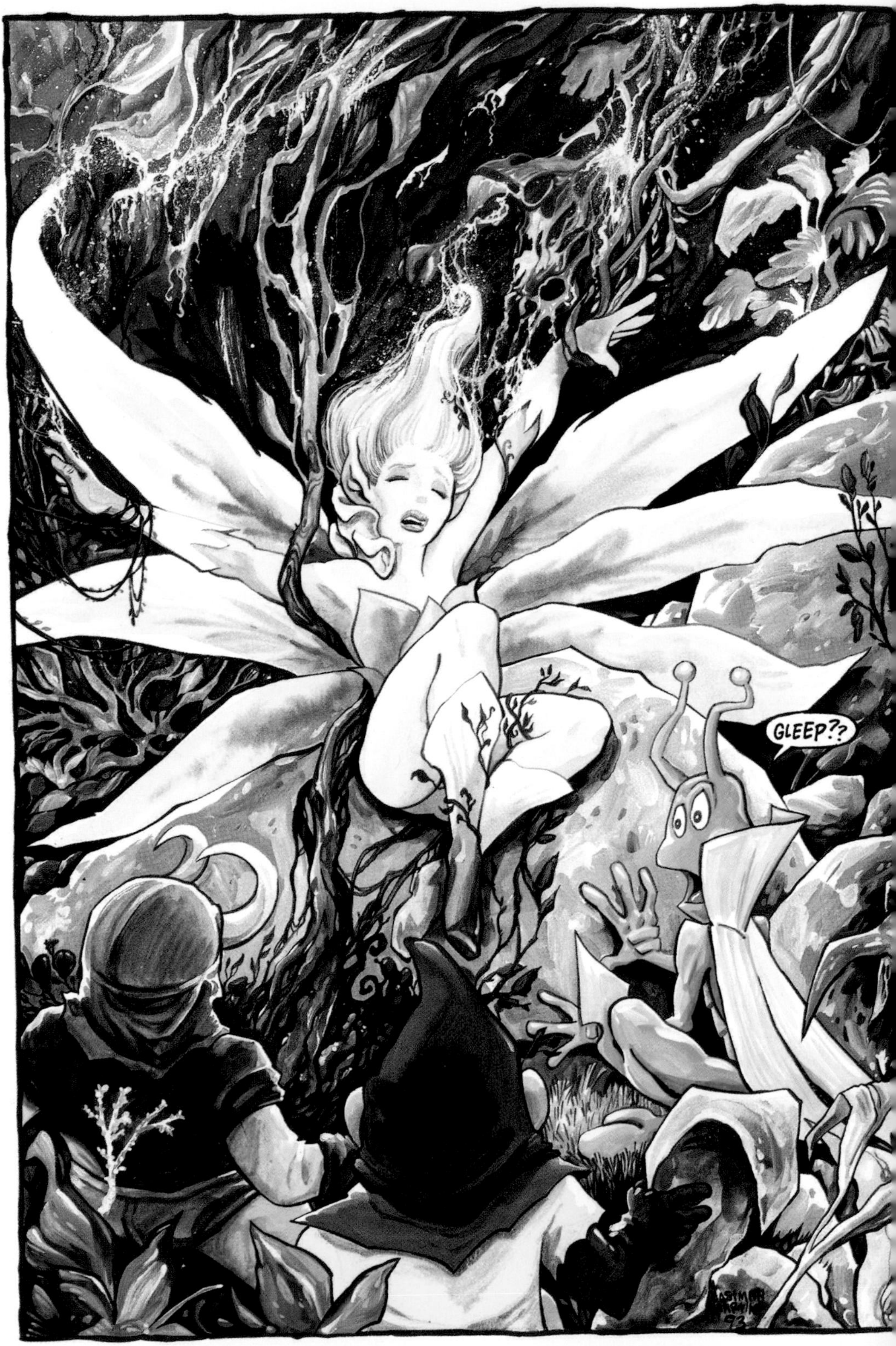
GLEEP??

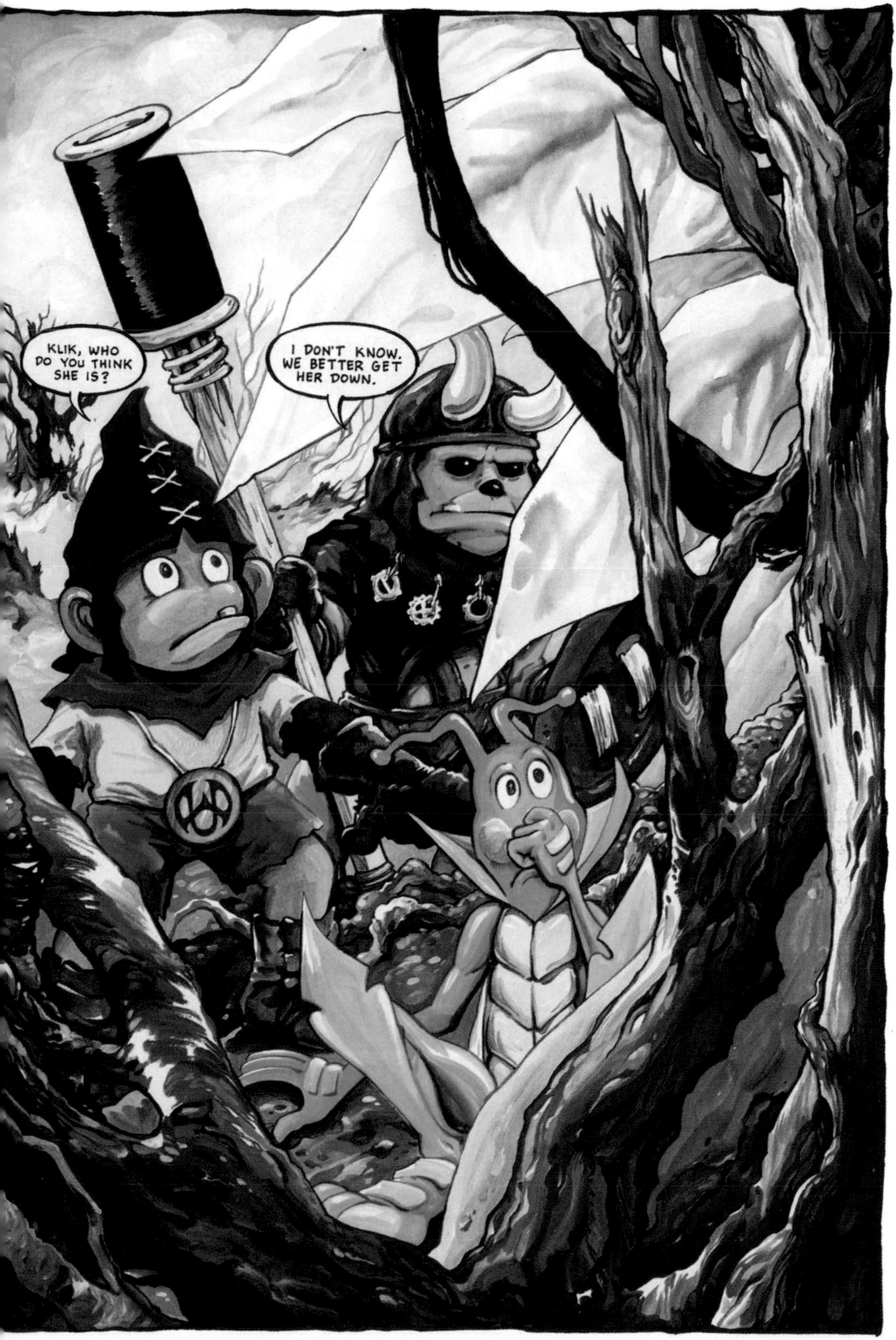
KLIK, WHO DO YOU THINK SHE IS?
I DON'T KNOW. WE BETTER GET HER DOWN.

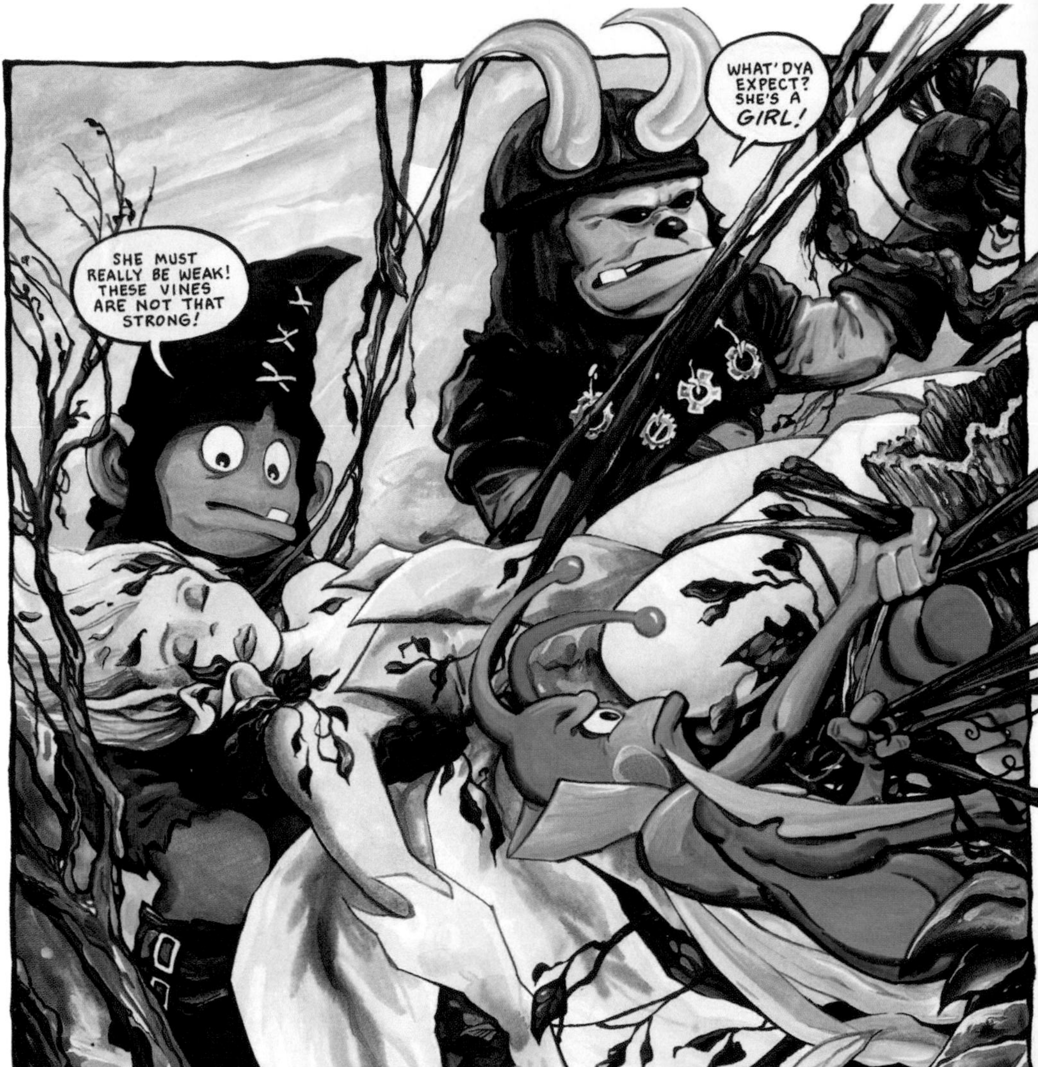
SHE MUST REALLY BE WEAK! THESE VINES ARE NOT THAT STRONG!
WHAT'DYA EXPECT? SHE'S A GIRL!

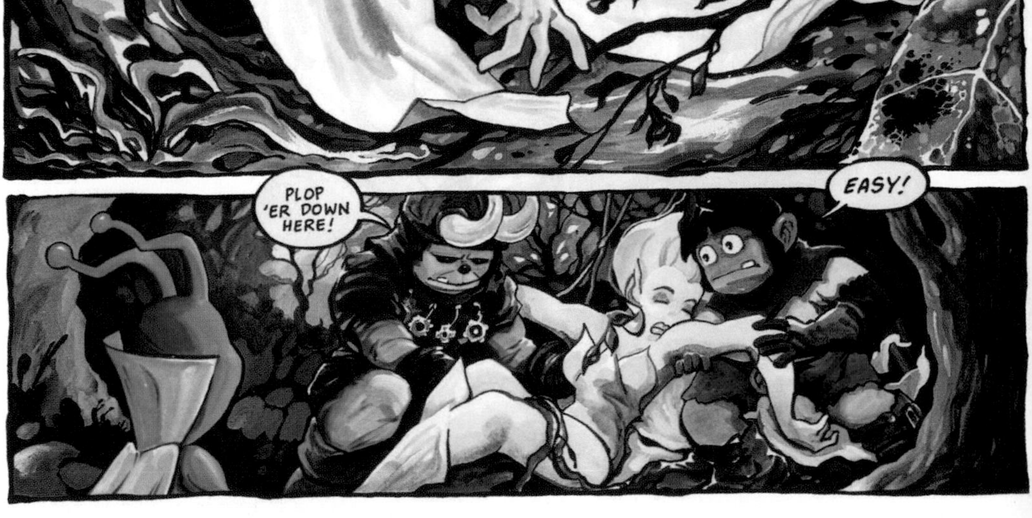
PLOP 'ER DOWN HERE!
EASY!

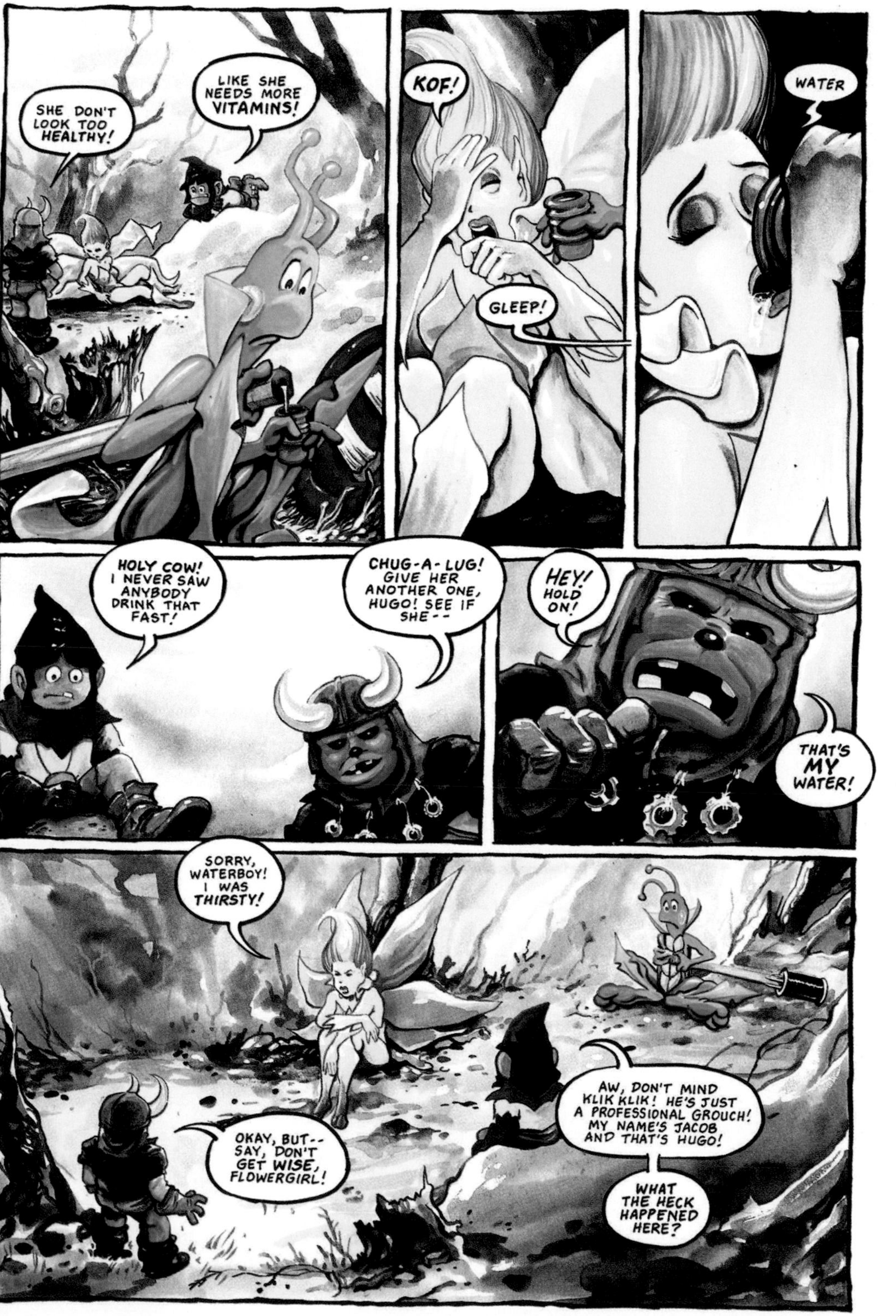
SHE DON'T LOOK TOO HEALTHY!
LIKE SHE NEEDS MORE VITAMINS!
KOF!
GLEEP!
WATER
HOLY COW! I NEVER SAW ANYBODY DRINK THAT FAST!
CHUG-A-LUG! GIVE HER ANOTHER ONE, HUGO! SEE IF SHE--
HEY! HOLD ON!
THAT'S MY WATER!
SORRY, WATERBOY! I WAS THIRSTY!
OKAY, BUT-- SAY, DON'T GET WISE, FLOWERGIRL!
AW, DON'T MIND KLIK KLIK! HE'S JUST A PROFESSIONAL GROUCH! MY NAME'S JACOB AND THAT'S HUGO!
WHAT THE HECK HAPPENED HERE?

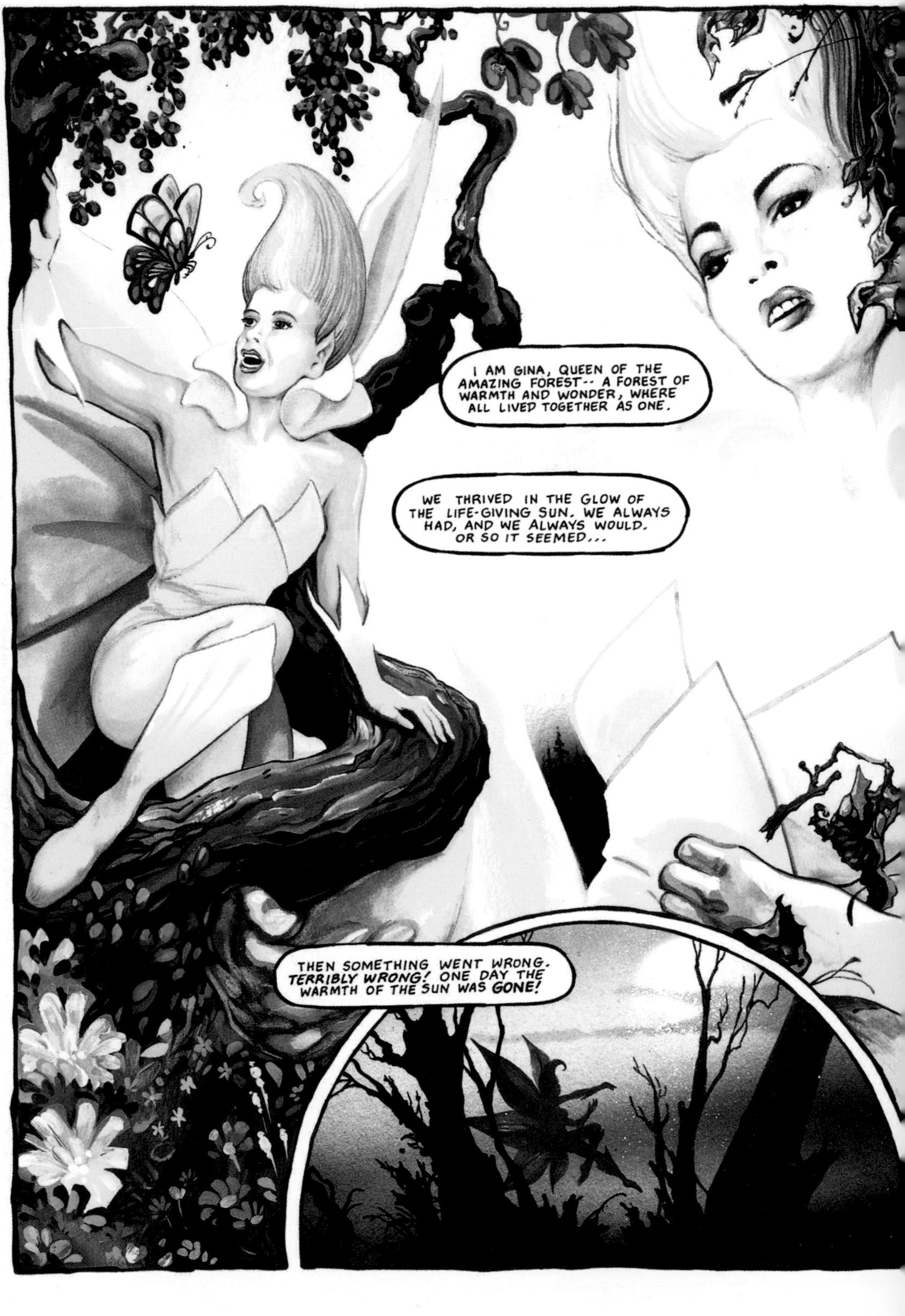
I AM GINA, QUEEN OF THE AMAZING FOREST-- A FOREST OF WARMTH AND WONDER, WHERE ALL LIVED TOGETHER AS ONE.
WE THRIVED IN THE GLOW OF THE LIFE-GIVING SUN. WE ALWAYS HAD, AND WE ALWAYS WOULD. OR SO IT SEEMED...
THEN SOMETHING WENT WRONG. TERRIBLY WRONG! ONE DAY THE WARMTH OF THE SUN WAS GONE!

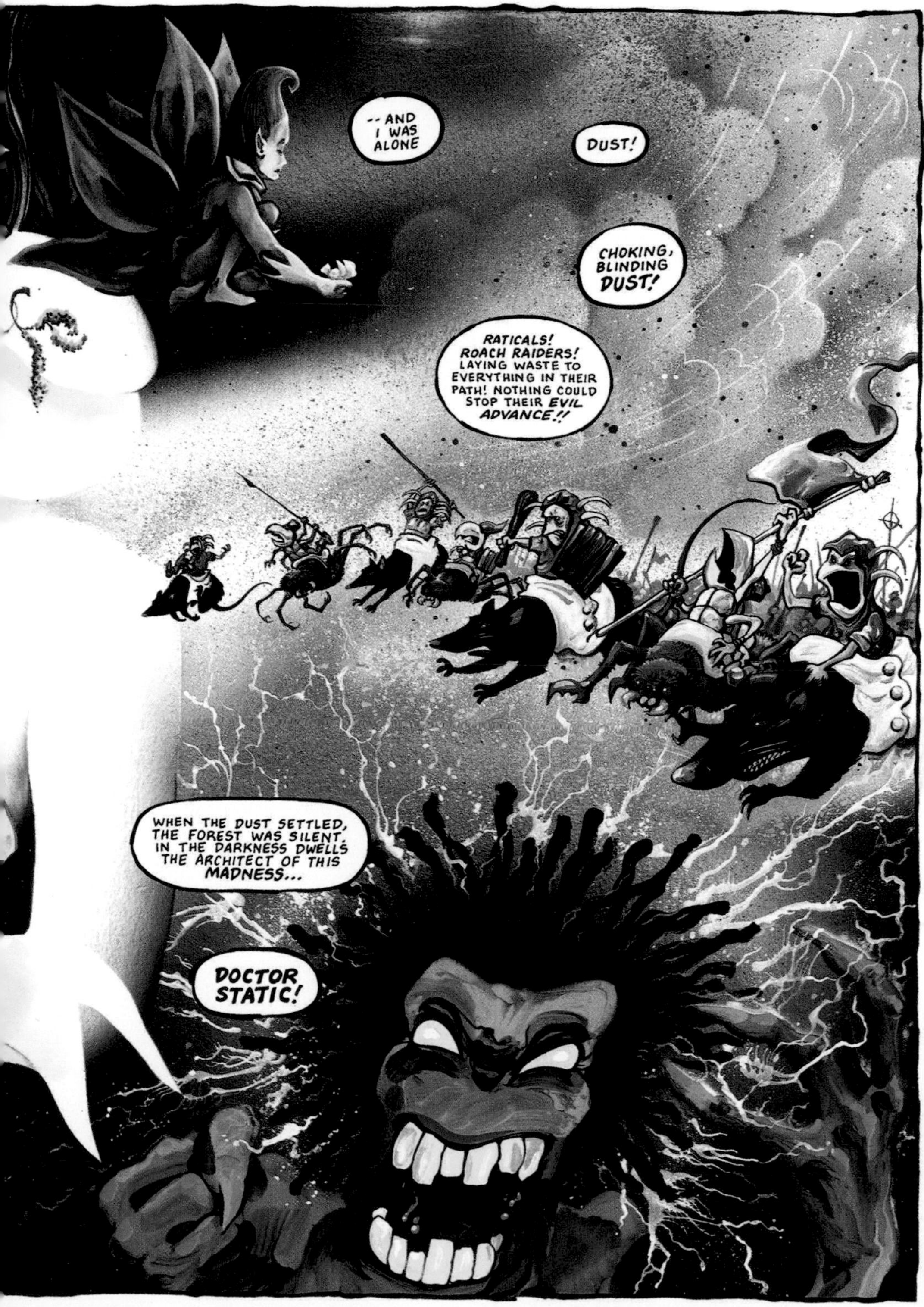
-- AND I WAS ALONE
DUST!
CHOKING, BLINDING DUST!
RATICALS! ROACH RAIDERS! LAYING WASTE TO EVERYTHING IN THEIR PATH! NOTHING COULD STOP THEIR EVIL ADVANCE!!
WHEN THE DUST SETTLED, THE FOREST WAS SILENT. IN THE DARKNESS DWELLS THE ARCHITECT OF THIS MADNESS...
DOCTOR STATIC!

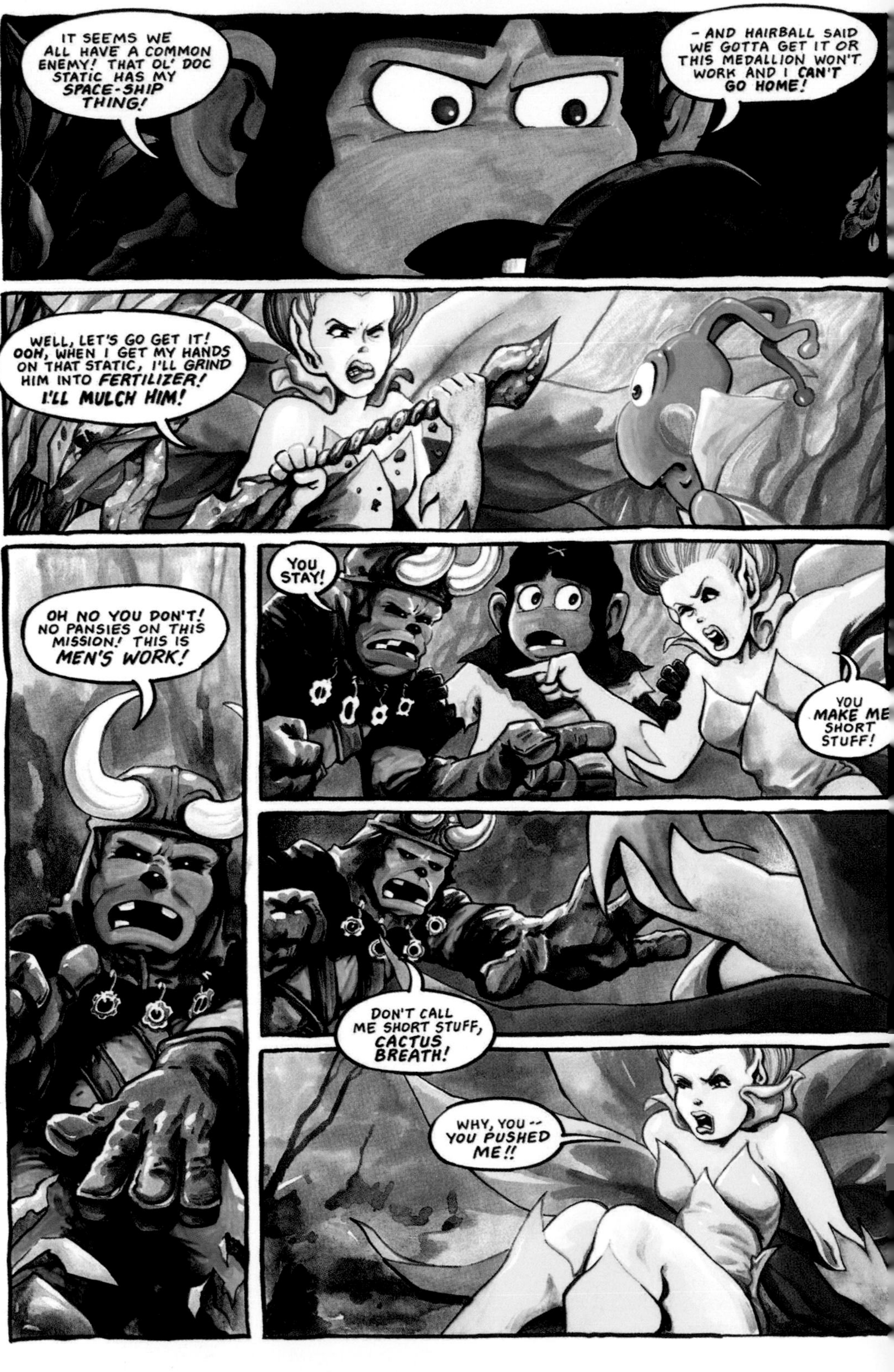
IT SEEMS WE ALL HAVE A COMMON ENEMY! THAT OL' DOC STATIC HAS MY SPACE-SHIP THING!
- AND HAIRBALL SAID WE GOTTA GET IT OR THIS MEDALLION WON'T WORK AND I CAN'T GO HOME!
WELL, LET'S GO GET IT! OOH, WHEN I GET MY HANDS ON THAT STATIC, I'LL GRIND HIM INTO FERTILIZER! I'LL MULCH HIM!
OH NO YOU DON'T! NO PANSIES ON THIS MISSION! THIS IS MEN'S WORK!
YOU STAY!
YOU MAKE ME SHORT STUFF!
DON'T CALL ME SHORT STUFF, CACTUS BREATH!
WHY, YOU -- YOU PUSHED ME!!

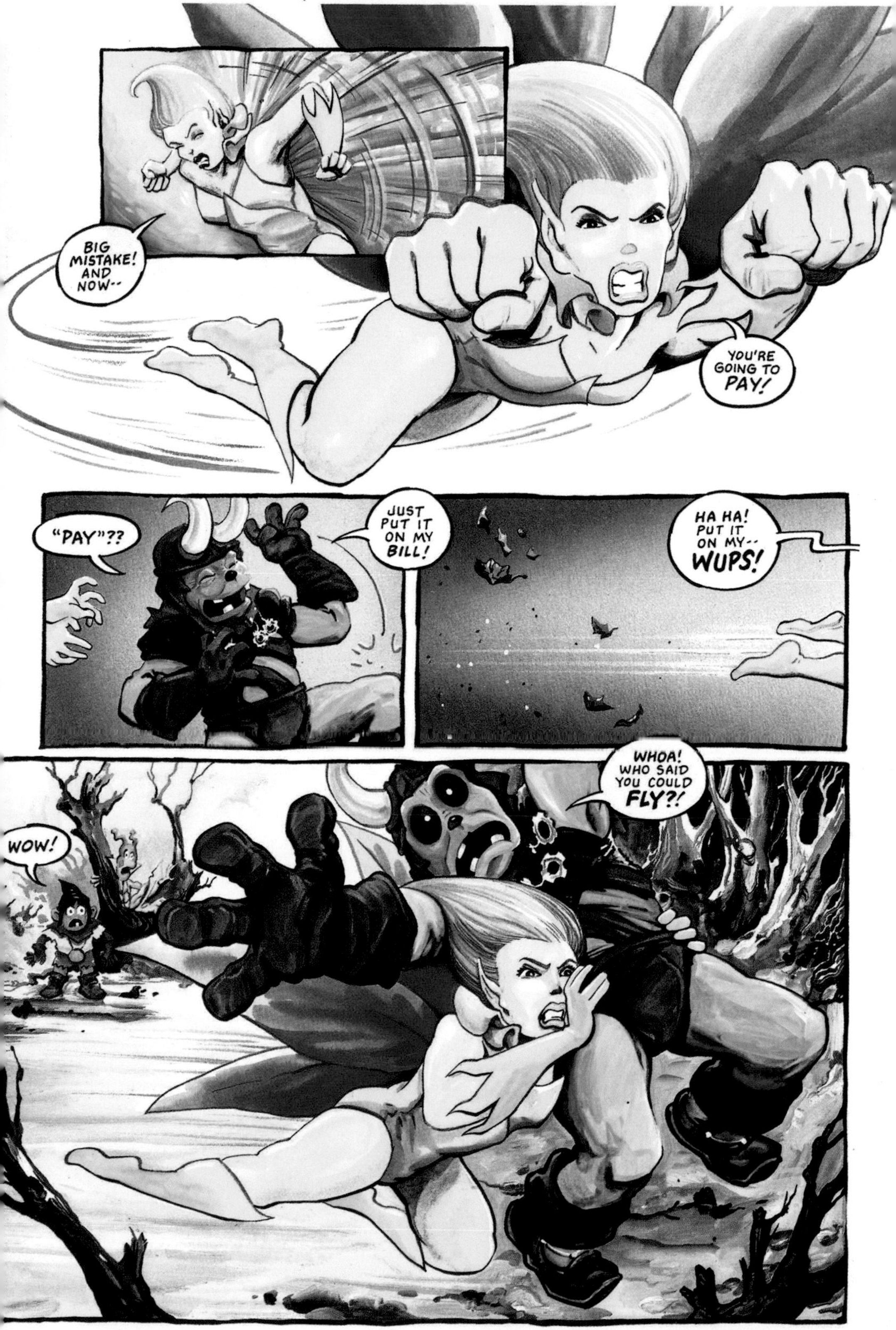
BIG MISTAKE! AND NOW--
YOU'RE GOING TO PAY!
"PAY"??
JUST PUT IT ON MY BILL!
HA HA! PUT IT ON MY-- WUPS!
WOW!
WHOA! WHO SAID YOU COULD FLY?!

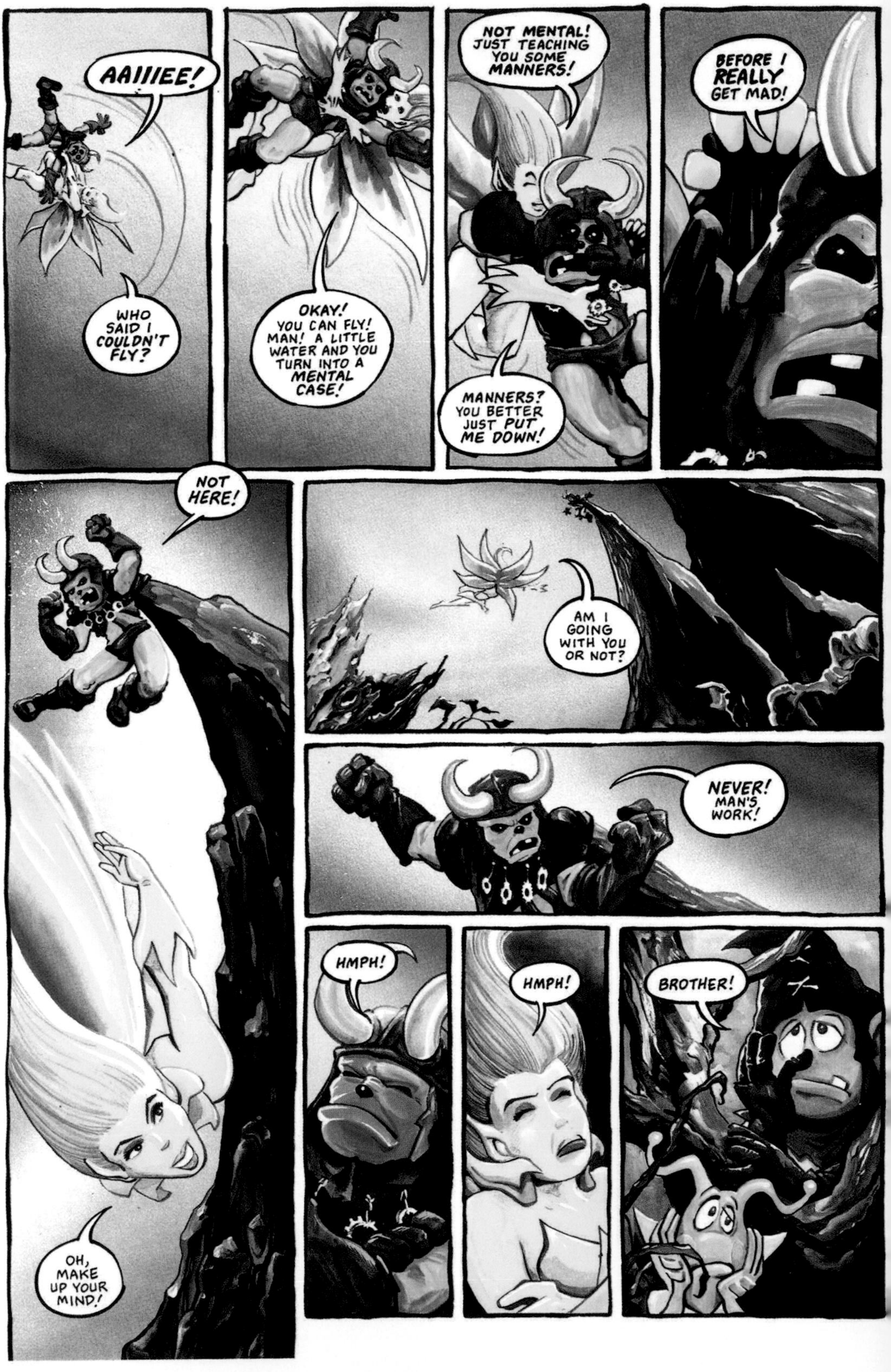
AAIIIEE!
WHO SAID I COULDN'T FLY?
OKAY! YOU CAN FLY! MAN! A LITTLE WATER AND YOU TURN INTO A MENTAL CASE!
NOT MENTAL! JUST TEACHING YOU SOME MANNERS!
MANNERS? YOU BETTER JUST PUT ME DOWN!
BEFORE I REALLY GET MAD!
NOT HERE!
OH, MAKE UP YOUR MIND!
AM I GOING WITH YOU OR NOT?
NEVER! MAN'S WORK!
HMPH!
HMPH!
BROTHER!

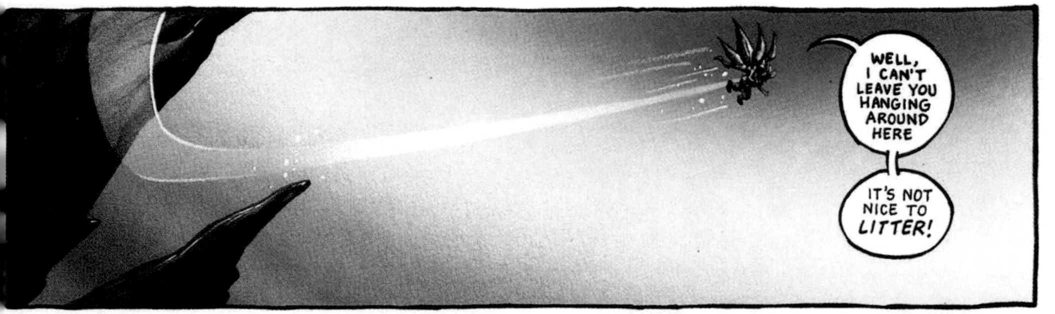
WELL, I CAN'T LEAVE YOU HANGING AROUND HERE
IT'S NOT NICE TO LITTER!

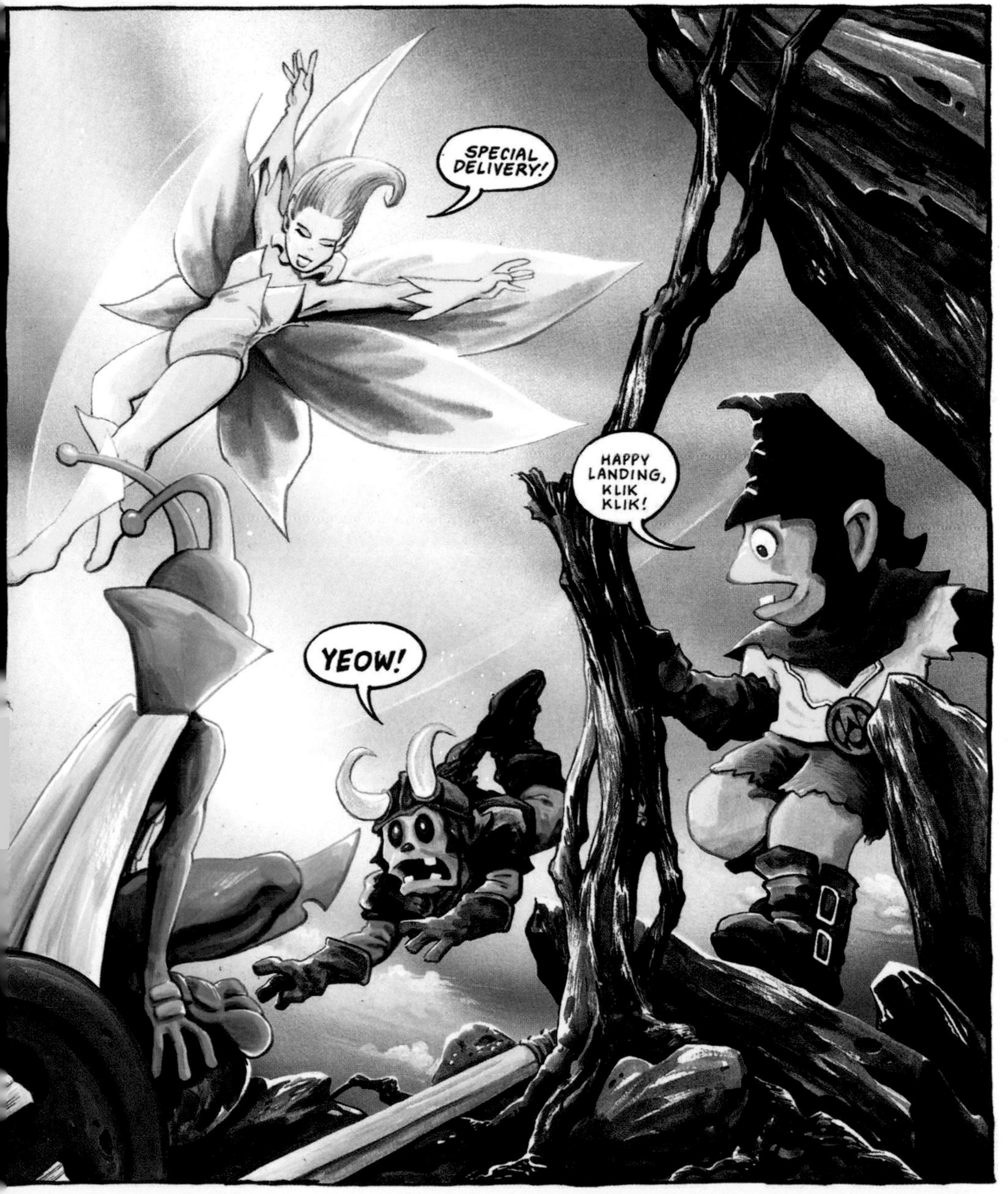
SPECIAL DELIVERY!
HAPPY LANDING, KLIK KLIK!
YEOW!

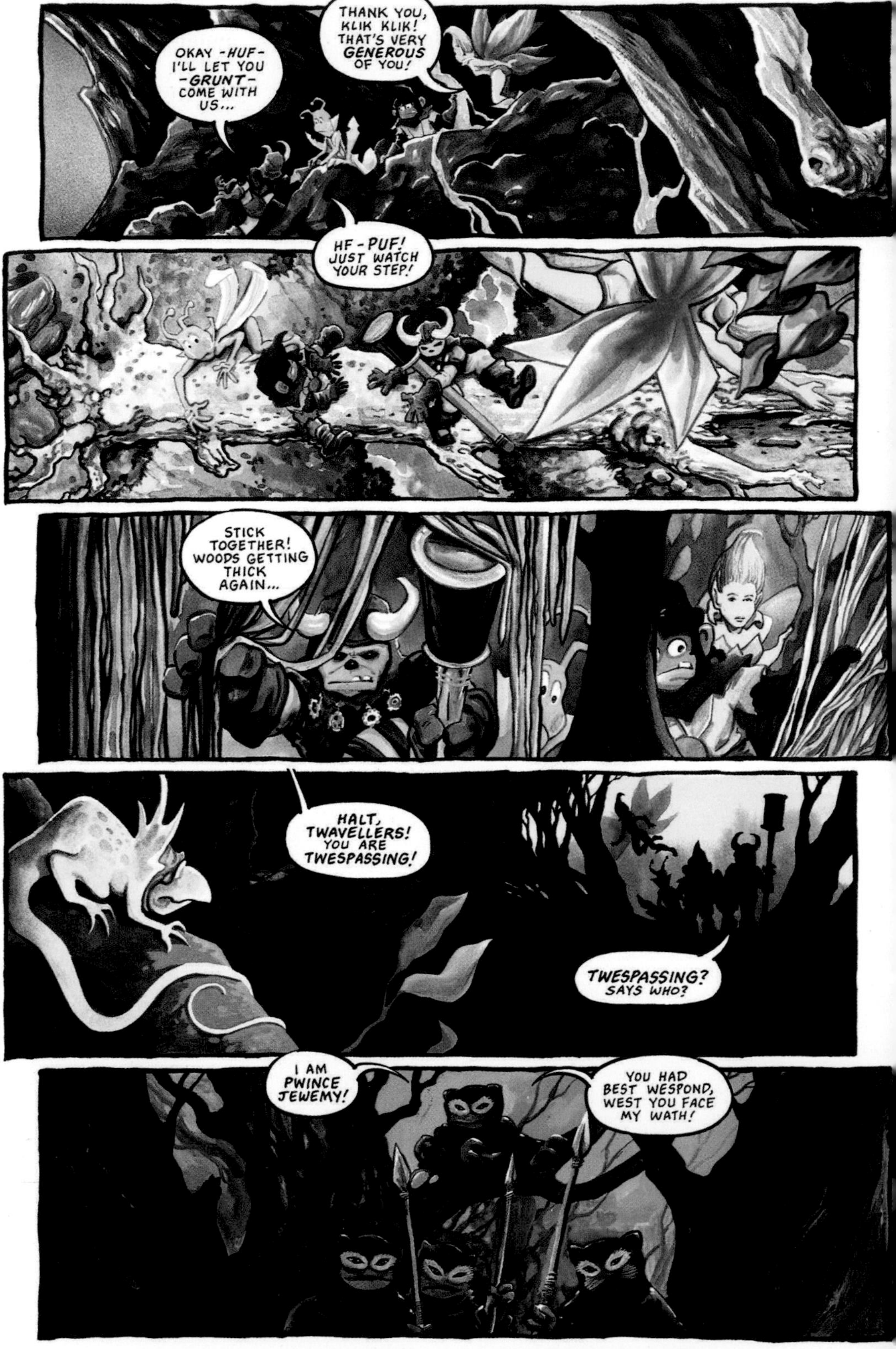
OKAY -HUF- I'LL LET YOU -GRUNT- COME WITH US...
THANK YOU, KLIK KLIK! THAT'S VERY GENEROUS OF YOU!
HF-PUF! JUST WATCH YOUR STEP!
STICK TOGETHER! WOODS GETTING THICK AGAIN...
HALT, TWAVELLERS! YOU ARE TWESPASSING!
TWESPASSING? SAYS WHO?
I AM PWINCE JEWEMY!
YOU HAD BEST WESPOND, WEST YOU FACE MY WATH!

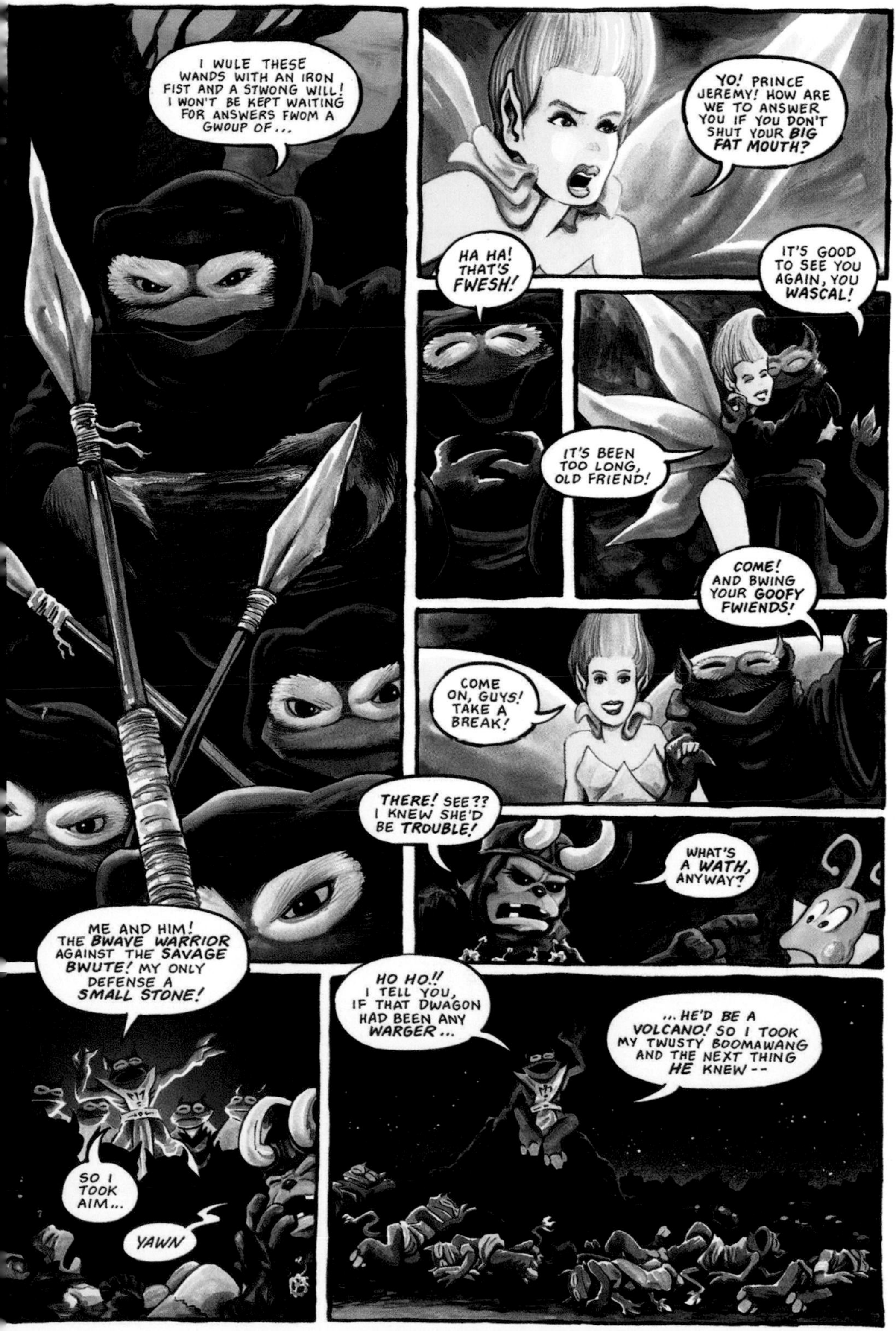
I WULE THESE WANDS WITH AN IRON FIST AND A STWONG WILL! I WON'T BE KEPT WAITING FOR ANSWERS FWOM A GWOUP OF...
YO! PRINCE JEREMY! HOW ARE WE TO ANSWER YOU IF YOU DON'T SHUT YOUR BIG FAT MOUTH?
HA HA! THAT'S FWESH!
IT'S GOOD TO SEE YOU AGAIN, YOU WASCAL!
IT'S BEEN TOO LONG, OLD FRIEND!
COME! AND BWING YOUR GOOFY FWIENDS!
COME ON, GUYS! TAKE A BREAK!
THERE! SEE?? I KNEW SHE'D BE TROUBLE!
WHAT'S A WATH, ANYWAY?
ME AND HIM! THE BWAVE WARRIOR AGAINST THE SAVAGE BWUTE! MY ONLY DEFENSE A SMALL STONE!
SO I TOOK AIM...
YAWN
HO HO!! I TELL YOU, IF THAT DWAGON HAD BEEN ANY WARGER...
...HE'D BE A VOLCANO! SO I TOOK MY TWUSTY BOOMAWANG AND THE NEXT THING HE KNEW--

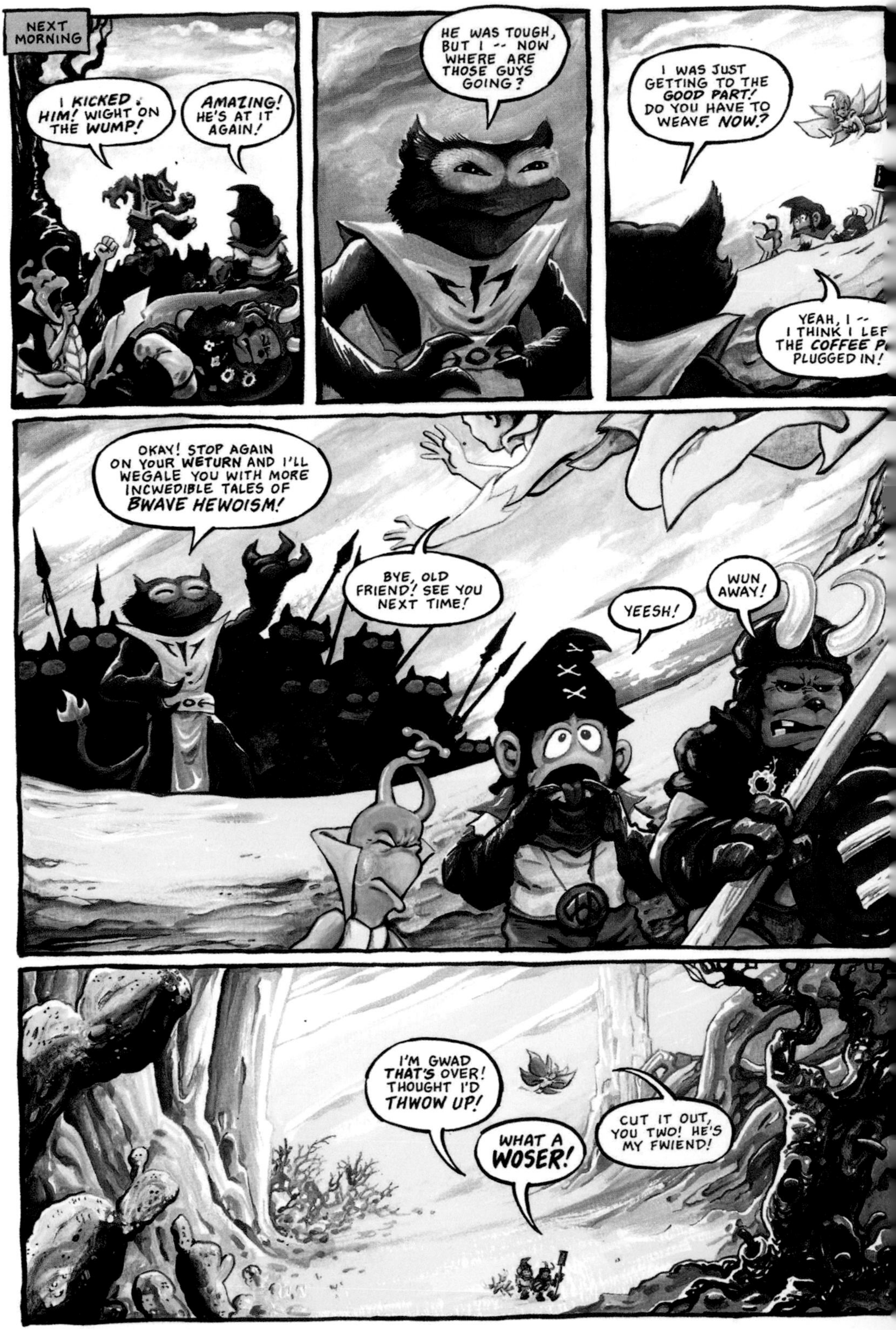
NEXT MORNING
I KICKED HIM! WIGHT ON THE WUMP!
AMAZING! HE'S AT IT AGAIN!
HE WAS TOUGH, BUT I -- NOW WHERE ARE THOSE GUYS GOING?
I WAS JUST GETTING TO THE GOOD PART! DO YOU HAVE TO WEAVE NOW?
YEAH, I -- I THINK I LEF THE COFFEE P PLUGGED IN!
OKAY! STOP AGAIN ON YOUR WETURN AND I'LL WEGALE YOU WITH MORE INCWEDIBLE TALES OF BWAVE HEWOISM!
BYE, OLD FRIEND! SEE YOU NEXT TIME!
YEESH!
WUN AWAY!
I'M GWAD THAT'S OVER! THOUGHT I'D THWOW UP!
WHAT A WOSER!
CUT IT OUT, YOU TWO! HE'S MY FWIEND!

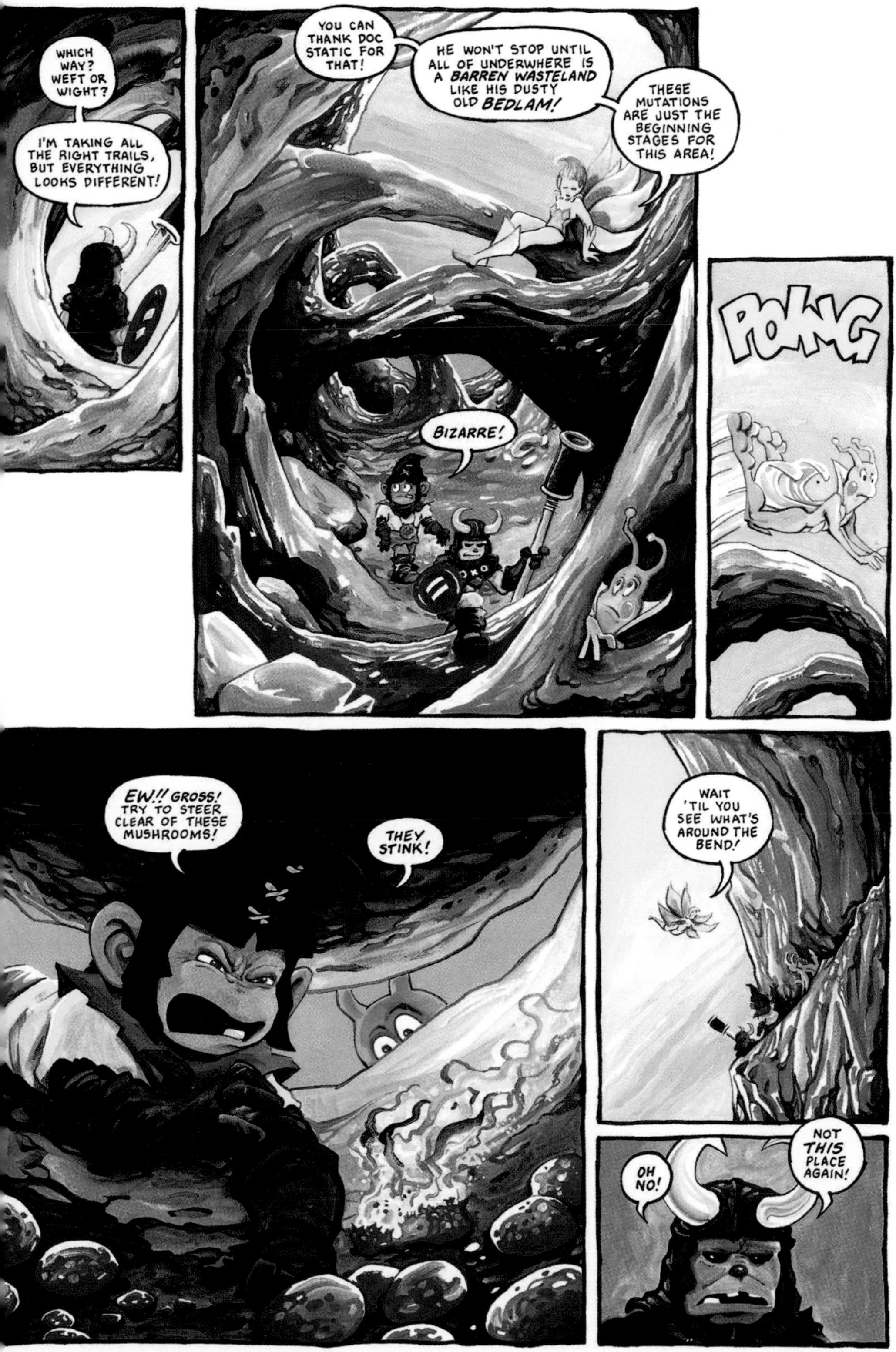
WHICH WAY? WEFT OR WIGHT?
I'M TAKING ALL THE RIGHT TRAILS, BUT EVERYTHING LOOKS DIFFERENT!
YOU CAN THANK DOC STATIC FOR THAT!
HE WON'T STOP UNTIL ALL OF UNDERWHERE IS A BARREN WASTELAND LIKE HIS DUSTY OLD BEDLAM!
THESE MUTATIONS ARE JUST THE BEGINNING STAGES FOR THIS AREA!
BIZARRE!
POING
EW!! GROSS! TRY TO STEER CLEAR OF THESE MUSHROOMS!
THEY STINK!
WAIT 'TIL YOU SEE WHAT'S AROUND THE BEND!
OH NO!
NOT THIS PLACE AGAIN!

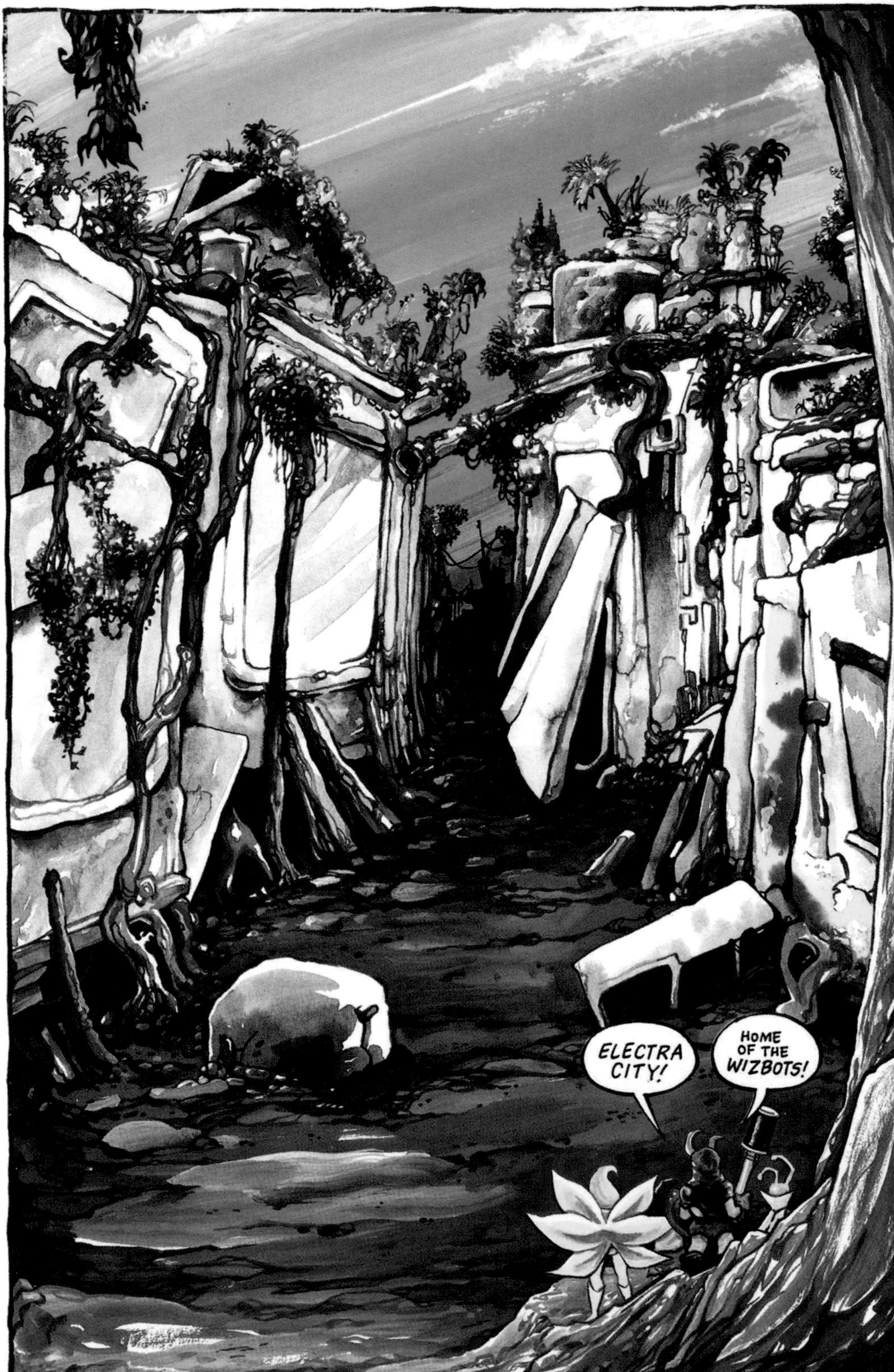
ELECTRA CITY!
HOME OF THE WIZBOTS!

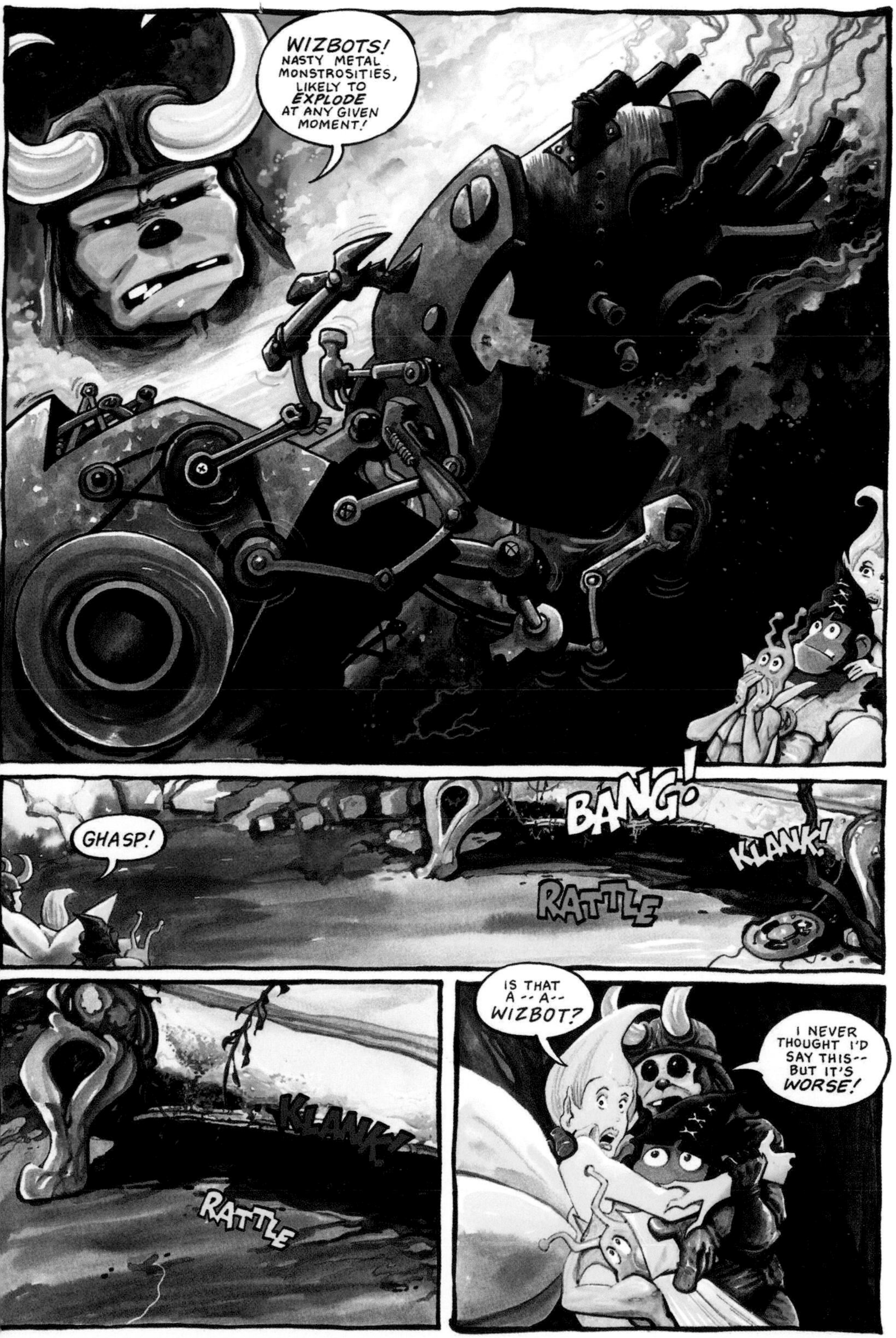
WIZBOTS! NASTY METAL MONSTROSITIES, LIKELY TO EXPLODE AT ANY GIVEN MOMENT!
GHASP!
BANG!
KLANK!
RATTLE
KLANK!
RATTLE
IS THAT A -- A-- WIZBOT?
I NEVER THOUGHT I'D SAY THIS-- BUT IT'S WORSE!

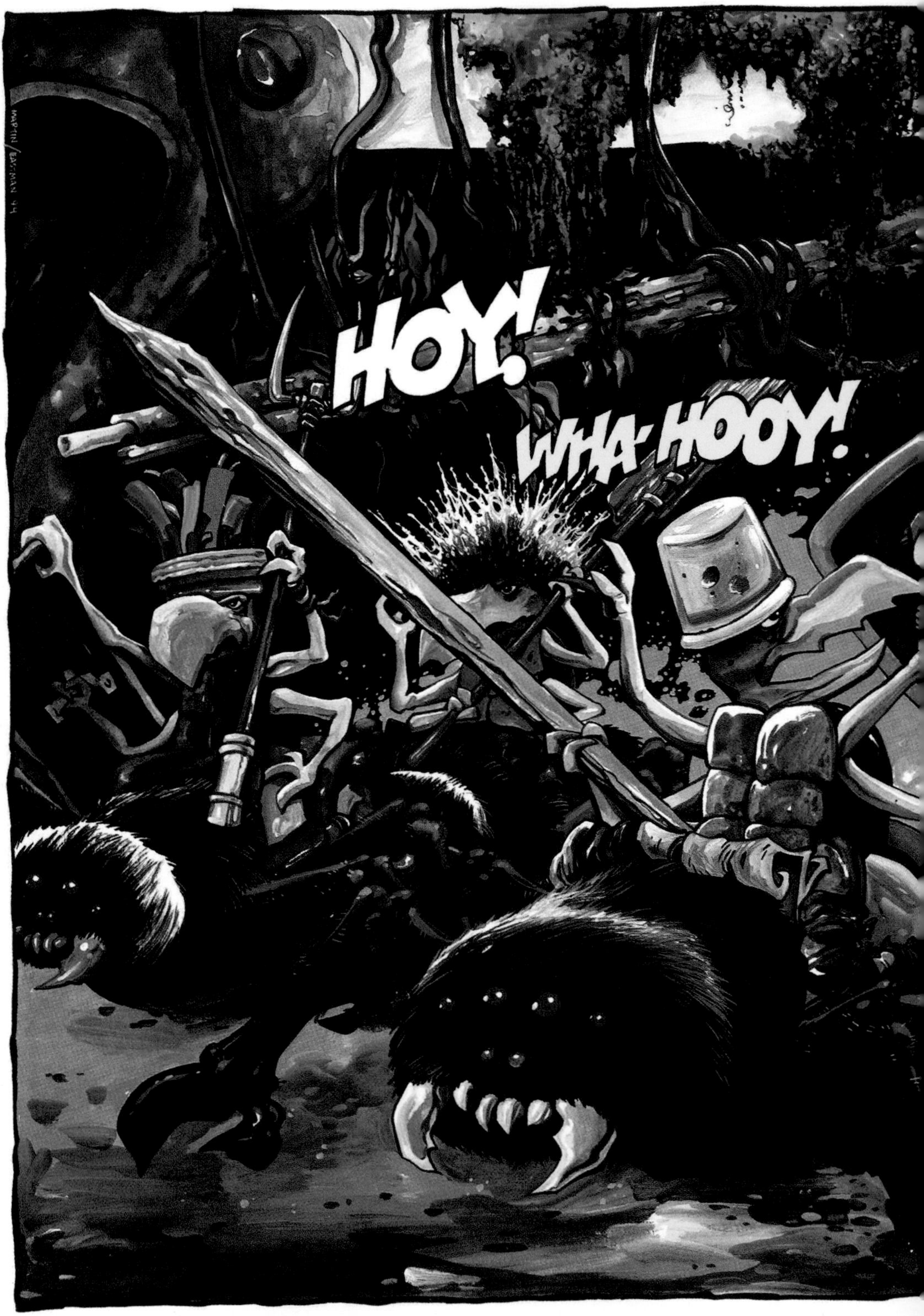
HOY!
WHA-HOOY!

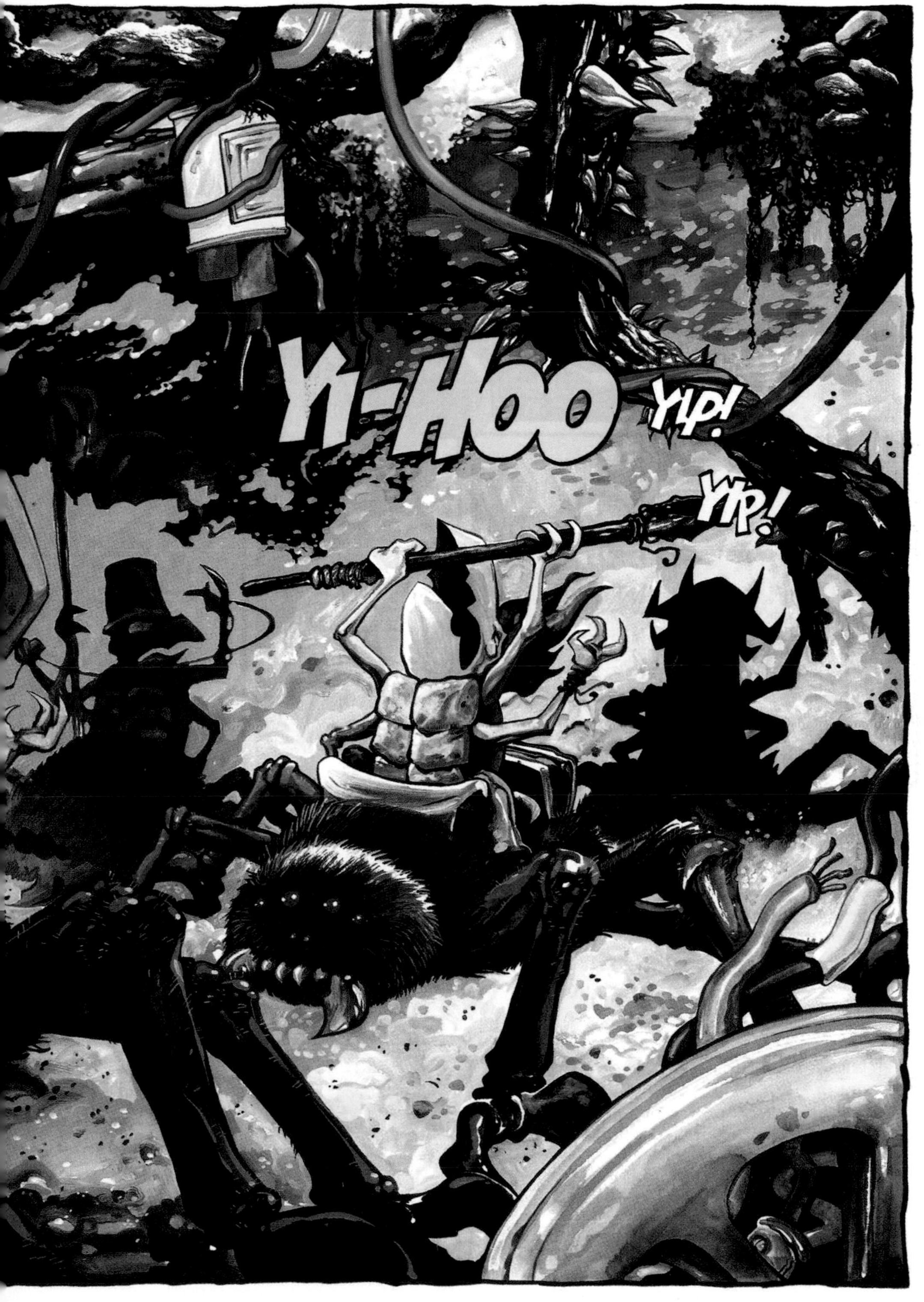

YI-HOO
YIP!
YIP!

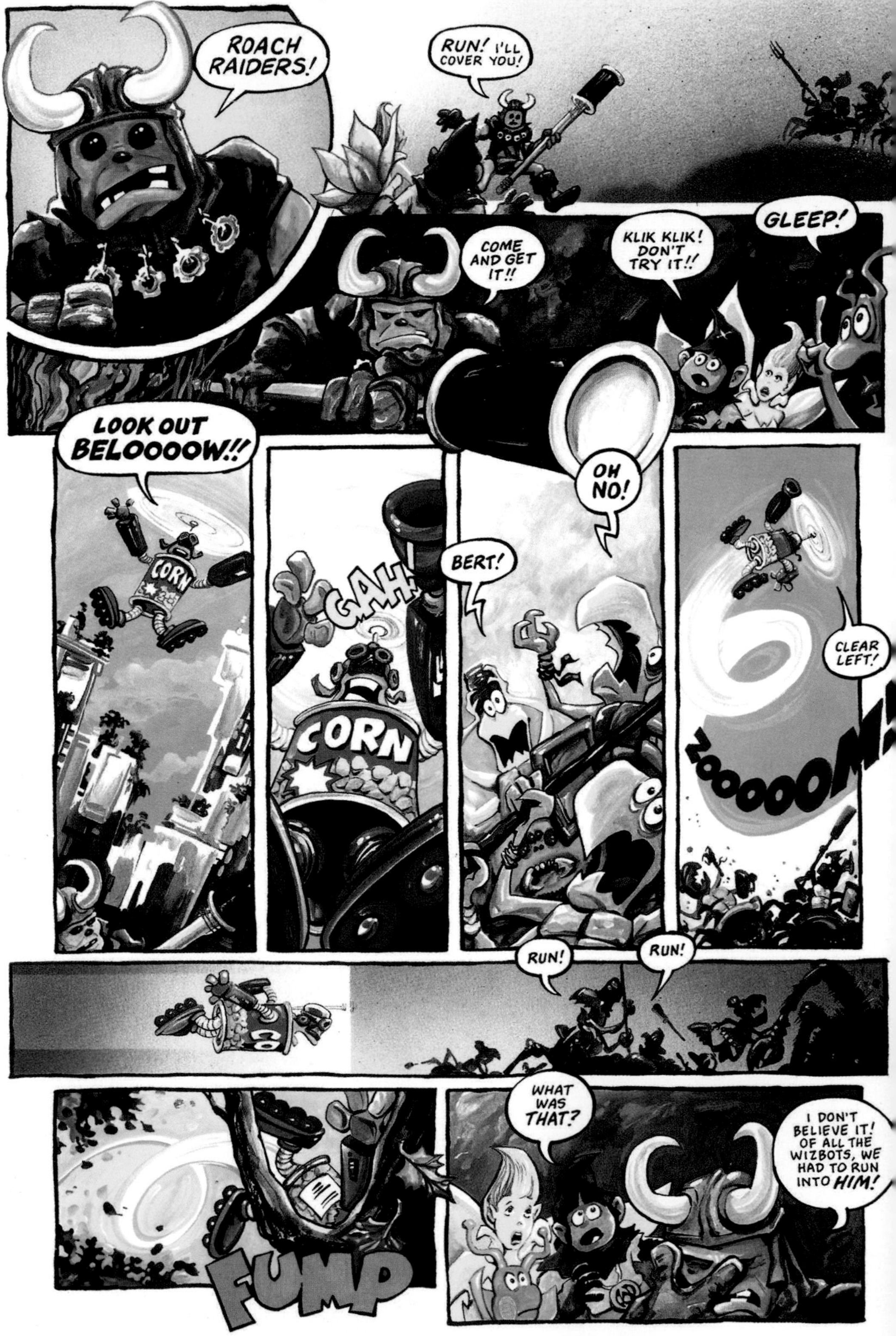
ROACH RAIDERS!
RUN! I'LL COVER YOU!
COME AND GET IT!!
KLIK KLIK! DON'T TRY IT!!
GLEEP!
LOOK OUT BELOOOOW!!
CORN
GAH
CORN
BERT!
OH NO!
CLEAR LEFT!
ZOOOOOOM!
RUN!
RUN!
FUMP
WHAT WAS THAT?
I DON'T BELIEVE IT! OF ALL THE WIZBOTS, WE HAD TO RUN INTO HIM!

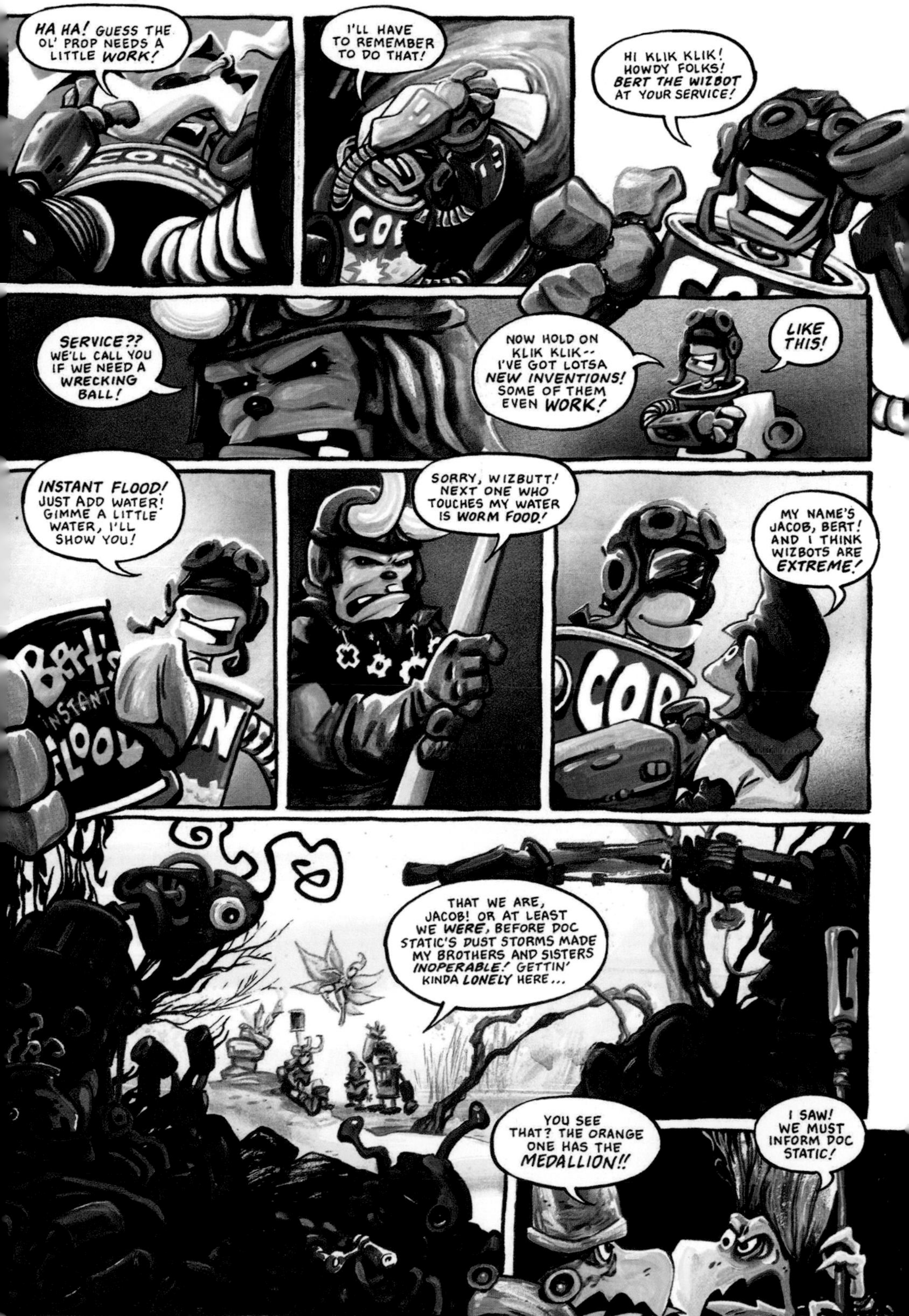
HA HA! GUESS THE OL' PROP NEEDS A LITTLE WORK!
I'LL HAVE TO REMEMBER TO DO THAT!
HI KLIK KLIK! HOWDY FOLKS! BERT THE WIZBOT AT YOUR SERVICE!
SERVICE?? WE'LL CALL YOU IF WE NEED A WRECKING BALL!
NOW HOLD ON KLIK KLIK-- I'VE GOT LOTSA NEW INVENTIONS! SOME OF THEM EVEN WORK!
LIKE THIS!
INSTANT FLOOD! JUST ADD WATER! GIMME A LITTLE WATER, I'LL SHOW YOU!
Bert's INSTANT FLOOD
SORRY, WIZBUTT! NEXT ONE WHO TOUCHES MY WATER IS WORM FOOD!
MY NAME'S JACOB, BERT! AND I THINK WIZBOTS ARE EXTREME!
THAT WE ARE, JACOB! OR AT LEAST WE WERE, BEFORE DOC STATIC'S DUST STORMS MADE MY BROTHERS AND SISTERS INOPERABLE! GETTIN' KINDA LONELY HERE...
YOU SEE THAT? THE ORANGE ONE HAS THE MEDALLION!!
I SAW! WE MUST INFORM DOC STATIC!

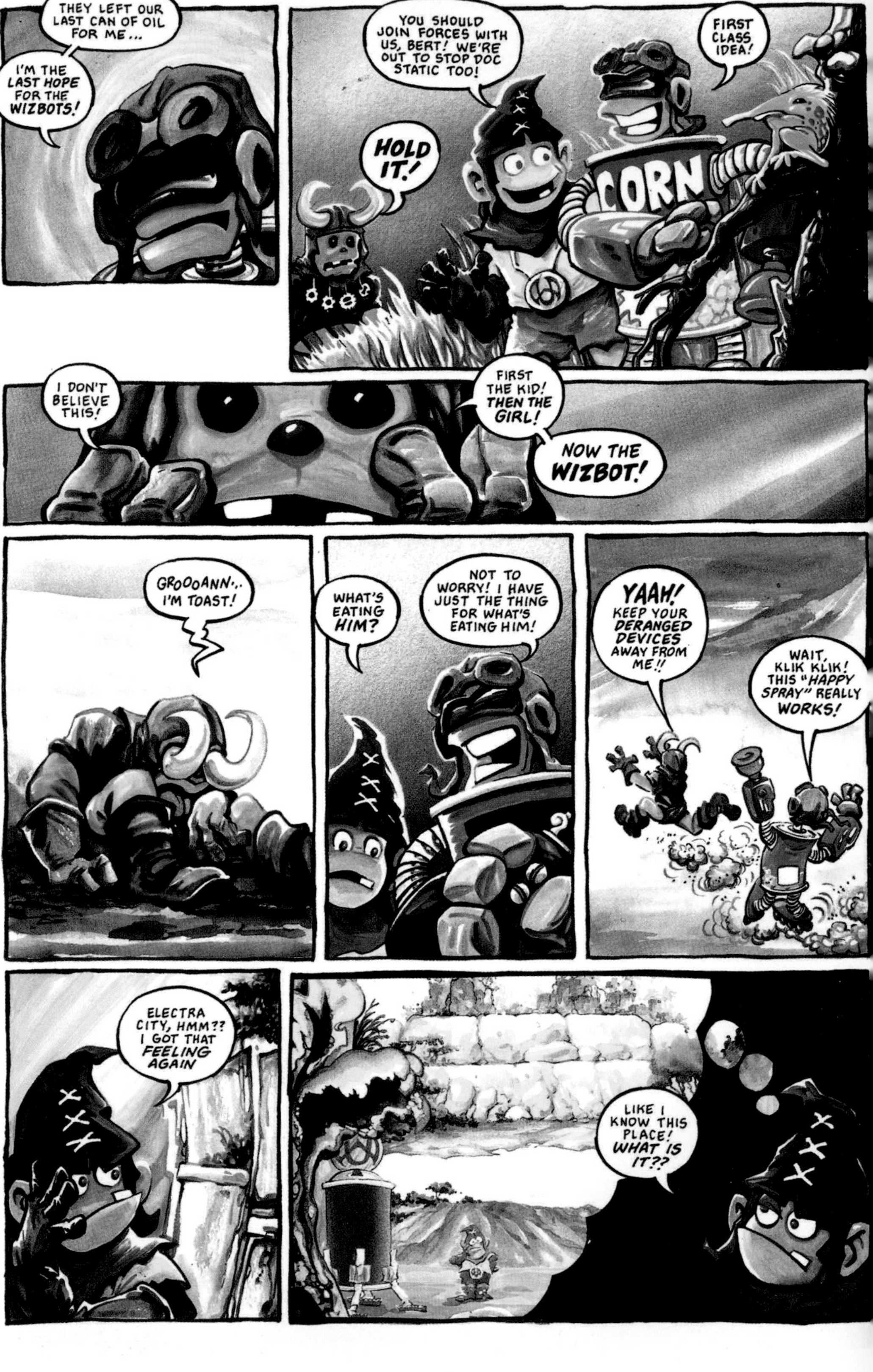
THEY LEFT OUR LAST CAN OF OIL FOR ME...
I'M THE LAST HOPE FOR THE WIZBOTS!
YOU SHOULD JOIN FORCES WITH US, BERT! WE'RE OUT TO STOP DOC STATIC TOO!
FIRST CLASS IDEA!
HOLD IT!
CORN
I DON'T BELIEVE THIS!
FIRST THE KID! THEN THE GIRL!
NOW THE WIZBOT!
GROOOANN... I'M TOAST!
WHAT'S EATING HIM?
NOT TO WORRY! I HAVE JUST THE THING FOR WHAT'S EATING HIM!
YAAH! KEEP YOUR DERANGED DEVICES AWAY FROM ME!!
WAIT, KLIK KLIK! THIS "HAPPY SPRAY" REALLY WORKS!
ELECTRA CITY, HMM?? I GOT THAT FEELING AGAIN
LIKE I KNOW THIS PLACE! WHAT IS IT??

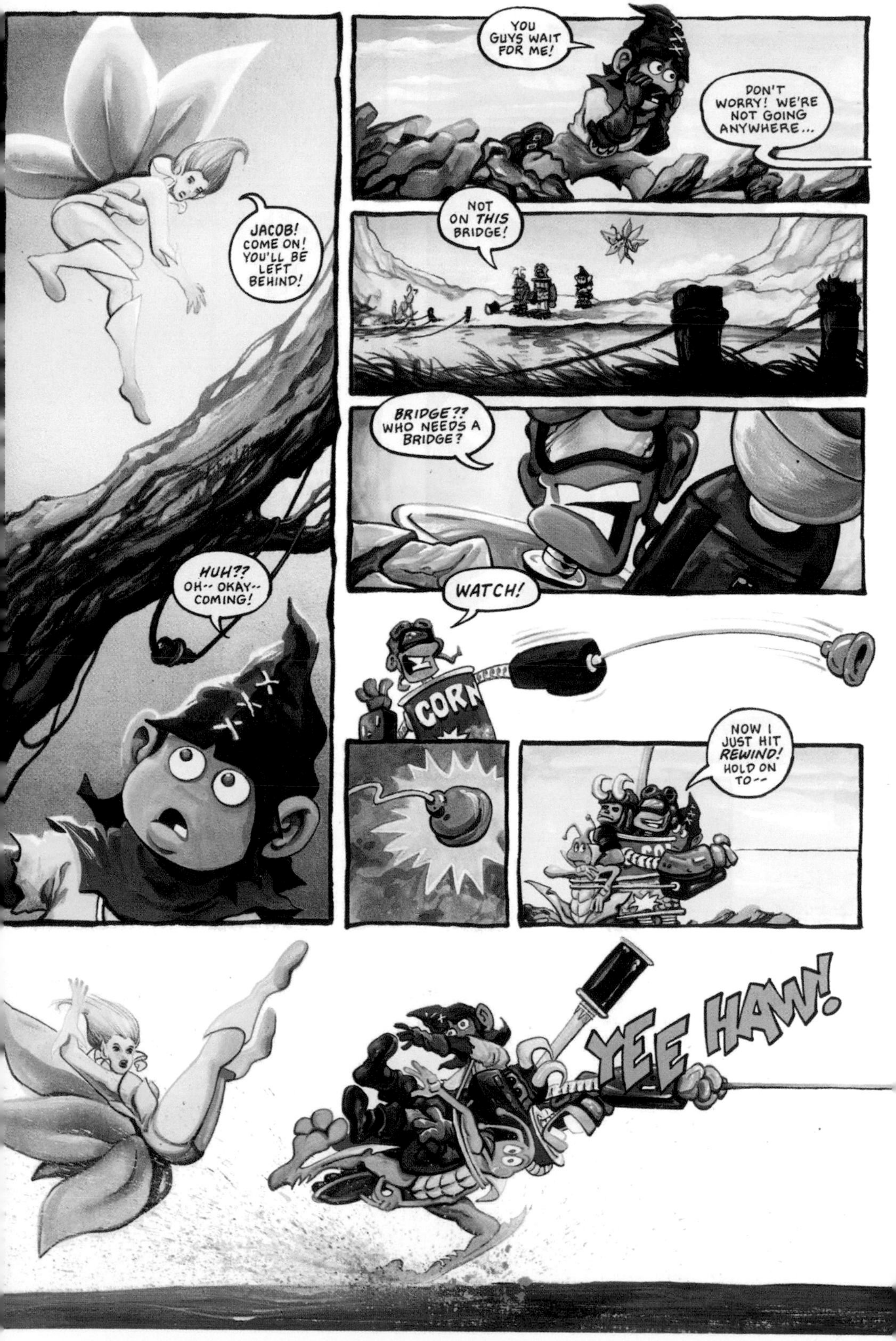
JACOB! COME ON! YOU'LL BE LEFT BEHIND!
HUH?? OH-- OKAY-- COMING!
YOU GUYS WAIT FOR ME!
DON'T WORRY! WE'RE NOT GOING ANYWHERE...
NOT ON THIS BRIDGE!
BRIDGE?? WHO NEEDS A BRIDGE?
WATCH!
CORN
NOW I JUST HIT REWIND! HOLD ON TO--
YEE HAW!

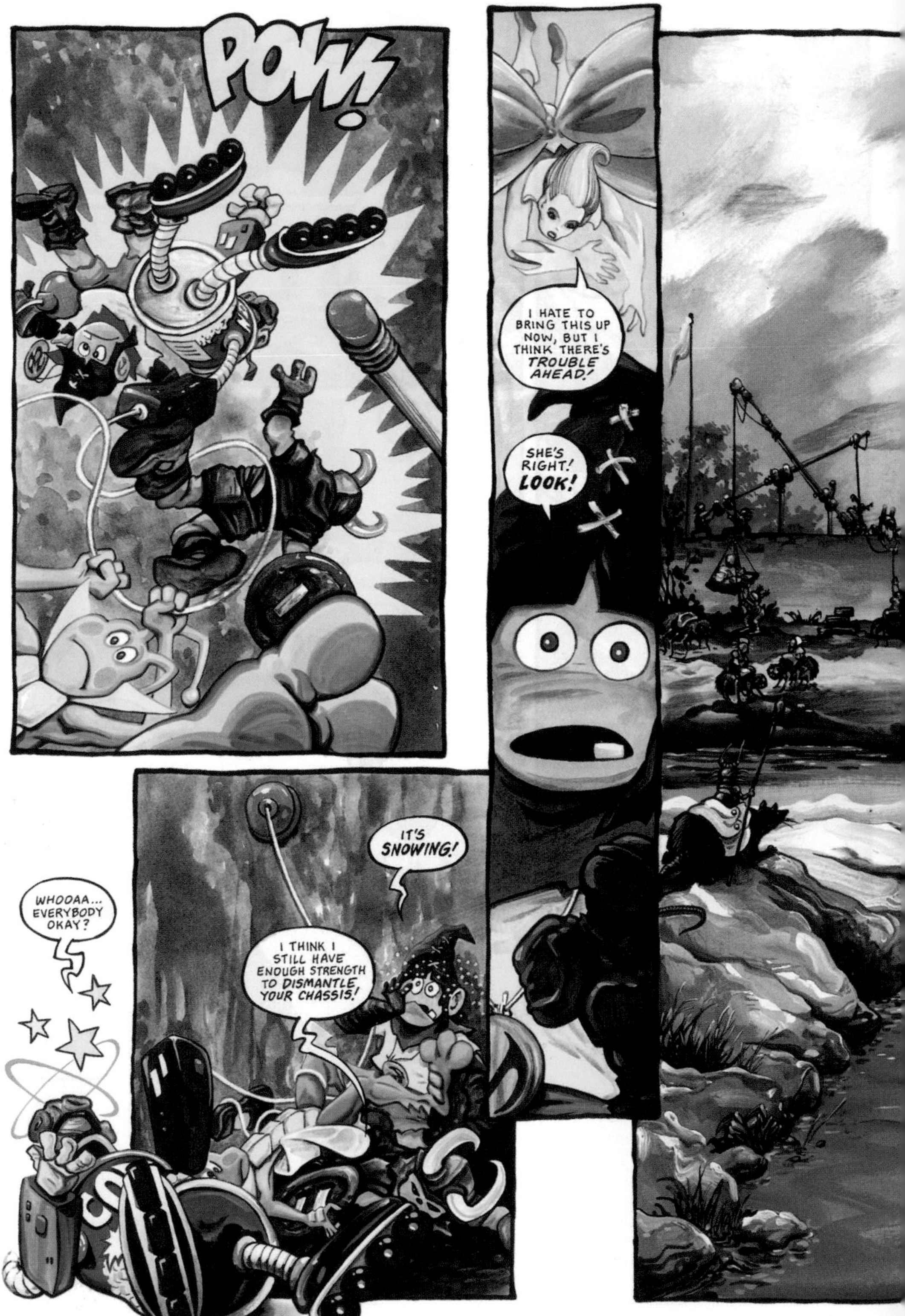
POW!
I HATE TO BRING THIS UP NOW, BUT I THINK THERE'S TROUBLE AHEAD!
SHE'S RIGHT! LOOK!
WHOOAA... EVERYBODY OKAY?
IT'S SNOWING!
I THINK I STILL HAVE ENOUGH STRENGTH TO DISMANTLE YOUR CHASSIS!

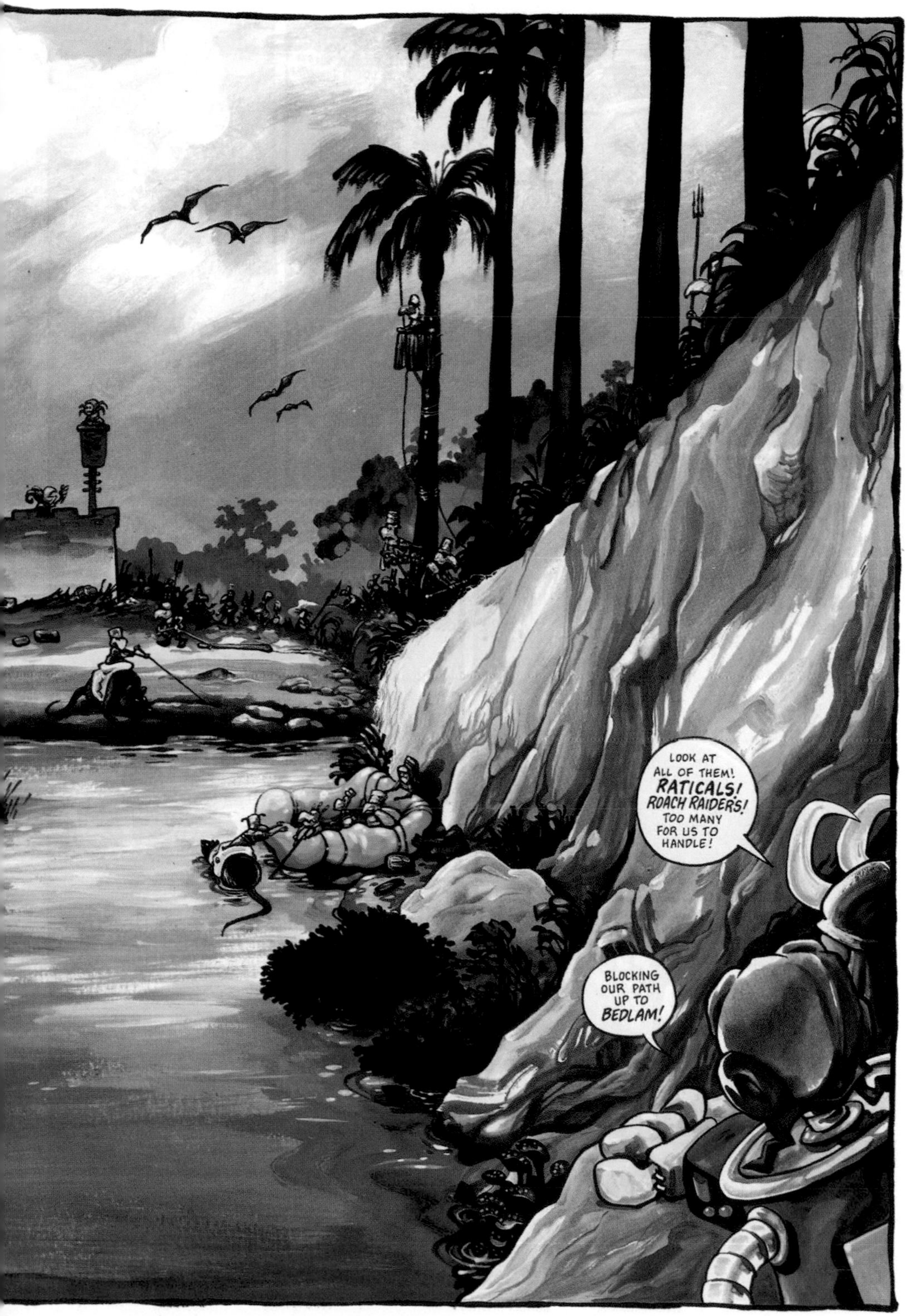
LOOK AT ALL OF THEM! RATICALS! ROACH RAIDERS! TOO MANY FOR US TO HANDLE!
BLOCKING OUR PATH UP TO BEDLAM!

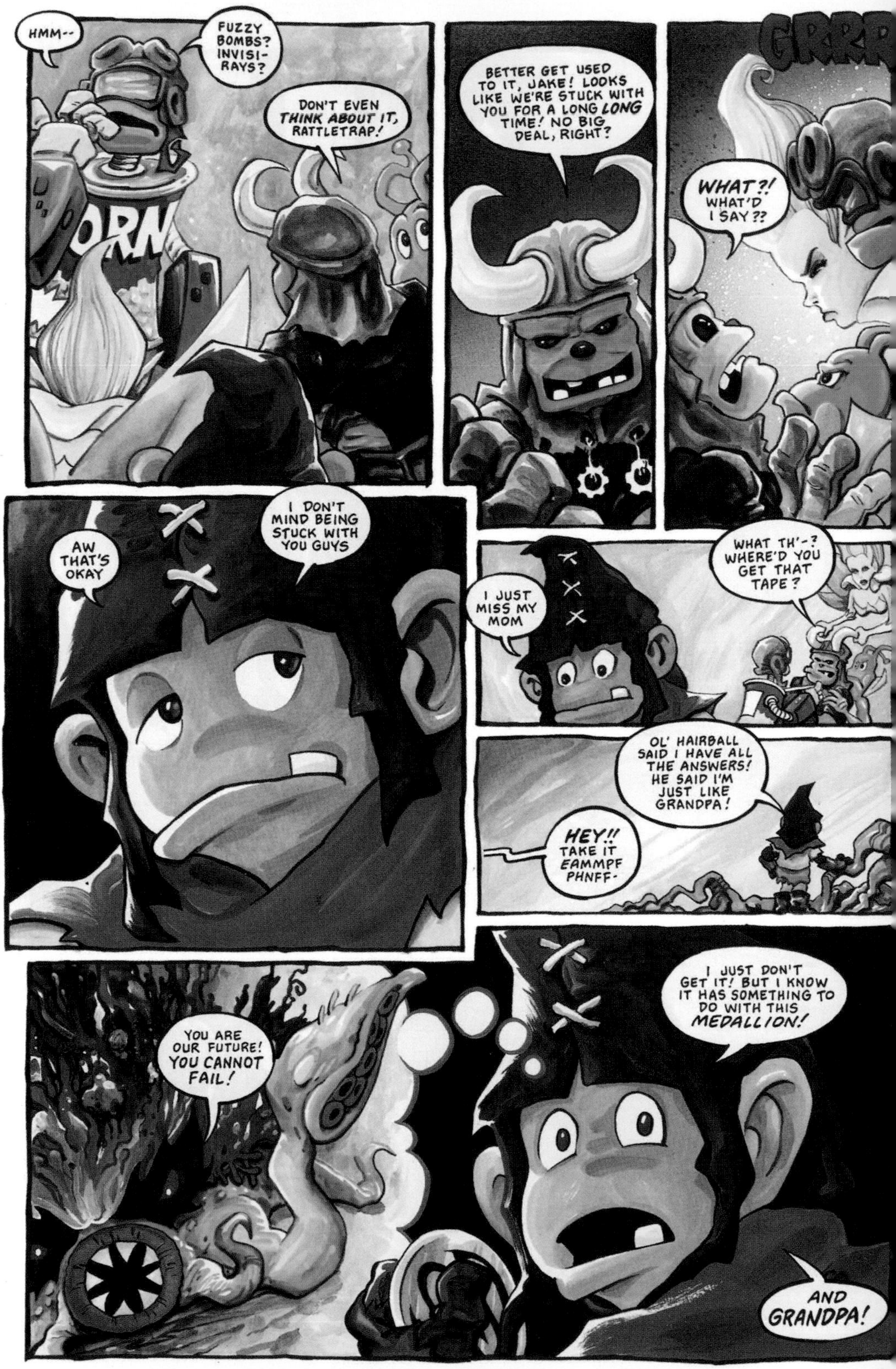
HMM--
FUZZY BOMBS? INVISI-RAYS?
DON'T EVEN THINK ABOUT IT, RATTLETRAP!
ORN
BETTER GET USED TO IT, JAKE! LOOKS LIKE WE'RE STUCK WITH YOU FOR A LONG LONG TIME! NO BIG DEAL, RIGHT?
GRRR
WHAT?! WHAT'D I SAY??
AW THAT'S OKAY
I DON'T MIND BEING STUCK WITH YOU GUYS
I JUST MISS MY MOM
WHAT TH'-? WHERE'D YOU GET THAT TAPE?
OL' HAIRBALL SAID I HAVE ALL THE ANSWERS! HE SAID I'M JUST LIKE GRANDPA!
HEY!! TAKE IT EAMMPF PHNFF-
YOU ARE OUR FUTURE! YOU CANNOT FAIL!
I JUST DON'T GET IT! BUT I KNOW IT HAS SOMETHING TO DO WITH THIS MEDALLION!
AND GRANDPA!

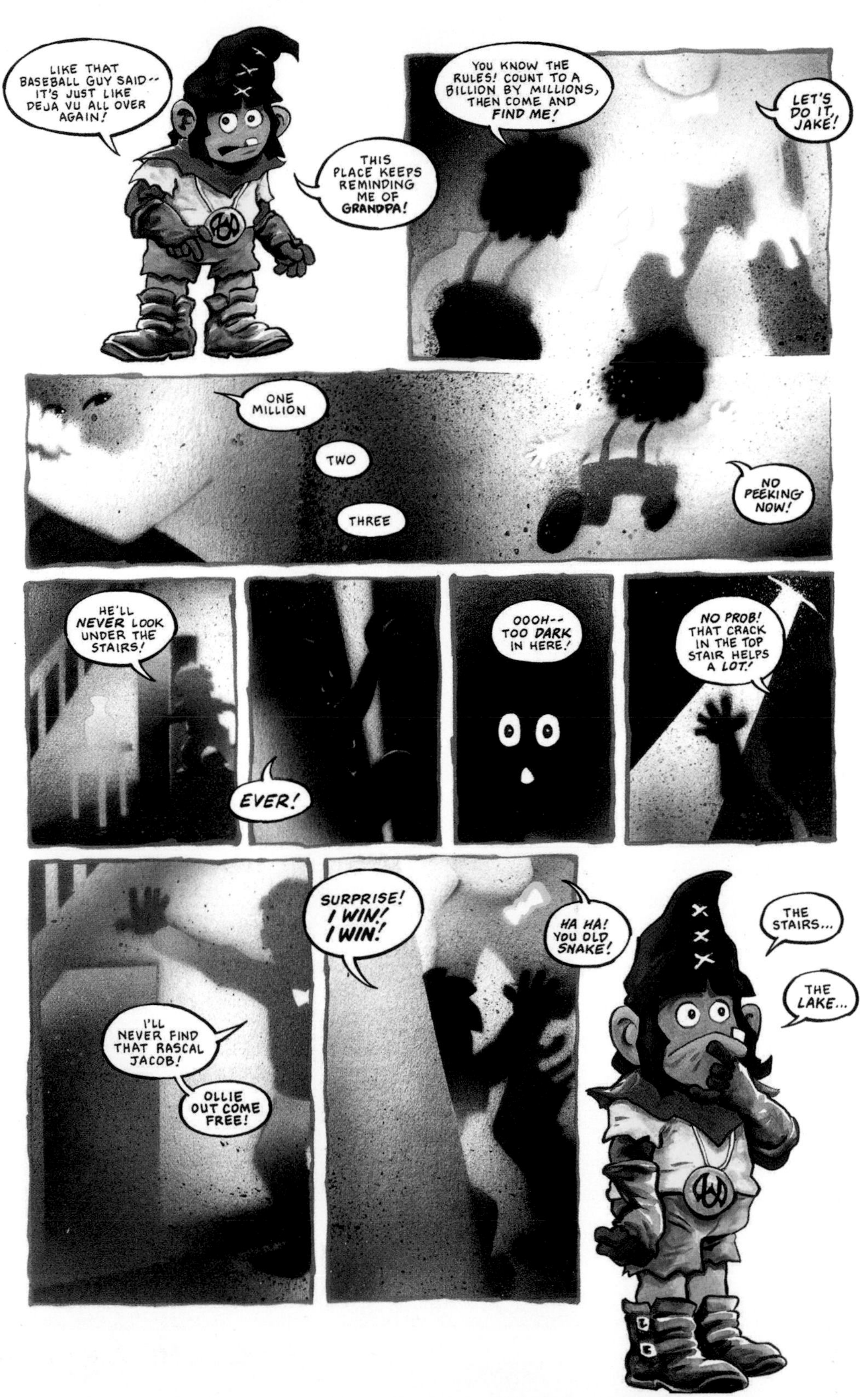
LIKE THAT BASEBALL GUY SAID-- IT'S JUST LIKE DEJA VU ALL OVER AGAIN!
THIS PLACE KEEPS REMINDING ME OF GRANDPA!
YOU KNOW THE RULES! COUNT TO A BILLION BY MILLIONS, THEN COME AND FIND ME!
LET'S DO IT, JAKE!
ONE MILLION
TWO
THREE
NO PEEKING NOW!
HE'LL NEVER LOOK UNDER THE STAIRS!
EVER!
OOOH-- TOO DARK IN HERE!
NO PROB! THAT CRACK IN THE TOP STAIR HELPS A LOT!
I'LL NEVER FIND THAT RASCAL JACOB!
OLLIE OUT COME FREE!
SURPRISE! I WIN! I WIN!
HA HA! YOU OLD SNAKE!
THE STAIRS...
THE LAKE...

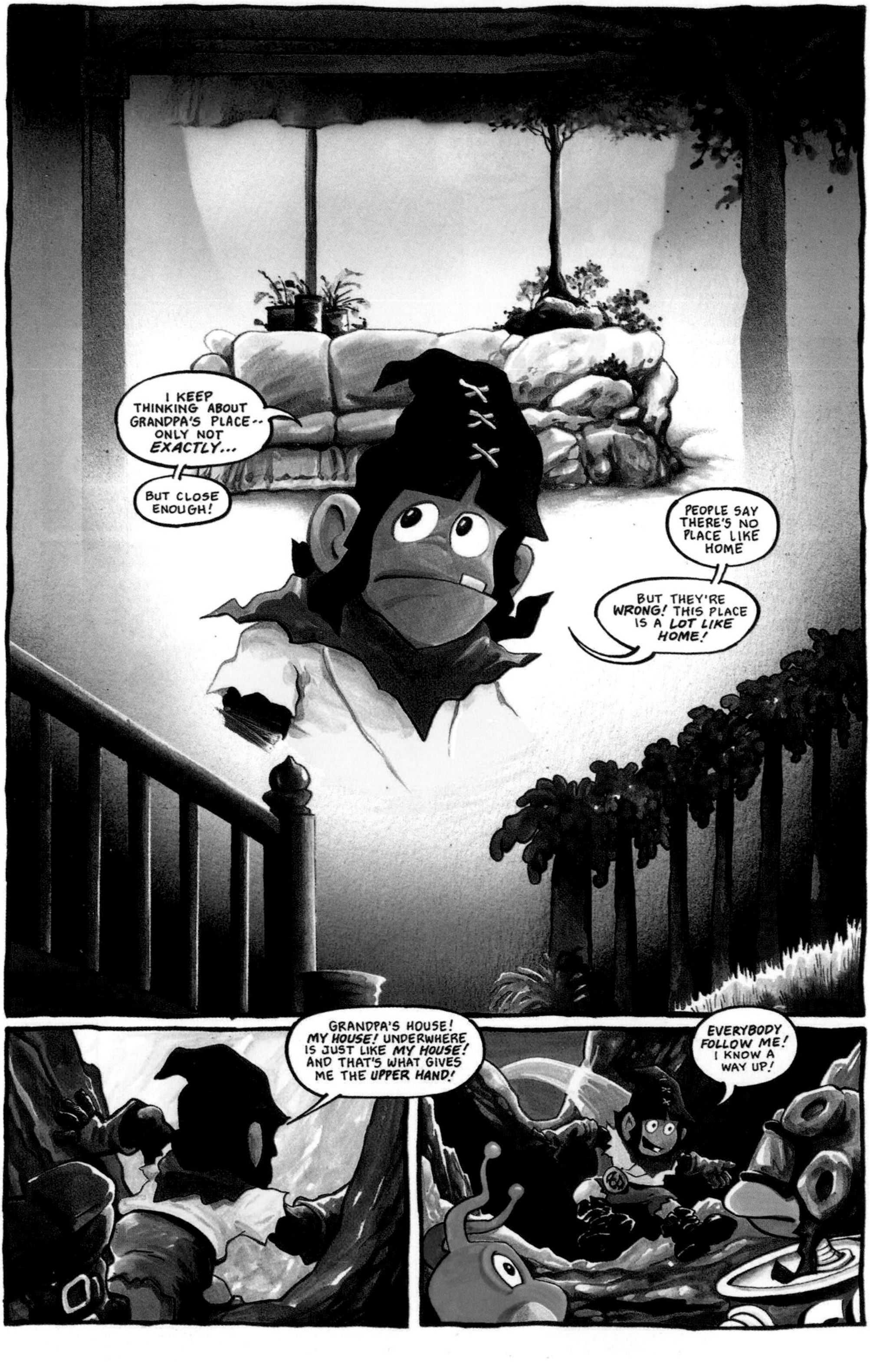
I KEEP THINKING ABOUT GRANDPA'S PLACE-- ONLY NOT EXACTLY...
BUT CLOSE ENOUGH!
PEOPLE SAY THERE'S NO PLACE LIKE HOME
BUT THEY'RE WRONG! THIS PLACE IS A LOT LIKE HOME!
GRANDPA'S HOUSE! MY HOUSE! UNDERWHERE IS JUST LIKE MY HOUSE! AND THAT'S WHAT GIVES ME THE UPPER HAND!
EVERYBODY FOLLOW ME! I KNOW A WAY UP!

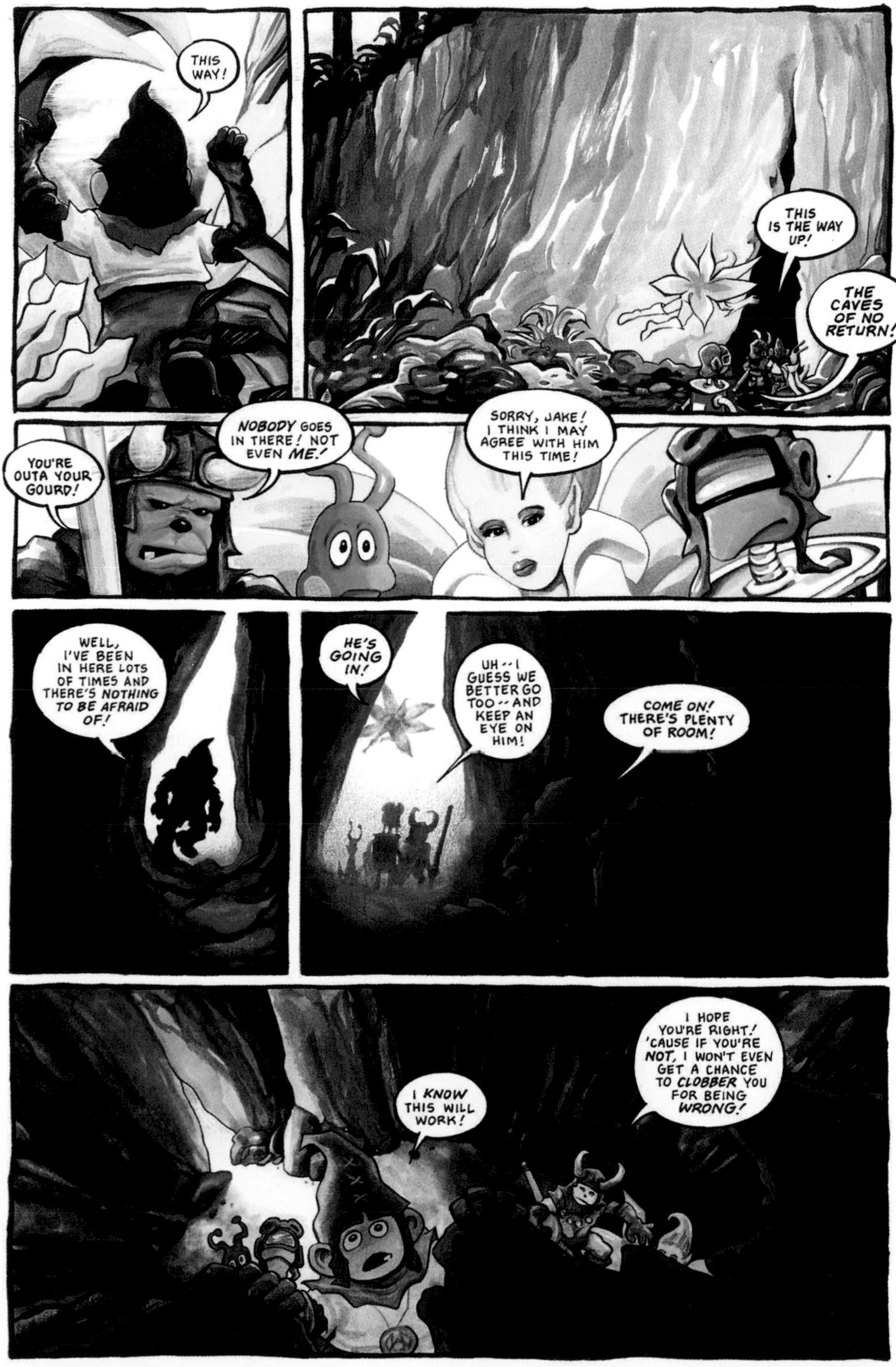
THIS WAY!
THIS IS THE WAY UP!
THE CAVES OF NO RETURN!
YOU'RE OUTA YOUR GOURD!
NOBODY GOES IN THERE! NOT EVEN ME.!
SORRY, JAKE! I THINK I MAY AGREE WITH HIM THIS TIME!
WELL, I'VE BEEN IN HERE LOTS OF TIMES AND THERE'S NOTHING TO BE AFRAID OF!
HE'S GOING IN!
UH -- I GUESS WE BETTER GO TOO -- AND KEEP AN EYE ON HIM!
COME ON! THERE'S PLENTY OF ROOM!
I KNOW THIS WILL WORK!
I HOPE YOU'RE RIGHT! 'CAUSE IF YOU'RE NOT, I WON'T EVEN GET A CHANCE TO CLOBBER YOU FOR BEING WRONG!

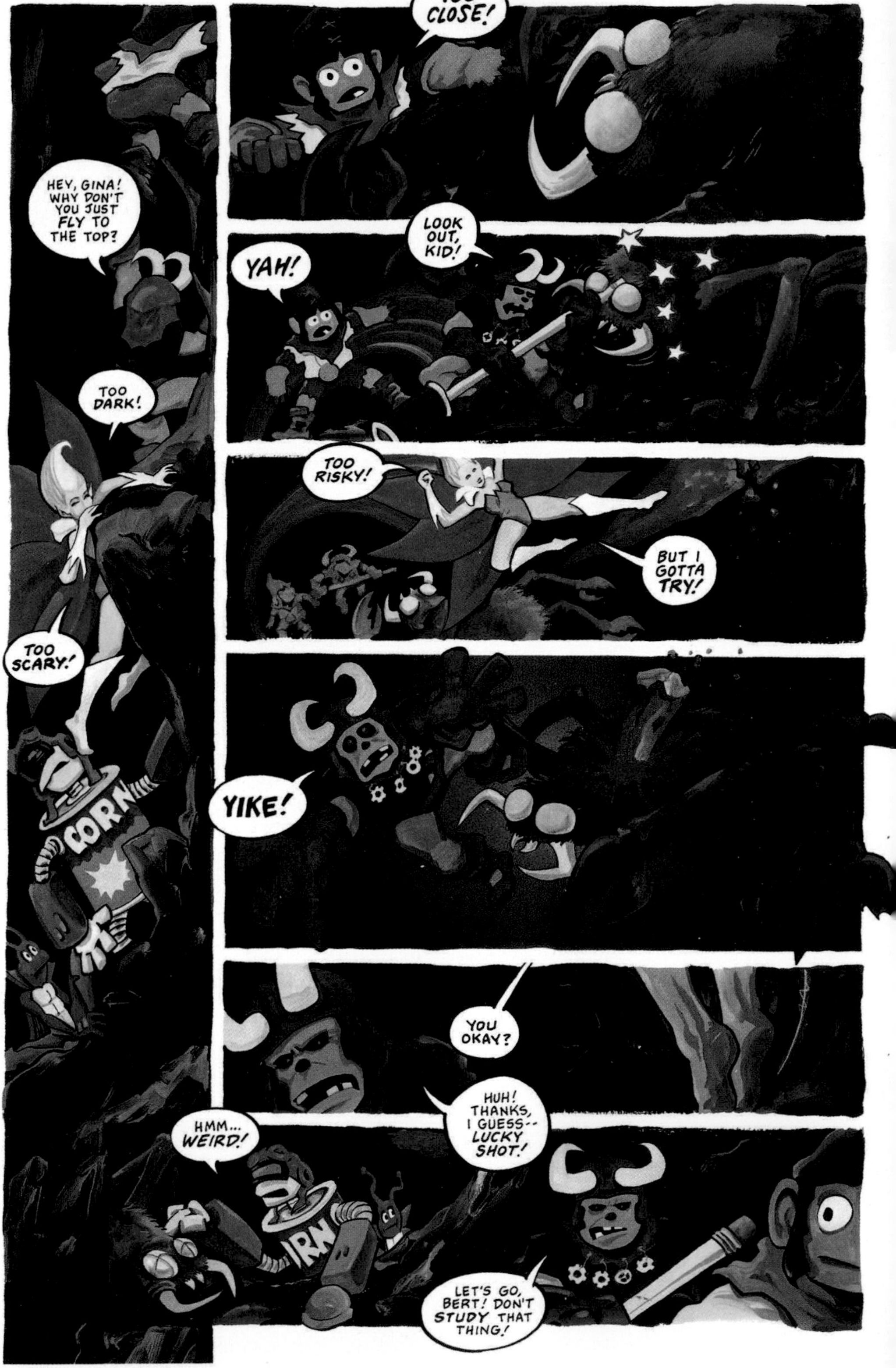
HEY, GINA! WHY DON'T YOU JUST FLY TO THE TOP?
TOO DARK!
TOO SCARY!
TOO CLOSE!
YAH!
LOOK OUT, KID!
TOO RISKY!
BUT I GOTTA TRY!
YIKE!
YOU OKAY?
HUH! THANKS, I GUESS-- LUCKY SHOT!
HMM... WEIRD!
CORN
LET'S GO, BERT! DON'T STUDY THAT THING!

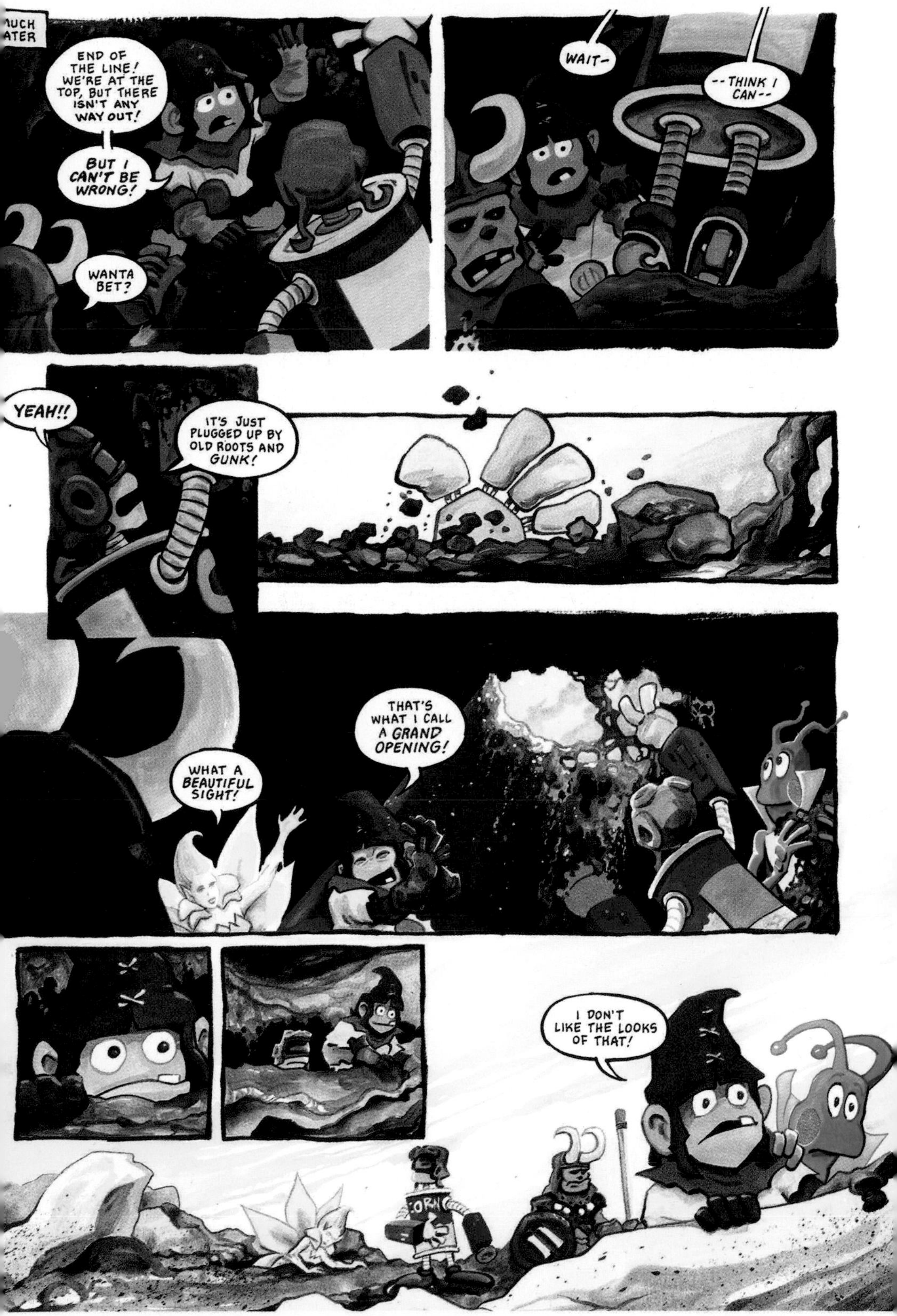
MUCH LATER
END OF THE LINE! WE'RE AT THE TOP, BUT THERE ISN'T ANY WAY OUT!
BUT I CAN'T BE WRONG!
WANTA BET?
WAIT-
--THINK I CAN--
YEAH!!
IT'S JUST PLUGGED UP BY OLD ROOTS AND GUNK!
THAT'S WHAT I CALL A GRAND OPENING!
WHAT A BEAUTIFUL SIGHT!
I DON'T LIKE THE LOOKS OF THAT!

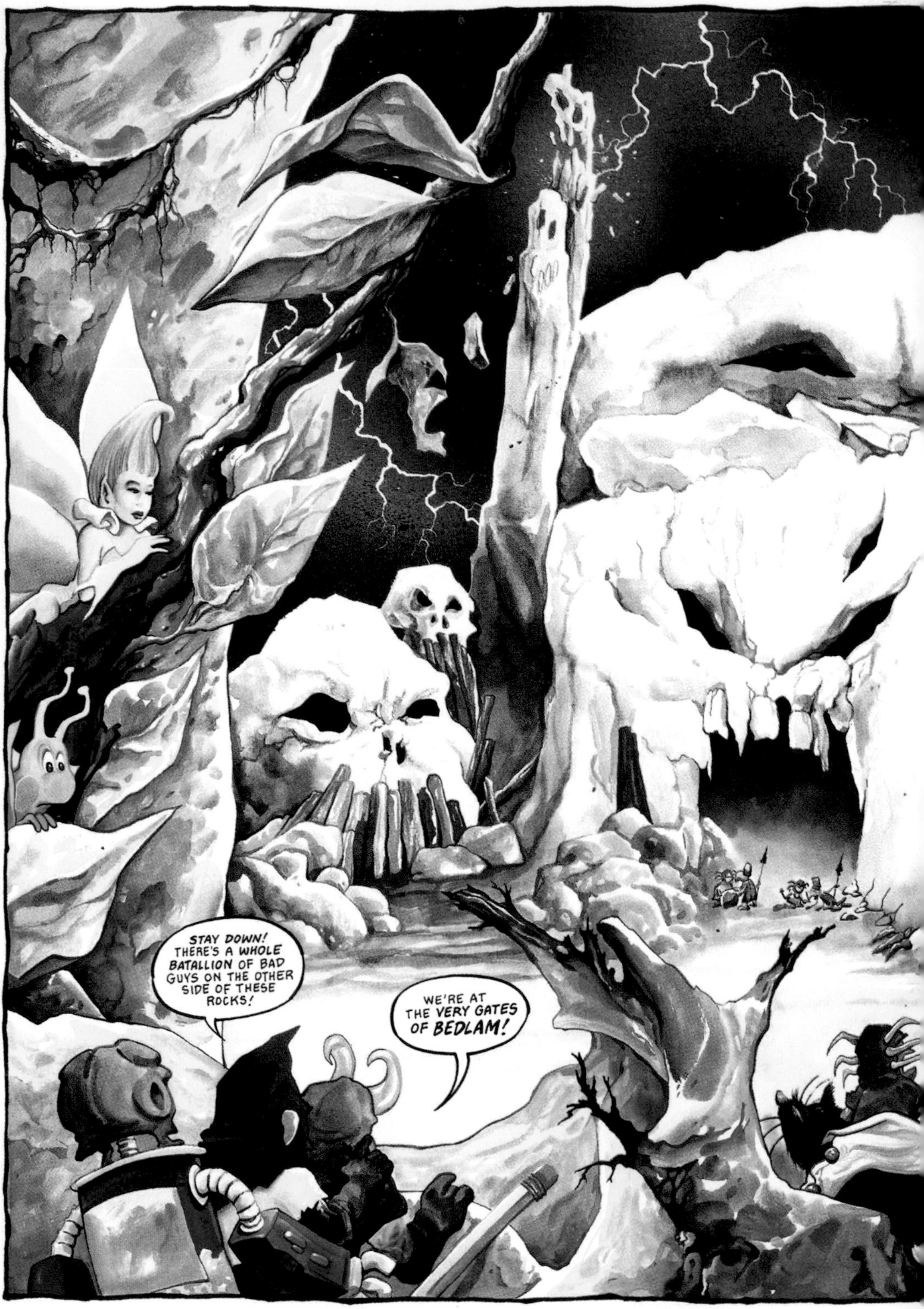
STAY DOWN! THERE'S A WHOLE BATALLION OF BAD GUYS ON THE OTHER SIDE OF THESE ROCKS!
WE'RE AT THE VERY GATES OF BEDLAM!

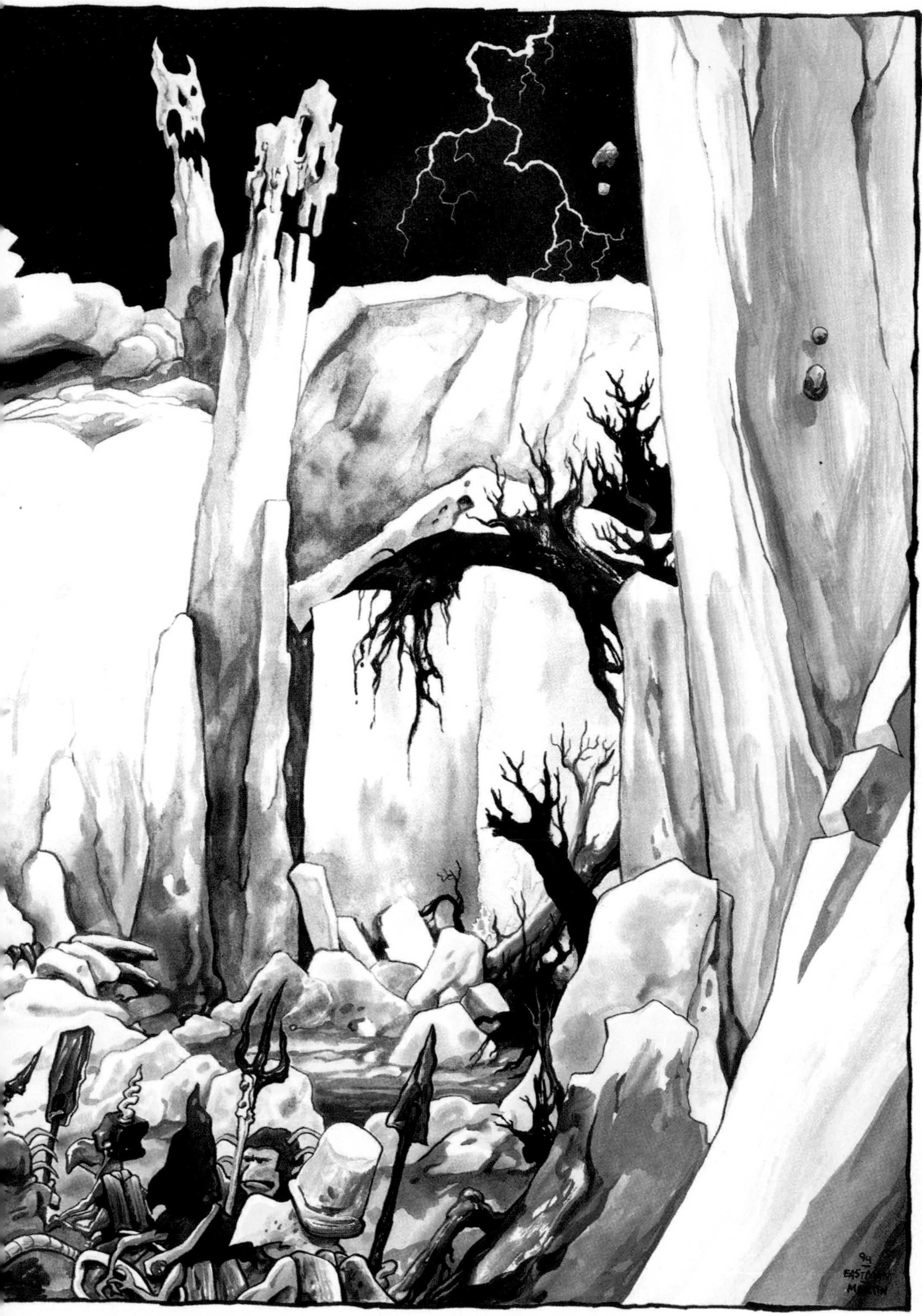

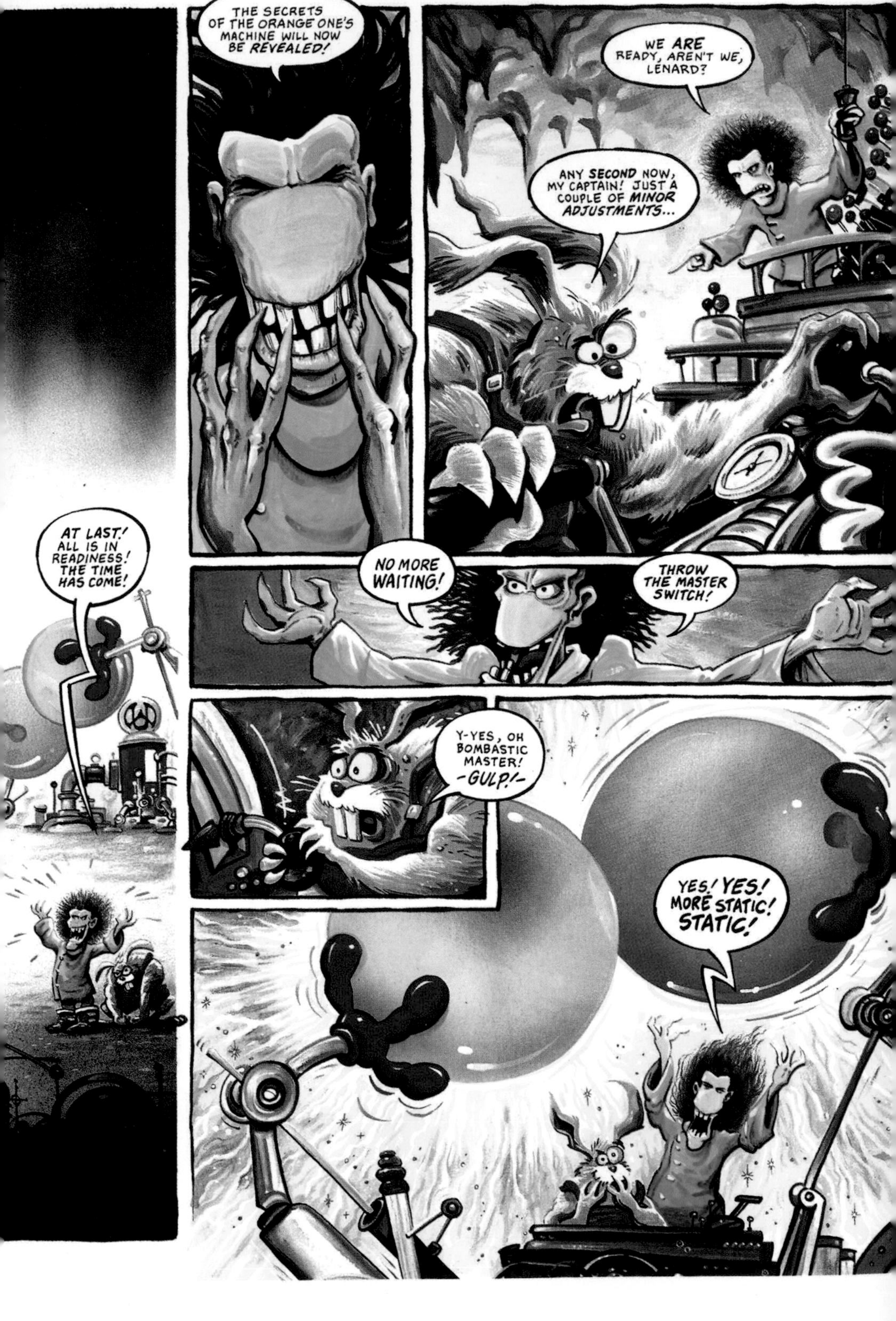
THE SECRETS OF THE ORANGE ONE'S MACHINE WILL NOW BE REVEALED!
WE ARE READY, AREN'T WE, LENARD?
ANY SECOND NOW, MY CAPTAIN! JUST A COUPLE OF MINOR ADJUSTMENTS...
AT LAST! ALL IS IN READINESS! THE TIME HAS COME!
NO MORE WAITING!
THROW THE MASTER SWITCH!
Y-YES, OH BOMBASTIC MASTER! -GULP!-
YES! YES! MORE STATIC! STATIC!

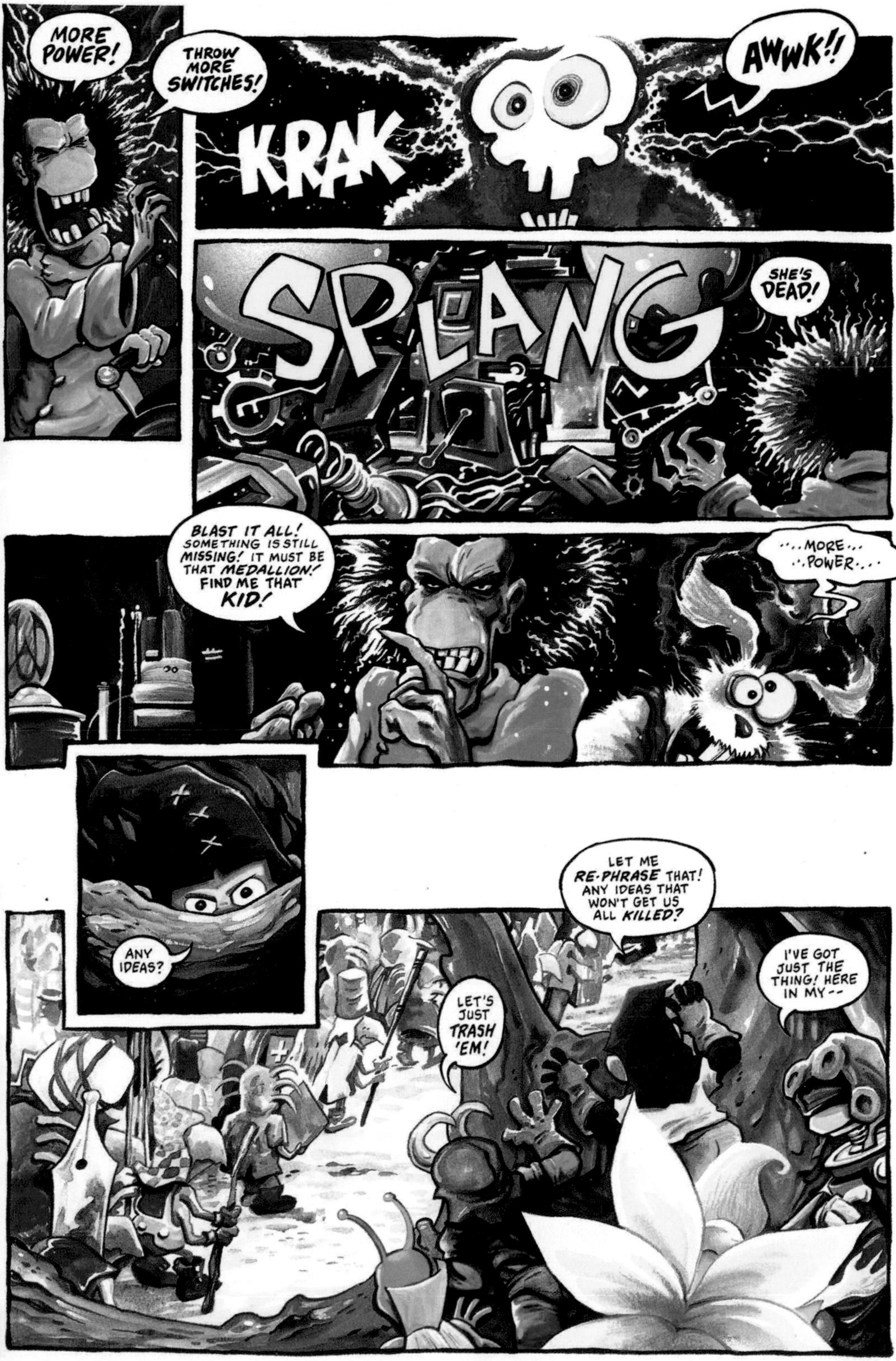
MORE POWER!
THROW MORE SWITCHES!
KRAK
AWWK!!
SPLANG
SHE'S DEAD!
BLAST IT ALL! SOMETHING IS STILL MISSING! IT MUST BE THAT MEDALLION! FIND ME THAT KID!
...MORE... ...POWER...
ANY IDEAS?
LET'S JUST TRASH 'EM!
LET ME RE-PHRASE THAT! ANY IDEAS THAT WON'T GET US ALL KILLED?
I'VE GOT JUST THE THING! HERE IN MY--

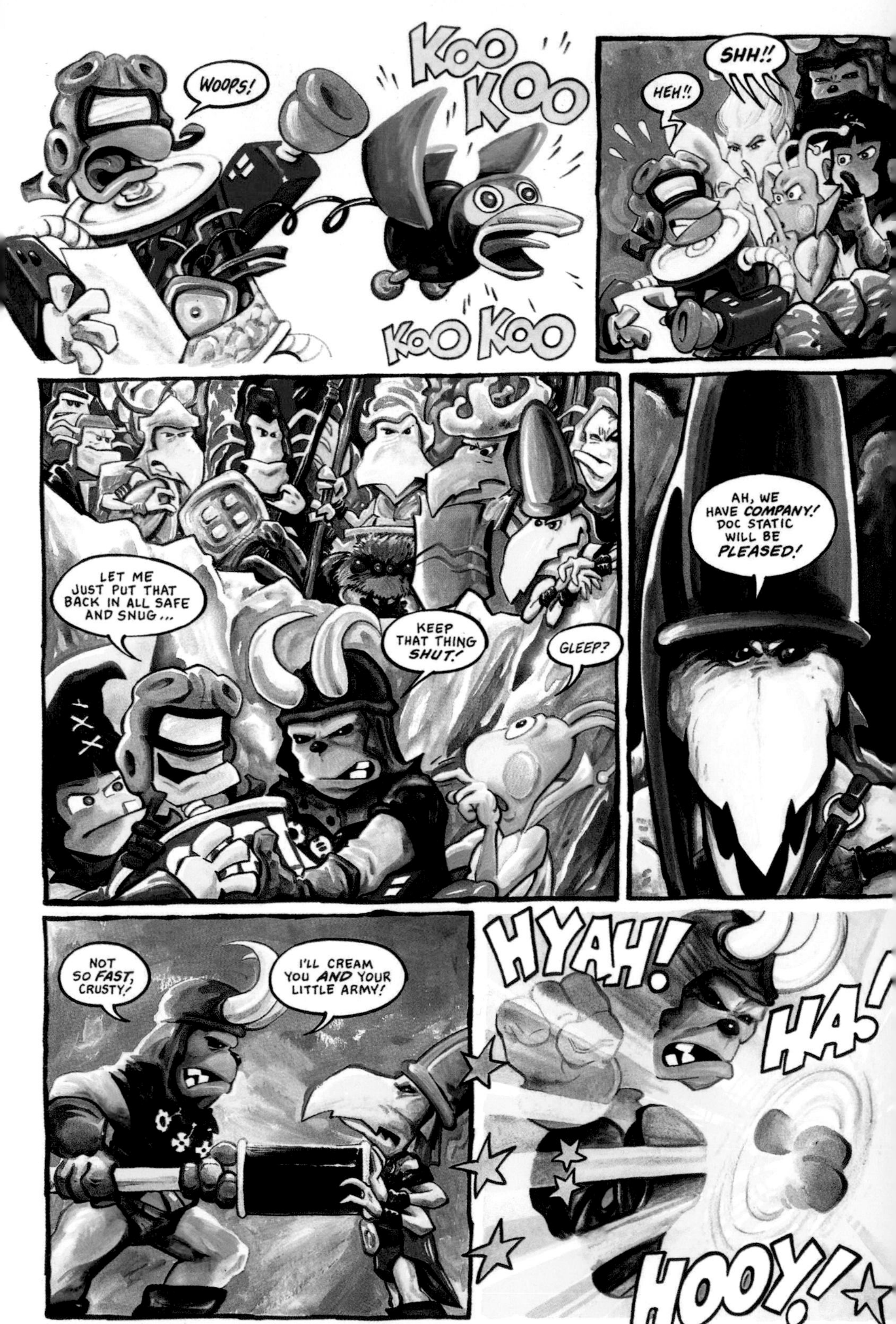
WOOPS!
KOO KOO
KOO KOO
HEH!!
SHH!!
LET ME JUST PUT THAT BACK IN ALL SAFE AND SNUG...
KEEP THAT THING SHUT!
GLEEP?
AH, WE HAVE COMPANY! DOC STATIC WILL BE PLEASED!
NOT SO FAST, CRUSTY!
I'LL CREAM YOU AND YOUR LITTLE ARMY!
HYAH!
HA!
HOOY!

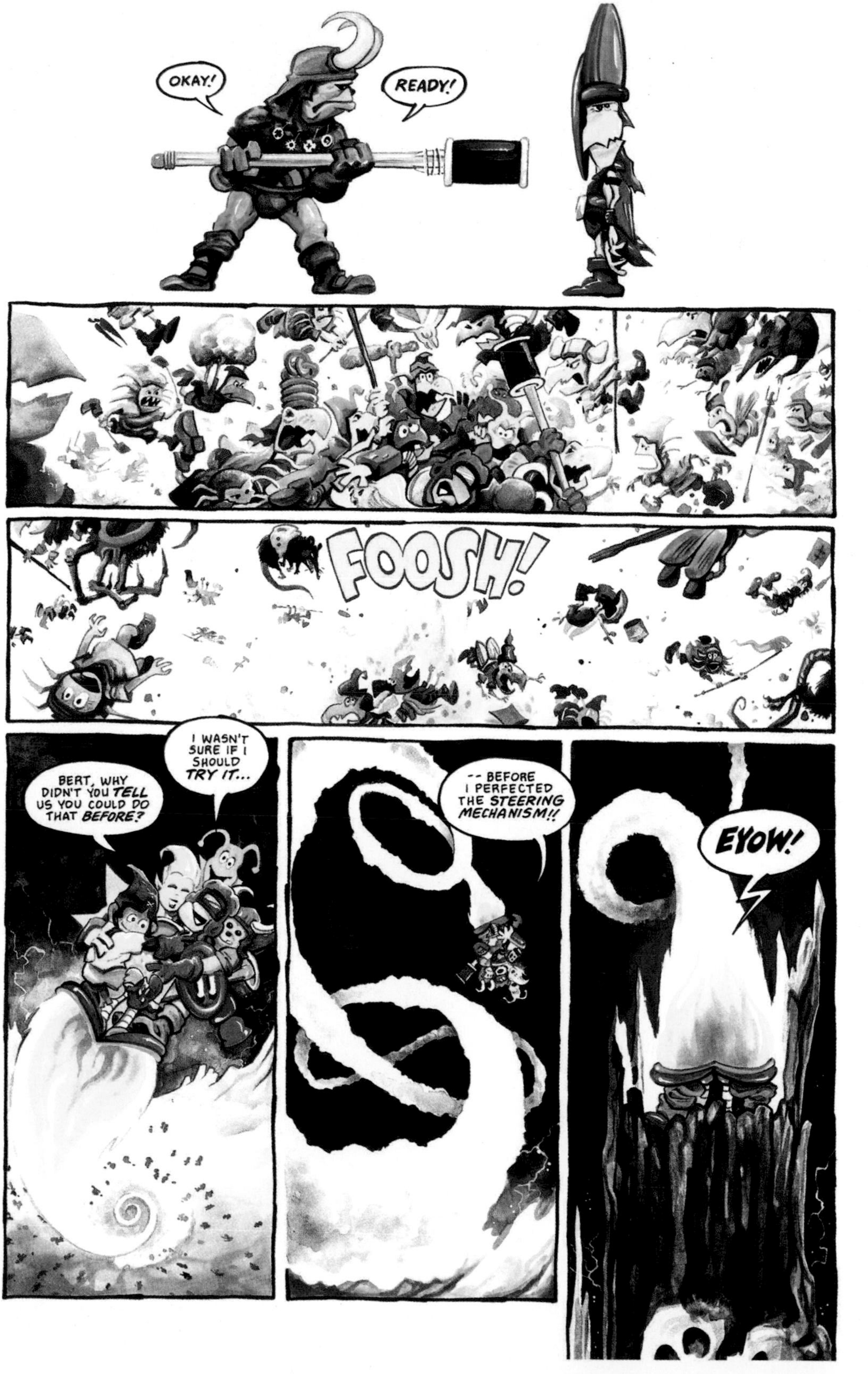
OKAY!
READY!
FOOSH!
BERT, WHY DIDN'T YOU TELL US YOU COULD DO THAT BEFORE?
I WASN'T SURE IF I SHOULD TRY IT...
-- BEFORE I PERFECTED THE STEERING MECHANISM!!
EYOW!

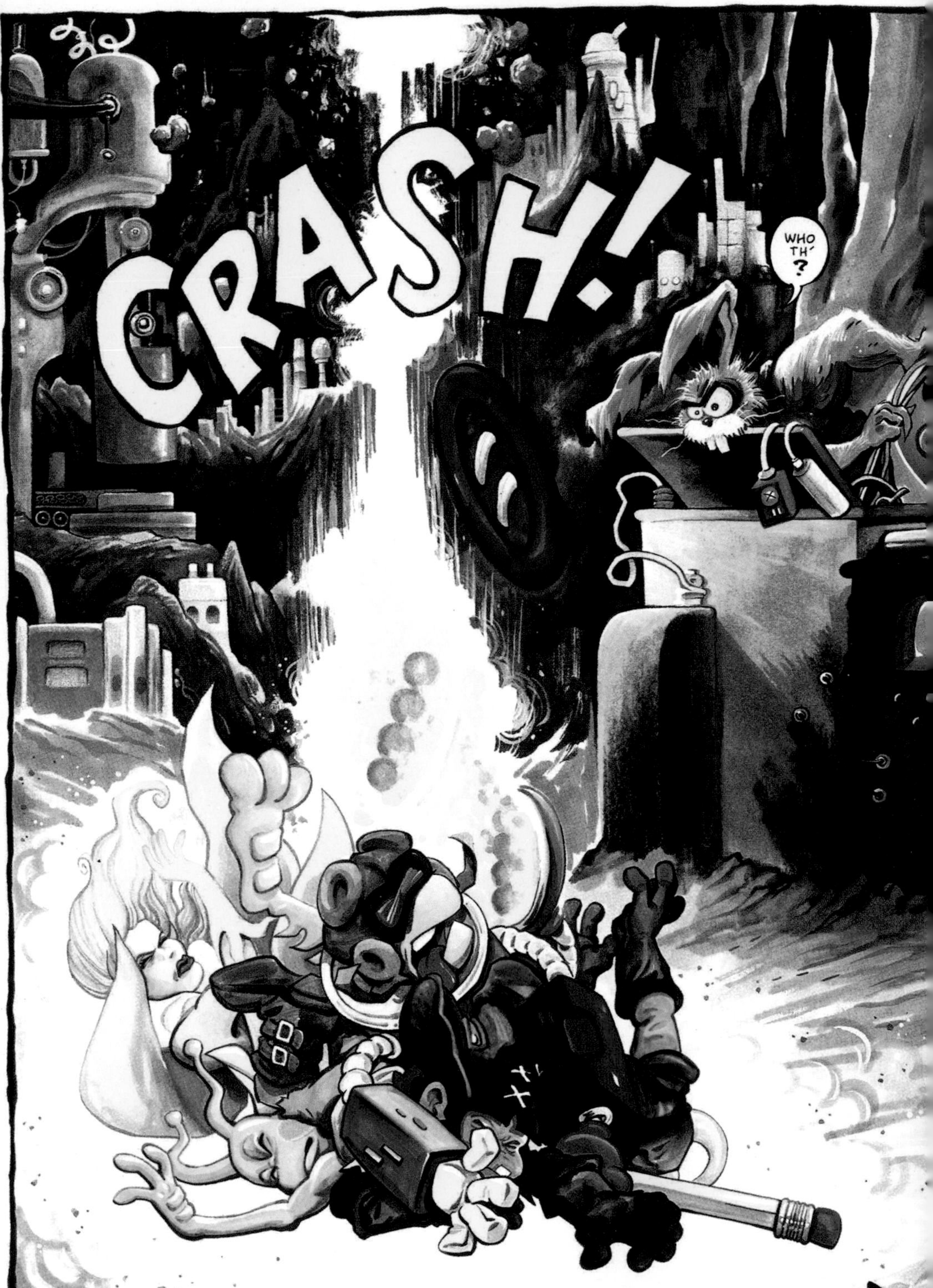
CRASH!
WHO TH' ?

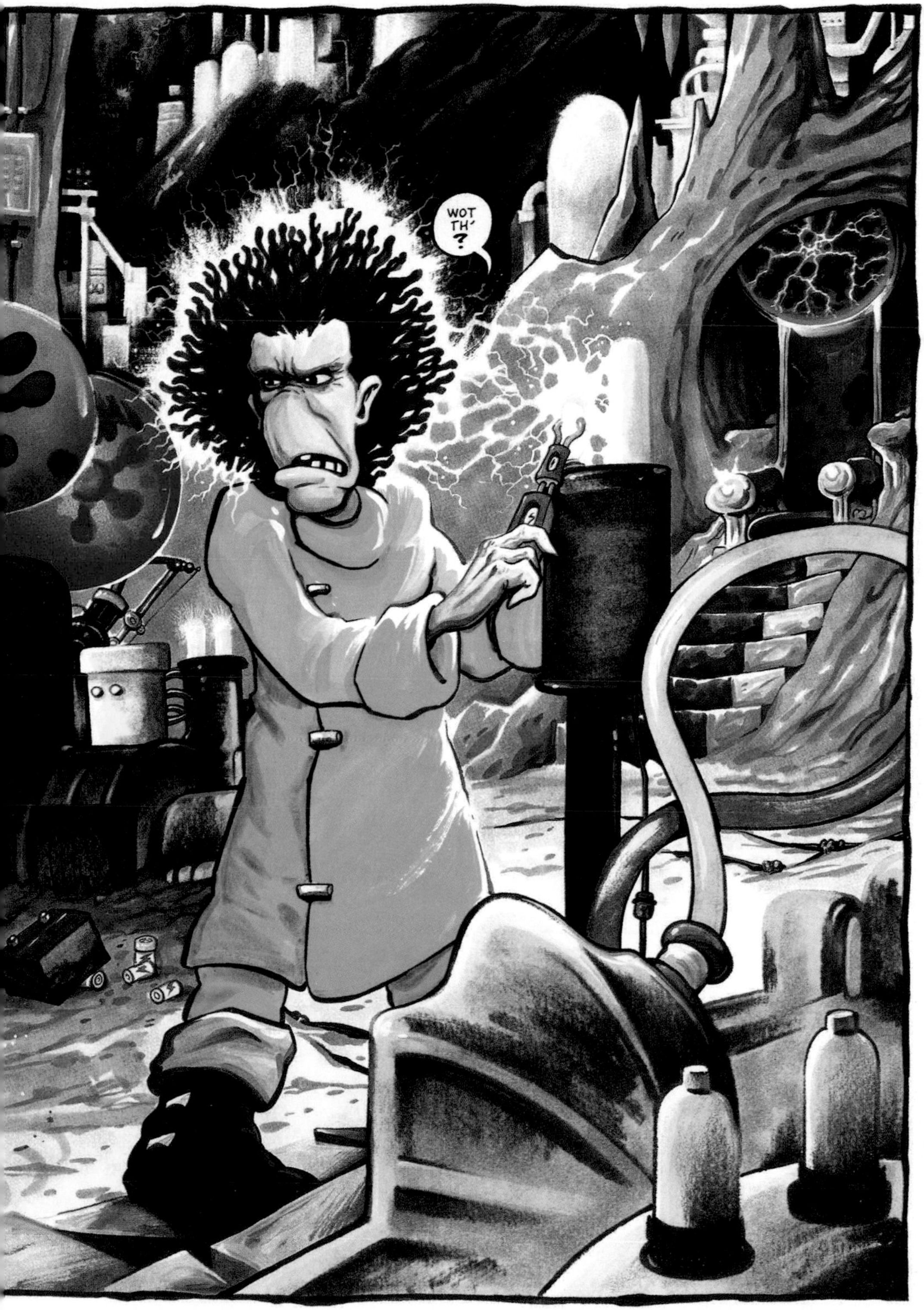
WOT TH'?

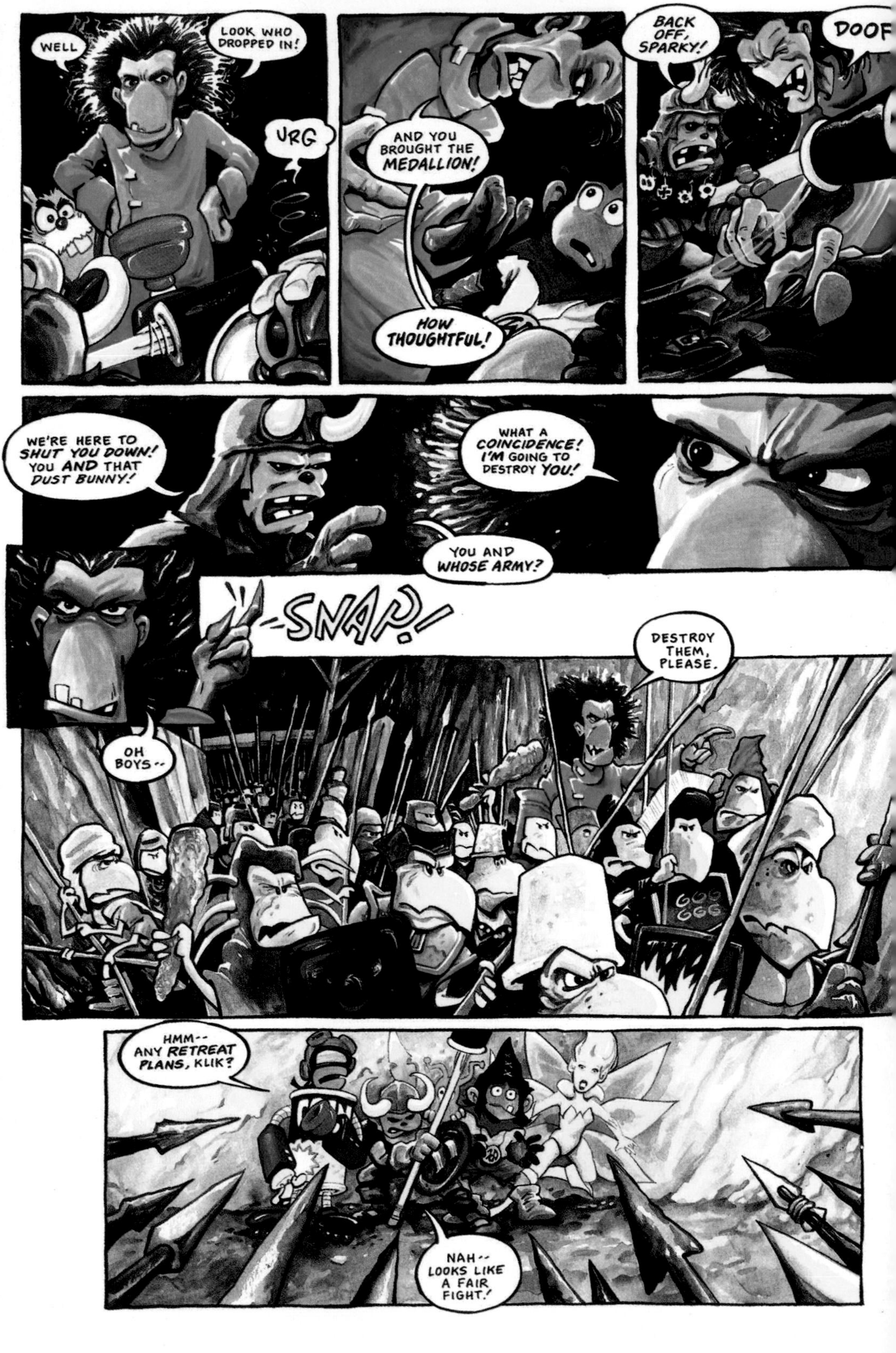
WELL
LOOK WHO DROPPED IN!
URG
AND YOU BROUGHT THE MEDALLION!
HOW THOUGHTFUL!
BACK OFF, SPARKY!
DOOF
WE'RE HERE TO SHUT YOU DOWN! YOU AND THAT DUST BUNNY!
WHAT A COINCIDENCE! I'M GOING TO DESTROY YOU!
YOU AND WHOSE ARMY?
SNAP!
DESTROY THEM, PLEASE.
OH BOYS--
HMM-- ANY RETREAT PLANS, KLIK?
NAH-- LOOKS LIKE A FAIR FIGHT!

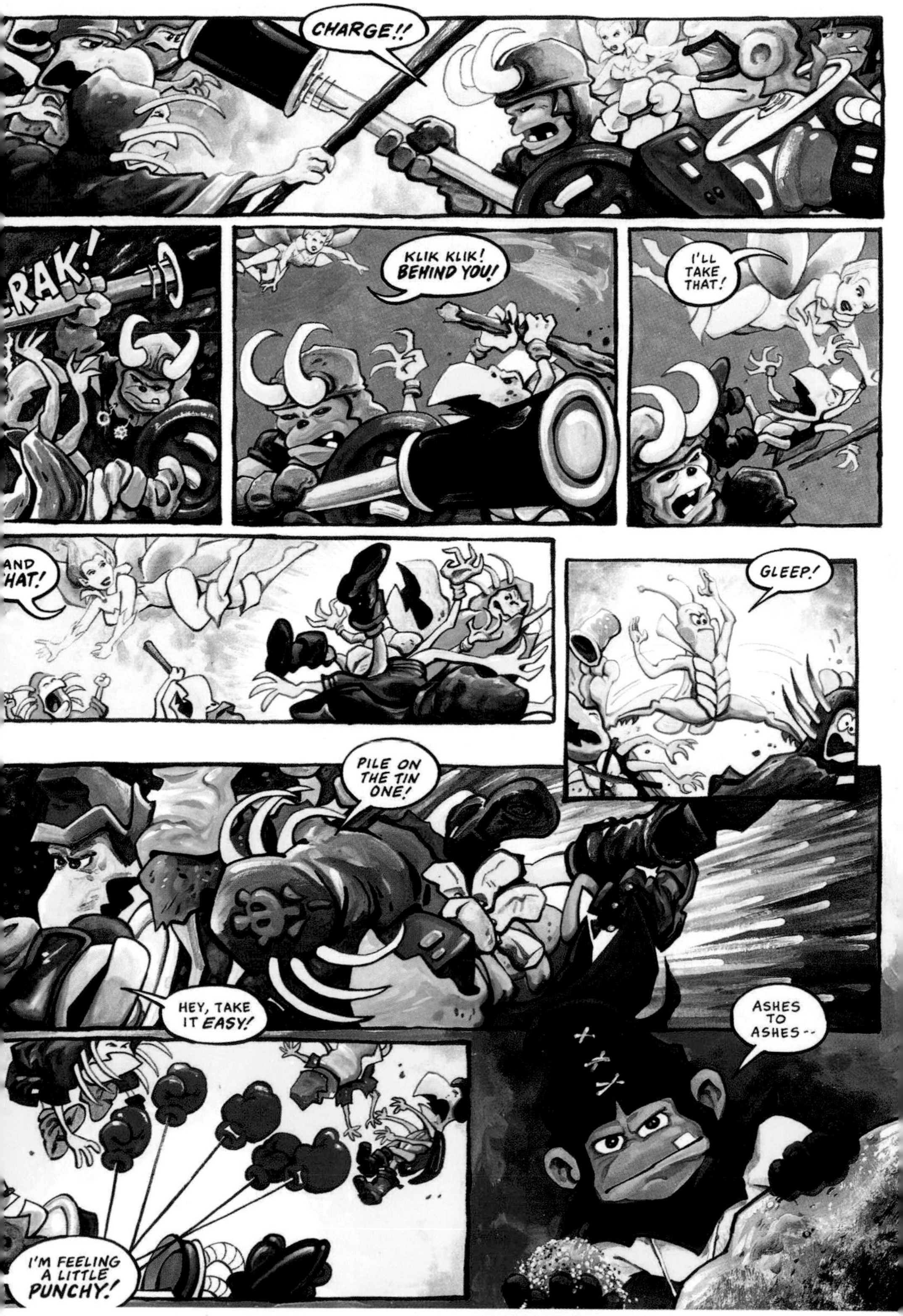
CHARGE!!
KRAK!
KLIK KLIK! BEHIND YOU!
I'LL TAKE THAT!
AND THAT!
GLEEP!
PILE ON THE TIN ONE!
HEY, TAKE IT EASY!
ASHES TO ASHES--
I'M FEELING A LITTLE PUNCHY!

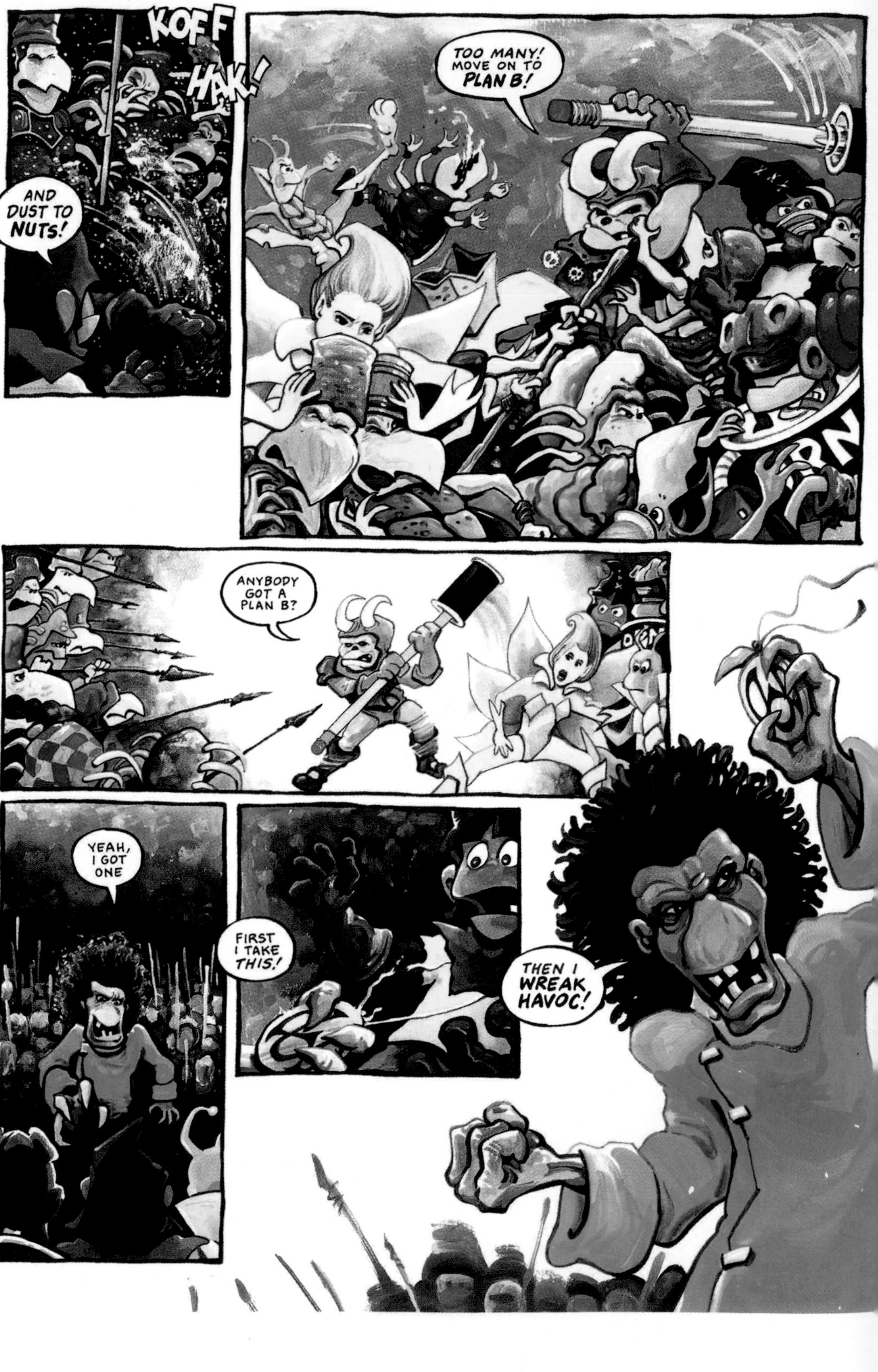
KOFF
HAK!
AND DUST TO NUTS!
TOO MANY! MOVE ON TO PLAN B!
ANYBODY GOT A PLAN B?
YEAH, I GOT ONE
FIRST I TAKE THIS!
THEN I WREAK HAVOC!

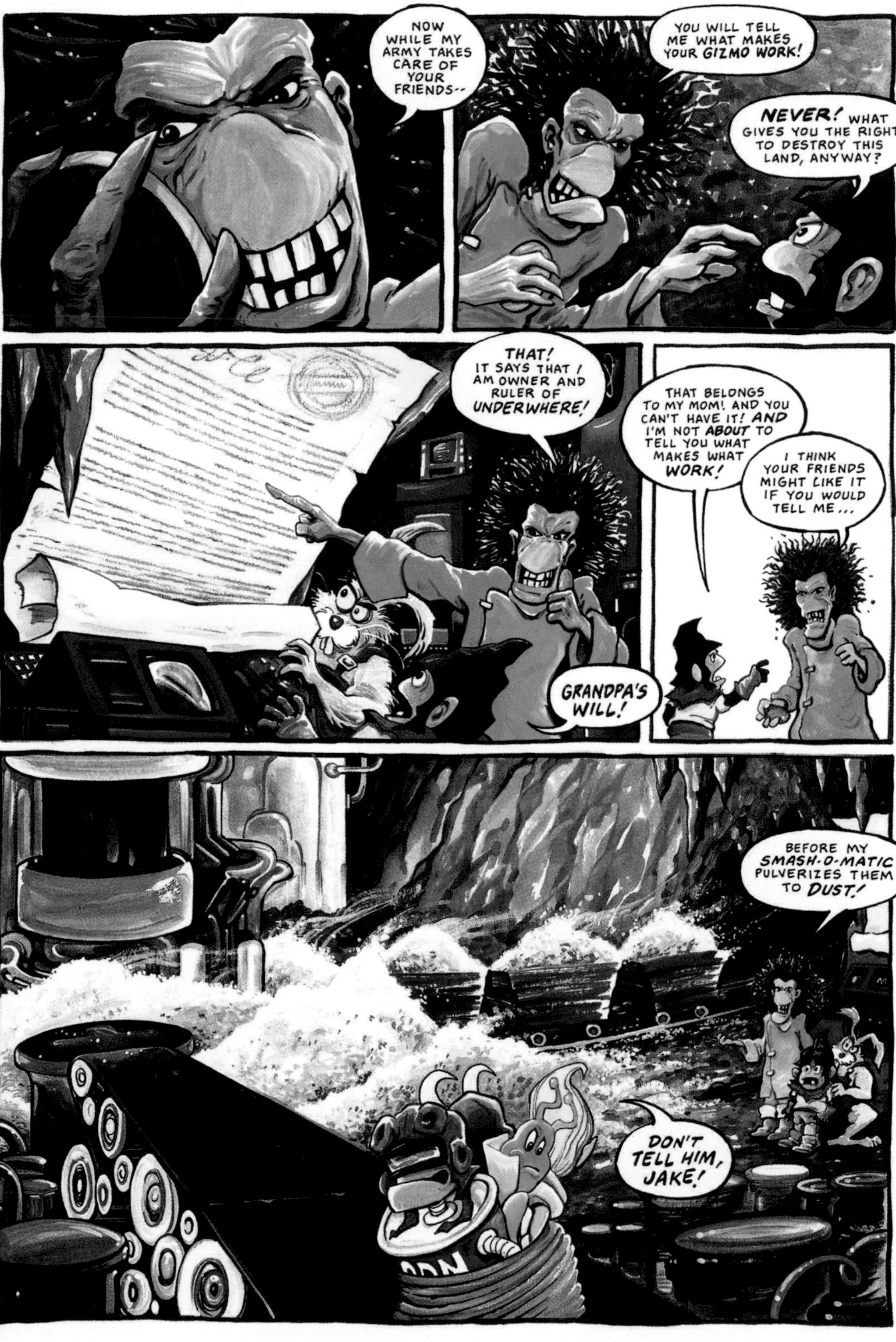
NOW WHILE MY ARMY TAKES CARE OF YOUR FRIENDS--
YOU WILL TELL ME WHAT MAKES YOUR GIZMO WORK!
NEVER! WHAT GIVES YOU THE RIGHT TO DESTROY THIS LAND, ANYWAY?
THAT! IT SAYS THAT I AM OWNER AND RULER OF UNDERWHERE!
GRANDPA'S WILL!
THAT BELONGS TO MY MOM! AND YOU CAN'T HAVE IT! AND I'M NOT ABOUT TO TELL YOU WHAT MAKES WHAT WORK!
I THINK YOUR FRIENDS MIGHT LIKE IT IF YOU WOULD TELL ME...
BEFORE MY SMASH-O-MATIC PULVERIZES THEM TO DUST!
DON'T TELL HIM, JAKE!

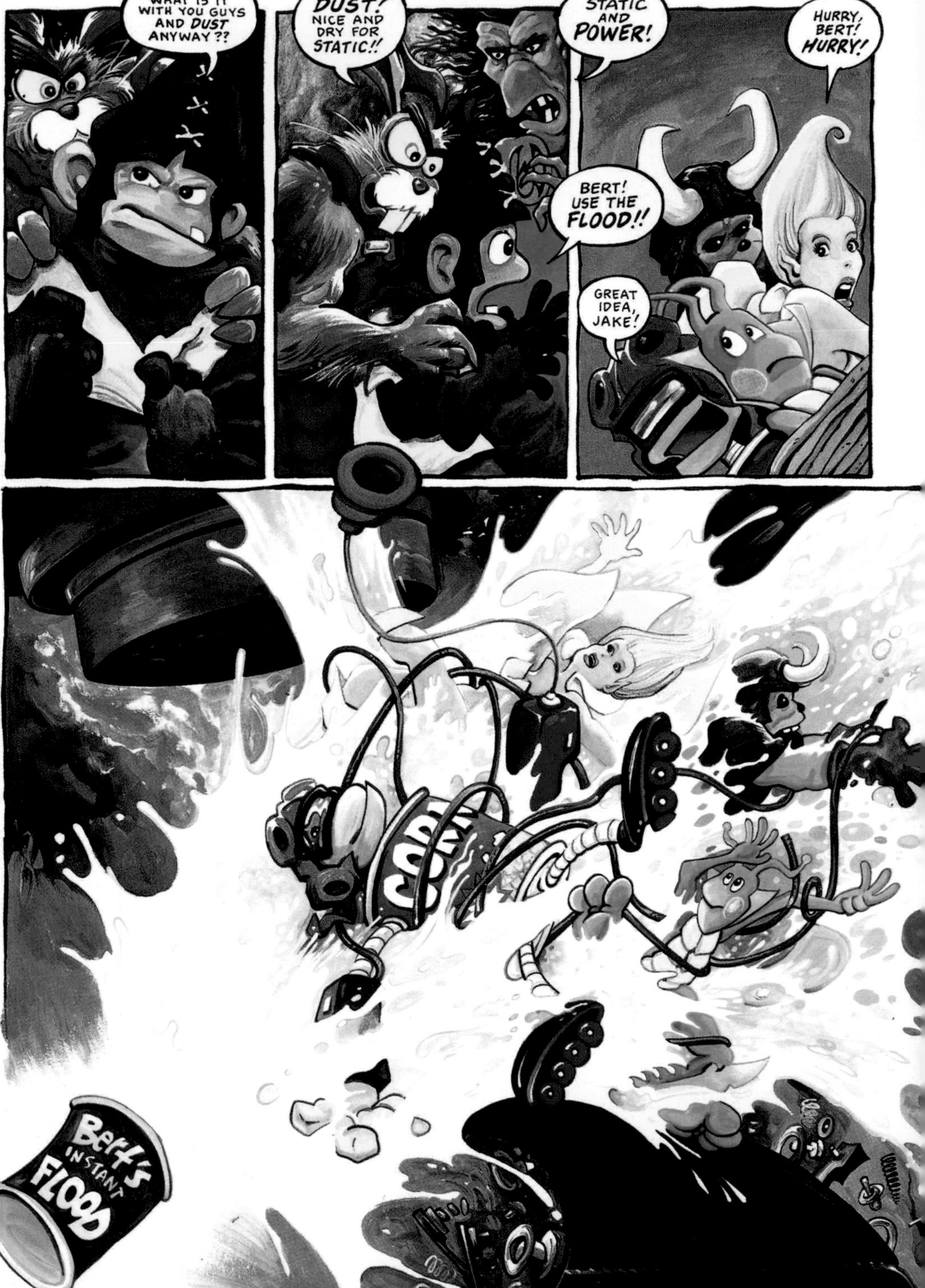
WHAT IS IT WITH YOU GUYS AND DUST ANYWAY??
DUST! NICE AND DRY FOR STATIC!!
STATIC AND POWER!
HURRY, BERT! HURRY!
BERT! USE THE FLOOD!!
GREAT IDEA, JAKE!
CORN
Bert's INSTANT FLOOD

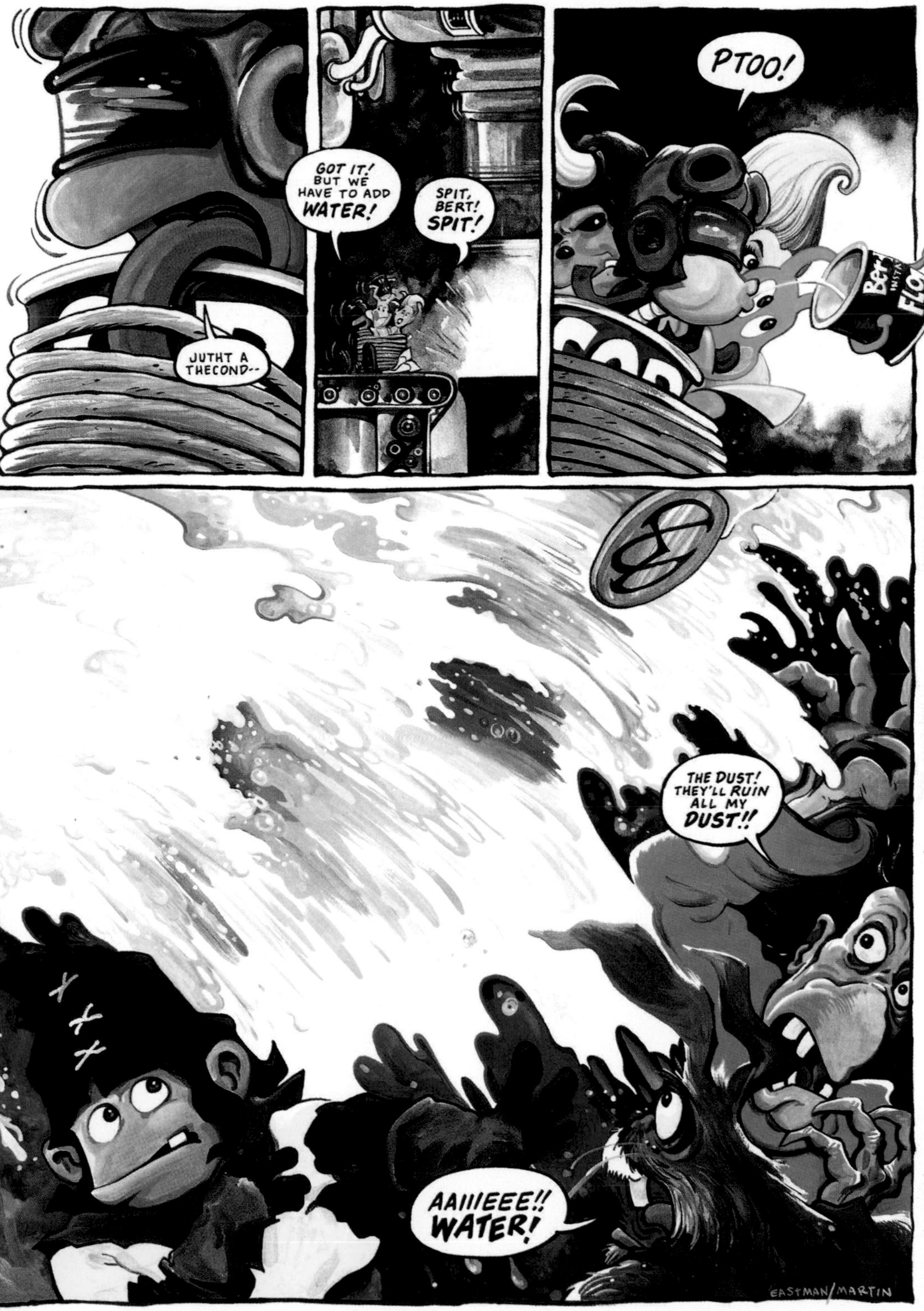
JUTHT A THECOND--
GOT IT! BUT WE HAVE TO ADD WATER!
SPIT, BERT! SPIT!
PTOO!
THE DUST! THEY'LL RUIN ALL MY DUST!!
AAIIIEEE!! WATER!
EASTMAN/MARTIN

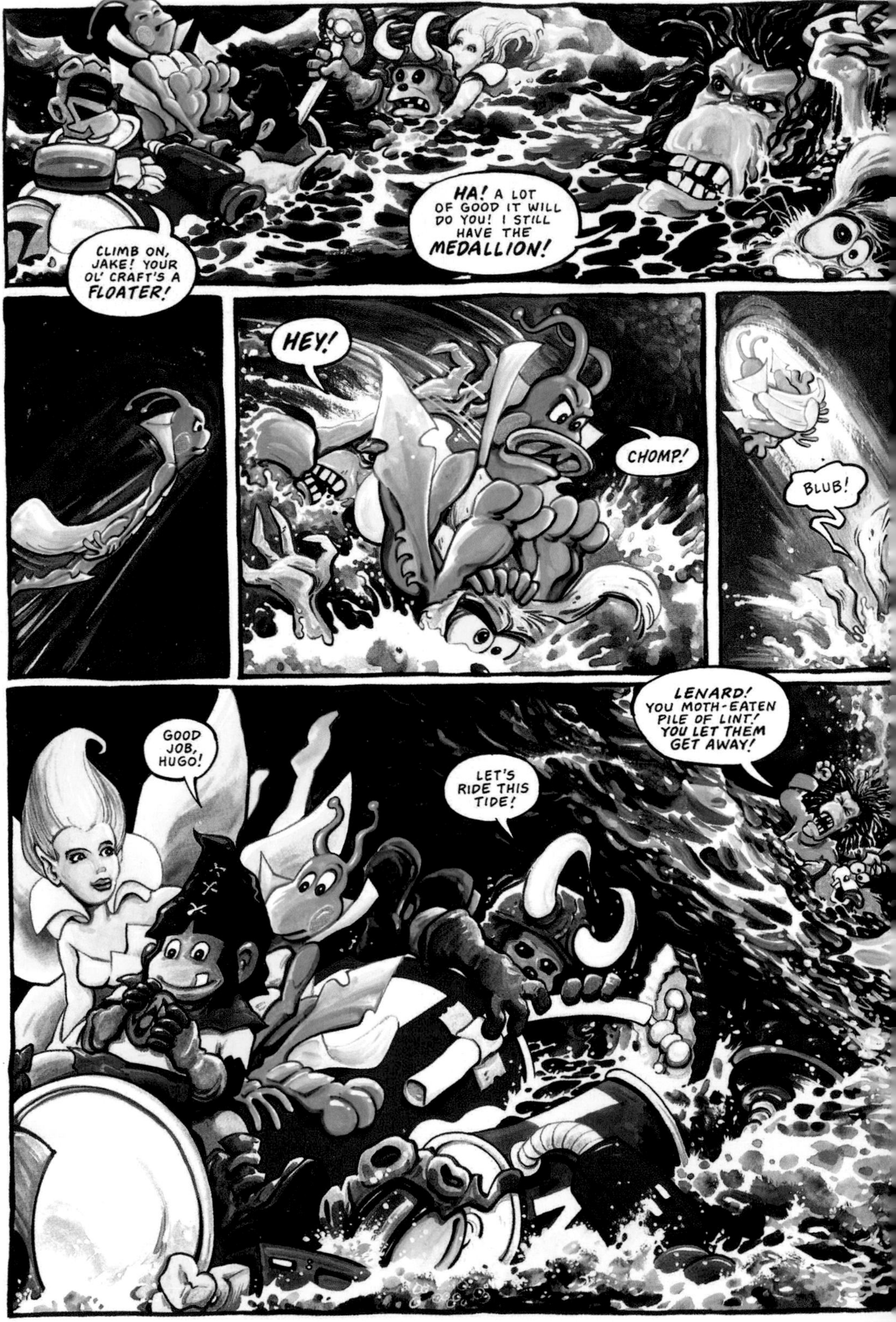
HA! A LOT OF GOOD IT WILL DO YOU! I STILL HAVE THE MEDALLION!
CLIMB ON, JAKE! YOUR OL' CRAFT'S A FLOATER!
HEY!
CHOMP!
BLUB!
GOOD JOB, HUGO!
LET'S RIDE THIS TIDE!
LENARD! YOU MOTH-EATEN PILE OF LINT! YOU LET THEM GET AWAY!

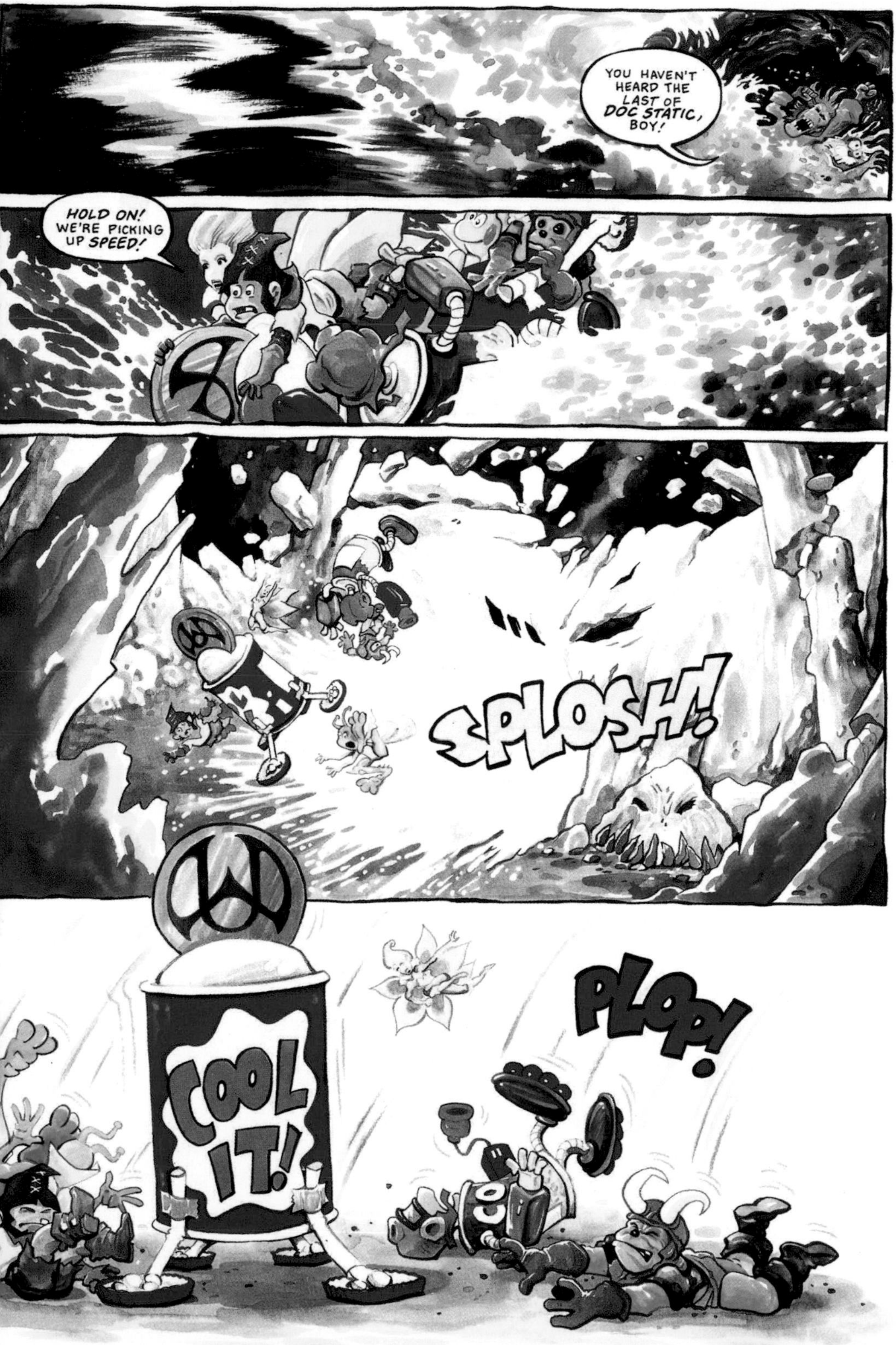
YOU HAVEN'T HEARD THE LAST OF DOC STATIC, BOY!
HOLD ON! WE'RE PICKING UP SPEED!
SPLOSH!
COOL IT!
PLOP!

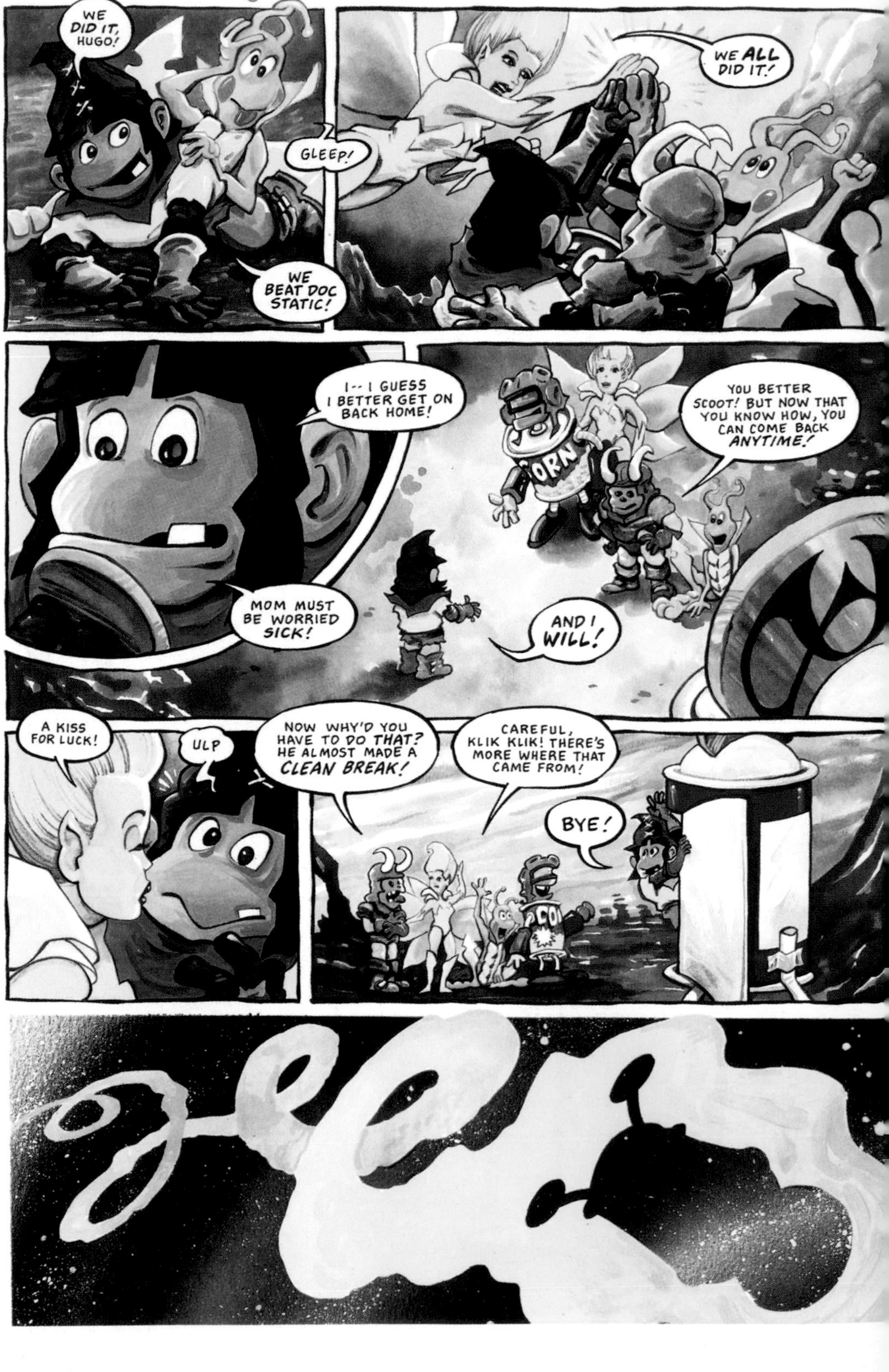
WE DID IT, HUGO!
GLEEP!
WE BEAT DOC STATIC!
WE ALL DID IT!
I-- I GUESS I BETTER GET ON BACK HOME!
MOM MUST BE WORRIED SICK!
YOU BETTER SCOOT! BUT NOW THAT YOU KNOW HOW, YOU CAN COME BACK ANYTIME!
AND I WILL!
A KISS FOR LUCK!
ULP
NOW WHY'D YOU HAVE TO DO THAT? HE ALMOST MADE A CLEAN BREAK!
CAREFUL, KLIK KLIK! THERE'S MORE WHERE THAT CAME FROM!
BYE!

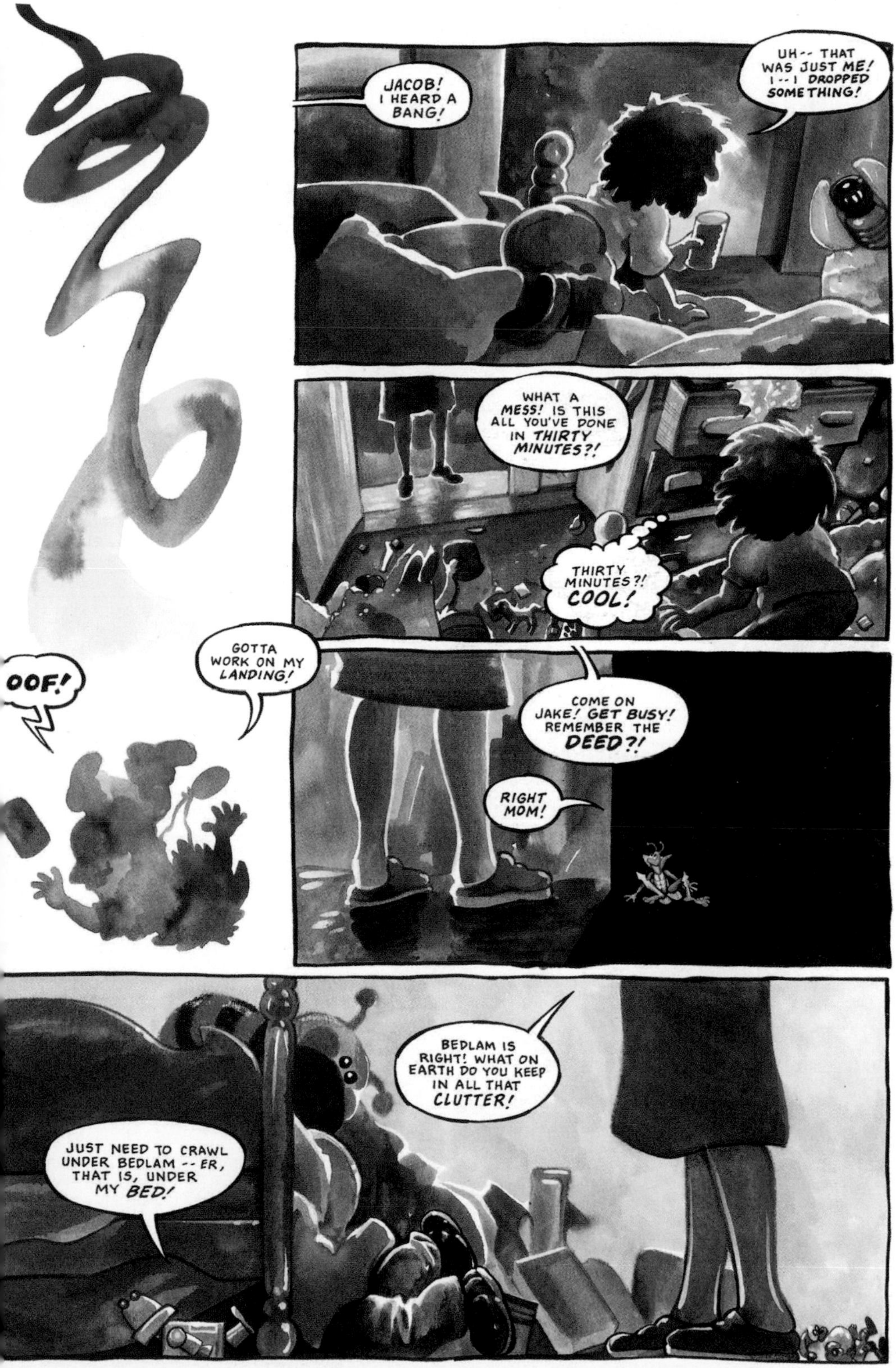

JACOB! I HEARD A BANG!
UH-- THAT WAS JUST ME! I--I DROPPED SOMETHING!
WHAT A MESS! IS THIS ALL YOU'VE DONE IN THIRTY MINUTES?!
THIRTY MINUTES?! COOL!
OOF!
GOTTA WORK ON MY LANDING!
COME ON JAKE! GET BUSY! REMEMBER THE DEED?!
RIGHT MOM!
BEDLAM IS RIGHT! WHAT ON EARTH DO YOU KEEP IN ALL THAT CLUTTER!
JUST NEED TO CRAWL UNDER BEDLAM -- ER, THAT IS, UNDER MY BED!

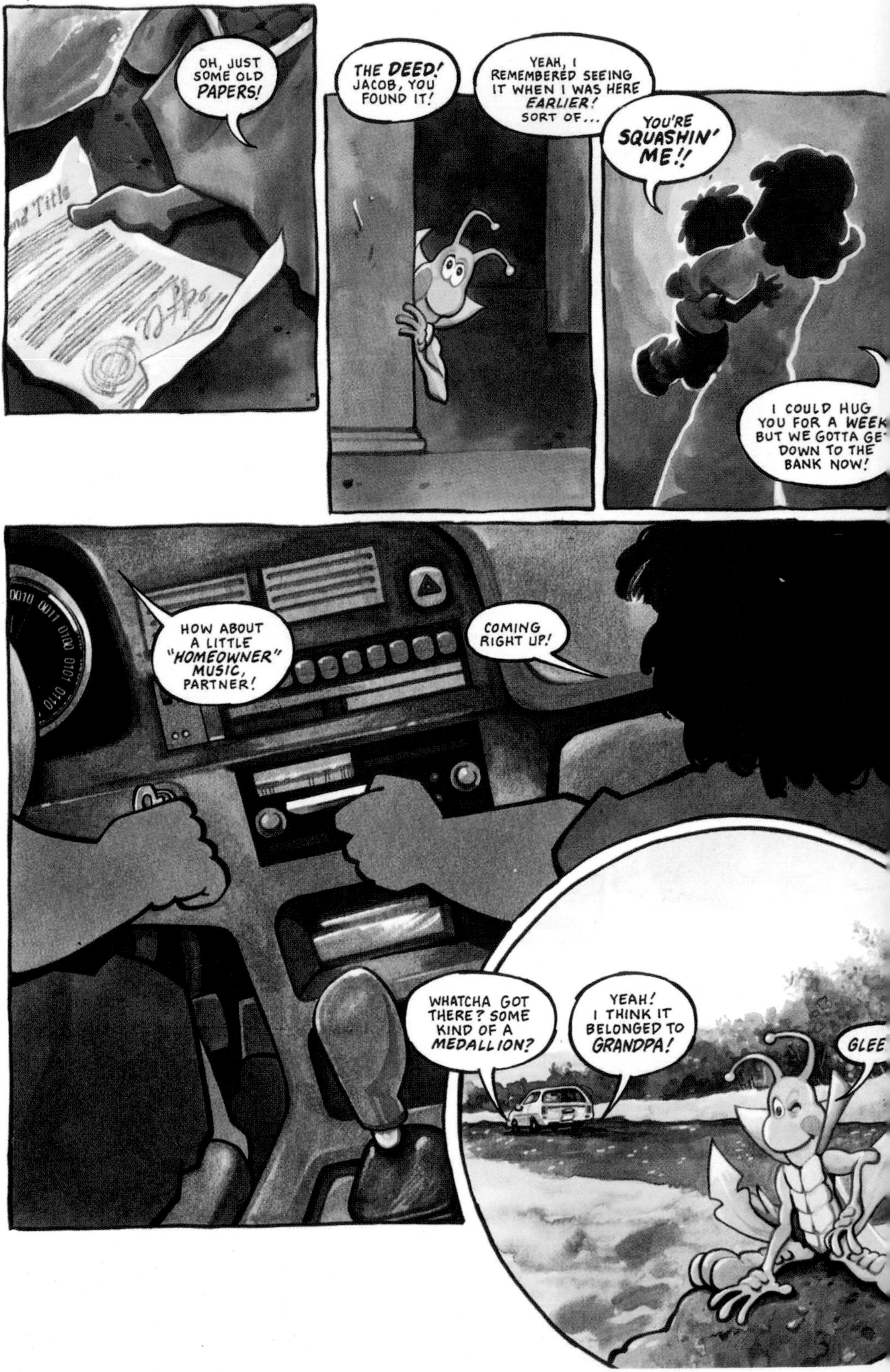
OH, JUST SOME OLD PAPERS!
THE DEED! JACOB, YOU FOUND IT!
YEAH, I REMEMBERED SEEING IT WHEN I WAS HERE EARLIER! SORT OF...
YOU'RE SQUASHIN' ME!!
I COULD HUG YOU FOR A WEEK BUT WE GOTTA GET DOWN TO THE BANK NOW!
HOW ABOUT A LITTLE "HOMEOWNER" MUSIC, PARTNER!
COMING RIGHT UP!
WHATCHA GOT THERE? SOME KIND OF A MEDALLION?
YEAH! I THINK IT BELONGED TO GRANDPA!
GLEE

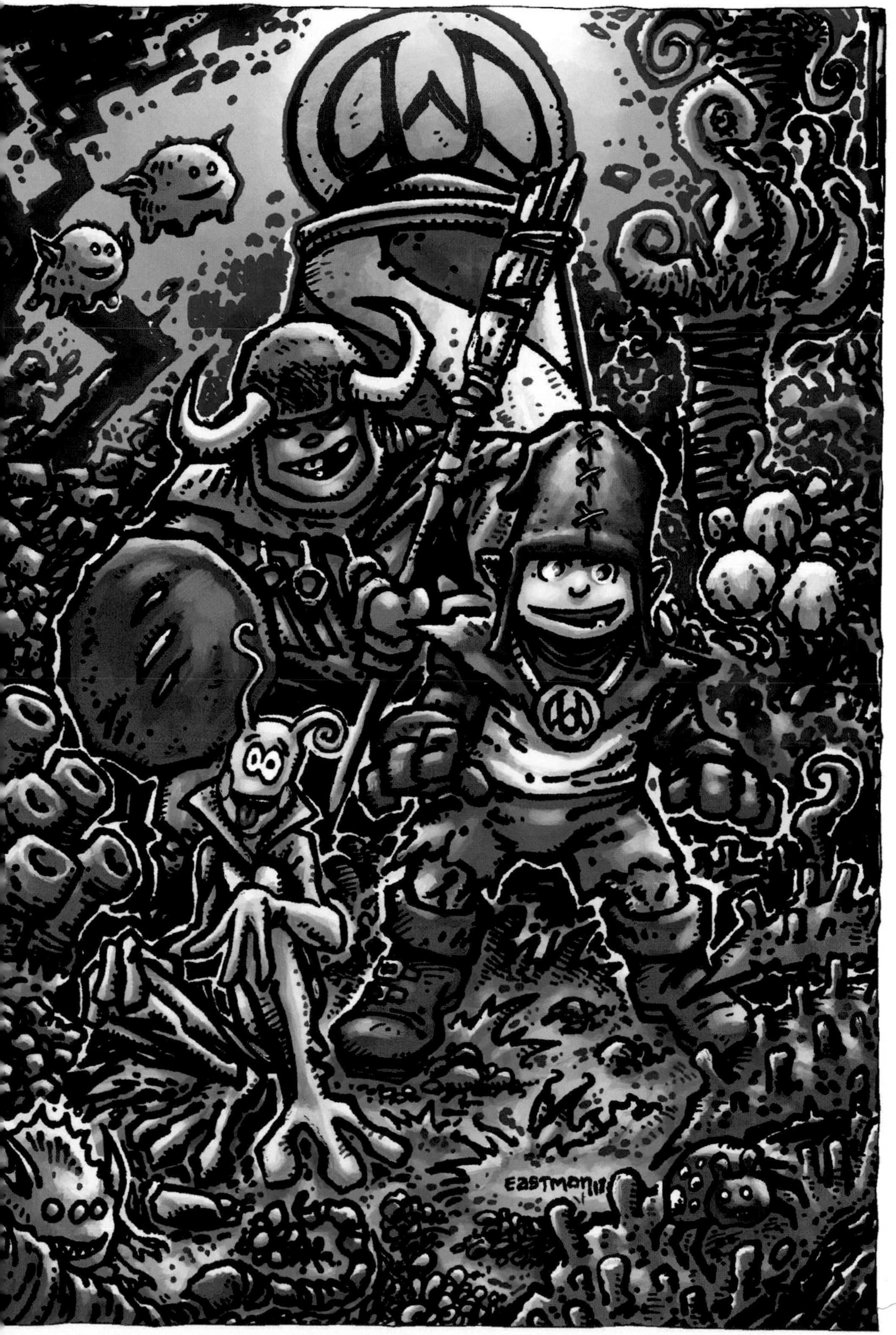
EASTMAN

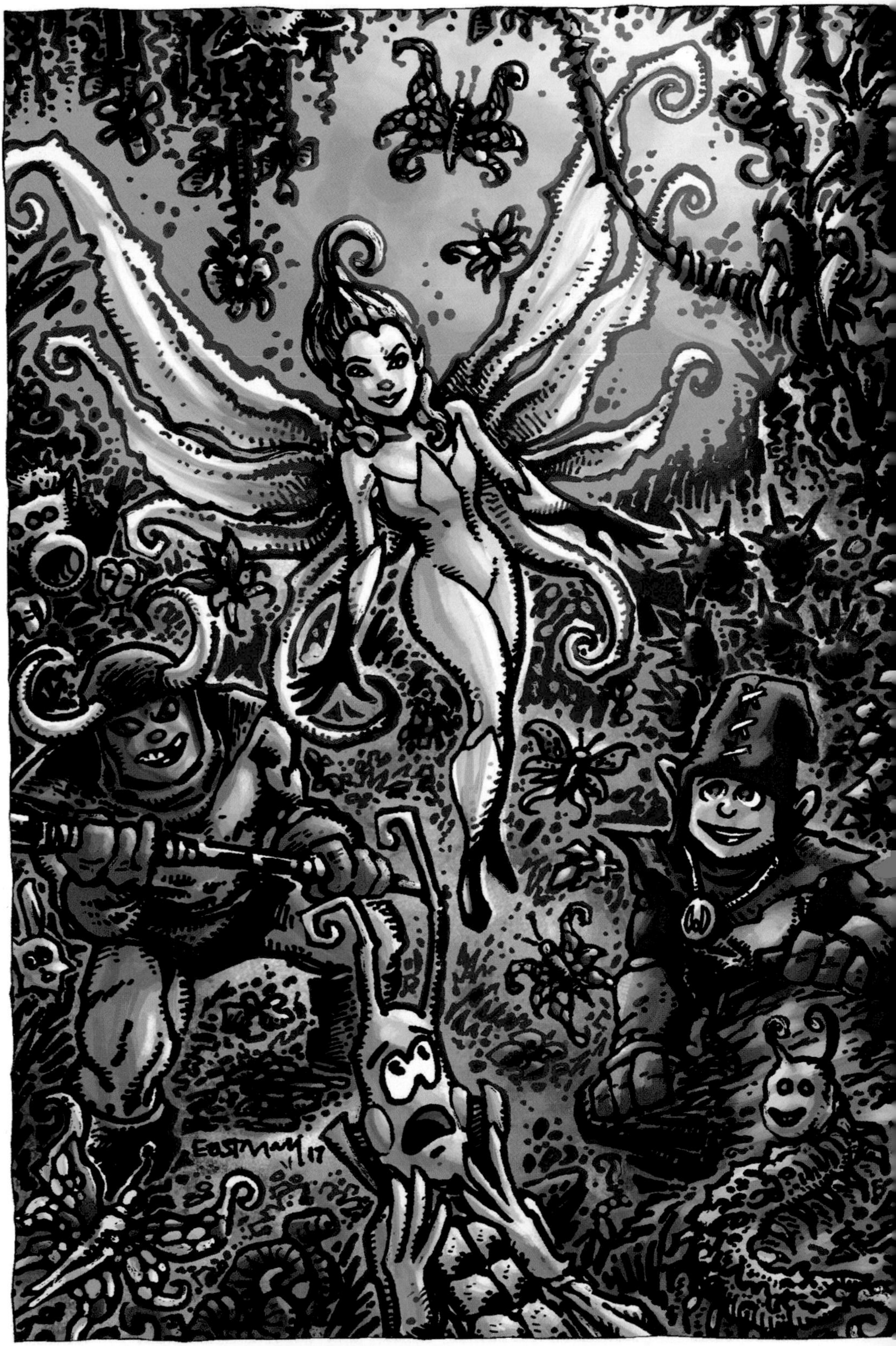

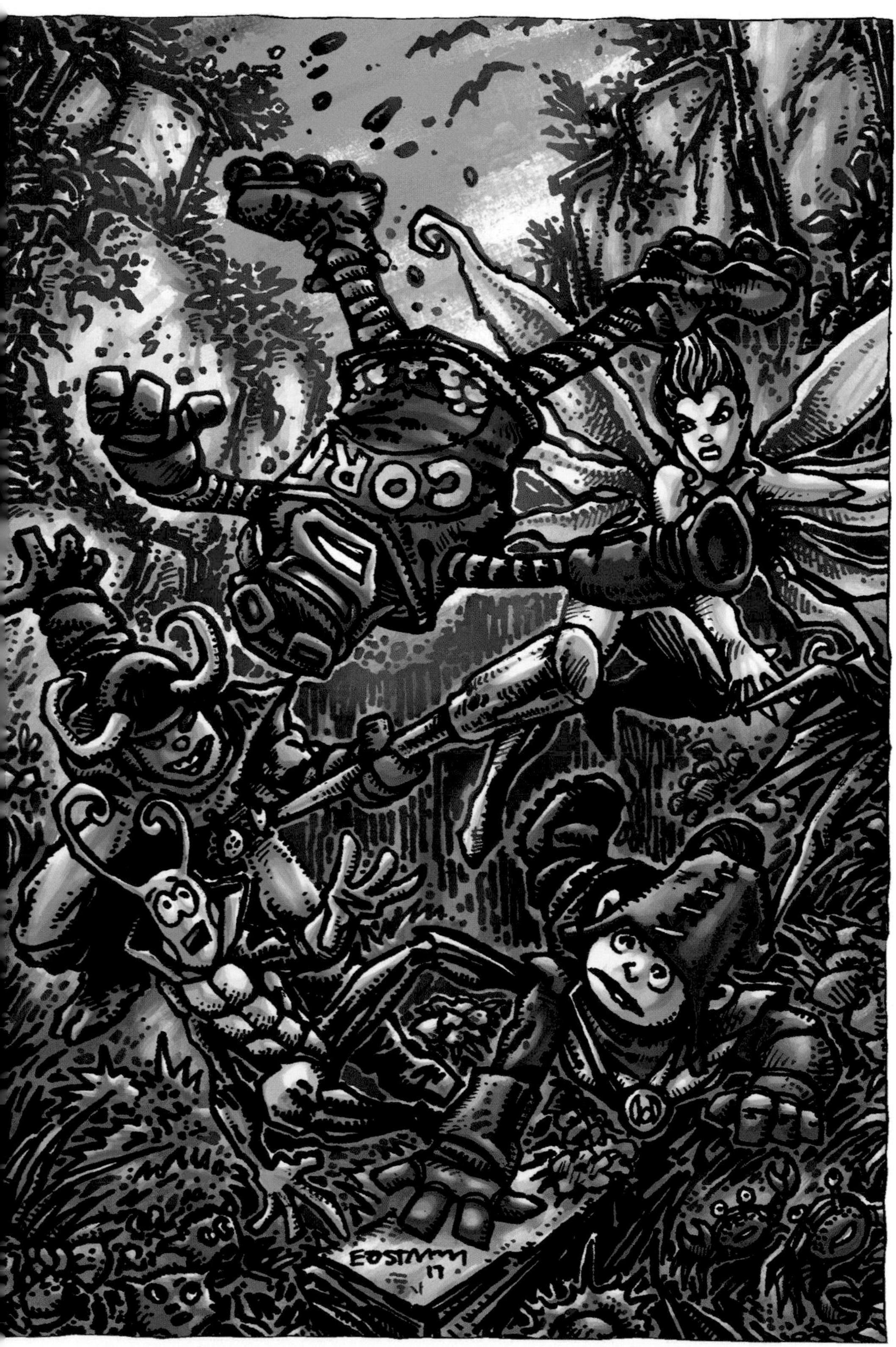

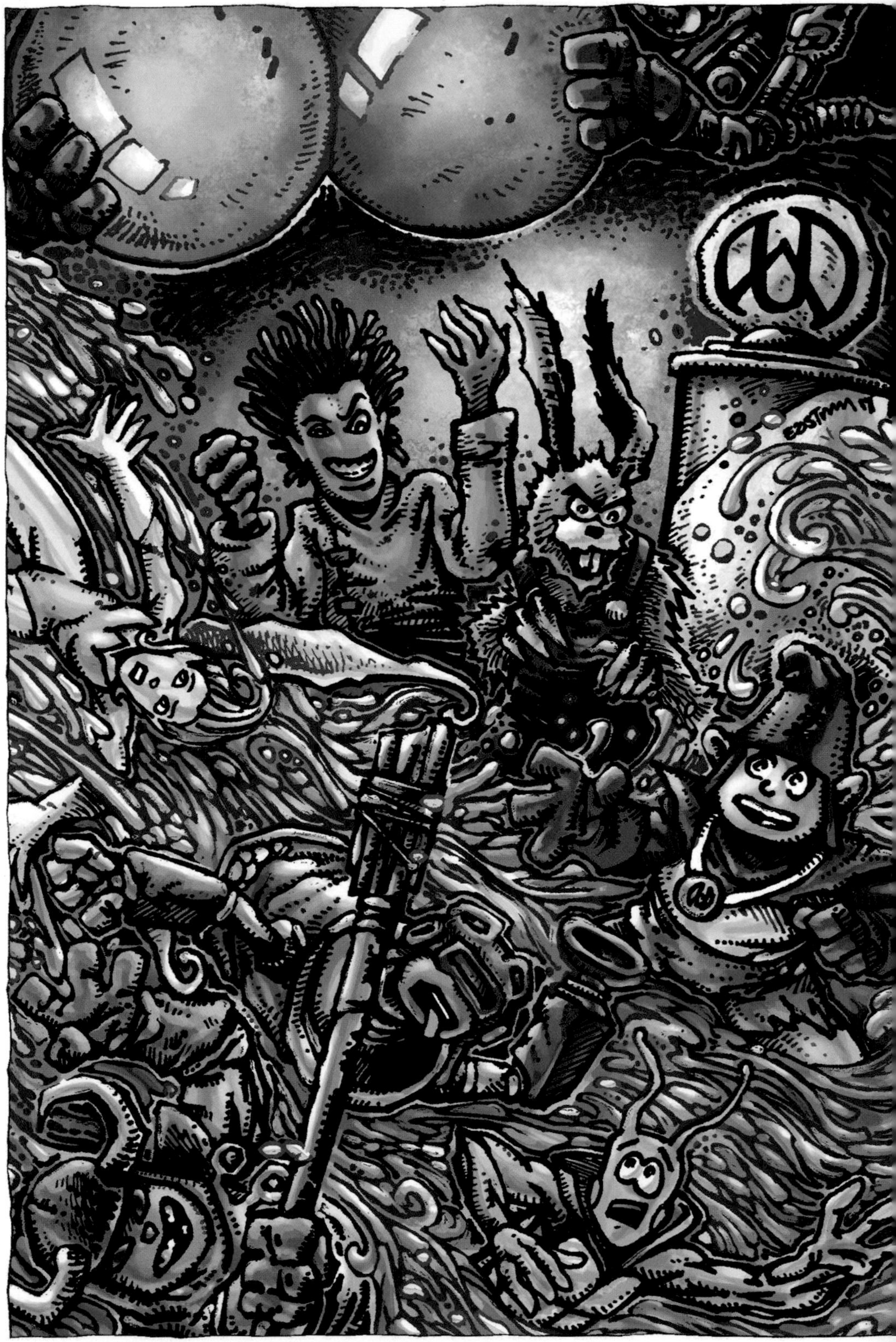

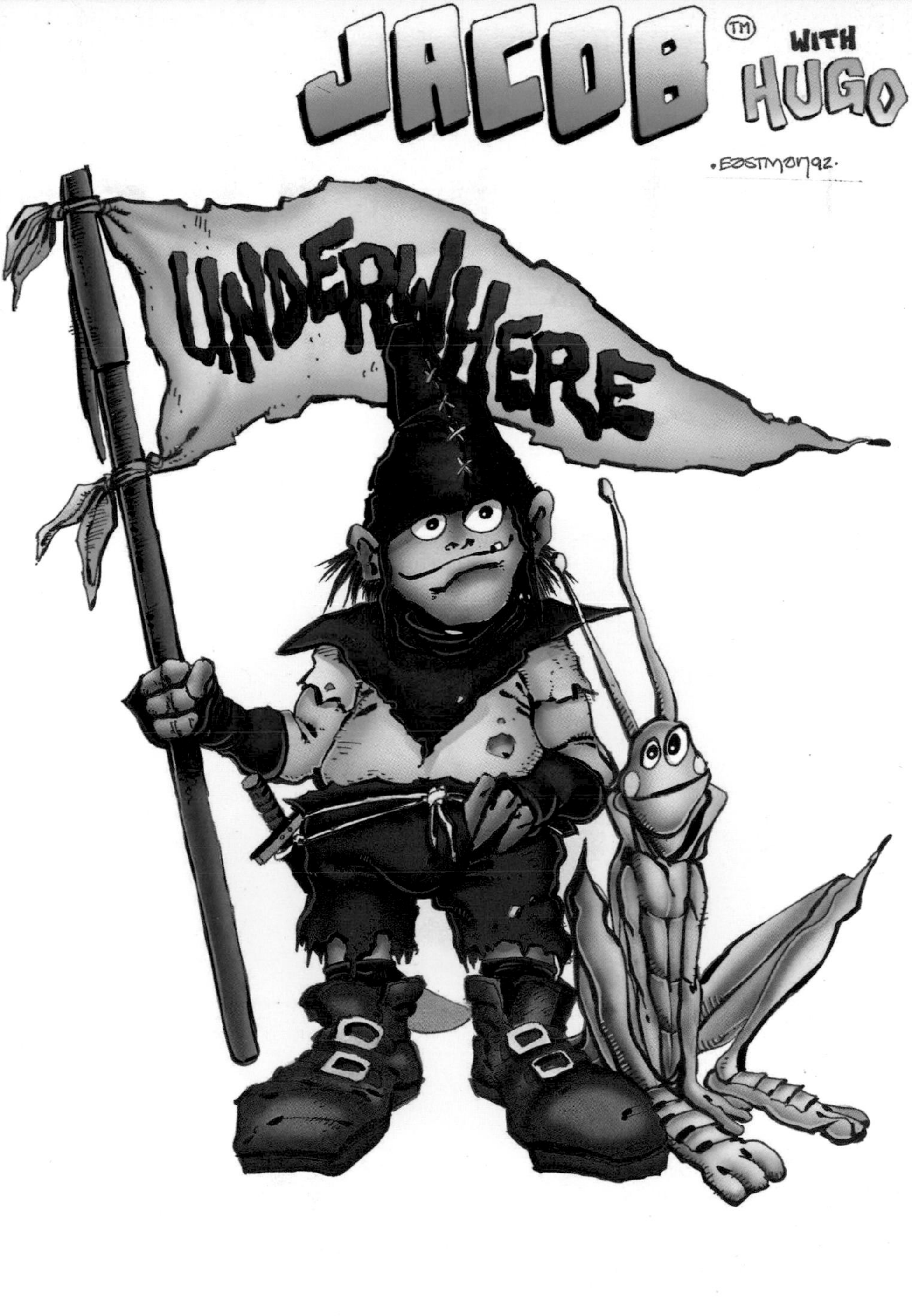
JACOB™ WITH HUGO
•EASTMAN'92•
UNDERWHERE

HUGO™ THE WONDER BUG

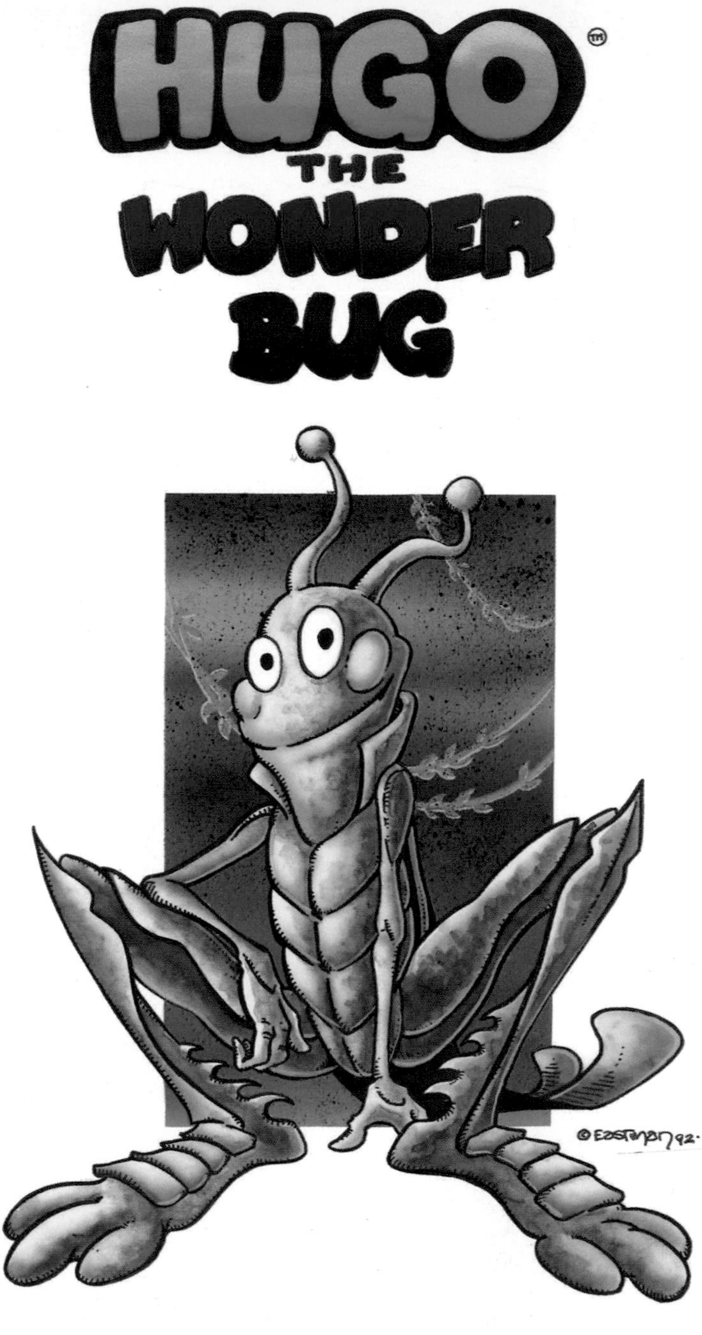
©EASTMAN 92

KLIK KLIK™ THE BRAVE

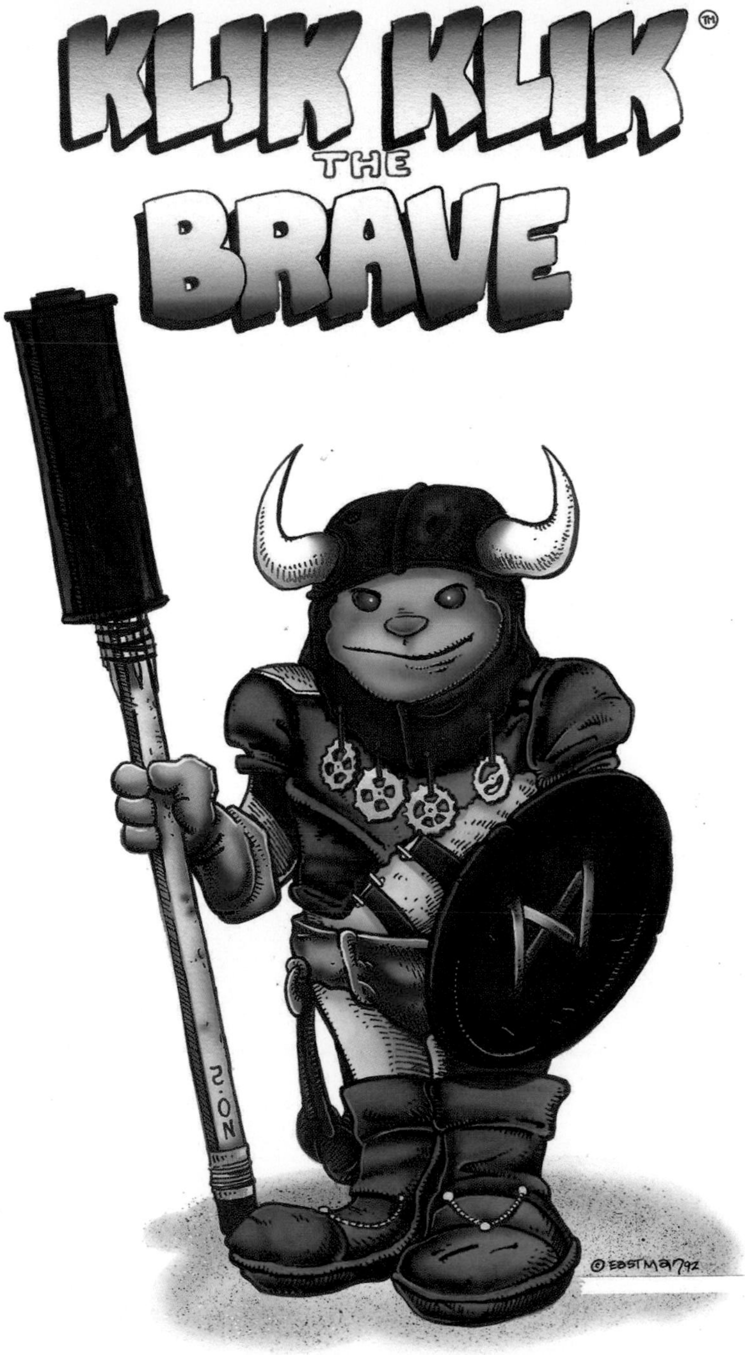
NO. 2
©EASTMAN '92

QUEEN GINA™

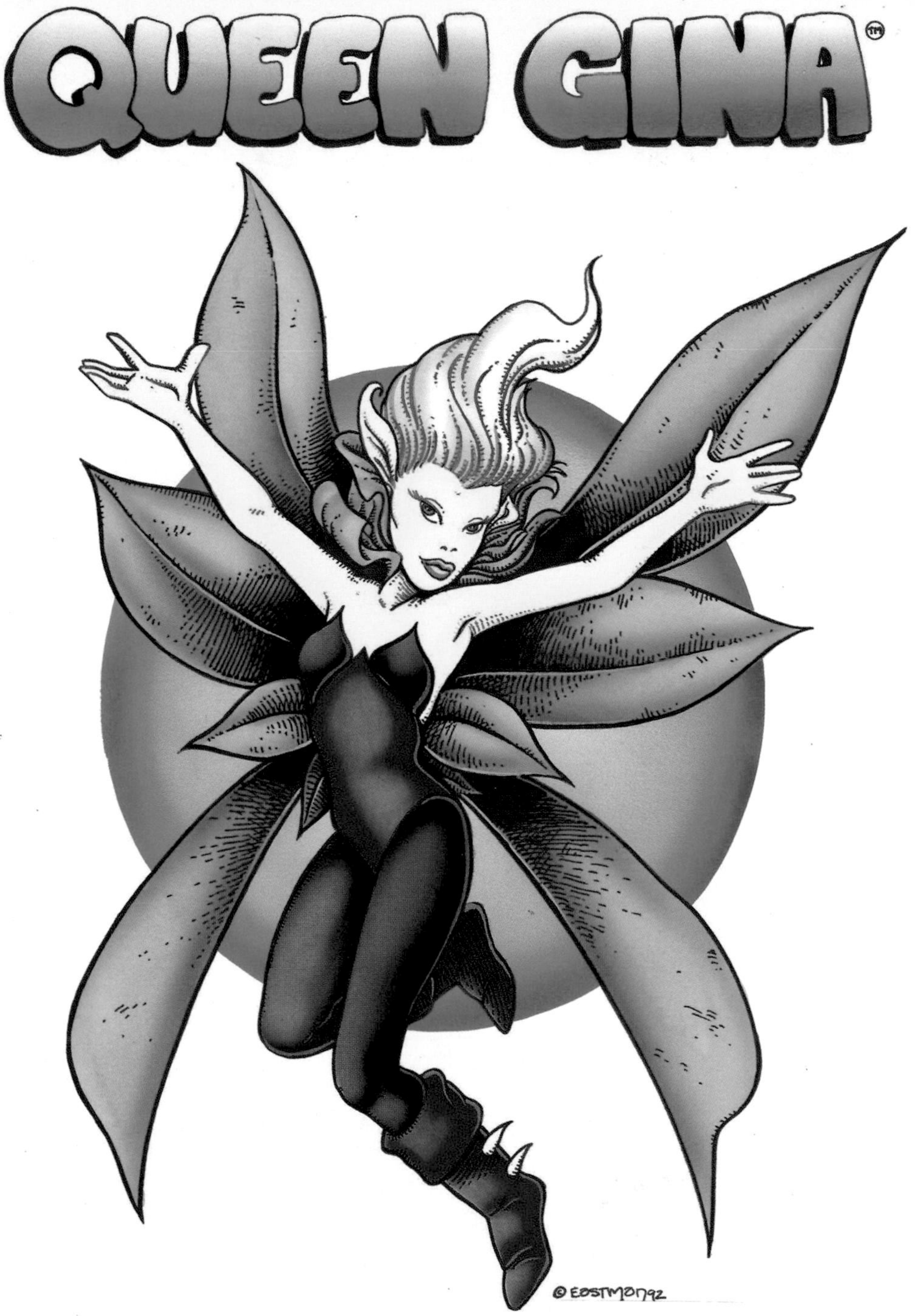
© EASTMAN92

BERT THE WIZBOT™

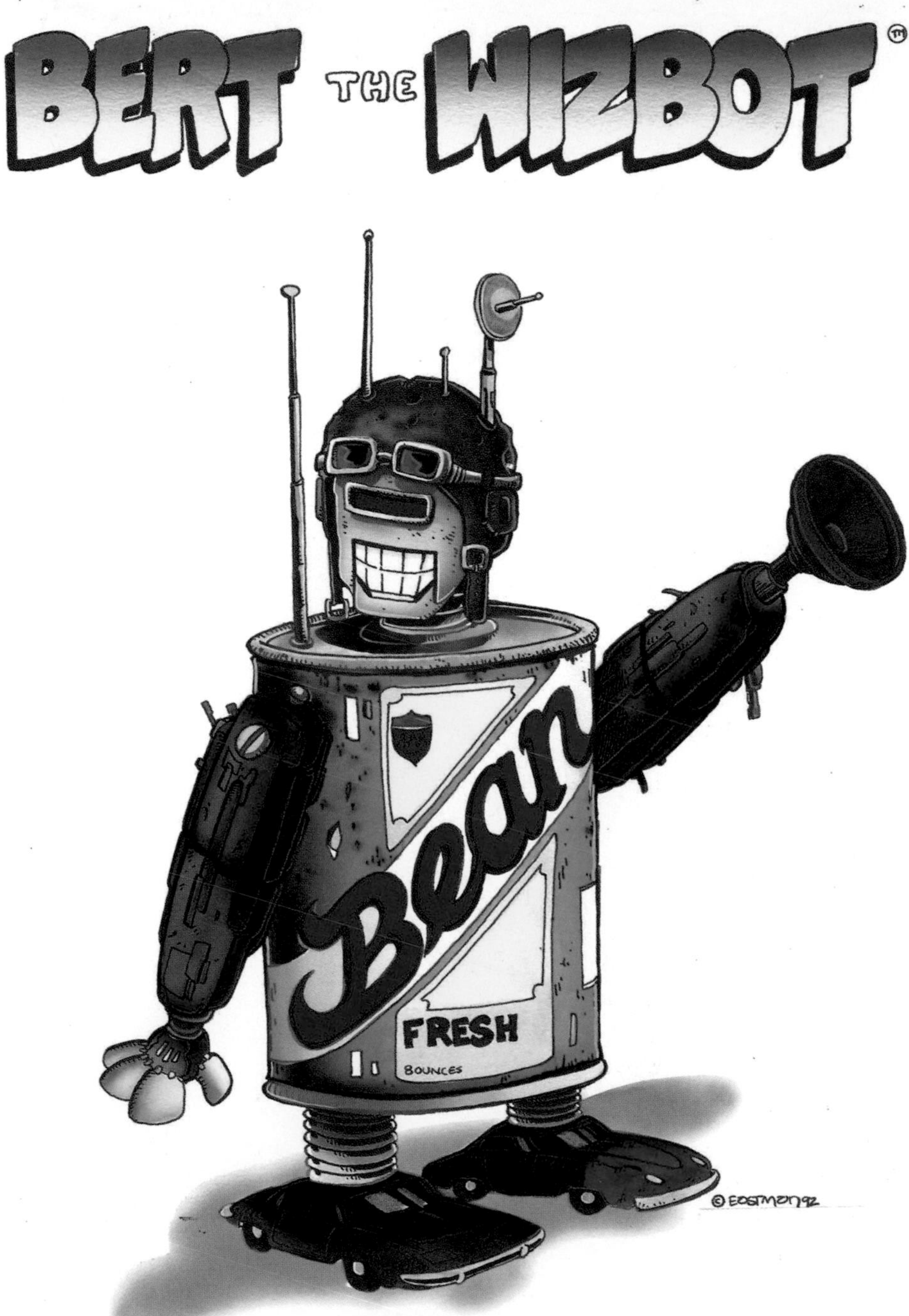
Bean
FRESH
BOUNCES
© EASTMAN 92

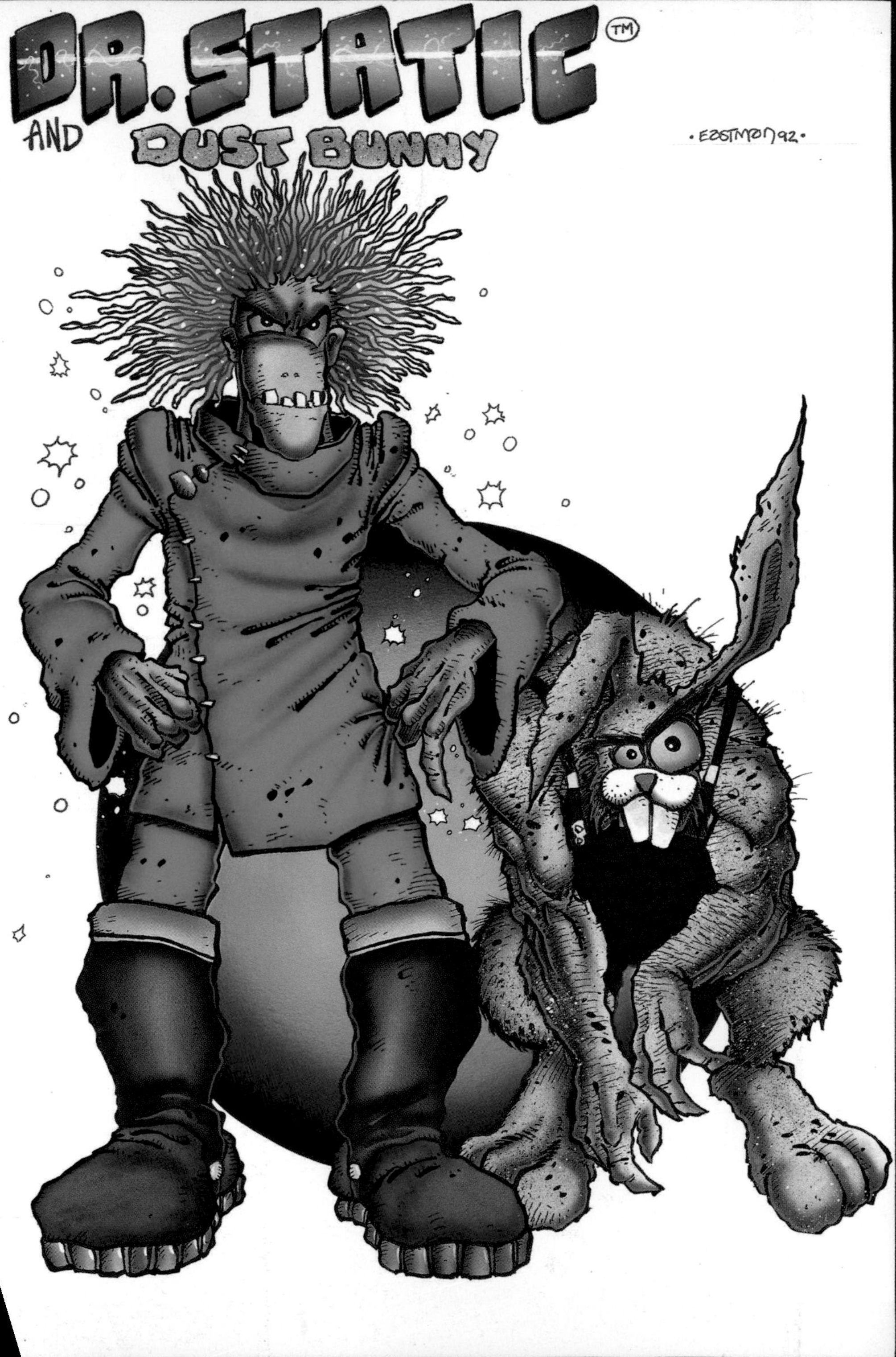
DR. STATIC™
AND
DUST BUNNY
·EASTMAN 92·

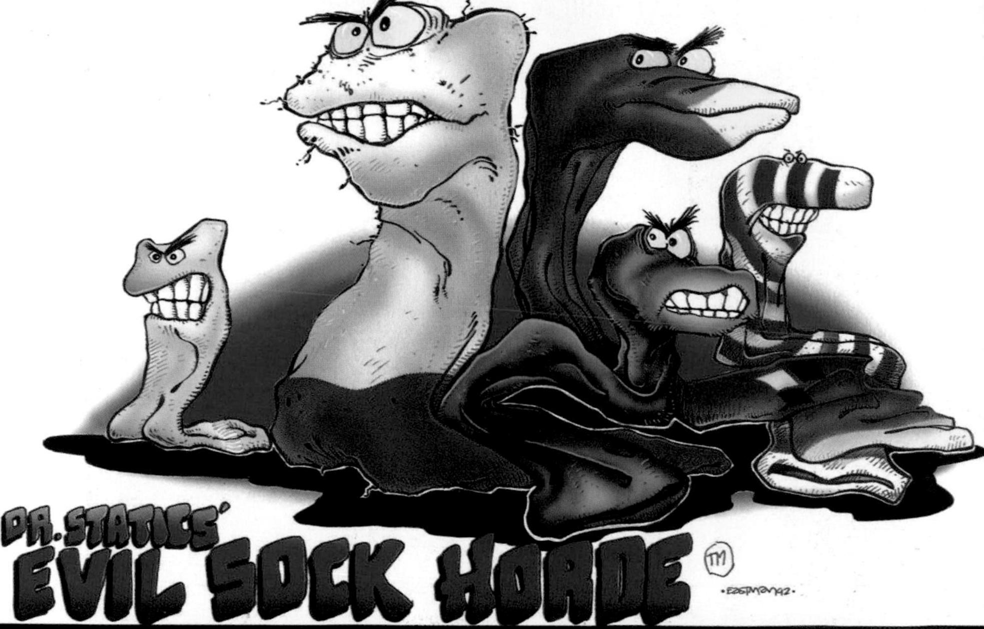
DR. STATICS'
EVIL SOCK HORDE ™
Eastman'92

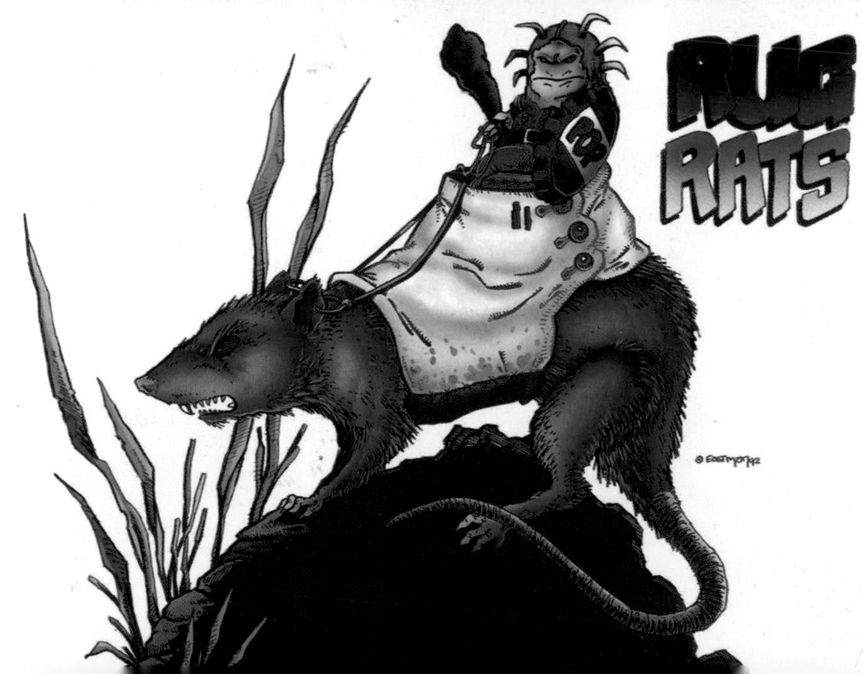
RUG RATS ™
© Eastman'92

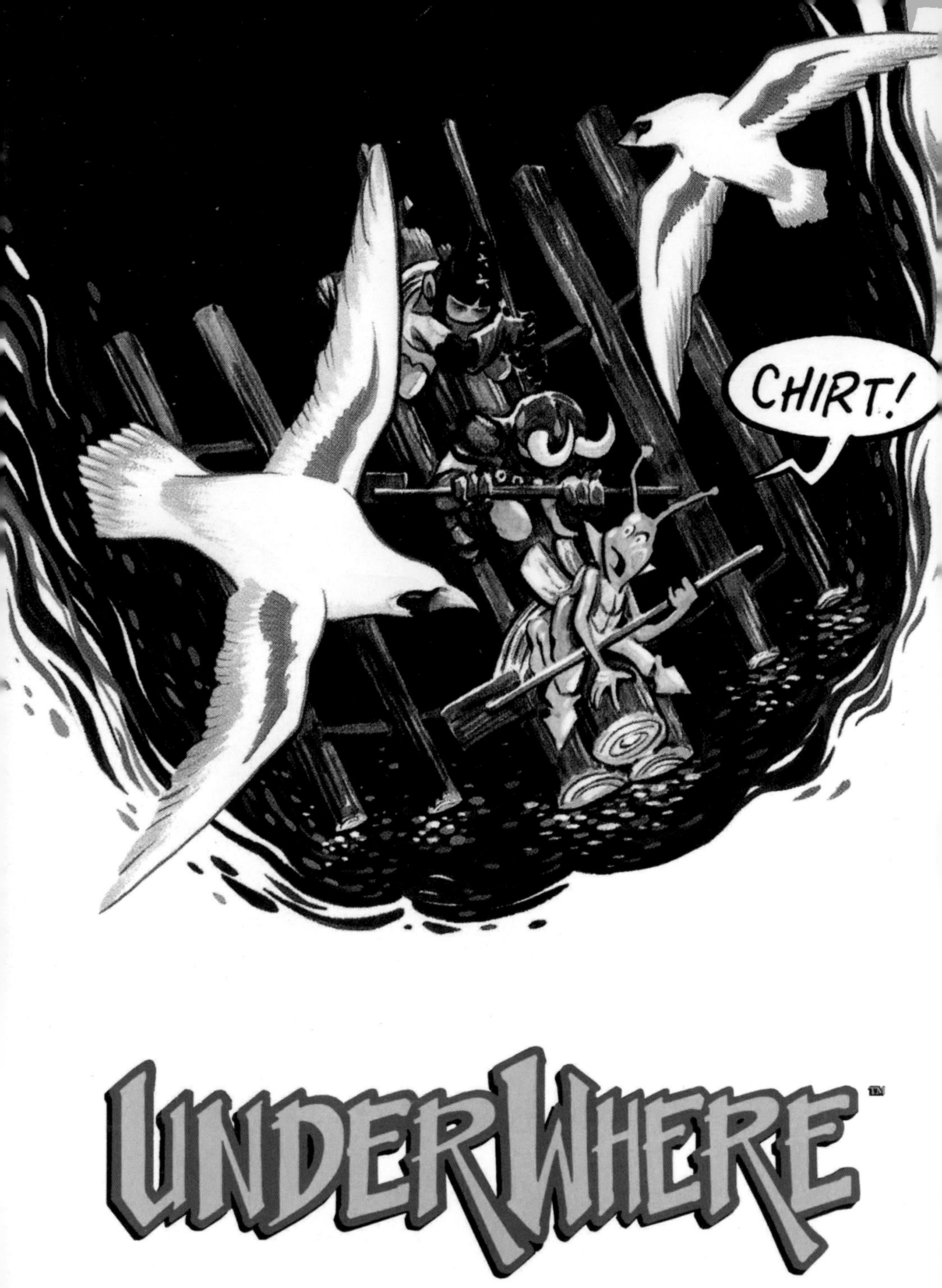
CHIRT!

UNDERWHERE™